Thomas Ruddiman

Rudiments of the Latin language

With an appendix. 24th Edition

Thomas Ruddiman

Rudiments of the Latin language
With an appendix. 24th Edition

ISBN/EAN: 9783337390365

Printed in Europe, USA, Canada, Australia, Japan

Cover: Foto ©Andreas Hilbeck / pixelio.de

More available books at **www.hansebooks.com**

Shakspeare's King Richard II. With Historical and Critical Introductions; Grammatical, Philological, and Miscellaneous Notes, etc. Adapted for the Use of Pupils in Training Colleges, Candidates for Civil-Service and other Examinations, and Students of English Literature generally. Edited by the Rev. H. G. ROBINSON, M.A., Rector of Bolton Abbey, Yorkshire, and Canon of York; late Principal of the Diocesan Training College, York. *First published, January* 1867. **2s.**

Wordsworth's Excursion. Book I. The Wanderer. With Notes to aid in Analysis and Paraphrasing. By Rev. Canon ROBINSON. **8d.** 3d Edition.

English Composition for the Use of Schools. By ROBERT ARMSTRONG, Madras College, St Andrews; and THOMAS ARMSTRONG, Heriot Foundation School, Edinburgh. Part I. 15th Edition. **1s. 6d.** ——Part II. 6th Edition. **2s.**——Both Parts in one, **3s.**——KEY, **2s.**

Economy of time in the class-room has been prominently kept in view in the compilation of the work. The exercises, which are so planned as to afford ample employment to the pupils when left to themselves, proceed upon a system of gradation intended to render their progress easy and interesting. They will also be found convenient for home work; and, when performed, it is recommended that they should be criticised by the master in presence of the class. Those prescribed for Oral Composition, in particular, will afford him a favourable opportunity of illustrating and suggesting in that familiar style so much calculated to give confidence, and produce advantageous results, in this branch of education.

Keeping in view that the great end of Composition is to cultivate habits of thought and discrimination, the authors have made it their aim to divest the exercises, as much as possible, of a mechanical character.

Armstrong's English Etymology for Schools. 3d Edition. **2s.**

Armstrong's English Etymology for Junior Classes. **4d.**

A System of English Grammar, founded on the Philosophy of Language and the Practice of the best Authors. With Copious Exercises, Constructive and Analytical. By C. W. CONNON, LL.D., formerly of Greenwich Hospital. **2s. 6d.** 8th Edition.

Connon's First Spelling-Book. **6d.** 4th Edition.

How to Train Young Eyes and Ears, A Manual of Object Lessons for Parents and Teachers. By MARY ANN ROSS, Mistress of the Church of Scotland Normal Infant School, Edinburgh. 3d Edit. **1s. 6d.**

Household Economy. A MANUAL intended for Female Training Colleges, and the Senior Classes of Girls' Schools. By MARGARET MARIA GORDON (Miss Brewster), Author of "Work, or Plenty to do and how to do it," etc. Ninth Thousand. **2s.**

[*Continued at end of Book.*

RUDIMENTS

OF THE

LATIN LANGUAGE,

WITH

AN APPENDIX.

FOR THE USE OF THE EDINBURGH ACADEMY.

TWENTY-FOURTH EDITION.

EDINBURGH:
OLIVER AND BOYD, TWEEDDALE COURT.
LONDON: SIMPKIN, MARSHALL, AND CO.
1867.

EDINBURGH ACADEMY CLASS BOOKS.

RUDIMENTS OF THE LATIN LANGUAGE. 12mo, 2s.

LATIN DELECTUS, with Vocabulary. 12mo, 3s.

RUDIMENTS OF THE GREEK LANGUAGE. 12mo, 3s. 6d.

GREEK EXTRACTS, with Vocabulary. 12mo, 3s. 6d.

SELECTIONS FROM CICERO. 18mo, *reduced to* 3s.

SELECTA E POETIS LATINIS. 12mo, 3s.

MODERN GEOGRAPHY. 12mo, 2s. 6d.

ANCIENT GEOGRAPHY. 12mo, 3s.

PRINTED BY OLIVER AND BOYD, EDINBURGH.

ADVERTISEMENT.

In revising the Latin Rudiments for a Fifth Edition, the attention of the Editor has been chiefly directed to the improvement of the latter part of the Appendix. He has introduced some farther remarks on Compound Verbs,— partly the result of his own investigations, and partly collected from other sources,—and has inserted Ruddiman's Rules for the Conjugation of Verbs, as the speediest and surest mode of fixing in the minds of young pupils this important part of elementary instruction. The remarks under the Rules for the Gender of Nouns have been extended and improved. For much of the additional matter which will be found under the Rules for the Quantity of Syllables, the Editor has to acknowledge his obligations to Professor Ramsay's excellent Treatise on Latin Prosody, a work in which the whole subject of Quantity and Versification has been treated with a degree of minuteness and skill which ought to recommend it to the careful study of every Teacher.

RUDIMENTS

LATIN LANGUAGE.

LETTERS AND SYLLABLES.

THERE are twenty-five Letters in the Latin language:
a, b, c, d, e, f, g, h, i, j, k, l, m, n, o, p, q, r, s, t, u, v,
x, y, z.

These are divided into Vowels and Consonants.

Six are Vowels: a, e, i, o, u, y.

Nineteen are Consonants: b, c, d, f, g, h, j, k, l, m, n,
p, q, r, s, t, v, x, z.

There are five Diphthongs: ae, oe,* au, eu, ei ; as, aetas,
poena, audio, euge, hei.

*These two are often printed thus ; æ, œ ; and are pronounced as
simple e.

WORDS, OR PARTS OF SPEECH.

There are eight Parts of Speech: Noun, Adjective,
Pronoun, Verb, Adverb, Preposition, Interjection, Conjunction.

These are divided into Declinable and Indeclinable.

Four are declinable: Noun, Adjective, Pronoun, Verb.

Four are indeclinable: Adverb, Preposition, Interjection, Conjunction.

NOUN.

A Noun, or Substantive, is the name of a person, place,
or thing.

It is declined by Genders, Cases, and Numbers.

There are three Genders: Masculine, Feminine, and
Neuter.

There are six Cases: Nominative, Genitive, Dative, Accusative, Vocative, and Ablative.

There are two Numbers: Singular and Plural.

There are five Declensions distinguished by the termination of the Genitive Singular.

GENERAL RULES.

1. Neuter Nouns have the Nominative, Accusative, and Vocative, alike in both Numbers; and these Cases in the Plural end always in *a*.

2. The Vocative, generally in the Singular, and always in the Plural, is like the Nominative.

3. The Dative and Ablative Plural are alike.

4. Proper names want the Plural.

FIRST DECLENSION.

The First Declension has the Genitive and Dative Singular in *æ* diphthong.

It has four Terminations: *a, e, as, es ;* as,

Penna, *a pen ;* Penelŏpe, *Penelope ;* Ænēas, *Æneas ;* Anchīses, *Anchises.*

PENNA, *a pen*, Substantive Feminine.

Singular.		*Plural.*	
Nom. Penn-a,	*a pen.*	*Nom.* Penn-æ,	*pens.*
Gen. Penn-æ,	*of a pen.*	*Gen.* Penn-ārum,	*of pens.*
Dat. Penn-æ,	*to a pen.*	*Dat.* Penn-is,	*to pens.*
Acc. Penn-am,	*a pen.*	*Acc.* Penn-as,	*pens.*
Voc. Penn-a,	*O pen.*	*Voc.* Penn-æ,	*O pens.*
Abl. Penn-a,	*with a pen.*	*Abl.* Penn-is,	*with pens.*

Ara, *an altar.* Galea, *a helmet.* Litĕra, *a letter.* Toga, *a gown.*

Additional Examples.

Ala, *a wing.*	Faba, *a bean.*	Ripa, *a bank.*
Arca, *a chest.*	Hora, *an hour.*	Turba, *a crowd.*
Casa, *a cottage.*	Mensa, *a table.*	Unda, *a wave.*
Causa, *a cause.*	Norma, *a rule.*	Virga, *a rod.*

Nouns in *a* and *e* are Feminine; in *as* and *es* Masculine.

RULE.—*Dea*, a goddess; *equa*, a mare; *filia*, a daughter; and *mula*, a she-mule, have sometimes *ābus* in the Dative and Ablative Plural, when it is necessary to distinguish them from the masculines in *us* of the Second Declension.

Note.—The same form may be employed in some other Nouns: as, *anima, asina, liberta,* and *nata ;* but is seldom, if ever, found.

Rules for the Declension of Nouns derived from the Greek.

1. Greek Nouns in *as* and *a* have sometimes the Accusative, with the poets, in *an :* as, Ænĕas, *the son of Anchises.*

ÆNEAS, *Æneas,* Subst. Masc.

Sing.	*Nom.* Ænĕas.	*Acc.* Ænĕam, or Ænĕan.
	Gen. Æneæ.	*Voc.* Ænea.
	Dat. Æneæ.	*Abl.* Enea.

Borĕas, *the north wind.*   Midas, *a king of Phrygia.*
Maia, *the daughter of Atlas.*   Ossa, *a mountain in Thessaly.*

2. Greek nouns in *es* have the Accusative in *en*, and the Vocative and Ablative in *e :* as, Anchĭses, *a celebrated Trojan.*

ANCHISES, *Anchises,* Subst. Masc.

Sing.	*Nom.* Anchĭses.	*Acc.* Anchĭsen.
	Gen. Anchĭsæ.	*Voc.* Anchise.
	Dat. Anchisæ.	*Abl.* Anchise.

Alcĭdes, *a name of Hercules.* Pelĭdes, *Achilles, the son of Peleus.*
Comētes, *a comet.*   Tydĭdes, *Diomedes, the son of Tydeus.*

Note.—Nouns in *es* have sometimes ă in the Vocative, and more rarely ā. Nouns in *stes* have stă. They also sometimes form the Accusative in *em*, and the Ablative in *a*.

3. Greek nouns in *e* have the Genitive in *es*, the Accusative in *en*, the Dative, Vocative, and Ablative in *e :* as, Penelŏpe, *the wife of Ulysses.*

PENELOPE, *Penelope,* Subst. Fem.

Sing.	*Nom.* Penelŏpe.	*Acc.* Penelŏpen.
	Gen. Penelopes.	*Voc.* Penelope.
	Dat. Penelope.	*Abl.* Penelope.

Circe, *a famous sorceress.*   Epitŏme, *an abridgement.*
Cybĕle, *the mother of the Gods.*   Grammatĭce, *grammar.*

SECOND DECLENSION.

The Second Declension has the Genitive Singular in *i*, and the Dative in *o*.

It has seven Terminations: *er, ir, ur ; us, um ; os, on ;* as,

Puer, *a boy ;* vir, *a man ;* satur, *full ;* domĭnus, *a lord ;* regnum, *a kingdom ;* synŏdos, *a synod ;* Albion, **Great** Britain.

PUER, *a boy*, Subst. Masc.

Singular.			Plural.		
Nom.	Puer,	a boy.	*Nom.*	Puĕr-i,	boys.
Gen.	Puĕr-i,	of a boy.	*Gen.*	Puer-ŏrum,	of boys.
Dat.	Puer-o,	to a boy.	*Dat.*	Puer-is,	to boys.
Acc.	Puer-um,	a boy.	*Acc.*	Puer-os,	boys.
Voc.	Puer,	O boy.	*Voc.*	Puer-i,	O boys.
Abl.	Puer-o,	with a boy.	*Abl.*	Puer-is,	with boys.

Gener,*a son-in-law.* Liber,*Bacchus.* Mulcĭber,*Vulcan.*Vir,*a man.*

But most Nouns in *er* lose the *e* in the Genitive : as,

LIBER, *a book*, Subst. Masc.

Singular.			Plural.		
Nom.	Lib-er,	a book.	*Nom.*	Lib-ri,	books.
Gen.	Lib-ri,	of a book.	*Gen.*	Lib-rŏrum,	of books.
Dat.	Lib-ro,	to a book.	*Dat.*	Lib-ris,	to books.
Acc.	Lib-rum,	a book.	*Acc.*	Lib-ros,	books.
Voc.	Lib-er,	O book.	*Voc.*	Lib-ri,	O books.
Abl.	Lib-ro,	with a book.	*Abl.*	Lib-ris,	with books.

Ager. *a field.*   Culter, *a knife.*   Magister, *a master.*

RULES.—1. Nouns in *us* have *e* in the Vocative : as, *ventus,
vente :* but Proper Names in *ius*, with *filius* and *genius*, have *i :*
as, *Georgius, Georgi.*

2. *Deus* has *Deus* in the Vocative ; and, in the Plural, more
frequently *Dii* than *Dei*, and *Diis* than *Deis*.

Note.—*Popŭlus,* a people, has sometimes *populus* in the Vocative.

DOMINUS, *a Lord*, Subst. Masc.

Singular.		Plural.	
Nom.	Domĭn-us.	*Nom.*	Domĭn-i.
Gen.	Domin-i.	*Gen.*	Domin-ŏrum.
Dat.	Domin-o.	*Dat.*	Domin-is.
Acc.	Domin-um.	*Acc.*	Domin-os.
Voc.	Domin-e.	*Voc.*	Domin-i.
Abl.	Domin-o.	*Abl.*	Domin-is

Annus, *a year.* Fluvius, *a river.* Hortus, *a garden.* Radius, *a ray.*

REGNUM, *a kingdom*, Subst. Neut.

Singular.		Plural.	
Nom.	Regn-um.	*Nom.*	Regn-a.
Gen.	Regn-i.	*Gen.*	Regn-ŏrum.
Dat.	Regn-o.	*Dat.*	Regn-is.
Acc.	Regn-um.	*Acc.*	Regn-a.
Voc.	Regn-um.	*Voc.*	Regn-a.
Abl.	Regn-o.	*Abl.*	Regn-is.

Antrum, *a cave.* Astrum, *a star.* Donum, *a gift.* Jugum, *a yoke.*

Additional Examples.

| Aper, *a wild boar.* | Bellum, *war.* | Caper, *a he-goat.* |
| Arbĭter, *a judge.* | Cadus, *a cask.* | Cervus, *a stag.* |

Collum, *the neck.*	Lupus, *a wolf.*	Ramus, *a branch.*
Equus, **a** *horse.*	Murus, *a wall.*	Saxum, *a stone.*
Faber, *an artist.*	Nidus, *a nest.*	Socer, *a father-in-law.*
Ficus, f. *a fig-tree.*	Ovum, **an egg.**	Telum, *a dart.*
Folium, *a leaf.*	Pomum, **an apple.**	Velum, **a sail.**
Gladius, **a sword.**	Prælium, *a battle.*	Virus, n. *poison.*

The terminations *er* and *us* are generally Masculine, and *um* is always Neuter. *Os* and *on* are Greek terminations, and are generally changed into *us* and *um.*

Greek Nouns in *os* or *us* have sometimes their Accusative singular in *on* : as, *Androgeos,* or *-us,* Androgeus; Gen. *Androge-o,* or *-i ;* Dat. *-o ;* Acc. *-on,* or *-um ;* Voc. *-o ;* Abl. *-o.*

Athos, Athos; Gen. *Ath-o,* or *-i ;* Dat. *-o ;* Acc. *-o, -on,* or *-um ;* Voc. *-o ;* Abl. *-o.*

Ilion, or *-um,* Troy; Gen. *Ili-i ;* Dat. *-o ;* Acc. *-on,* or *-um ,* Voc. *-on,* or *-um ;* Abl. *-o.*

THIRD DECLENSION.

The Third Declension has the Genitive Singular in *is,* and the Dative in *i.*

It has eleven final Letters : *a, e, o, c, d, l, n, r, s, t, x ;* as,

Poëma, *a poem ;* sedile, *a seat ;* sermo, *speech ;* lac, *milk ;* David, *David ;* animal, *an animal ;* pecten, *a comb ;* pater, *a father ;* rupes, *a rock ;* caput, *the head ;* rex, *a king.*

Sermo, *speech,* Subst. Masc.

Singular.		*Plural.*
Nom. Sermo.	*Nom.*	Sermŏ-nes.
Gen. Sermŏ-nis.	*Gen.*	Sermo-num.
Dat. Sermo-ni.	*Dat.*	Sermo-nĭbus.
Acc. Sermo-nem.	*Acc.*	Sermo-nes.
Voc. Sermo.	*Voc.*	Sermo-nes.
Abl. Sermo-ne.	*Abl.*	Sermo-nibus.

Carbo, *a coal.* Leo, *a lion.* Pavo, *a peacock.* Prædo, *a robber.*

Color, *a colour,* Subst. Masc.

Singular.		*Plural.*
Nom. Color.	*Nom.*	Colŏr-es.
Gen. Colŏr-is.	*Gen.*	Color-um.
Dat. Color-i.	*Dat.*	Color-ĭbus.
Acc. Color-em.	*Acc.*	Color-es.
Voc. Color.	*Voc.*	Color-es.
Abl. Colŏr-e.	*Abl.*	Color-ibus.

Honor, *honour.* Lector, *a reader.* Pastor, *a shepherd.*

MILES, *a soldier*, Subst. Com.

Singular.		*Plural.*	
Nom.	Mil-es.	*Nom.*	Mil-ītes
Gen.	Mil-ĭtis.	*Gen.*	Mil-itum.
Dat.	Mil-iti.	*Dat.*	Mil-itĭbus.
Acc.	Mil-item.	*Acc.*	Mil-ites.
Voc.	Mil-es.	*Voc.*	Mil-ites.
Abl.	Mil-ite.	*Abl.*	Mil-itibus.

Comes, *a companion*. Limes, m. *a limit*. Trames, m. *a path*.

RULE.—Nouns in *es* and *is* not increasing in the Genitive Singular, have *ium* in the Genitive Plural.

Except *canis*, a dog; *panis*, bread; *vates*, a prophet; *juvĕnis*, a young man; and *volucris*, a bird.

RUPES, *a rock*, Subst. Fem.

Singular.		*Plural.*	
Nom.	Rup-es.	*Nom.*	Rup-es.
Gen.	Rup-is.	*Gen.*	Rup-ium.
Dat.	Rup-i.	*Dat.*	Rup-ībus.
Acc.	Rup-em.	*Acc.*	Rup-es.
Voc.	Rup-es.	*Voc.*	Rup-es.
Abl.	Rup-e.	*Abl.*	Rup-ibus.

Classis, *a fleet*. Nubes, *a cloud*. Vitis, *a vine*. Vulpes, *a fox*.

RULE.—Nouns of one syllable in *as, is*, and *s* or *x* preceded by a consonant, have *ium* in the Genitive Plural.

PARS, *a part*, Subst. Fem.

Singular.		*Plural.*	
Nom.	Pars.	*Nom.*	Part-es.
Gen.	Part-is.	*Gen.*	Part-ium.
Dat.	Part-i.	*Dat.*	Part-ībus.
Acc.	Part-em.	*Acc.*	Part-es.
Voc.	Pars.	*Voc.*	Part-es.
Abl.	Part-e.	*Abl.*	Part-ibus.

Vas, -dis, c. *a surety*. Lis, -tis, *a lawsuit*. Arx, -cis, *a castle*.

RULE.—Nouns of two or more syllables in *as* and *ns* have *um*, and sometimes *ium :* as, *cliens*, a client, *clientum*, or *clientium*.

Note.—Nouns which have *ium* in the Genitive Plural, have *es, eis*, or *is*, in the Nominative, Accusative, and Vocative Plural.

PECTUS, *the breast*, Subst. Neut.

Singular.		*Plural.*	
Nom.	Pect-us.	*Nom.*	Pect-ŏra.
Gen.	Pect-ŏris.	*Gen.*	Pect-orum.
Dat.	Pect-ori.	*Dat.*	Pect-orībus.
Acc.	Pect-us.	*Acc.*	Pect-ora.
Voc.	Pect-us.	*Voc.*	Pect-ora.
Abl.	Pect-ore.	*Abl.*	Pect-oribus.

Corpus, *a body*. Littus, *a shore*. Nemus, *a grove*. Pignus, *a pledge*.

RULE.—Neuter Nouns in *e*, *al*, and *ar*, have *i* in the Ablative Singular; *ium* in the Genitive Plural; and *ia* in the Nominative, Accusative, and Vocative.

Note.—Proper Names in *e* have *e* in the Ablative: as, *Præneste*, n. a town in Italy; Ablative, *Præneste.*

SEDILE, *a seat*, Subst. Neut.

Singular.		Plural.	
Nom.	Sedil-e.	*Nom.*	Sedil-ia.
Gen.	Sedil-is.	*Gen.*	Sedil-ium.
Dat.	Sedil-i.	*Dat.*	Sedil-ĭbus.
Acc.	Sedil-e.	*Acc.*	Sedil-ia.
Voc.	Sedil-e.	*Voc.*	Sedil-ia.
Abl.	Sedil-i.	*Abl.*	Sedil-ibus.

Ancile, *a shield.*   Mantile, *a towel.*   Mare, *the sea.*   Rete, *a net.*

ANIMAL, *an animal*, Subst. Neut.

Singular.		Plural.	
Nom.	Anĭmal.	*Nom.*	Animal-ia.
Gen.	Anĭmăl-is.	*Gen.*	Animal-ium.
Dat.	Anĭmal-i.	*Dat.*	Animal-ĭbus.
Acc.	Anĭmal.	*Acc.*	Animal-ia.
Voc.	Anĭmal.	*Voc.*	Animal-ia.
Abl.	Anĭmal-i.	*Abl.*	Animal-ibus.

Cubĭtal, *a cushion.*   Calcar, -ăris, *a spur.*   Vectĭgal, *a tax.*

Additional Examples.

Acer, -ĕris, n. *a maple tree.*
Æstas, -ātis, f. *summer.*
Arbor, -ŏris, f. *a tree.*
Aries, ĕtis, m. *a ram.*
Ars, artis, f. *an art.*
Canon, -ŏnis, m. *a rule.*
Carcer, -ĕris, m. *a prison.*
Cardo, -ĭnis, m. *a hinge.*
Carmen, -ĭnis, n. *a song.*
Cervix, -ĭcis, f. *the neck.*
Codex, -ĭcis, m. *a book.*
Consul, -ŭlis, m. *a consul.*
Cor, cordis, n. *the heart.*
Crux, -ucis, f. *a cross.*
Cubĭle, -is, n. *a couch.*
Dens, -tis, m. *a tooth.*
Dos, dotis, f. *a dowry.*
Femur, -ŏris, n. *the thigh.*
Formĭdo, -ĭnis, f. *fear.*
Fornax, -ācis, f. *a furnace.*
Frater, -tris, m. *a brother.*
Fur, furis, c. *a thief.*
Genus, -ĕris, n. *a kind.*
Hæres, -ēdis, c. *an heir.*

Homo, -ĭnis, m. *a man.*
Imāgo, -ĭnis, f. *an image.*
Iter, itinĕris, n. *a journey.*
Lac, -tis, n. *milk.*
Lapis, -ĭdis, m. *a stone.*
Laus, -dis, f. *praise.*
Lex, legis, f. *a law.*
Monĭle, -is, n. *a necklace.*
Mons, -tis, m. *a mountain.*
Munus, -ĕris, n. *a gift.*
Nox, noctis, f. *night.*
Onus, -ĕris, n. *a burden.*
Ovĭle, -is, n. *a sheepfold.*
Pecten, -ĭnis, m. *a comb.*
Regio, -ōnis, f. *a country.*
Salar, -ăris, m. *a trout.*
Serpens, -tis, c. *a serpent.*
Toral, -ālis, n. *a bedcover.*
Trabs, -abis, f. *a beam.*
Turris, -is, f. *a tower.*
Uter, utris, m. *a bottle.*
Virgo, -ĭnis, f. *a virgin.*
Voluptas, -ātis, f. *pleasure.*
Vulnus, -ĕris, n. *a wound.*

GREEK NOUNS through all the Cases.

Nom.	Gen.	Dat.	Acc.	Voc.	Abl.
Sing. Lamp-as;	-ădis, *or* -ădos;	-adi ;	-adem, *or* -ada ;	-as :	-ade.
Plur. Lamp-ădes;-adum ;		-adĭbus ;	-ades, *or* -adas;	-ades ;	-adibus.
Sing. Tro-as ;	-ădis, *or* -ădos;	-adi ;	-adem, *or* -ada ;	-as ;	-ade.
Plur. Tro-ădes;	-adum ;	-adĭbus, -ăsi, *or* -ăsin ;	-ades, *or* -adas ;	-ades ;	-adibus, -asi,*or*-asin
Sing. Tros;	Trois ;	Troi ;	Troem, *or* Troa ; Tros ;	Troe.	
Sing. Phyll-is ;	-ĭdis, *or* ĭdos ;	-idi ;	-idem, *or* -ida ;	-i,*or*-is ;	-ide.
Sing. Par-is ;	-ĭdis, *or* ĭdos ;	-idi ;	-idem,-im,*or*-in; -i ;		-ide.
Sing. Chlam-ys ;	-ȳdis, *or* ȳdos ;	-ydi ;	-ydem, *or* -yda ;	-ys ;	-yde.
Sing. Cap-ys ;	-yis, *or* yos ;	-yi ;	-ym, *or* -yn ·	-y ;	-ye, *or* -y.
Sing. Hærēs-is ;	-is, *or* -eos ;	-i ;	-im, *or* -in ;	-i ;	-i.
Sing. Orph-eus;	-eos, -ĕi,*or*-ei;	-ĕi, *or* -ei ;	-ea ;	-eu ;	-eo.
Sing. Did-o ;	-us, *or* -ōnis ;	-o, *or* -oni ;	-o, *or* -onem ;	-o ;	-o, *or* -one.

FOURTH DECLENSION.

The Fourth Declension has the Genitive Singular in *us*, and the Dative in *ui*.

It has two Terminations : *us* and *u ;* as, Fructus, *fruit ;* Cornu, *a horn*.

FRUCTUS, *fruit*, Subst. Masc.

Singular.		Plural.	
Nom.	Fruct-us.	*Nom.*	Fruct-us.
Gen.	Fruct-ûs.	*Gen.*	Fruct-uum.
Dat.	Fruct-ui.	*Dat.*	Fruct-ĭbus.
Acc.	Fruct-um.	*Acc.*	Fruct-us.
Voc.	Fruct-us.	*Voc.*	Fruct-us.
Abl.	Fruct-u.	*Abl.*	Fruct-ĭbus.

Casus, *a fall.* Currus, *a chariot.* Fluctus, *a wave.* Gradus, *a step.*

CORNU, *a horn*, Subst. Neut.

Singular.		Plural.	
Nom.	Cornu.	*Nom.*	Corn-ua.
Gen.	Cornu.	*Gen.*	Corn-uum.
Dat.	Cornu.	*Dat.*	Corn-ĭbus.
Acc.	Cornu.	*Acc.*	Corn-ua.
Voc.	Cornu.	*Voc.*	Corn-ua.
Abl.	Cornu.	*Abl.*	Corn-ibus.

Gelu, *ice.* Genu, *the knee.* Tonĭtru, *thunder.* Veru, *a spit.*

Additional Examples.

Flatus, *a blast.*	Motus, *a motion.*	Ritus, *a ceremony.*
Ictus, *a stroke.*	Nutus, *a nod.*	Sinus, *a bosom.*
Manus, f. *the hand.*	Passus, *a pace.*	Situs, *a situation.*

Nouns in *us* of the Fourth Declension are generally Masculine, and those in *u* are all Neuter, and indeclinable in the Singular Number.

RULE.—*Acus,* a needle; *arcus,* a bow; *artus,* a joint; *genu,* the knee; *lacus,* a lake; *partus,* a birth; *pecu,* cattle; *portus,* a har_bour; *specus,* a den; *tribus,* a tribe; and *veru,* a spit; have *ŭbus* in the Dative and Ablative Plural. *Portus, genu,* and *veru,* have likewise *ĭbus.*

Domus, a house, is partly of the Second, and partly of the Fourth Declension: thus,

DOMUS, *a house,* Subst. Fem.

Singular.		*Plural.*	
Nom.	Domus.	*Nom.*	Domus.
Gen.	Domûs, or _mi.	*Gen.*	Domuum, or _ōrum.
Dat.	Domui, or _mo.	*Dat.*	Domĭbus.
Acc.	Domum.	*Acc.*	Domus, or _os.
Voc.	Domus.	*Voc.*	Domus.
Abl.	Domo.	*Abl.*	Domibus.

Note.—Domûs, in the Genitive, signifies *of a house;* and *domi* is only used to signify *at home,* or *of home.*

FIFTH DECLENSION.

The Fifth Declension has the Genitive and Dative Singular in *ēi.*

It has one Termination: *es;* as Dies, *a day.*

DIES, *a day,* Subst. Masc. or Fem.

Singular.		*Plural.*	
Nom.	Di_es.	*Nom.*	Di_es.
Gen.	Di_ēi.	*Gen.*	Di_ērum.
Dat.	Di_ei.	*Dat.*	Di_ēbus.
Acc.	Di_em.	*Acc.*	Di_es.
Voc.	Di_es.	*Voc.*	Di_es.
Abl.	Di_e.	*Abl.*	Di_ebus.

Res, ĕi, f. *a thing.*   Glacies, f. *ice.*   Macies, f. *leanness.*

FACIES, *a face,* Subst. Fem.

Singular.		*Plural.*	
Nom.	Faci_es.	*Nom.*	Faci_es.
Gen.	Faci_ēi.	*Gen.*	——
Dat.	Faci_ei.	*Dat.*	——
Acc.	Faci_em.	*Acc.*	Faci_es.
Voc.	Faci_es.	*Voc.*	Faci_es.
Abl.	Faci_e.	*Abl.*	——

Effigies, *an image.*   Series, *an order.*   Spes, _ĕi, *hope.*

Additional Examples.

Acies, *the edge.*   Fides, _ĕi, *faith.*   Rabies, *madness.*
Caries, *rottenness.*   Materies, *matter.*   Species, *an appearance.*

Dies and *res* are the only Nouns of the Fifth **Declension** which have the Plural complete; *acies, effigies, facies, series, species,* and *spes,* have the Nominative, Accusative, and Vocative; the others have no plural.

Nouns of the Fifth Declension are all Feminine, except *dies,* which is Masc. or Fem. in the Singular, Masc. only in the Plural; and *meridies,* the mid-day, or noon, which is Masculine only, and does not occur in the Plural.

ADJECTIVE.

An Adjective is a word added to a Noun, to express its quality.

Adjectives are either of the First and Second Declension, or of the Third only.

Adjectives of three Terminations* are of the First and Second Declension; but Adjectives of one or two Terminations are of the Third.

ADJECTIVES OF THE FIRST AND SECOND DECLENSION.

Adjectives of the First and Second Declension have the Masculine in *us* or *er;* the Feminine always in *a;* and the Neuter always in *um;* as,

Bonus for the Masc. *bona* for the Fem. *bonum* for the Neut. good.

BONUS, BONA, BONUM, *good,* Adj.

	Singular.				Plural.		
	Masc.	Fem.	Neut.		Masc.	Fem.	Neut.
Nom.	Bon-us,	-a,	-um.	Nom.	Bon-i,	-æ,	-a.
Gen.	Bon-i,	-æ,	-i.	Gen.	Bon-ōrum,	-ārum,	-ōrum.
Dat.	Bon-o,	-æ,	-o.	Dat.	Bon-is,	-is,	-is.
Acc.	Bon-um,	-am,	-um.	Acc.	Bon-os,	-as,	-a.
Voc.	Bon-e,	-a,	-um.	Voc.	Bon-i,	-æ,	-a.
Abl.	Bon-o,	-a,	-o.	Abl.	Bon-is,	-is,	-is.

Altus, *high.*   Carus, *dear.*   Durus, *hard.*   Lætus, *joyful.*

---

* Except eleven, *acer,* sharp; *alăcer,* cheerful; *campester,* belonging to a plain; *celĕber,* famous; *celer,* swift; *equester,* belonging to a horse; *paluster,* marshy; *pedester,* on foot; *salūber,* wholesome; *sylvester,* woody; *volŭcer,* swift; which are of the Third, and have the Masculine in *er* or *is,* the Feminine in *is,* and the Neuter in *e.*

TENER, TENERA, TENERUM, *tender,* Adj.

	Singular.			Plural.	
M.	F.	N.	M.	F.	N.
N. Tener,	-a,	-um.	N. Tenĕr-i,	-æ,	-a.
G. Tenĕr-i,	-æ,	-i.	G. Tener-ōrum,	-ārum,	-ōruin.
D. Tener-o,	-æ,	-o.	D. Tener-is,	-is,	-is.
A. Tener-um,	-am	-um.	A. Tener-os,	-as,	-a.
V. Tener,	-a,	-um.	V. Tener-i,	-æ,	-a.
A. Tener-o,	-a,	-o.	A. Tener-is,	-is,	-is.

Asper, *rough.* Dexter, *right.* Liber, *free.* Miser, *wretched.*

Also all the compounds of *gero* and *fero :* as, *laniger,* bearing wool ; *opifer,* bringing help.

But most Adjectives in *er* lose the *e :* as,

ATER, ATRA, ATRUM, *black,* Adj.

	Singular.			Plural.	
M.	F.	N.	M.	F.	N.
N. Ater,	atra,	atrum.	N. Atri,	atræ,	atra.
G. Atri,	atræ,	atri.	G. Atrōruin,	atrārum,	atrōruin
D. Atro,	atræ,	atro.	D. Atris,	atris,	atris.
A. Atrum,	atram,	atrum.	A. Atros,	atras,	atra.
V. Ater,	atra,	atrum.	V. Atri,	atræ,	atra.
A. Atro,	atra,	atro.	A. Atris,	atris,	atris.

Niger, *black.* Pulcher, *fair.* Ruber, *red.* Sacer, *sacred.*

Additional Examples.

Æger, *sick. Gen.* -ri.	Longus, *long.*	Prosper, *prosperous.*
Lacer, *torn.*	Macer, *lean. Gen.* -ri.	Satur, *full.*
Latus, *broad.*	Novus, *new.*	Verus, *true.*

The following **Adjectives** have *ius* in the **Genitive Singular,** and in the **Dative :—**

Alius, *another of many.*	Solus, *alone.*	Uterlĭbet, *which of the*
Alter, *the other of two.*	Totus, *whole.*	*two you please.*
Alterŭter, *the one or the other.*	Ullus, *any.*	Uterque, *both.*
	Unus, *one.*	Utervis, *which of the*
Neuter, *neither.*	Uter, *whether.*	*two you please.*
Nullus, *none.*		

TOTUS, TOTA, TOTUM, *whole,* Adj.

	Singular.			Plural.	
M.	F.	N.	M.	F.	N.
N. Tot-us,	-a,	-um.	N. Tot-i,	-æ,	-a.
G. Tot-ius,	-ius,	-ius.	G. Tot-ōrum,	-ārum,	-ōrum.
D. Tot-i,	-i,	-i.	D. Tot-is,	-is,	-is.
A. Tot-um,	-am,	-um.	A. Tot-os,	-as,	-a.
V. Tot-e,	-a,	-um.	V. Tot-i,	-æ,	-a.
A. Tot-o,	-a,	-o.	A. Tot-is,	-is,	-is.

ADJECTIVES OF THE THIRD DECLENSION.

RULES.—1. Adjectives of the Third Declension have *e* or *i* in the Ablative Singular; but if the Neuter be in *e*, the Ablative has *i* only.

2. The Genitive Plural ends in *ium*, and the Neuter of the Nominative, Accusative, and Vocative, in *ia*.

3. Comparatives have *um* in the Genitive Plural, and *a* in the Nominative, Accusative, and Vocative Neuter.

1. *Of one Termination.*

FELIX, *happy*, Adj.

	Singular.			Plural.	
M.	*F.*	*N.*	*M.*	*F.*	*N.*
N. Fel-ix,	-ix,	-ix.	*N.* Fel-ĭces,	-ĭces,	-ĭcia.
G. Fel-ĭcis,	-ĭcis,	-ĭcis.	*G.* Fel-icium,	-icium,	-icium.
D. Fel-ici,	-ici,	-ici.	*D.* Fel-icĭbus,	-icĭbus,	-icĭbus.
A. Fel-icem,	-icem,	-ix.	*A.* Fel-ices,	-ices,	-icia.
V. Fel-ix,	-ix,	-ix.	*V.* Fel-ices,	-ices,	-icia.
A. Fel-ice, *or* -ici, &c.			*A.* Fel-icibus,	-icibus,	-icibus.

Ingens, -entis, *huge.* Trux, -ucis, *cruel.* Velox, -ōcis, *swift.*

2. *Of two Terminations.*

MITIS, MITE, *meek*, Adj.

	Singular.			Plural.	
M.	*F.*	*N.*	*M.*	*F.*	*N.*
N. Mitis,	mitis,	mite.	*N.* Mites,	mites,	mitia.
G. Mitis,	mitis,	mitis.	*G.* Mitium,	mitium,	mitium.
D. Miti,	miti,	miti.	*D.* Mitĭbus,	mitĭbus,	mitĭbus.
A. Mitem,	mitem,	mite.	*A.* Mites,	mites,	mitia.
V. Mitis,	mitis,	mite.	*V.* Mites,	mites,	mitia.
A. Miti,	miti,	miti.	*A.* Mitibus,	mitibus,	mitibus.

Brevis, *short.* Fortis, *brave.* Gravis, *heavy.* Mollis, *soft.*

MITIOR, MITIUS, *more meek*, Adj.

	Singular.			Plural.	
M.	*F.*	*N.*	*M.*	*F.*	*N.*
N. Miti-or,	-or,	-us.	*N.* Miti-ōres,	-ōres,	-ōra.
G. Miti-ōris,	-ōris,	-ōris.	*G.* Miti-orum,	-orum,	-orum.
D. Miti-ori,	-ori,	-ori.	*D.* Miti-orĭbus,	-orĭbus,	-orĭbus.
A. Miti-orem,	-orem,	-us.	*A.* Miti-ores,	-ores,	-ora.
V. Miti-or,	-or,	-us.	*V.* Miti-ores,	-ores,	-ora.
A. Miti-ore, *or* -ori, &c.			*A.* Miti-oribus,	-oribus,	-oribus.

Brevior, *shorter;* Fortior, *braver;* Mollior, *softer;* and all other Comparatives.

3. *Of three* Terminations.

ACER, *or* ACRIS, ACRE, *sharp,* Adj.

	Singular.				Plural.	
M.	*F.*	*N.*		*M.*	*F.*	*N.*
N. A-cer, *or* -cris,	-cris,	-cre.		*N.* A-cres,	-cres,	-cria.
G. A-cris,	-cris,	-cris.		*G.* A-crium,	-crium,	-crium.
D. A-cri,	-cri,	-cri.		*D.* A-crĭbus,	-crĭbus,	-crĭbus.
A. A-crem,	-crem,	-cre.		*A.* A-cres,	-cres,	-cria.
V. A-cer, *or* -cris,	-cris,	-cre.		*V.* A-cres,	-cres,	-cria.
A. A-cri,	-cri,	-cri.		*A.* A-cribus,	-cribus,	-cribus.

Alăcer, *or* alacris, *cheerful,* &c. See page 10.

Additional Examples.

Atrox, -ōcis, *cruel.*	Elĕgans, -tis, *elegant.*	Tristis, *sad.*
Audax, -ācis, *bold.*	Ferox, -ōcis, *fierce.*	Turpis, *base.*
Clemens, -tis, *gentle.*	Levis, *light.*	Utĭlis, *useful.*
Dulcis, *sweet.*	Recens, -tis, *fresh.*	Vilis, *worthless.*

Adjectives and Substantives to be declined together, and varied through the different degrees of comparison.

Parva casa, *a small cottage.*	Cæca mens, *a blinded understanding.*
Clarus poēta, *a famous poet.*	Alta arbor, *a high tree.*
Pulchra filia, *a beautiful daughter.*	Sacrum poēma, *a sacred poem.*
Dulce pomum, *a sweet apple.*	Inepta res, *a foolish thing.*
Docĭlis puer, *a docile boy.*	Minax fluctus, *a threatening wave.*
Breve ævum, *a short life.*	Priscus mos, *an ancient custom.*
Capax antrum, *a capacious den.*	Calĭda æstas, *a warm summer.*
Magnum opus, *a large work.*	Tutus portus, *a safe harbour.*
Tener pes, *a tender foot.*	Volŭcris ala, *a swift wing.*
Serēnus dies, *a clear day.*	Libĕra palus, *a free marsh.*
Densa nubes, *a thick cloud.*	Solers vir, *an ingenious man.*
Acūta acus, *a sharp needle.*	Sublīmis arx, *a lofty castle.*
Valĭda manus, *a strong hand.*	Mœsta vox, *a sorrowful voice.*
Longa pinus, *a tall pine.*	Ferus draco, *a cruel dragon.*
Ferax ager, *a fertile field.*	Cava navis, *a hollow ship.*
Fidus pastor, *a faithful shepherd.*	Ardua turris, *a lofty tower.*
Potens dea, *a powerful goddess.*	Magna dos, *a large dowry.*
Nova opinio, *a new opinion.*	Unus niger bos, *one black ox.*
Nobĭle carmen, *a noble poem.*	Ænea lampas, *a brazen lamp.*
Antīqua urbs, *an ancient city.*	Fortis heros, *a brave hero.*
Rarum rete, *a thin net.*	Militāris chlamys, *a military cloak.*
Fessus advĕna, *a wearied stranger.*	Culpātus Paris, *wicked Paris.*
Gelĭdus fons, *a cold fountain.*	Miser Tros, *a miserable Trojan.*
Acris acies, *a sharp edge.*	Infēlix Dido, *unhappy Dido.*

NUMERAL ADJECTIVES.

Adjectives which signify Number, are divided into four classes: *Cardinal,* denoting number simply; *Ordinal,* denoting the place or number in succession; *Distributive*, denoting how many to each: and *Multiplicative*, denoting how many fold.

The *Cardinal*, or *Principal* Numbers are:

Unus, *one.*	Triginta, *thirty.*
Duo, *two.*	Quadraginta, *forty.*
Tres, *three.*	Quinquaginta, *fifty.*
Quatuor, *four.*	Sexaginta, *sixty.*
Quinque, *five.*	Septuaginta, *seventy.*
Sex, *six.*	Octoginta, *eighty.*
Septem, *seven.*	Nonaginta, *ninety.*
Octo, *eight.*	Centum, *a hundred.*
Novem, *nine.*	Ducenti, -æ, -a, *two hundred.*
Decem, *ten.*	Trecenti, -æ, -a, *three hundred.*
Undĕcim, *eleven.*	Quadringenti, *four hundred.*
Duodĕcim, *twelve.*	Quingenti, *five hundred.*
Tredĕcim, *thirteen.*	Sexcenti, *six hundred.*
Quatuordĕcim, *fourteen.*	Septingenti, *seven hundred.*
Quindĕcim, *fifteen.*	Octingenti, *eight hundred.*
Sexdĕcim, *sixteen.*	Nongenti, *nine hundred.*
Septemdĕcim, *seventeen.*	Mille, *a thousand.*
Octodĕcim, *eighteen.*	Duo millia, *or*
Novemdĕcim, *nineteen.*	Bis mille, } *two thousand.*
Viginti, *twenty.*	Decem millia, *or*
Viginti unus, *or* } Unus et Viginti, } *twenty-one.*	Decies mille, } *ten thousand.*
	Viginti millia, *or* } Vicies mille, } *twenty thousand.*
Viginti duo, *or* } Duo et Viginti, } *twenty-two.*	

Eighteen and *nineteen* are more properly expressed by *duodeviginti*, and *undeviginti*; from which Ordinals, Distributives, and Adverbs, are likewise formed. The same form may be employed in the corresponding numbers of each of the other decades: as, *duodetriginta*, twenty-eight; *undetriginta*, twenty-nine; &c.

The Cardinal Numbers, except *unus* and *mille*, want the Singular.

Unus is not used in the Plural, except when joined with a substantive which wants the Singular: as, *una mœnia*, one wall; or when several particulars are considered as one whole: as, *una vestimenta*, one suit of clothes.

Duo, *two*, and Tres, *three*, are thus declined:

	Plural.				Plural.		
	M.	*F.*	*N.*		*M.*	*F.*	*N.*
N.	Duo,	duæ,	duo.	*N.*	Tres,	tres,	tria.
G.	Duōrum,	duārum,	duōrum.	*G.*	Trium,	trium,	trium.
D.	Duōbus,	duābus,	duōbus.	*D.*	Tribus,	tribus,	tribus.
A.	Duos, -o,	duas,	duo.	*A.*	Tres,	tres,	tria.
V.	Duo,	duæ,	duo.	*V.*	Tres,	tres,	tria.
A	Duōbus,	duābus,	duōbus.	*A.*	Tribus,	tribus,	tribus.

Ambo, both, is declined as *duo.*

All the *Cardinal* Numbers from *quatuor* to **centum** inclusive, are indeclinable ; and, from **centum** to **mille**, they are declined as the Plural of *bonus*.

Mille, when placed before a Genitive Plural, is a Substantive indeclinable in the Singular, and, in the **Plural**, declined *millia*, *millium*, *millibus*, &c., but, when it has a Substantive joined to it in any other case, it is a **Plural Adjective indeclinable.**

Ordinal.	*Distributive.*	*Numeral* *Adverbs.*
1. primus, -a, -um, *first.*	singŭli, -æ, -a, *one by one.*	semel, *once.*
2. secundus, *second.*	bini, *two by two.*	bis, *twice.*
3. tertius, *third.*	terni, *three by three.*	ter, *thrice.*
4. quartus, *&c.*	quaterni, *&c.*	quater, *four times.*
5. quintus.	quini.	quinquies, *&c.*
6. **sextus.**	seni.	sexies.
7. septĭmus.	septēni.	septies.
8. **octăvus.**	octōni.	octies.
9. **nonus.**	novēni.	**novies.**
10. decĭmus.	deni.	**decies.**
11. undecĭmus.	**undēni.**	**undecies.**
12. duodecĭmus.	**duodēni.**	duodecies.
13. decĭmus tertius.	**tredēni, terni deni.**	**tredecies.**
14. decĭmus quartus.	**quaterni deni.**	quatuordecies.
15. decĭmus quintus.	**quindēni.**	**quindecies.**
16. decĭmus sextus.	**seni deni.**	sexdecies.
17. decĭmus septĭmus.	septēni deni.	decies et septies.
18. decĭmus octăvus.	octōni deni.	decies et octies.
19. decĭmus nonus.	novēni deni.	decies et novies.
20. vigesĭmus, vicesĭmus.	vicēni.	vicies.
21. vigesĭmus primus.	vicēni singŭli.	vicies semel.
30. trigesĭmus, tricesĭmus.	tricēni.	tricies.
40. quadragesĭmus.	quadragēni.	quadragies.
50. quinquagesĭmus.	quinquagēni.	quinquagies.
60. sexagesĭmus.	**sexagēni.**	sexagies.
70. septuagesĭmus.	**septuagēni.**	**septuagies.**
80. octogesĭmus.	octogēni.	**octogies.**
90. nonagesĭmus.	nonagēni.	nonagies.
100. centesĭmus.	centēni.	centies.
200. ducentesĭmus.	ducēni.	**ducenties.**
300. trecentesĭmus.	trecentēni.	**trecenties.**
400. **quadringentesĭmus.**	**quater centēni.**	quadringenties.
500. **quingentesĭmus.**	**quinquies centēni.**	quingenties.
600. **sexcentesĭmus.**	**sexies centēni.**	sexcenties.
700. **septingentesĭmus.**	**septies centēni.**	septingenties.
800. octingentesĭmus.	octies centēni.	octingenties.
900. **nongentesĭmus.**	novies centēni.	nongenties.
1000. millesĭmus.	millēni.	millies.
2000. bis millesĭmus.	**bis millēni.**	bis millies.

The Multiplicative Numbers are *simplex*, simple ; *duplex*, double ; *triplex*, triple ; *quadrŭplex*, fourfold, &c.

Note.—The *Distributive* Number, when used in the sense of the Cardinal, is often found in the Singular: as, *centena arbore*, for *centum arboribus*, VIRG.

COMPARISON OF ADJECTIVES.

Those Adjectives only can be compared whose signification can be increased or diminished.

There are three degrees of Comparison: Positive, Comparative, and Superlative.

The Positive is an Adjective of the First and Second Declension, or of the Third only; the Comparative is always of the Third; the Superlative is always of the First and Second.

RULES.—1. The Comparative is formed from the first case of the Positive in *i*, by adding *or* for the Masculine and Feminine, and *us* for the Neuter : as,

> *Doctus*, learned, Gen. *docti* ; Comparative. *docti-or* for the Masc. *docti-or* for the Fem. *docti-us* for the Neuter, more learned.
> *Mitis*, meek, Dat. *miti* ; Comparative, *miti-or* for the Masc. *miti-or* for the Fem. *miti-us* for the Neuter, more meek.

2. The Superlative is formed from the first case of the Positive in *i* by adding *ssĭmus* : as,

> Gen. *Docti* ; Superlative, *docti-ssĭmus*, -a, -um, most learned.
> Dat. *Miti* ; Sup. *miti-ssĭmus*, -a, -um, most meek.

3. If the Positive end in *er*, the Superlative is formed by adding *rĭmus* to the Nominative Singular Masculine : as,

> Nom. *Pulcher*, fair ; Sup. *pulcher-rĭmus*, -a, -um, most fair.
> Nom. *Pauper*, poor ; Sup. *pauper-rĭmus*, -a, -um, most poor.

Pos.			Comp.	Sup.
Firmus,	*strong ;*	Gen. -i,	Firmior,	Firmissĭmus.
Fortis,	*brave ;*	Dat. -i,	Fortior,	Fortissĭmus.
Liber,	*free :*	Gen. -i,	Liberior,	Liberrĭmus.
Piger,	*slow ;*	Gen. -ri,	Pigrior,	Pigerrĭmus.
Prudens,	*wise ;*	Dat. -ti,	Prudentior,	Prudentissĭmus.
Velox,	*swift ;*	Dat. -ci,	Velocior,	Velocissĭmus.

IRREGULAR COMPARISONS.

Pos.	Comp.	Sup.	Pos.	Comp.	Sup.
Bonus,	Melior,	Optĭmus,	*Good,*	*better,*	*best.*
Magnus,	Major,	Maxĭmus,	*Great,*	*greater,*	*greatest.*
Malus,	Pejor,	Pessĭmus,	*Bad,*	*worse,*	*worst.*
Multus,	Plus, n.	Plurĭmus,	*Much,*	*more,*	*most.*
Parvus,	Minor,	Minĭmus,	*Little,*	*less,*	*least.*

Note.—Plus is used only in the Neuter Gender in the Singular; it is regular in the Plural, and has *plura,* and sometimes *pluria,* in the Nom. Acc. and Voc. Neuter.

See Appendix, page 103.

Different kinds of Nouns and Adjectives.

A *Collective* Noun signifies " many" in the Singular number: as, *popŭlus,* a people; *exercĭtus,* an army.

An *Abstract* Noun expresses the quality of an Adjective: as, *bonĭtas,* goodness, from *bonus,* good. Abstract Nouns commonly end in *a. as,* or *do.*

A *Patronymic* Noun is generally derived from the name of the father: as, *Priamĭdes,* the son of Priam. The poets derive them also from some other remarkable person of the family, or from the founder of a nation: as, *Æacĭdes,* the son, grandson, or one of the descendants of *Æacus; Romulĭdæ,* the Romans, from *Romŭlus.* Patronymics of men end in *des;* of women in *is, as,* and *ne.* Those in *des* and *ne* are of the First Declension, and those in *is* and *as* are of the Third.

A *Diminutive* Noun, or Adjective, expresses a diminution, or lessening of the signification of the word from which it is derived: as, *libellus,* a little book, from *liber; parvŭlus,* very little, from *parvus.* Diminutives generally end in *lus, la,* or *lum;* and the Nouns are usually of the same gender with their primitives.

A *Verbal* Noun, or Adjective, is derived from a Verb: as, *amor,* love; *amabĭlis,* lovely, from *amo.* Verbal Nouns commonly end in *is, io, or, men, us,* or *ūra;* and Adjectives in *ax,* or *ĭlis.*

An *Interrogative* word is used to ask a question: as, *uter,* which of the two? *quis,* who? *cur,* why? These words, when they do not ask a question, are called *Indefinites.*

PRONOUN.

A *Pronoun* is a word which supplies the place of a Noun.

There are eighteen simple Pronouns: *Ego, tu, sui;*

ille, ipse, iste, hic, is, quis, qui ; meus, tuus, suus, noster, vester ; nostras, vestras, **and** *cujas.*

Three of these are Substantives: *ego, tu, sui ;* the other fifteen are Adjectives.

Ego, *I ;* Plur. *we.*

Singular.		Plural.	
Nom.	Ego, *I.*	*Nom.*	Nos, *we.*
Gen.	Mei, *of me.*	*Gen.*	Nostrûm, *or* nostri, *of us.*
Dat.	Mihi, *to me.*	*Dat.*	Nobis, *to us.*
Acc.	Me, *me.*	*Acc.*	Nos, *us.*
Voc.	———	*Voc.*	———
·Abl.	Me, *with me.*	*Abl.*	Nobis, *with us.*

Tu, *thou,* or *you ;* Plur. *ye,* or *you.*

Singular.		Plural.	
N.	Tu, *thou,* or *you.*	*N.*	Vos, *ye,* or *you.*
G.	Tui, *of thee,* or *you.*	*G.*	Vestrûm, *or* vestri, *of you.*
D.	Tibi, *to thee,* or *you.*	*D.*	Vobis, *to you.*
A.	Te, *thee,* or *you.*	*A.*	Vos, *you.*
V.	Tu, *O thou,* or *you.*	*V.*	Vos, *O ye,* or *you.*
A.	Te, *with thee,* or *you.*	*A.*	Vobis, *with you.*

Sui, *of himself, of herself, of itself ;* Plur. *of themselves.*

Singular.		Plural.	
Nom.	———	*Nom.*	———
Gen.	Sui, *of himself, &c.*	*Gen.*	Sui, *of themselves.*
Dat.	Sibi, *to himself, &c.*	*Dat.*	Sibi, *to themselves.*
Acc.	Se, *himself, &c.*	*Acc.*	Se, *themselves.*
Voc.	———	*Voc.*	———
Abl.	Se, *with himself, &c.*	*Abl.*	Se, *with themselves.*

Ille, illa, illud, *he, she, it ; that ;* Plur. *they, those.*

	Singular.				Plural.		
	M.	*F.*	*N.*		*M.*	*F.*	*N.*
Nom.	Ille,	illa,	illud.	*Nom.*	Illi,	illæ,	illa.
Gen.	Illius,	illius,	illius.	*Gen.*	Illorum,	illarum,	illorum.
Dat.	Illi,	illi,	illi.	*Dat.*	Illis,	illis,	illis.
Acc.	Illum,	illam,	illud.	*Acc.*	Illos,	illas,	illa.
Voc.	Ille,	illa,	illud.	*Voc.*	Illi,	illæ,	illa.
Abl.	Illo,	illa,	illo.	*Abl.*	Illis,	illis,	illis.

Ipse, *he* **himself,** ipsa, *she herself,* ipsum, *itself ;* Plur. *they themselves ;* and iste, *he,* ista, *she,* istud, *that ;* Plur. *those ;* are declined as *ille ;* **except that** *ipse* has *ipsum* in the Nom. Acc. and Voc. Singular Neuter.

Hic, hæc, hoc, *this;* Plur. *these.*

	Singular.				Plural.		
	M.	F.	N.		M.	F.	N.
Nom.	Hic,	hæc,	hoc.	Nom.	Hi,	hæ,	hæc.
Gen.	Hujus,	hujus,	hujus.	Gen.	Horum,	harum,	horum.
Dat.	Huic,	huic,	huic.	Dat.	His,	his,	his.
Acc.	Hunc,	hanc,	hòc.	Acc.	Hos,	has,	hæc.
Voc.	Hic,	hæc,	hoc.	Voc.	Hi,	hæ,	hæc.
Abl.	Hoc,	hac,	hoc.	Abl.	His,	his,	his.

Is, ea, id, *he, she, it; that;* Plur. *they, those.*

	Singular.				Plural.		
	M.	F.	N.		M.	F.	N.
Nom.	Is,	ea,	id.	Nom.	Ii,	eæ,	ea.
Gen.	Ejus,	ejus,	ejus.	Gen.	Eōrum,	eārum,	eōrum.
Dat.	Ei,	ei,	ei.	Dat.	Iis, *or* ëis, iis, *or* ëis, iis, *or* ëis.		
Acc.	Eum,	eam,	id.	Acc.	Eos,	eas,	ea.
Voc.	—	—	—	Voc.	—	—	—
Abl.	Eo,	ea,	eo.	Abl.	Iis, *or* ëis, iis, *or* ëis, iis, *or* ëis.		

Quis, quæ, quod, *or* quid, *who, which, what?*
Interrogative.

	Singular.				Plural.		
	M.	F.	N.		M.	F.	N.
N.	Quis,	quæ,	quod, *or* quid	N.	Qui,	quæ,	quæ.
G.	Cujus,	cujus,	cujus.	G.	Quorum,	quarum,	quorum.
D.	Cui,	cui,	cui.	D.	Queis, *or* quibus, &c.		
A.	Quem,	quam,	quod, *or* quid.	A.	Quos,	quas,	quæ.
V.	—	—	—	V.	—	—	—
A.	Quo,	qua,	quo.	A.	Queis, *or* quibus, &c.		

Qui, quæ, quod, *who, which, that.*
Relative.

	Singular.				Plural.		
	M.	F.	N.		M.	F.	N.
N.	Qui,	quæ,	quod.	N.	Qui,	quæ,	quæ.
G.	Cujus,	cujus,	cujus.	G.	Quorum,	quarum,	quorum.
D.	Cui,	cui,	cui.	D.	Queis *or* quibus, &c.		
A.	Quem,	quam,	quod.	A.	Quos,	quas,	quæ.
V.	—	—	—	V.	—	—	—
A.	Quo,	qua,	quo.	A.	Queis, *or* quibus, &c.		

The Relative *qui* has also *quí* in the Ablative in all genders and in both numbers. *Qui* is sometimes used interrogatively for *quis.*

Meus, my, *or* mine; *tuus,* thy, *or* thine; *suus,* his own, her own, its own, their own; are declined like *bonus;* and *noster,* our, *or* ours; *vester,* your, *or* yours; like *ater,* of the First and

Second Declension. *Tuus, suus,* and *vester,* want the Vocative; *noster* and *meus* have it; the latter having *mi,* and sometimes *meus* in the Masculine Singular.

Nostras, of our country; *vestras,* of your country; *cujas,* of
what, *or* which country, are declined like *felix* of the Third
Declension; Gen. *nostrātis,* Dat. *nostrāti,* &c.

COMPOUND PRONOUNS.

In the Compounds of *quis* and *qui, quis* is sometimes the first, and
sometimes the last part of the word compounded; but *qui* is always
the first.

1. The Compounds of *quis,* when *quis* is put first, are *quisnam,*
who? *quispiam, quisquam,* any one; *quisque,* every one; *quisquis,*
whosoever.

QUISNAM, *who, which, what ?*

	Singular.			Plural.	
M.	*F.*	*N.*	*M.*	*F.*	*N.*
N. Quisnam,	quænam,	quodnam.	*N.* Quinam,	quænam,	quænam.
	or quidnam.				
G. Cujusnam,	cujusnam,	cujus-	*G.* Quorumnam,	quarumnam,	
	nam.			quorumnam.	
D. Cuinam,	cuinam,	cuinam.	*D.* Quibusnam,	quibusnam,	qui-
				busnam.	
A. Quemnam,	quamnam,	quod-	*A.* Quosnam,	quasnam,	quænam.
	nam, *or* quidnam.				
V. ———	———	———	*V.* ———	———	———
A. Quonam,	quanam,	quonam.	*A.* Quibusnam,	quibusnam,	qui-
				busnam.	

M.	*F.*	*N.*
Quispiam,	quæpiam,	quodpiam, *or* quidpiam.
Quisquam,	quæquam,	quidquam, *or* quicquam.
Quisque,	quæque,	quodque, *or* quidque.
Quisquis,	———	quidquid, *or* quicquid.

Quisquam has *quenquam* in the Accusative, without the Feminine.
The Plural is scarcely used. *Quisque* has also *quicque* for *quidque.*
Quisquis has no Feminine termination, except in the Ablative, and
the Neuter only in the Nominative and Accusative. *Quisquis* is
sometimes used for the Feminine.

2. The Compounds of *quis,* when *quis* is put last, have *qua* in the
Nom. Sing. Fem. and in the Nom. and Acc. Plur. Neuter. These
are *aliquis,* some; *ecquis,* whether any? *nequis,* lest any; *numquis,*
whether any? and *siquis,* if any. The last three are frequently read
separately; *ne quis, num quis, si quis.*

| | *Singular.* | | | *Plural.* | |
| M. | F. | N. | M. | F. | N. |

. Alĭquis, alĭqua, alĭquod, *or* N. Alĭqui, alĭquæ, alĭqua.
   alĭquid.

. Alicujus, alicujus, alicujus.   G. Aliquŏrum, aliquārum, aliquŏrum.

. Alicui, alicui, alicui.   D. Aliquĭbus, aliquĭbus, aliquĭbus.

. Aliquem, aliquaın, aliquod, *A.* Aliquos, aliquas, aliqua.
   or aliquid.

. Aliquis, aliqua, aliquod, *or* V. Aliqui, aliquæ, aliqua.
   aliquid.

Aliquo, aliqua, aliquo.   *A.* Aliquĭbus, aliquĭbus, aliquĭbus.

M.	F.	N.
Ecquis,	ecquæ, *or* ecqua,	ecquod, *or* ecquid.
Ne quis,	ne qua,	ne quod, *or* ne quid.
Num quis,	num qua,	num quod, *or* num quid.
Si quis,	si qua, *or* si quæ,	si quod, *or* si quid.

3. The Compounds of *qui* are *quicunque,* whosoever; *quidam,* me; *quilĭbet, quivis,* any one, whom you please.

QUICUNQUE, *whosoever, whatsoever.*

| | *Singular.* | | | *Plural.* | |
| M. | F. | N. | M. | F. | N. |

. Quicunque, quæcunque, quod- N. Quicunque, quæcunque, quæcunque.   cunque.

. Cujuscunque, cujuscunque, cu- G. Quorumcunque, quarumcun-
   juscunque; *&c.*   que, quorumcunque; *&c.*

M.	F.	N.
Quidam,	quædam,	quoddam, *or* quiddam.
Quilĭbet,	quælĭbet,	quodlĭbet, *or* quidlĭbet.
Quivis,	quævis,	quodvis, *or* quidvis.

Quidam has *quendam, quandam, quoddam,* or *quiddam,* in the Accusative Singular, and *quorundam, quarundam, quorundam,* in the Genitive Plural.

Some of these are twice compounded: as, *ecquisnam, ecquænam, quodnam,* or *ecquidnam,* who? *unusquisque, unaquæque, unumquodte,* or *unumquidque,* every one; Gen. *uniuscujusque, &c.* The former is scarcely declined beyond the Nom. Sing.; and the latter wants the Plural.

All these compounds want the Vocative except *quisque, alĭquis, tilĭbet,* and *quicunque;* and have seldom or never *queis,* but *quibus,* in the Dative and Ablative Plural.

B

IDEM, *the same*, is compounded of *is* and *dem*, and is thus declined:

Singular.			Plural.		
M.	F.	N.	M.	F.	N.
N. Īdem,	eădem,	ïdem.	*N.* Iidem,	eædem,	eădem.
G. Ejusdem,	ejusdem,	ejusdem.	*G.* Eorundem,	earundem,	eorundem.
D. Eīdem,	eīdem,	eīdem.	*D.* Iisdem,	*or* eïsdem,	&c.
A. Eundem,	eandem,	idem.	*A.* Eosdem,	easdem,	eadem.
V. Idem,	eadem,	idem.	*V.* Iidem,	eædem,	eadem.
A. Eōdem,	eădem,	eōdem.	*A.* Iisdem, *or* eïsdem,		&c.

Of *iste* and *hic* is compounded *isthic, isthæc, isthoc,* or *isthuc ;* and of *ille* and *hic, illic, illæc, illoc,* or *illuc,* which are used only in the Nom. Acc. and Abl. Sing. and in the Neut. Plural *isthæc,* and *illæc.*

The syllables *te, ce, pte, cĭne,* are sometimes added to pronouns to increase their demonstrative force ; as, *tute, hujusce,* &c.

Pronouns are divided into four Classes :

1. *Demonstratives,* which point out a person or thing present: *ego, tu, sui.*

2. *Relatives,* which refer to something going before; *ille, ipse, iste, hic, is, quis, qui.*

3. *Possessives,* which denote possession; *meus, tuus, suus, noster, vester.*

4. *Gentiles* or *Patrials,* which signify one's country: *nostras, vestras, cujas.*

Quis and *cujas* are called also *Interrogatives.*

VERB.

A Verb is a word which expresses what is affirmed or said of things.

Verbs are declined by Voices, Moods, Tenses, Numbers, and Persons.

They have two Voices: Active ending in *o ;* and Passive ending in *or.*

They have four Moods: Indicative, Subjunctive,* Imperative, and Infinitive.

They have six Tenses: Present, Imperfect, Perfect, Pluperfect, Future, and Future-Perfect.

They have two Numbers: Singular and Plural.

They have three Persons in each Number.

----

* The Subjunctive Mood is also called Potential or Conditional.

There are four Conjugations, or modes of varying Verbs, distinguished by the Infinitive Mood.

The First Conjugation has *ā* long before *re* of the Infinitive, as *amāre ;* the Second has *ē* long, as *monēre ;* the Third has *ĕ* short, as *regĕre ;* the Fourth has *i* long, as *audīre.*

There are four Principal Parts of a Verb from which the other Tenses are formed: the Present ending in *o ;* the Perfect in *i ;* the Supine in *um ;* and the Infinitive in *re ;* as, Pres. *amo ;* Perf. *amāvi ;* Sup. *amātum ;* Inf. *amāre.*

FORMATION OF THE TENSES.

From the **Present Indicative** are formed,

1. The Imperfect Indicative, in the First Conjugation, by the change of *o* into *ābam ;* in the second, of *eo* into *ēbam ;* and in the Third and Fourth, of *o* into *ēbam.*

2. The Future Indicative, in the First Conjugation, by the change of *o* into *ābo ;* in the Second, of *eo* into *ēbo ;* and in the Third and Fourth, of *o* into *am.*

3. The Present Subjunctive, in the First Conjugation, by the change of *o* into *em ;* and in the Second, Third, and Fourth, into *am.*

4. The Present Participle, in the First Conjugation, by the change of *o* into *ans ;* in the Second, of *eo* into *ens ;* and in the Third and Fourth, of *o* into *ens.*

5. The Gerund is formed from the Present Participle, by the change of *s* into *dum.*

From the **Perfect Indicative** are formed,

1. The Pluperfect Indicative, by the change of *i* into *ĕram.*
2. The Future-Perfect, by the change of *i* into *ĕro.*
3. The Perfect Subjunctive, by the change of *i* into *ĕrim.*
4. The Pluperfect Subjunctive, by the change of *i* into *issem.*
5. The Perfect Infinitive, by the change of *i* into *isse.*

From the **Supine** are formed,

1. The Future Participle, by the change of *um* into *ūrus.*
2. The Future Subjunctive is made up of the Future Participle, and *sim.*
3. The Future Infinitive is made up of the Future Participle, and *esse* or *fuisse.*

From the **Present Infinitive** are formed,

1. The Imperfect Subjunctive, by adding *m.*
2. The Present Imperative, by dropping **re.**

Sum is an irregular Verb, and is thus conjugated:

Principal Parts.

Pres. Ind.	*Perf. Ind.*	*Pres Inf.*
Sum.	fui.	esse, *to be.*

Indicative Mood.

Present Tense.

Persons.
Sing. 1. *Ego* Sum, *I am.*
2. *Tu* Es, *thou art,* or *you are.*
3. *Ille** Est, *he is.*
Plur. 1. *Nos* Sŭmus, *we are.*
2. *Vos* Estis, *ye,* or *you are.*
3. *Illi†* Sunt, *they are.*

Imperfect Tense.

Sing. 1. *Ego* Eram, *I was.*
2. *Tu* Eras, *thou wast,* or *you were.*
3. *Ille* Erat, *he was.*
Plur. 1. *Nos* Erāmus, *we were.*
2. *Vos* Erātis, *ye,* or *you were.*
3. *Illi* Erant, *they were.*

Perfect Tense.

Sing. 1. *Ego* Fui, *I was,* or *have been.*
2. *Tu* Fuisti, *thou wast,* or *hast been.*
3. *Ille* Fuit, *he was,* or *has been.*
Plur. 1. *Nos* Fuĭmus, *we were,* or *have been.*
2. *Vos* Fuistis, *ye,* or *you were,* or *have been.*
3. *Illi* Fuērunt, *or* fuēre, *they were,* or *have been.*

Pluperfect Tense.

Sing. 1. *Ego* Fuĕram, *I had been.*
2. *Tu* Fueras, *thou hadst been.*
3. *Ille* Fuerat, *he had been.*
Plur. 1. *Nos* Fuerāmus, *we had been.*
2. *Vos* Fuerātis, *ye,* or *you had been.*
3. *Illi* Fuerant, *they had been.*

Future Tense.

Sing. 1. *Ego* Ero, *I shall,* or *will be.*
2. *Tu* Eris, *thou shall,* or *wilt be.*
3. *Ille* Erit, *he shall,* or *will be.*
Plur. 1. *Nos* Erimus, *we shall,* or *will be.*
2. *Vos* Eritis, *ye,* or *you shall,* or *will be.*
3. *Illi* Erunt, *they shall,* or *will be.*

---

* Or any Noun in the Nom. Singular: as, *liber est*, the book is.
† Or any Noun in the Nom. Plural: as, *libri sunt*, the books are.

Future-Perfect Tense.

Sing. 1. *Ego* Fuĕro, *I shall have been.*
  2. *Tu* Fueris, *thou shalt have been.*
  3. *Ille* Fuerit, *he shall have been.*

Plur. 1. *Nos* Fuerimus,* *we shall have been.*
  2. *Vos* Fueritis,* *ye, or you shall have been.*
  3. *Illi* Fuerint, *they shall have been.*

Subjunctive Mood.

Present Tense.

Sing. 1. *Ego* Sim, *I may, or can be.*
  2. *Tu* Sis, *thou mayest, or canst be.*
  3. *Ille* Sit, *he may, or can be.*

Plur. 1. *Nos* Sīmus, *we may, or can be.*
  2. *Vos* Sītis, *ye, or you may, or can be.*
  3. *Illi* Sint, *they may, or can be.*

Imperfect Tense.

Sing. 1. *Ego* Essem, *I might, could, would, or should be.*
  2. *Tu* Esses, *thou mightst, couldst, wouldst, or shouldst be.*
  3. *Ille* Esset, *he might, could, would, or should be.*

Plur. 1. *Nos* Essēmus, *we might, could, would, or should be.*
  2. *Vos* Essētis, *ye, or you might, could, would, or should be.*
  3. *Illi* Essent, *they might, could, would, or should be.*

Perfect Tense.

Sing. 1. *Ego* Fuĕrim, *I may have been.*
  2. *Tu* Fueris, *thou mayest have been.*
  3. *Ille* Fuerit, *he may have been.*

Plur. 1. *Nos* Fuerĭmus, *we may have been.*
  2. *Vos* Fuerĭtis, *ye, or you may have been.*
  3. *Illi* Fuerint, *they may have been.*

Pluperfect Tense.

Sing. 1. *Ego* Fuissem, *I might, could, would, or should have been.*
  2. *Tu* Fuisses, *thou mightst, couldst, &c. have been.*
  3. *Ille* Fuisset, *he might, could, &c. have been.*

Plur. 1. *Nos* Fuissēmus, *we might, could, &c. have been.*
  2. *Vos* Fuissētis, *ye, or you might, could, &c. have been.*
  3. *Illi* Fuissent, *they might, could, &c. have been.*

---

* The quantity of the *i*, in the First and Second Persons Plural of the Future-Perfect of every Verb, is doubtful.

Future Tense.*

Sing. 1. *Ego* Futūr-us sim, *I may be about to be,* or *will be.*
2. *Tu* Futur-us sis, *thou mayest be about to be,* or *wilt be ; &c.*

Imperative Mood.

Present Tense.

Sing. 2. *Tu* Es, or esto, *be thou.*
3. *Ille* Esto, *let him be.*

Plur. 2. *Vos* Este, or estōte, *be ye,* or *be you.*
3. *Illi* Sunto, *let them be.*

Infinitive Mood.

Present and Imperfect Tense.

Esse, *to be,* that *I am,* that *I was.*

Perfect and Pluperfect Tense.

Fuisse, *to have been,* that *I have been,* that *I had been.*

Future Tense.

Futūrus, -a, -um esse, *to be about to be,* that *I will be,* that *I would be ;*
and Futūrus, -a, -um fuisse, *to have been about to be,* that *I would have been.*

Participle.

Future.

Futūrus, -a, -um, *about to be.*

FIRST CONJUGATION.

Active Voice.

Amo, *I love.*

Creo, *I create.*   Domo, *I tame.*

Principal Parts.

Pres. Indic.	Perfect.	Supine.	Pres. Infin.
Amo,	amāvi,	amātum,	amāre, *to love.*
Creo,	creāvi,	creātum,	creāre, *to create.*
Domo,	domui,	domĭtum,	domāre, *to tame.*

---

* There is no Simple Future Subjunctive, but, instead of it, the Future Participle is used with *sim.*

Indicative Mood.

Present Tense.—(*Principal Part.*)

Sing. 1. Am-o, *I love, do love,* or *am loving.*
2. Am-as, *thou lovest, dost love,* or *art loving.*
3. Am-at, *he loves, does love,* or *is loving.*

Plur. 1. Am-āmus, *we love, do love,* or *are loving.*
2. Am-ātis, *ye love, do love,* or *are loving.*
3. Am-ant, *they love, do love,* or *are loving.*

Cre-o.   Dom-o.

Imperfect Tense.—(*From the Present.*)

Sing. 1. Am-ābam, *I loved, did love,* or *was loving.*
2. Am-abas, *thou lovedst, didst love,* or *wast loving*
3. Am-abat, *he loved, did love,* or *was loving.*

Plur. 1. Am-abāmus, *we loved, did love,* or *were loving.*
2. Am-abātis, *ye loved, did love,* or *were loving.*
3. Am-abant, *they loved, did love,* or *were loving.*

Cre-ābam.   Dom-ābam.

Perfect Tense.—(*Principal Part.*)

Sing. 1. Amāv-i, *I loved,* or *have loved.*
2. Amav-isti, *thou lovedst,* or *hast loved.*
3. Amav-it, *he loved,* or *has loved.*

Plur. 1. Amav-ĭmus, *we loved,* or *have loved.*
2. Amav-istis, *ye loved,* or *have loved.*
3. Amav-ērunt, *or -ēre, they loved,* or *have loved.*

Creāv-i.   Domu-i.

Pluperfect Tense.—(*From the Perfect.*)

Sing. 1. Amav-ĕram, *I had loved.*
2. Amav-eras, *thou hadst loved.*
3. Amav-erat, *he had loved.*

Plur. 1. Amav-erāmus, *we had loved.*
2. Amav-erātis, *ye had loved.*
3. Amav-erant, *they had loved.*

Creav-ĕram.   Domu-ĕram.

Future Tense.—(*From the Present.*)

Sing. 1. Am-ăbo, *I shall,* or *will love.*
2. Am-abis, *thou shall,* or *wilt love.*
3. Am-abit, *he shall,* or *will love.*

Plur. 1. Am-abĭmus, *we shall,* or *will love.*
2. Am-abĭtis, *ye shall,* or *will love.*
3. Am-abunt, *they shall,* or *will love.*

Cre-ăbo.   Dom-ăbo.

Future-Perfect Tense.—(*From the Perfect.*)

Sing. 1. Amav-ĕro, *I shall have loved.*
2. Amav-eris, *thou shalt have loved.*
3. Amav-erit, *he shall have loved.*
Plur. 1. Amav-erimus, *we shall have loved.*
2. Amav-eritis, *ye shall have loved.*
3. Amav-erint, *they shall have loved.*
  Creav-ĕro.   Domu-ĕro.

Subjunctive Mood.*

Present Tense.—(*From the Present.*)

Sing. 1. Am-em, *I may*, or *can love.*
2. Am-es, *thou mayest*, or *canst love.*
3. Am-et, *he may*, or *can love.*
Plur. 1. Am-ēmus, *we may*, or *can love.*
2. Am-ētis, *ye may*, or *can love.*
3. Am-ent, *they may*, or *can love.*
  Cre-em.   Dom-em.

Imperfect Tense.—(*From the Present Infinitive.*)

Sing. 1. Am-ārem, *I might, could, would,* or *should love.*
2. Am-ares, *thou mightst, couldst, wouldst, &c. love.*
3. Am-aret, *he might, could, would,* or *should love.*
Plur. 1. Am-arēmus, *we might, could, &c. love.*
2. Am-arētis, *ye might, could, would,* or *should love.*
3. Am-arent, *they might, could, would,* or *should love.*
  Cre-ārem.   Dom-ārem.

Perfect Tense.—(*From the Perfect.*)

Sing. 1. Amav-ĕrim, *I may have loved.*
2. Amav-eris, *thou mayest have loved.*
3. Amav-erit, *he may have loved.*
Plur. 1. Amav-erĭmus, *we may have loved.*
2. Amav-erĭtis, *ye may have loved.*
3. Amav-erint, *they may have loved.*
  Creav-ĕrim.   Domu-ĕrim.

Pluperfect Tense.—(*From the Perfect.*)

Sing. 1. Amav-issem, *I might, could, would, &c. have loved.*
2. Amav-isses, *thou mightst, couldst, &c. have loved.*
3. Amav-isset, *he might, could, &c. have loved.*

---

* The Subjunctive Tenses, when preceded by Conjunctions, or Indefinites, are often translated like the corresponding Tenses of the Indicative: as, *si amem,* if I love: *nescio quis amet,* I know not who loves.

The Third Person Singular, and the First and Third Persons Plural of the Present, are often translated by *let :* as, *amet,* let him love.

Plur. 1. Amav-issēmus, *we might, could, &c. have loved.*
2. Amav-issētis, *ye might, could, &c. have loved.*
3. Amav-issent, *they might, could, &c. have loved.*

      Creav-issem.   Domu-issem.

Future Tense.—(*Fut. Participle* and *sim.*)

Sing. 1. Amat-ūrus sim, *I may be about to love*, or *will love.*
2. Amat-urus sis, *thou mayest be about to love*, or *wilt love; &c.*

      Creat-ūrus sim.   Domit-ūrus sim.

Imperative Mood.

Present Tense.—(*From the Pres. Inf.*)

Sing. 2. Am-a, *or* -āto, *love thou*, or *do thou love.*
3. Am-āto, *let him love.*

Plur. 2. Am-āte, *or* -atōte, *love ye*, or *do ye love.*
3. Am-anto, *let them love.*

      Cre-a, *or* -āto.   Dom-a, *or* -āto.

Infinitive Mood.*

Present and Imperfect Tense.—(*Principal Part.*)

Am-āre, *to love*, that *I love*, that *I was loving.*

      Cre-āre.   Dom-āre.

Perfect and Pluperfect Tense.—(*From the Perfect.*)

Amav-isse, *to have loved*, that *I have loved*, that *I had loved.*

      Creav-isse.   Domu-isse.

Future Tense.—(*Fut. Participle* and *esse*, or *fuisse.*)

Amat-ūrus, -a, -um esse, *to be about to love*, that *I will love*, that *I would love;*
and Amat-ūrus, -a, -um fuisse, *to have been about to love*, that *I would have loved.*

Creat-ūrus esse, *or* fuisse.   Domit-ūrus esse, *or* fuisse.

Participles.

Present and Imperfect.—(*From the Present.*)

Am-ans, *loving; Gen.* am-antis.

      Cre-ans.   Dom-ans.

Future.—(*From the Supine.*)

Amat-ūrus, -a, -um, *about to love.*

      Creat-ūrus.   Domit-ūrus.

---

* The Infinitive Tenses, when preceded by an Accusative, are commonly translated like the corresponding Tenses of the Indicative, the Particle *that* being sometimes expressed, but often understood.

Gerunds.—(From the Pres. Participle.)

Nom. Aman-dum, *loving.*
Gen. Aman-di, *of loving.*
Dat. Aman-do, *to loving.*
Acc. Aman-dum, *loving.*
Abl. Aman-do, *with loving.*
Crean-dum.   Doman-dum.

Supines.—(Principal Part.)

Amāt-um, *to love.*
Amāt-u, *to love, or to be loved.*
Creāt-um.   Domĭt-um.

Pres. Ind.	Perfect.	Supine.	Pres. Inf.
Muto,	mutāvi,	mutātum,	mutāre, *to change.*
Seco,	secui,	sectum,	secāre, *to cut.*
Voco,	vocāvi,	vocātum,	vocāre, *to call.*
Mico,	micui,	———	micāre, *to glitter.*

PASSIVE VOICE.

FORMATION OF THE TENSES.

1. The Present Indicative Passive is formed from the Present Indicative Active by adding *r*.
2. The Imperfect Indicative Passive is formed from the Imperfect Indicative Active, by the change of *m* into *r*.
3. The Perfect Indicative Passive is made up of the Perfect Participle and *sum*, or *fui.*
4. The Pluperfect Indicative Passive is made up of the Perfect Participle and *eram*, or *fuĕram.*
5. The Future Indicative Passive is formed from the Future Indicative Active, in the First and Second Conjugations, by adding *r*, and in the Third and Fourth, by the change of *m* into *r*.
6. The Future-Perfect Passive is made up of the Perfect Participle and *ero*, or *fuĕro.*
7. The Present Subjunctive Passive is formed from the Present Subjunctive Active, by the change of *m* into *r*.
8. The Imperfect Subjunctive Passive is formed from the Imperfect Subjunctive Active, by the change of *m* into *r*.
9. The Perfect Subjunctive Passive is made up of the Perfect Participle and *sim*, or *fuĕrim.*
10. The Pluperfect Subjunctive Passive is made up of the Perfect Participle and *essem*, or *fuissem.*
11. The Present Imperative Passive is formed from the Present Imperative Active by adding *re.*

12. The Present Infinitive Passive is formed from the Present Infinitive Active, in the First, Second, and Fourth Conjugations, by the change of *e* into *i*, and in the Third, by the change of *ĕre* into *i*.

13. The Perfect Infinitive Passive is made up of the Perfect Participle and *esse*, or *fuisse*.

14. The Future Infinitive Passive is made up of the First Supine and *iri*.

15. The Perfect Participle is formed from the First Supine, by the change of *um* into *us*.

16. The Future Participle Passive is formed from the Gerund by the change of *dum* into *dus*.

Pres. Indicative.	Perf. Participle.	Pres. Infinitive.
Amor,	amātus,	amāri, *to be loved*.
Creor,	creātus,	creāri, *to be created*.
Domor,	domĭtus,	domāri, *to be tamed*.

Indicative Mood.

Present Tense.—(*From the Pres. Ind. Active.*)

Sing. 1. Am-or, *I am loved.**
     2. Am-āris, *or* -āre, *thou art loved.*
     3. Am-ātur, *he is loved.*

Plur. 1. Am-āmur, *we are loved.*
     2. Am-amĭni, *ye are loved.*
     3. Am-antur, *they are loved.*

           Cre-or.   Dom-or.

Imperfect Tense.—(*From the Imp. Ind. Active.*)

Sing. 1. Am-ābar, *I was loved.†*
     2. Am-abāris, *or* -abāre, *thou wast loved.*
     3. Am-abātur, *he was loved.*

Plur. 1. Am-abāmur, *we were loved.*
     2. Am-abamĭni, *ye were loved.*
     3. Am-abantur, *they were loved.*

           Cre-ābar.   Dom-ābar.

---

* The true meaning of *amor* is, I am in the state of being loved, or I am being loved; as, *domus ædificatur*, the house is building, is being built; not the house is built.

† *Amabar* properly signifies, I was being loved, I was in the state of being loved: as, *domus ædificabatur*, the house was building, was being built; not the house was built.

Perfect Tense.—(*Perfect Part.* and *sum,* or *fui.*)

Sing. 1. *Amăt_us sum, *or* fui, *I was,* or *have been loved.*
     2. Amat_us es, *or* fuisti, *thou wast,* or *hast been loved.*
     3. Amat_us est, *or* fuit, *he was,* or *has been loved.*

Plur. 1. Amat_i sumus, *or* fuĭmus, *we were,* or *have been loved.*
     2. Amat_i estis, *or* fuistis, *ye were,* or *have been loved.*
     3. Amat_i sunt, fuĕrunt, *or* fuĕre, *they were,* or *have been loved.*

     Creăt-us sum, *or* fui.   Domĭt-us sum, *or* fui.

Pluperfect Tense.—(*Perf. Part.* and *eram,* or *fuĕram.*)

Sing. 1. Amăt_us eram, *or* fuĕram, *I had been loved.*
     2. Amat_us eras, *or* fueras, *thou hadst been loved.*
     3. Amat_us erat, *or* fuerat, *he had been loved.*

Plur. 1. Amat_i erāmus, *or* fuerāmus, *we had been loved.*
     2. Amat_i erātis, *or* fuerătis, *ye had been loved.*
     3. Amat_i erant, *or* fuerant, *they had been loved.*

     Creăt-us eram, *or* fuĕram.   Domĭt-us eram, *or* fuĕram.

Future Tense.—(*From the Fut. Ind. Active.*)

Sing. 1. Am-ābor, *I shall,* or *will be loved.*
     2. Am-abĕris, *or* -abĕre, *thou shalt,* or *wilt be loved.*
     3. Am-abĭtur, *he shall,* or *will be loved.*

Plur. 1. Am-abĭmur, *we shall,* or *will be loved.*
     2. Am-abimĭni, *ye shall,* or *will be loved.*
     3. Am-abuntur, *they shall,* or *will be loved.*

     Cre-ābor.   Dom-ābor.

Future-Perfect Tense.—(*Perf. Part.* and *ero,* or *fuĕro.*)

Sing. 1. Amăt_us ero, *or* fuĕro, *I shall have been loved.*
     2. Amat_us eris, *or* fueris, *thou shalt have been loved.*
     3. Amat_us erit, *or* fuerit, *he shall have been loved.*

Plur. 1. Amat_i erimus, *or* fuerimus, *we shall have been loved.*
     2. Amat_i eritis, *or* fueritis, *ye shall have been loved.*
     3. Amat_i erunt, *or* fuerint, *they shall have been loved.*

     Creăt-us ero, *or* fuĕro.   Domĭt-us ero, *or* fuĕro.

---

* Properly *amatus, -a, -um sum,* or *fui,* I have been loved. The Perfect Participle, in all the Tenses of which it forms a part, must agree in Gender and Number with the Nominative of the Verb : as, *vir amatus est,* the man is loved; *fœmina amata est,* the woman is loved; *animal amatum est,* the animal is loved. *Fui, fuisti,* &c. are very seldom found with the Perfect Participle.

Subjunctive Mood.

Present Tense.—(*From the Pres. Sub. Active.*)

Sing. 1. Am-er, *I may,* or *can be loved.*
2. Am-ēris, *or* -ēre, *thou mayest,* or *canst be loved.*
3. Am-ētur, *he may,* or *can be loved.*

Plur. 1. Am-ēmur, *we may,* or *can be loved.*
2. Am-emīni, *ye may,* or *can be loved.*
3. Am-entur, *they may,* or *can be loved.*

Cre-er.   Dom-er.

Imperfect Tense.—(*From the Imp. Sub. Active.*)

Sing. 1. Am-ārer, *I might, could, &c. be loved.*
2. Am-arēris, *or* -arēre, *thou mightst, &c. be loved.*
3. Am-arētur, *he might, &c. be loved.*

Plur. 1. Am-arēmur, *we might, &c. be loved.*
2. Am-aremīni, *ye might, &c. be loved.*
3. Am-arentur, *they might, &c. be loved.*

Cre-ārer.   Dom-ārer.

Perfect Tense.—(*Perf. Part.* and *sim,* or *fuĕrim.*)

Sing. 1. **Amāt-us sim,** *or* fuĕrim, *I may have been loved.*
2. Amat-us sis, *or* fueris, *thou mayest have been loved.*
3. Amat-us sit, *or* fuerit, *he may have been loved.*

Plur. 1. Amat-i simus, *or* fuerīmus, *we may have been loved.*
2. Amat-i sitis, *or* fuerītis, *ye may have been loved.*
3. Amat-i sint, *or* fuerint, *they may have been loved.*

Creāt-us sim, *or* fuĕrim.   Domĭt-us sim, *or* fuĕrim.

Pluperfect Tense.—(*Perf. Part.* and *essem,* or *fuissem.*)

Sing. 1. Amāt-us essem, *or* fuissem, *I might, &c. have been loved.*
2. Amat-us esses, *or* fuisses, *thou mightst, &c. have been loved.*
3. Amat-us esset, *or* fuisset, *he might, &c. have been loved.*

Plur. 1. Amat-i essēmus, *or* fuissēmus, *we might, &c. have been loved.*
2. Amat-i essētis, *or* fuissētis, *ye might, &c. have been loved.*
3. Amat-i essent, *or* fuissent, *they might, &c. have been loved.*

Creāt-us essem, *or* fuissem.   Domĭt-us essem, *or* fuissem.

Imperative Mood.

Present Tense.—(*From the Pres. Imper. Active.*)

Sing. 2. Am-āre, *or* -ātor, *be thou loved.*
3. Am-ātor, *let him be loved.*

Plur. 2. Am-amīni, *be ye loved.*
3. Am-antor, *let them be loved.*

Cre-āre, *or* -ātor.   Dom-āre, *or* -ātor.

Infinitive Mood.

Present and Imperfect Tense.—(*From the Pres. Inf. Active.*)
Am-āri, *to be loved*, that *I am loved*, that *I was loved.*
Cre-āri. Dom-āri.

Perfect and Pluperfect Tense.—(*Perf. Part.* and *esse*, or *fuisse.*)
Amāt-us, -a, -um esse, *or* fuisse, *to have been loved*, that *I have
been loved*, that *I had been loved.*
Creāt-us esse, *or* fuisse. Domĭt-us esse, *or* fuisse.

Future Tense.—(*Supine* and *iri.*)
Amāt-um iri, *to be about to be loved*, that *I will be loved*,
that *I would be loved.*
Creāt-um iri. Domĭt-um iri.

Participles.

Perfect.—(*From the Supine.*)
Amāt-us, -a, -um, *loved*, or *being loved.*
Creāt-us, -a, -um. Domĭt-us, -a, -um.

Future.—(*From the Gerund.*)
Aman-dus, -da, -dum, *to be loved, deserving*, or *requiring to be
loved.*
Crean-dus. Doman-dus.

Pres. Ind.	Perf. Part.	Pres. Inf.
Mutor,	mutātus,	mutāri, *to be changed.*
Secor,	sectus,	secāri, *to be cut.*
Vocor,	vocātus,	vocāri, *to be called.*

SECOND CONJUGATION.

Active Voice.

MONEO, *I advise.*
Doceo, *I teach.* Jubeo, *I order.*

Principal Parts.

Pres. Ind.	Perfect.	Supine.	Pres. Inf.
Moneo,	Monui,	monĭtum,	monēre, *to advise.*
Doceo,	docui,	doctum,	docēre, *to teach.*
Jubeo,	jussi,	jussum,	jubēre, *to order.*

Indicative Mood.

Present Tense.—(*Principal Part.*)

Sing. 1. Mon-eo, *I advise, do advise,* or *am advising.*
2. Mon-es, *thou advisest, dost advise,* or *art advising.*
3. Mon-et, *he advises, does advise,* or *is advising.*

Plur. 1. Mon-ēmus, *we advise, do advise,* or *are advising.*
2. Mon-ētis, *ye advise, do advise,* or *are advising.*
3. Mon-ent, *they advise, do advise,* or *are advising.*

Doc-eo.   Jub-eo.

Imperfect Tense.—(From the Present.)

Sing. 1. Mon-ēbam, *I advised, did advise,* or *was advising.*
2. Mon-ebas, *thou advisedst, didst advise,* or *wast advising.*
3. Mon-ebat, *he advised, did advise,* or *was advising.*
Plur. 1. Mon-ebāmus, *we advised, did advise,* or *were advising.*
2. Mon-ebātis, *ye advised, did advise,* or *were advising.*
3. Mon-ebant, *they advised, did advise,* or *were advising.*

Doc-ēbam.   Jub-ēbam.

Perfect Tense.—(Principal Part.)

Sing. 1. Monu-i, *I advised,* or *have advised.*
2. Monu-isti, *thou advisedst,* or *hast advised.*
3. Monu-it, *he advised,* or *has advised.*
Plur. 1. Monu-ĭmus, *we advised,* or *have advised.*
2. Monu-istis, *ye advised,* or *have advised.*
3. Monu-ērunt, *or -ēre, they advised,* or *have advised.*

Docu-i.   Juss-i.

Pluperfect Tense.—(From the Perfect.)

Sing. 1. Monu-ĕram, *I had advised.*
2. Monu-eras, *thou hadst advised.*
3. Monu-erat, *he had advised.*
Plur. 1. Monu-erāmus, *we had advised.*
2. Monu-erātis, *ye had advised.*
3. Monu-erant, *they had advised.*

Docu-ĕram.   Juss-ĕram.

Future Tense.—(From the Present.)

Sing. 1. Mon-ēbo, *I shall,* or *will advise.*
2. Mon-ebis, *thou shalt,* or *wilt advise.*
3. Mon-ebit, *he shall,* or *will advise.*
Plur. 1. Mon-ebĭmus, *we shall,* or *will advise.*
2. Mon-ebĭtis, *ye shall,* or *will advise.*
3. Mon-ebunt, *they shall,* or *will advise.*

Doc-ēbo.   Jub-ēbo.

Future-Perfect Tense.—(From the Perfect.)

Sing. 1. Monu-ĕro, *I shall have advised.*
2. Monu-eris, *thou shalt have advised.*
3. Monu-erit, *he shall have advised.*
Plur 1. Monu-erimus, *we shall have advised.*
2. Monu-eritis, *ye shall have advised.*
3. Monu-erint, *they shall have advised.*

Docu-ĕro.   Juss-ĕro.

Subjunctive Mood.

Present Tense.—(*From the Present.*)

Sing. 1. Mone-am, *I may,* or *can advise.*
2. Mone-as, *thou mayest,* or *canst advise.*
3. Mone-at, *he may,* or *can advise.*

Plur. 1. Mone-āmus, *we may,* or *can advise.*
2. Mone-ātis, *ye may,* or *can advise.*
3. Mone-ant, *they may,* or *can advise.*
Doce-am.   Jube-am.

Imperfect Tense.—(*From the Present Infinitive.*)
Sing. 1. Mon-ērem, *I might, could, would,* or *should advise.*
2. Mon-eres, *thou mightst, couldst, &c. advise.*
3. Mon-eret, *he might, could, would, &c. advise.*

Plur. 1. Mon-erēmus, *we might, could, would, &c. advise.*
2. Mon-erētis, *ye might, could, would, &c. advise.*
3. Mon-erent, *they might, could, would, &c. advise.*
Doc-ērem.   Jub-ērem.

Perfect Tense.—(*From the Perfect.*)
Sing. 1. Monu-ĕrim, *I may have advised.*
2. Monu-eris, *thou mayest have advised.*
3. Monu-erit, *he may have advised.*
Plur. 1. Monu-erĭmus, *we may have advised.*
2. Monu-erĭtis, *ye may have advised.*
3. Monu-erint, *they may have advised.*
Docu-ĕrim.   Juss-ĕrim.

Pluperfect Tense.—(*From the Perfect.*)
Sing. 1. Monu-issem, *I might, could, &c. have advised.*
2. Monu-isses, *thou mightst, couldst, &c. have advised.*
3. Monu-isset, *he might, could, &c. have advised.*
Plur. 1. Monu-issēmus, *we might, could, &c. have advised.*
2. Monu-issētis, *ye might, could, &c. have advised.*
3. Monu-issent, *they might, could, &c. have advised.*
Docu-issem.   Juss-issem.

Future Tense.—(*Fut. Participle* and *sim.*)
Sing. 1. Monit-ūrus sim, *I may be about to advise,* or *will advise.*
2. Monit-urus sis, *thou mayest be about to advise,* or *wilt advise; &c.*
Doct-ūrus sim.   Juss-ūrus sim.

Imperative Mood.

Present Tense.—(*From the Pres. Inf.*)
Sing. 2. Mon-e, *or* -ēto, *advise thou,* or *do thou advise.*
3. Mon-ēto, *let him advise.*

Plur. 2. Mon-ēte, *or* -etòte, *advise ye,* or *do ye advise.*
  3. Mon-ento, *let them advise.*
    Doc-e, *or* -ēto.   Jub-e, *or* -ēto.

Infinitive Mood.

Present and Imperfect Tense.—(*Principal Part.*)
Mon-ēre, *to advise,* that *I advise,* that *I was advising.*
    Doc-ēre.   Jub-ēre.

Perfect and Pluperfect Tense.—(*From the Perfect.*)
Monu-isse, *to have advised,* that *I have advised,* that *I had advised.*
    Docu-isse.   Juss-isse.

Future Tense.—(*Fut. Participle* and *esse,* or *fuisse.*)
Monit-ūrus, -a, -um esse, *to be about to advise,* that *I will advise,* that *I would advise ;*
and Monit-ūrus, -a, -um fuisse, *to have been about to advise,* that *I would have advised.*
 Doct-ūrus esse, *or* fuisse. Juss-ūrus esse, *or* fuisse.

Participles.

Present and Imperfect.—(*From the Present.*)
    Mon-ens, *advising.*
    Doc-ens.   Jub-ens.

Future.—(*From the Supine.*)
  Monit-ūrus, -a, -um, *about to advise.*
    Doct-ūrus.   Juss-ūrus.

Gerunds.—(*From the Pres. Participle.*)
Nom. Monen-dum, *advising.*
Gen. Monen-di, *of advising.*
Dat. Monen-do, *to advising.*
Acc. Monen-dum, *advising.*
Abl. Monen-do, *with advising.*
  Docen-dum.   Juben-dum.

Supines.—(*Principal Part.*)
Monĭt-um, *to advise.*
Monĭt-u, *to advise,* or *to be advised.*
    Doct-um.   Juss-um.

Pres. Ind.	*Perf.*	*Sup.*	*Pres. Inf.*
Præbeo,	præbui,	præbĭtum,	præbēre, *to afford.*
Torqueo,	torsi,	tortum,	torquēre, *to twist.*
Video,	vidi,	visum,	vidēre, *to see.*
Lugeo,	luxi,	———	lugēre, *to mourn.*

PASSIVE VOICE.

Pres. Ind.	Perf. Participle.	Pres. Infinitive.
Moneor,	monĭtus,	monēri, *to be advised.*
Doceor,	doctus,	docēri, *to be taught.*
Jubeor,	jussus,	jubēri, *to be ordered.*

Indicative Mood.

Present Tense.—(*From the Pres. Ind. Active.*)

Sing. 1. Mon-eor, *I am advised.*
　　　2. Mon-ēris, *or* -ēre, *thou art advised.*
　　　3. Mon-ētur, *he is advised.*

Plur. 1. Mon-ēmur, *we are advised.*
　　　2. Mon-emĭni, *ye are advised.*
　　　3. Mon-entur, *they are advised.*

　　　　Doc-eor.　　　　Jub-eor.

Imperfect Tense.—(*From the Imp. Ind. Active.*)

Sing. 1. Mon-ēbar, *I was advised.*
　　　2. Mon-ebāris, *or* -ebāre, *thou wast advised.*
　　　3. Mon-ebātur, *he was advised.*

Plur. 1. Mon-ebāmur, *we were advised.*
　　　2. Mon-ebamĭni, *ye were advised.*
　　　3. Mon-ebantur, *they were advised.*

　　　　Doc-ēbar.　　　　Jub-ēbar.

Perfect Tense.—(*Perf. Part.* and *sum,* or *fui.*)

Sing. 1. Monĭt-us sum, *or* fui, *I was,* or *have been advised.*
　　　2. Monĭt-us es, *or* fuisti, *thou wast,* or *hast been advised.*
　　　3. Monĭt-us est, *or* fuit, *he was,* or *has been advised.*

Plur. 1. Monĭt-i sumus, *or* fuĭmus, *we were,* or *have been advised.*
　　　2. Monĭt-i estis, *or* fuistis, *ye were,* or *have been advised.*
　　　3. Monĭt-i sunt, fuērunt, *or* fuēre, *they were,* or *have been advised.*

　　　　Doct-us sum, *or* fui.　　　Juss-us sum, *or* fui.

Pluperfect Tense.—(*Perf. Part.* and *eram,* or *fuĕram.*)

Sing. 1. Monĭt-us eram, *or* fuĕram, *I had been advised.*
　　　2. Monĭt-us eras, *or* fueras, *thou hadst been advised.*
　　　3. Monĭt-us erat, *or* fuerat, *he had been advised.*

Plur. 1. Monĭt-i erāmus, *or* fuerāmus, *we had been advised.*
　　　2. Monĭt-i erātis, *or* fuerātis, *ye had been advised.*
　　　3. Monĭt-i erant, *or* fuerant, *they had been advised.*

　　　　Doct-us eram, *or* fuĕram.　　　Juss-us eram, *or* fuĕram.

Future Tense.—(*From the Fut. Ind. Active.*)

Sing. 1. Mon-ēbor, *I shall*, or *will be advised.*
2. Mon-ebĕris, *or -ebĕre, thou shalt*, or *wilt be advised.*
3. Mon-ebĭtur, *he shall*, or *will be advised.*

Plur. 1. Mon-ebĭmur, *we shall*, or *will be advised.*
2. Mon-ebimĭni, *ye shall*, or *will be advised.*
3. Mon-ebuntur, *they shall*, or *will be advised.*

Doc-ēbor.   Jub-ēbor.

Future-Perfect Tense.—(*Perf. Part.* and *ero*, or *fuĕro.*)

Sing. 1. Monĭt-us ero, *or* fuĕro, *I shall have been advised.*
2. Monĭt-us eris, *or* fueris, *thou shalt have been advised.*
3. Monĭt-us erit, *or* fuerit, *he shall have been advised.*

Plur. 1. Monĭt-i erimus, *or* fuerimus, *we shall have been advised.*
2. Monĭt-i eritis, *or* fuerĭtis, *ye shall have been advised.*
3. Monĭt-i erunt, *or* fuerint, *they shall have been advised.*

Doct-us ero, *or* fuĕro.   Juss-us ero, *or* fuĕro.

Subjunctive Mood.

Present Tense.—(*From the Pres. Sub. Active.*)

Sing. 1. Mon-ear, *I may*, or *can be advised.*
2. Mon-eāris, *or -eāre, thou mayest*, or *canst be advised.*
3. Mon-eātur, *he may*, or *can be advised.*

Plur. 1. Mon-eāmur, *we may*, or *can be advised.*
2. Mon-eamĭni, *ye may*, or *can be advised.*
3. Mon-eantur, *they may*, or *can be advised.*

Doc-ear.   Jub-ear.

Imperfect Tense.—(*From the Imp. Sub. Active.*)

Sing. 1. Mon-ĕrer, *I might, could, would, &c. be advised.*
2. Mon-erĕris, *or -erĕre, thou mightst, &c. be advised.*
3. Mon-erētur, *he might, &c. be advised.*

Plur. 1. Mon-erēmur, *we might, &c. be advised.*
2. Mon-eremĭni, *ye might, &c. be advised.*
3. Mon-erentur, *they might, &c. be advised.*

Doc-ērer.   Jub-ērer.

Perfect Tense.—(*Perf. Part.* and *sim*, or *fuĕrim.*)

Sing. 1. Monĭt-us sim, *or* fuĕrim, *I may have been advised.*
2. Monĭt-us sis, *or* fueris, *thou mayest have been advised.*
3. Monĭt-us sit, *or* fuerit, *he may have been advised.*

Plur. 1. Monĭt-i simus, *or* fuerĭmus, *we may have been advised.*
2. Monĭt-i sitis, *or* fuerĭtis, *ye may have been advised.*
3. Monĭt-i sint, *or* fuerint, *they may have been advised.*

Doct-us sim, *or* fuĕrim.   Juss-us sim, *or* fuĕrim.

Pluperfect Tense.—(*Perf. Part.* and *essem,* or *fuissem.*)

Sing. 1. Monĭt-us essem, *or* fuissem, *I might, &c. have been advised.*
  2. Monit-us esses, *or* fuisses, *thou mightst, &c. have been advised.*
  3. Monit-us esset, *or* fuisset, *he might, &c. have been advised.*

Plur. 1. Monĭt-i essēmus, *or* fuissēmus, *we might, &c. have been advised.*
  2. Monit-i essētis, *or* fuissētis, *ye might, &c. have been advised.*
  3. Monit-i essent, *or* fuissent, *they might, &c. have been advised.*

Doct-us essem, *or* fuissem. Juss-us essem, *or* fuissem.

Imperative Mood.

Present Tense.—(*From the Pres. Imper. Active.*)

Sing. 2. Mon-ēre, *or* -ētor, *be thou advised.*
  3. Mon-ētor, *let him be advised.*

Plur. 2. Mon-emĭni, *be ye advised.*
  3. Mon-entor, *let them be advised.*

  Doc-ēre, *or* -ētor. Jub-ēre, *or* -ētor.

Infinitive Mood.

Present and Imperfect Tense.—(*From the Pres. Inf. Active.*)

Mon-ēri, *to be advised,* that *I am advised,* that *I was advised.*

  Doc-ēri. Jub-ēri.

Perfect and Pluperfect Tense.—(*Perf. Part.* and *esse,* or *fuisse.*)

Monĭt-us, -a, -um esse, *or* fuisse, *to have been advised,* that *I have been advised,* that *I had been advised.*

  Doct-us esse, *or* fuisse. Juss-us esse, *or* fuisse.

Future Tense.—(*Supine* and *iri.*)

Monĭt-um iri, *to be about to be advised,* that *I will be advised,* that *I would be advised.*

  Doct-um iri. Juss-um iri.

Participles.

Perfect.—(*From the Supine.*)

Monĭt-us, -a, -um, *advised,* or *being advised.*

  Doct-us, -a, -um. Juss-us, -a, -um.

Future.—(*From the Gerund.*)

Monen-dus, -da, -dum, *to be advised, deserving,* or *requiring to be advised.*

  Docen-dus. Juben-dus.

Pres. Ind.	*Perf. Part.*	*Pres. Inf.*
Præbeor,	præbĭtus,	præbēri, *to be afforded.*
Torqueor,	tortus,	torquēri, *to be twisted.*
Videor,	visus,	vidēri, *to be seen.*

THIRD CONJUGATION.

Active Voice.

Rego, *I rule.*

Lego, *I read.*   Capio, *I take.*

Principal Parts.

Pres. Ind.	*Perf.*	*Sup.*	*Pres. Inf.*
Rego,	rexi,	rectum,	regĕre, *to rule*
Lego,	legi,	lectum,	legĕre, *to read.*
Capio,	cepi,	captum,	capĕre, *to take.*

Indicative Mood.

Present Tense.—(*Prin. Part.*)
Reg-o, *I rule, do rule,* or *am ruling.*

Singular.			*Plural.*		
1.	2.	3.	1.	2.	3.
Reg-o.	-is.	-it.	-ĭmus.	-ĭtis.	-unt.
	Leg-o.		Cap-io.		

Imperfect Tense.—(*Present.*)
Reg-ĕbam, *I ruled, did rule,* or *was ruling.*

Reg-ĕbam	-ebas.	-ebat.	-ebāmus.	-ebātis.	-ebant.
	Leg-ĕbam.		Capi-ĕbam.		

Perfect Tense.—(*Prin. Part.*)
Rexi, *I ruled,* or *have ruled.*

Rex-i.	-isti.	-it.	-ĭmus.	-istis.	-ērunt, *or* -ēre.
	Leg-i.		Cep-i.		

Pluperfect Tense.—(*Perfect.*)
Rex-ĕram, *I had ruled.*

Rex-ĕram.	-eras.	-erat.	-erāmus.	-erātis.	-erant.
	Leg-ĕram.		Cep-ĕram.		

Future Tense.—(*Present.*)
Reg-am, *I shall,* or *will rule.*

Reg-am.	-es.	-et.	-ēmus.	-ētis.	-ent.
	Leg-am.		Capi-am.		

Future-Perfect Tense.—(*Perfect.*)
Rex-ĕro, *I shall have ruled.*

Rex-ĕro.	-eris.	-erit.	-erimus.	-eritis.	-erint.
	Leg-ĕro.		Cep-ĕro.		

Subjunctive Mood.

Present Tense.—(*Present.*)

Reg-am, *I may,* or *can rule.*

Reg-am.	-as.	-at.	-āmus.	-ātis.	-ant.
	Leg-am.	Capi-am.			

Imperfect Tense.—(*Pres. Inf.*)

Reg-ĕrem, *I might, could, &c. rule.*

Reg-ĕrem.	-eres.	-eret.	-erēmus.	-erētis.	-erent.
	Leg-ĕrem.	Cap-ĕrem.			

Perfect Tense.—(*Perfect.*)

Rex-ĕrim, *I may have ruled.*

Rex-ĕrim.	-eris.	-erit.	-erĭmus.	-erĭtis.	-erint.
	Leg-ĕrim.	Cep-ĕrim.			

Pluperfect Tense.—(*Perfect.*)

Rex-issem, *I might, could, &c. have ruled.*

Rex-issem.	-isses.	-isset.	-issēmus.	-issētis.	-issent.
	Leg-issem.	Cep-issem.			

Future Tense.—(*Fut. Part.* and *sim.*)

Rect-ūrus sim, *I may be about to rule, &c.*

Rect-ūrus sim.	sis.	sit.	-ūri simus.	sitis.	sint.
	Lect-ūrus sim.	Capt-ūrus sim.			

Imperative Mood.

Present Tense.—(*Pres. Inf.*)

Reg-e, or **-ĭto,** *rule thou,* or *do thou rule.*

— Reg-e, or -ĭto.	-ĭto.	— -ĭte, or -itōte.	-unto.
	Leg-e, *or* -ĭto.	Cap-e, *or* -ĭto.	

Infinitive Mood.

Present and Imperfect Tense.—(*Prin. Part.*)

Reg-ĕre, *to rule,* that *I rule,* that *I was ruling.*

Leg-ĕre.   Cap-ĕre.

Perfect and Pluperfect Tense.—(*Perfect.*)

Rex-isse, *to have ruled,* that *I have ruled,* that *I had ruled.*

Leg-isse.   Cep-isse.

Future Tense.—(*Fut. Part.* and *esse,* or *fuisse.*)

Rect-ūrus, -a, -um esse, *to be about to rule,* that *I will rule,*
that *I would rule ;*

and Rect-ūrus, -a, -um fuisse, *to have been about to rule,* that
I would have ruled.

Lect-ūrus esse, *or* fuisse.   Capt-ūrus esse, *or* fuisse.

Participles.

Present and Imperfect.—(*Present.*)

Reg-ens, *ruling.*
Leg-ens.   Capi-ens.

Future.—(*Supine.*)

Rect-ūrus, -a, -um, *about to rule.*
Lect-ūrus.   Capt-ūrus.

Gerunds.—(*Pres. Participle.*)

Regen-dum, *ruling,* &c.
Legen-dum.   Capien-dum.

Supines.—(*Prin. Part.*)

Rect-um, *to rule.*   Rect-u, *to rule,* or *to be ruled.*
Lect-um.   Capt-um.

Pres. Ind.	*Perf.*	*Sup.*	*Pres. Inf.*
Jacio,	jeci,	jactum,	jacĕre, *to throw.*
Mitto,	misi,	missum,	mittĕre, *to send.*
Tango,	tetĭgi,	tactum,	tangĕre, *to touch.*
Viso,	visi,	————	visĕre, *to visit.*

PASSIVE VOICE.

Pres. Ind.	*Perf. Part.*		*Pres. Inf.*
Regor,	rectus,		regi, *to be ruled.*
Legor,	lectus,	legi,	*to be read.*
Capior,	captus,	capi,	*to be taken.*

Indicative Mood.

Present Tense.—(*Pres. Ind. Active.*)

Regor, *I am ruled.*

	Singular.				*Plural.*	
1.	2.	3.	1.	2.	3.	
Reg-or.	-ĕris, *or* -ĕre.	-ĭtur.	-ĭmur.	-imĭni.	-untur.	
		Leg-or. Capi-or.				

Imperfect Tense.—(*Imp. Ind. Active.*)

Reg-ēbar, *I was ruled.*

Reg-ēbar. { -ebāris,   -ebātur.   -ebāmur.   -ebamĭni.   -ebantur.
          { *or* -ebāre.

Leg-ēbar.   Capi-ēbar.

Perfect Tense.—(*Perf. Part.* and *sum*, or *fui.*)

Rect-us sum, *or* fui, *I was,* or *have been* ruled.

Rect-us sum, *or* fui, &c.   -i sumus, *or* fuĭmus, &c.

Lect-us sum, *or* fui.   Capt-us sum, *or* fui.

Pluperfect Tense.—(*Perf. Part.* and *eram*, or *fŭĕram.*)

Rect-us eram, *or* fuĕram, *I had been* ruled.

Rect-us eram, *or* fuĕram, &c.   -i erāmus, *or* fuerāmus, &c.

Lect-us eram, *or* fuĕram.   Capt-us eram, *or* fuĕram.

Future Tense.—(*Fut. Ind. Active.*)

Reg-ar, *I shall,* or *will be ruled.*

Reg-ar.   -ēris, *or* -ēre.   -ētur.   -ēmur.   -emĭni.   -entur.

Leg-ar.   Capi-ar.

Future-Perfect Tense.—(*Perf. Part.* and *ero*, or *fŭĕro.*)

Rect-us ero, *or* fuĕro, *I shall have been ruled.*

Rect-us ero, *or* fuĕro, &c.   -i erimus, *or* fuerimus, &c.

Lect-us ero, *or* fuĕro.   Captus ero, *or* fuĕro.

Subjunctive Mood.

Present Tense.—(*Pres. Sub. Active.*)

Reg-ar, *I may,* or *can be ruled.*

Reg-ar.   -āris, *or* -āre.   -ātur.   -āmur.   -amĭni.   -antur.

Leg-ar.   Capi-ar.

Imperfect Tense.—(*Imp. Sub. Active.*)

Reg-ĕrer, *I might, could, &c. be ruled.*

Reg-ĕrer, { -erēris,   -erētur.   -erēmur.   -eremĭni.   -erentur.
          { *or* -erēre.

Leg-ĕrer.   Cap-ĕrer.

Perfect Tense.—(*Perf. Part.* and *sim*, or *fŭĕrim.*)

Rect-us sim, *or* fuĕrim, *I may have been ruled.*

Rect-us sim, *or* fuĕrim, &c.   -i simus, *or* fuerĭmus, &c.

Lect-us sim, *or* fuĕrim.   Capt-us sim, *or* fuĕrim.

Pluperfect Tense.—(*Perf. Part.* and *essem,* or *fuissem.*)

Rect-us essem, or fuissem, *I might, &c. have been ruled.*
Rect-us essem, or fuissem, &c.   -i essēmus, or fuissēmus, &c.
Lect-us essem, or fuissem.   Capt-us essem, or fuissem.

Imperative Mood.

Present Tense.—(*Pres. Imper. Active.*)
Reg-ĕre, or -ĭtor, *be thou ruled.*
——   Reg-ĕre, *or -*ĭtor.   -ĭtor.   ——   -imĭni.   -untor.
Leg-ĕre, or -ĭtor.   Cap-ĕre, or -ĭtor.

Infinitive Mood.

Present and Imperfect Tense.—(*Pres. Inf. Active.*)
Reg-i, *to be ruled,* that *I am ruled,* that *I was ruled.*
Leg-i.   Cap-i.

Perfect and Pluperfect Tense.—(*Perf. Part.* and *esse,* or *fuisse.*)
Rect-us, -a, -um esse, or fuisse, *to have been ruled,* that *I have
been ruled,* that *I had been ruled.*
Lect-us esse, or fuisse.   Capt-us esse, or fuisse.

Future Tense.—(*Supine* and *iri.*)
Rect-um iri, *to be about to be ruled,* that *I will be ruled,* that *I
would be ruled.*
Lect-um iri.   Capt-um iri.

Participles.

Perfect.—(*Supine.*)
Rect-us, -a, -um, *ruled,* or *being ruled.*
Lect-us.   Capt-us.

Future.—(*Gerund.*)
Regen-dus, -da, -dum, *to be ruled, deserving,* or *requiring to
be ruled.*
Legen-dus.   Capien-dus.

Pres. Ind.	Perf. Part.	Pres. Inf.
Jacior,	jactus,	jaci, *to be thrown.*
Mittor,	missus,	mitti, *to be sent.*
Tangor,	tactus,	tangi, *to be touched.*

FOURTH CONJUGATION.

Active Voice.
AUDIO, *I hear.*
Polio, *I polish.*   Vincio, *I bind.*

C

Principal Parts.

Pres. Ind.	*Perf.*	*Sup.*	*Pres. Inf.*
Audio,	audīvi,	audītum,	audīre, *to hear.*
Polio,	polīvi,	polītum,	polīre, *to polish.*
Vincio,	vinxi,	vinctum,	vincīre, *to bind.*

Indicative Mood.

Present Tense.—(*Prin. Part.*)

Aud-io, *I hear, do hear,* or *am hearing.*

Singular.			*Plural.*		
1.	2.	3.	1.	2.	3.
Aud-io.	-is.	-it.	-īmus.	-ītis.	-iunt.
		Pol-io.	Vinc-io.		

Imperfect Tense.—(*Present.*)

Audi-ēbam, *I heard, did hear,* or *was hearing.*

Audi-ēbam.	-ebas.	-ebat.	-ebāmus.	-ebātis.	-ebant.
	Poli-ēbam.		Vinci-ēbam.		

Perfect Tense.—(*Prin. Part.*)

Audīv-i, *I heard,* or *have heard.*

Audīv-i.	-isti.	-it.	-īmus.	-istis.	-ērunt, *or* -ēre.
		Polīv-i.	Vinx-i.		

Pluperfect Tense.—(*Perfect.*)

Audiv-ĕram, *I had heard.*

Audiv-ĕram.	-eras.	-erat.	-erāmus.	-erātis.	-erant.
	Poliv-ĕram.		Vinx-ĕram.		

Future Tense.—(*Present.*)

Audi-am, *I shall,* or *will hear.*

Audi-am.	-es.	-et.	-ēmus.	-ētis.	-ent.
	Poli-am.		Vinci-am.		

Future-Perfect Tense.—(*Perfect.*)

Audiv-ĕro, *I shall have heard.*

Audiv-ĕro.	-eris.	-erit.	-erimus.	-eritis.	-erint.
	Poliv-ĕro.		Vinx-ĕro.		

Subjunctive Mood.

Present Tense.—(*Present.*)

Audi-am, *I may,* or *can hear.*

Audi-am.	-as.	-at.	-āmus.	-ātis.	-ant.
	Poli-am.		Vinci-am.		

Imperfect Tense.—(*Pres. Inf.*)

Aud-īrem, *I might, could, &c. hear.*

Aud-īrem.　-ires.　-iret.　　　-irēmus.　-irētis.　-irent.
　　　　　Pol-īrem.　　　Vinc-īrem.

Perfect Tense.—(*Perfect.*)

Audiv-ĕrim, *I may have heard.*

Audiv-ĕrim.　-eris.　-erit.　　　-erĭmus.　-erītis.　-erint.
　　　　　Poliv-ĕrim.　　　Vinx-ĕrim.

Pluperfect Tense.—(*Perfect.*)

Audiv-issem, *I might, could, &c. have heard.*

Audiv-issem.　-isses.　-isset.　　-issēmus.　-issĕtis.　-issent.
　　　　　Poliv-issem.　　　Vinx-issem.

Future Tense.—(*Fut. Part. and sim.*)

Audit-ūrus sim, *I may be about to hear, &c.*

Audit-ūrus sim.　sis.　sit.　　-uri simus.　sitis.　sint.
　　　　　Polit-ūrus sim.　　　Vinct-ūrus sim.

Imperative Mood.

Present Tense.—(*Pres. Inf.*)

Aud-i, *or* -īto, *hear thou,* or *do thou hear.*

— Aud-i, *or* -īto.　-īto.　— -īte, *or* -itōte.　-iunto.
　　　　Pol-i, *or* -īto.　　　Vinc-i, *or* -īto.

Infinitive Mood.

Present and Imperfect Tense.—(*Prin. Part.*)

Aud-īre, *to hear,* that *I hear,* that *I was hearing.*
　　　　Pol-īre.　　　Vinc-īre.

Perfect and Pluperfect Tense.—(*Perfect.*)

Audiv-isse, *to have heard,* that *I have heard,* that *I had heard.*
　　　　Poliv-isse.　　　Vinx-isse.

Future Tense.—(*Fut. Part. and esse, or fuisse.*)

Audit-ūrus, -a, -um esse, *to be about to hear,* that *I will hear,* that *I would hear;*

and Audit-ūrus, -a, -um fuisse, *to have been about to hear,* that *I would have heard.*

Polit-ūrus esse, *or* fuisse.　　Vinct-ūrus esse, *or* fuisse.

Participles.

Present and Imperfect.—(*Present.*)

Audi-ens, *hearing.*
　　　Poli-ens.　　　Vinci-ens.

Future.—(*Supine.*)

Audit-ūrus, -a, -um, *about to hear.*

Polit-ūrus.   Vinct-ūrus.

Gerunds.—(*Pres. Participle.*)

Audien-dum, *hearing,* &c.

Polien-dum.   Vincien-dum.

Supines.—(*Prin. Part.*)

Audit-um, *to hear.*   Audīt-u, *to hear,* or *to be heard.*

Polit-um.   Vinct-um.

Pres. Ind.	Perf.	Sup.	Pres. Inf.
Condio,	condīvi,	condĭtum,	condīre, *to season.*
Nutrio,	nutrīvi,	nutrītum,	nutrīre, *to nourish.*
Sepio,	sepsi,	septum,	sepīre, *to enclose.*
Gestio,	gestīvi,	————	gestīre, *to exult.*

PASSIVE VOICE.

Pres. Ind.	Perf. Part.	Pres. Inf.
Audior,	audītus,	audīri, *to be heard.*
Polior,	polītus,	polīri, *to be polished.*
Vincior,	vinctus,	vincīri, *to be bound.*

Indicative Mood.

Present Tense.—(*Pres. Ind. Active.*)

Aud-ior, *I am heard.*

Singular.			Plural.		
1.	2.	3.	1.	2.	3.
Aud-ior.	-ĭris, *or* -ĭre.	-ītur.	-īmur.	-imĭni.	-iuntur.
	Pol-ior.		Vinc-ior.		

Imperfect Tense.—(*Imp. Ind. Active.*)

Audi-ēbar, *I was heard.*

Audi-ēbar. } -ebāris, *or* -ebāre.   -ebātur.   -ebāmur.   -ebamĭni.   -ebantur.

Poli-ēbar.   Vinci-ēbar.

Perfect Tense.—(*Perf. Part.* and *sum,* or *fui.*)

Audit-us sum, *or* fui, *I was,* or *have been heard.*

Audīt-us sum, *or* fui, &c.   -i sumus, *or* fuĭmus, &c.

Polīt-us sum, *or* fui.   Vinct-us sum, *or* fui.

Pluperfect Tense.—(*Perf. Part.* and *eram,* or *fuĕram.*)

Audīt-us eram, *or* fuĕram, *I had been heard.*

Audīt-us eram, *or* fuĕram, &c.   -i erāmus, *or* fuerāmus, &c.

Polīt-us eram, *or* fuĕram.   Vinct-us eram, *or* fuĕram.

Future Tense.—(*Fut. Ind. Active.*)

Audi-ar, *I shall*, or *will be heard.*

Audi-ar. -ēris, *or* -ēre. -ētur.   -ēmur. -emīni. -entur.

Poli-ar.   Vinci-ar.

Future-Perfect Tense.—(*Perf. Part.* and *ero*, or *fuĕro.*)

Audĭt-us ero, *or* **fuĕro,** *I shall have been heard.*

Audĭt-us ero, *or* **fuĕro,** &c.   -i erimus, *or* fuerimus, &c.

Polĭt-us ero, *or* fuĕro.   Vinct-us ero, *or* fuĕro.

Subjunctive Mood.

Present Tense.—(*Pres. Sub. Active.*)

Audi-ar, *I may*, or *can be heard.*

Audi-ar. -āris, *or* -āre. -ātur.   -āmur. -amīni, -antur.

Poli-ar.   Vinci-ar.

Imperfect Tense.—(*Imp. Sub. Active.*)

Aud-īrer, *I might, could, &c. be heard.*

Aud-īrer. -irēris, *or* -irēre. -irētur.   -irēmur, -iremīni. -irentur.

Pol-īrer.   Vinc-īrer.

Perfect Tense.—(*Perf. Part.* and *sim*, or *fuĕrim.*)

Audĭt-us sim, *or* **fuĕrim,** *I may have been heard.*

Audĭt-us sim, *or* fuĕrim, &c.   -i simus, *or* fuerĭmus, &c.

Polĭt-us sim, *or* fuĕrim.   Vinct-us sim, *or* fuĕrim.

Pluperfect Tense.—(*Perf. Part.* and *essem*, or *fuissem.*)

Audĭt-us essem, *or* **fuissem,** *I might, &c. have been heard.*

Audĭt-us essem, *or* **fuissem,** &c.   -i essēmus, *or* fuissēmus, &c.

Polĭt-us essem, *or* fuissem.   Vinct-us essem, *or* fuissem.

Imperative Mood.

Present Tense.—(*Pres. Imper. Active.*)

Aud-īre, *or* -ītor, *be thou heard.*

—— Aud-īre, *or* -ītor. -ītor.   —— -imīni. -iuntor.

Pol-īre, *or* -ītor.   Vinc-īre, *or* -ītor.

Infinitive Mood.

Present and Imperfect Tense.—(*Pres. Inf. Active.*)

Aud-īri, *to be heard*, that *I am heard,* that *I was heard.*

Pol-īri.   Vinc-īri.

Perfect and Pluperfect Tense.—(*Perf. Part.* and *esse*, or *fuisse.*)

Audĭt-us, -a, -um esse, *or* fuisse, *to have been heard*, that *I have been heard*, that *I had been heard.*

    Polĭt-us esse, *or* fuisse.   Vinct-us esse, *or* fuisse.

Future Tense.—(*Supine* and *iri.*)

Audĭt-um **iri**, *to be about to be heard*, that *I will be heard*, that
    • *I would be heard.*

    Polĭt-um iri.   Vinct-um iri.

Participles.

Perfect.—(*Supine.*)

Audĭt-us, -a, -um, **heard**, or *being heard.*

    Polĭt-us.   Vinct-us.

Future.—(*Gerund.*)

Audien-dus, -da, -dum, *to be heard, deserving*, or *requiring to be heard.*

    Polien-dus.   Vincien-dus.

Pres. Ind.	*Perf. Part.*	*Pres. Inf.*
Condior,	condĭtus,	condīri, *to be seasoned.*
Nutrior,	nutrītus,	nutrīri, *to be nourished.*
Sepior,	septus,	sepīri, *to be enclosed.*

Exercise showing the signification of the different Tenses of the Infinitive Mood, when preceded by a Verb and an Accusative.

Dicit me scribĕre, he says *that* I write, do write, *or* am writing.
Dixit me scribere, he said *that* I wrote, did write, *or* was writing.
Dicit me scripsisse, he says *that* I wrote, did write, *or* have written.
Dixit me scripsisse, he said *that* I had written.
Dicit me scriptūrum esse, he says *that* I will write.
Dixit me scripturum esse, he said *that* I would write.
Dicit me scripturum fuisse, he says *that* I would have written.
Dicit literas scribi, he says *that* letters are writing, are in the state of being written, *or* are being written.
Dixit literas scribi, he said *that* letters were writing, *or* being written.
Dicit literas scriptas esse, he says *that* letters are, *or* were written.
Dicit literas scriptas fuisse, he says *that* letters have been written.
Dixit literas scriptas fuisse, he said *that* letters had been written.
Dicit literas scriptum iri, he says *that* letters will be written.
Dixit literas scriptum iri, he said *that* letters would be written.

In Verbs which want the Supine, the Future Infinitive is supplied by *fore ut*, or *futurum esse ut*, with the Subjunctive: as, *scio fore*, or *futurum esse ut lugeat*, I know that he will mourn; *scivi fore*, or *futurum esse ut lugeret*, I knew that he would mourn.

Different kinds of Verbs.

An *Active* Verb expresses some action of its nominative: as, *amo*, I love. When the action implied in the Verb is communicated to some other object, it is called *Active Transitive :* as, *amo patrem*, I love my father. When the action does not pass from the agent to any other object, the Verb is called *Active Intransitive :* as, *curro*, I run.

A *Passive* Verb denotes that its nominative is suffering, or is acted upon: as, *amor*, I am loved.

A *Neuter* Verb expresses neither action nor suffering, but simply the state, posture, or quality of its nominative: as, *palleo*, I am pale ; *sedeo*, I sit; *gaudeo*, I am glad.

A *Substantive* Verb expresses being or existence. The Substantive Verbs are, *sum*, I am ; *fio*, I am made ; *forem*, I might be ; *existo*, I exist.

A *Deponent* Verb has a Passive Termination, with an Active, or Neuter signification: as, *loquor*, I speak ; *morior*, I die. Verbs are called *Deponent* because they have laid aside their Passive signification.

A *Common* Verb has a Passive termination with an Active and Passive signification: as, *criminor*, I accuse, *or* I am accused.

A *Neuter-Passive* Verb is partly Active and partly Passive in termination ; and is Active, Passive, or Neuter in signification : as, *audeo*, I dare ; *fio*, I am made ; *gaudeo*, I rejoice.

A *Frequentative* Verb expresses a frequent repetition of the action, or an increase of the signification denoted by the primitive: as, *clamito*, I cry frequently, from *clamo*. Frequentatives are formed from the last Supine, by the change of *atu* into *ito*, in Verbs of the First, and of *u* into *o*, in Verbs of the other Conjugations. They are all of the First Conjugation, and end in *ito, so, xo*, and, when Deponent, in *or*.

An *Inceptive* Verb expresses the beginning or continued increase of the action or state denoted by the primitive: as, *caleo*, I am warm ; *calesco*. I grow warm. Inceptives are formed from the Second Person Singular of the Present Indicative, by adding *co :* as, *caleo, cales, cales-co*. They are all of the Third Conjugation, and want both Perfect and Supine. Inceptives are likewise formed from Nouns and Adjectives: as, *puerasco*, from *puer ; dulcesco*, from *dulcis*.

A *Desiderative* Verb expresses a desire to do something. Desideratives are formed from the Future Participle Active, by changing *rus* into *rio*, and shortening the penultima: as, *cæno*, I sup ; *cænaturus, cænaturio*, I desire to sup. They are all of the Fourth Conjugation, and want both Perfect and Supine, except *esurio*, which is regularly conjugated, and *parturio*, and *nupturio*, which have the Perfect.

Participle.

A *Participle* is a kind of Adjective derived from a Verb, which, in its signification, implies time. When Participles are divested of the idea of time, they admit degrees of Comparison.

There are four Participles; the Present and Imperfect, ending in *ns*; the Perfect, in *tus, sus, xus*; the Future Active, in *rus*; and the Future Passive, in *dus*. Those which end in *ns* and *rus* are generally Active; those in *dus* are always Passive; and those in *tus, sus, xus*, are generally Passive, but sometimes Active, or Commen, according to the nature of the Verbs from which they come.

Active Verbs have two Participles, the Present and Future: as, *amans*, loving; *amatūrus*, about to love. Active Verbs have no Perfect Participle, but this defect is supplied by *quum*, with the Pluperfect Subjunctive: as, *quum amavisset*, when he had loved, *or* having loved.

Active Intransitive Verbs have frequently three Participles: as, *carens, caritūrus, carendus*, from *careo*; and sometimes four: as, *vigĭlans, vigilātus, vigilatūrus, vigilandus*, from *vigĭlo*.

Passive Verbs have two Participles, the Perfect and Future: as, *amōtus*, loved; *amandus*, to be loved. The Future Participle often supplies the place of a Present Participle Passive.

Neuter Verbs have two Participles: as, *sedens, sessūrus*, from *sedeo*.

Deponent Verbs of an Active signification have generally four Participles: as, *loquens, locūtus, locutūrus, loquendus*, from *loquor*. Those of a Neuter signification have generally three: as, *labens, lapsus, lapsūrus*, from *labor*. The Perfect Participle of *Deponent* Verbs has an Active signification, and corresponds to the English Perfect Participle with *having*: as, *locūtus*, having spoken.

Common Verbs have generally four Participles: as, *crimĭnans, crimĭnātus, criminatūrus, criminandus*, from *crimĭnor*. Their Perfect Participle has sometimes an Active, and sometimes a Passive signification: as, *crimĭnātus*, having accused, *or* being accused.

Neuter Passive Verbs have generally three Participles: as, *gaudens, gavīsus, gavisūrus*, from *gaudeo*.

DEPONENT VERBS.*

FIRST CONJUGATION.

CONOR, *I attempt.*

Pres. Ind.	*Perf. Part.*	*Pres. Inf.*
Conor,	conātus,	conāri, *to attempt.*

---

* Deponent Verbs are conjugated like the Passive Voice of the Conjugations to which they belong, except that they have four Participles, with the Gerunds, Supines, and Future of the Infinitive like Active Verbs. The Perfect Participle has an Active signification: ?s, conātus, *having attempted*, not *being attempted*.

Indicative Mood.

Present Tense.

Con-or, *I attempt, do attempt, or am attempting.*

	Singular.			*Plural.*	
1.	2.	3.	1.	2.	3.
Con-or.	-āris, *or* -āre.	-ātur.	-āmur.	-amĭni.	-antur.

Imperfect Tense.

Con-ābar, *I attempted, did attempt, or was attempting.*

Con-ābar. { -abāris, *or* -abāre. } -abātur. -abāmur. -abamĭni. -abantur.

Perfect Tense.

Conāt-us sum, *or* fui, *I attempted, or have attempted.*

Conāt-us sum, *or* fui, &c.   -i sumus, *or* fuimus, &c.

Pluperfect Tense.

Conāt-us eram, **or fuĕram, *I had attempted.***

Conāt-us eram, *or* fuĕram, &c.   -i erāmus, *or* fuerāmus, &c.

Future Tense.

Con-ābor, *I shall, or will attempt.*

Con-ābor. { -abĕris, *or* -abēre. } -abĭtur. -abĭmur. -abimĭni. -abuntur.

Future-Perfect Tense.

Conāt-us ero, *or* fuĕro, *I shall have attempted.*

Conāt-us ero, *or* fuĕro, &c.   -i erimus, *or* fuerĭmus, &c.

Subjunctive Mood.

Present Tense.

Con-er, *I may, or can attempt.*

Con-er. -ēris, *or* -ēre. -ētur. -ēmur. -emĭni. -entur.

Imperfect Tense.

Con-ārer, *I might, could, &c. attempt.*

Con-ārer, { -arēris, *or* -arēre. } -arētur. -arēmur. -aremĭni. -arentur

Perfect Tense.

Conāt-us sim, *or* fuĕrim, *I may have attempted.*

Conāt-us sim, *or* fuĕrim, &c.   -i simus, *or* fuerĭmus, &c

Pluperfect Tense.

Conāt-us essem, *or* fuissem, *I might, &c. have attempted.*

Conāt-us essem, *or* fuissem, &c. -i essēmus, *or* fuissēmus, &c.

Imperative Mood.
Present Tense.

Con-āre, *or* -ātor, *attempt thou,* or *do thou attempt.*
—— Con-āre, *or* -ātor. -ātor.   —— -amĭni.   -antor.

Infinitive Mood.
Present and Imperfect Tense.

Con-āri, *to attempt,* that *I attempt,* that *I was attempting.*

Perfect and Pluperfect Tense.

Conāt-us, -a, -um esse, *or* fuisse, *to have attempted,* that *I have attempted,* that *I had attempted.*

Future Tense.

Conat-ūrus, -a, -um esse, *to be about to attempt,* that *I will attempt,* that *I would attempt ;*

and Conat-ūrus, -a, -um fuisse, *to have been about to attempt,* that *I would have attempted.*

Participles.

Present and Imperfect.—Conans, *attempting.*
Perfect.—Conāt-us, -a, -um, *having attempted.*
Fut. Active.—Conat-ūrus, -a, -um, *about to attempt.*
Fut. Passive.—Conan-dus, -da, -dum, *to be attempted, deserving,* or *requiring to be attempted.*

Gerunds.

Nom. Conan-dum, *attempting.*   *Gen.* Conan-di, &c.

Supines.

Conāt-um, *to attempt.* Conāt-u, *to attempt,* or *to be attempted.*

Pres. Ind.	Perf. Part.	Pres. Inf.
Causor,	causātus,	causāri, *to blame.*
Lætor,	lætātus,	lætāri, *to rejoice.*
Prædor,	prædātus,	prædāri, *to plunder.*

SECOND CONJUGATION.

Pres. Ind.	Perf. Part.	Pres. Inf.
Mereor,	merĭtus,	merēri, *to deserve.*
Fateor,	fassus,	fatēri, *to confess.*
Polliceor	pollicĭtus,	pollicēri, *to promise.*

Conjugated like *Moneor,* page 38.

THIRD CONJUGATION.

Pres. Ind.	*Perf. Part.*	*Pres. Inf.*
Utor,	usus,	uti, *to use.*
Morior,	mortuus,	mori, *to die.*
Sequor,	secûtus,	sequi, *to follow.*

Conjugated like *Regor*, page 43.

FOURTH CONJUGATION

Pres. Ind.	*Perf. Part.*	*Pres. Inf.*
Blandior,	blandîtus,	blandîri, *to flatter.*
Metior,	mensus,	metîri, *to measure.*
Ordior,	orsus,	ordîri, *to begin.*

Conjugated like *Audior*, page 48.

NEUTER-PASSIVE VERBS.

Audeo, *I dare.*

Pres. Ind.	*Perf. Part.*	*Pres. Inf.*
Audeo,	ausus,	audêre, *to dare.*

Indicative Mood.

Present Tense.

Aud-eo, *I dare, do dare,* or *am daring.*

	Singular.			*Plural.*	
1.	2.	3.	1.	2.	3.
Aud-eo.	-es.	-et.	-ēmus.	-ētis.	-ent.

Imperfect Tense.

Aud-ēbam, *I dared, did dare,* or *was daring.*

Aud-ēbam.	-ebas.	-ebat.	-ebāmus.	-ebātis.	-ebant.

Perfect Tense.

Aus-us sum, *or* fui, *I dared,* or *have dared.*

Aus-us sum, *or* fui, &c.		-i sumus, *or* fuĭmus, &c.

Pluperfect Tense.

Aus-us eram, *or* fuĕram, *I had dared.*

Aus-us eram, *or* fuĕram, &c.	-i erāmus, *or* fuerāmus, &c.

Future Tense.

Aud-ēbo, *I shall,* or *will dare.*

Aud-ēbo,	-ebis.	-ebit.	-ebĭmus.	-ebĭtis.	-ebunt.

Future-Perfect Tense.

Aus-us ero, *or* fuĕro, *I shall have dared.*

Aus-us ero, *or* fuĕro, &c.   -i erimus, *or* fuerimus, &c.

Subjunctive Mood.

Present Tense.

Aude-am, *I may,* or *can dare.*

Aude-am.   -as.   -at.   -āmus.   -ātis.   -ant.

Imperfect Tense.

Aud-ērem, *I might, could, &c. dare.*

Aud-ērem.   -eres.   -eret.   -erēmus.   -erētis.   -erent.

Perfect Tense.

Aus-us sim, *or* fuĕrim, *I may have dared.*

Aus-us sim, *or* fuĕrim, &c.   -i simus, *or* fuerĭmus, &c.

Pluperfect Tense.

Aus-us essem, *or* fuissem, *I might, &c. have dared.*

Aus-us essem, *or* fuissem, &c.   -i essēmus, *or* fuissēmus, &c.

Imperative Mood.

Present Tense.

Aud-e, *or* -ēto, *dare thou,* or *do thou dare.*

Aud-e, *or* -ēto.   -ēto.   — -ēte, *or* -etōte.   -ento.

Infinitive Mood.

Present and Imperfect Tense.

Aud-ēre, *to dare,* that *I dare,* that *I was daring.*

Perfect and Pluperfect Tense.

Aus-us, -a, -um esse, *or* fuisse, *to have* dared, that *I have dared,* that *I had dared.*

Future Tense.

Aus-ūrus, -a, -um essé, *to be about to dare,* that *I will dare,* that *I would dare ;*

and Aus-ūrus, -a, -um fuisse, *to have been about to dare,* that *I would have dared.*

Participles.

Present and Imperfect.—Aud-ens, *daring.*

Perfect.—Aus-us, -a, -um, *having dared.*

Fut. Active—Aus-ūrus -a, -um, *about to dare.*

Fut. P.—Auden-dus, -da, -dum, *to be dared, &c.* (seldom used.)

Gerunds.

Nom. Auden-dum, *daring.*   *Gen.* Auden-di, &c.

Supines.

Aus-um, *to dare.*   Aus-u, *to dare,* or *to be dared.*

The other Neuter-Passive Verbs are,

Gaudeo,	gavīsus,	gaudēre, *to rejoice.*
Soleo,	solītus,	solēre, *to be wont.*
Fido,	fisus,	fidēre, *to trust,* with its com-

pounds *confīdo,* I trust, and *diffīdo,* I distrust, which have also *confīdi,* and *diffīdi,* in the Perfect.

IRREGULAR VERBS.

There are six Irregular Verbs: *sum, eo, queo, volo, fero,* and *fio,* with their Compounds.

The Compounds *absum, adsum, &c.* are declined like *sum* (see p. 24), except *subsum,* which wants the Perfect and the Tenses formed from it.

In *Prosum,* a *d* is inserted where *sum* begins with *e.*

PROSUM, *I do good.*

Prosum,   profui,   prodesse, *to do good.*

Indicative Mood.

Pres. Pro-sum. prod-es. prod-est. pro-sŭmus. prod-estis, pro-sunt.

Imp. Prod-ĕram. -eras. -erat. -erāmus. -erātis. -erant.

Fut. Prod-ĕro. -eris. -erit. -erimus. -eritis. -erunt.

Subjunctive Mood.

Imp. Prod-essem. -esses. -esset. -essēmus. -essētis. -essent.

Imperative Mood.

Pres. Prod-es, *or* -esto. -esto. -este, *or* -estōte. pro-sunto.

Infinitive Mood.

Pres. and *Imp.* Prod-esse.

In the other Tenses, *prosum* is declined like *sum* ; *pro-fui, pro-fuĕram, pro-sim, &c.*

POSSUM, *I am able.*

Possum,   potui,   posse, *to be able.*

Indicative Mood.

Pres.	Pos–sum.	pot–es.	pot–est.	pos–sŭmus.	pot–estis.	pos–sunt.
Imp.	Pot–ĕram.	–eras.	–erat.	–erāmus.	–erātis.	–erant.
Perf.	Potu–i.	–isti.	–it.	–ĭmus.	–istis.	–ĕrunt, or–ēre.
Plup.	Potu–ĕram.	–eras.	–erat.	–erāmus.	–erātis.	–erant.
Fut.	Pot–ĕro.	–eris.	–erit.	–erimus.	–eritis.	–erunt.
Fut.-P.	Potu–ĕro.	–eris.	–erit.	–erimus.	–eritis.	–erint.

Subjunctive Mood.

Pres.	Pos–sim.	–sis.	–sit.	–sīmus.	–sītis.	–sint.
Imp.	Pos–sem.	–ses.	–set.	–sĕmus.	–sĕtis.	–sent.
Perf.	Potu–ĕrim.	–eris.	–erit.	–erīmus.	–erĭtis.	–erint.
Plup.	Potu–issem.	–isses.	–isset.	–issēmus.	–issētis.	–issent.

(*No Imperative.*)

Infinitive Mood.

Pres. and *Imp.* Posse.   *Perf.* and *Plup.* Potuisse.
Participle, Pres. and *Imp.* Potens, *able,* is always used as an Adjective. *The rest not used.*

Possum is compounded of *potis,* able, and *sum.*

Eo, *I go.*

Eo, ĭvi, ĭtum, īre, *to go.*

Indicative Mood.

Pres.	Eo.	is.	it.	īmus.	ītis.	eunt.
Imp.	Ibam.	ības.	ibat.	ibāmus.	ibātis.	ibant.
Perf.	Ivi.	īvisti.	ivit.	ivīmus.	ivistis.	ivĕrunt, or ivēre.
Plup.	Ivĕram.	īveras.	iverat.	iverāmus.	iverātis.	iverant.
Fut.	Ibo.	ībis.	ibit.	ibĭmus.	ibĭtis.	ibunt.
Fut.-P.	Ivĕro.	īveris.	iverit.	iverimus.	iveritis.	iverint.

Subjunctive Mood.

Pres.	Eam.	eas.	eat.	eāmus.	eātis.	eant.
Imp.	Irem.	īres.	iret.	irēmus.	irētis.	irent.
Perf.	Ivĕrim.	īveris.	iverit.	iverīmus.	iverītis.	iverint.
Plup.	Ivissem.	īvisses.	ivisset.	ivissēmus.	ivissētis.	ivissent.
Fut.	Itūrus sim.	sis.	sit.	–i simus.	sitis.	sint.

Imperative Mood.

Pres.	——	I, *or* ĭto.	ĭto.	——	īte, *or* itōte.	eunto.

Infinitive Mood.

Pres. and *Imp.* Ire.
Perf. and *Plup.* Ivisse.
Fut. It–ūrus, -a, –um esse ;
and It–ūrus, -a, –um fuisse.

Participles.

Pres. and *Imp.* Iens.   *Gen.* euntis.
Fut. It–ūrus, -a, –um.

	Gerunds.		*Supines.*
Nom.	Eundum.		Itum.
Gen.	Eundi, -do ; &c.		Itu.

Eo is, for the most part, formed regularly according to the Fourth Conjugation. It is used in the Passive as an Impersonal only : as, *itur, ibātur, &c.*

The Compounds of *eo* generally reject *v* in the Perfect and the Tenses formed from it : as, *abeo, abii,* seldom *abīvi, abĭtum, abīre,* to go away. *Ambio, -īvi, -ītum, -īre,* to surround, is a regular Verb of the Fourth Conjugation.

Queo, I can, *nequeo,* I cannot, and *veneo,* I am sold, are conjugated like *eo,* except that they want the Imperative and Gerunds, and *veneo* has no Participles or Supines.

Volo, *I am willing, I wish.*

Vŏlo,   volui,   velle, *to be willing, to wish.*

Indicative Mood.

Pres.	Vŏlo.	vis.	vult.	volŭmus.	vultis.	volunt.
Imp.	Vol-ēbam.	-ebas.	-ebat.	-ebāmus.	-ebātis.	-ebant.
Perf.	Volu-i.	-isti.	-it.	-ĭmus.	-istis.	{ -ērunt, or -ēre.
Plup.	Volu-ĕram.	-eras.	-erat.	-erāmus.	-erātis.	-erant.
Fut.	Vol-am.	-es.	-et.	-ēmus.	-ētis.	-ent.
Fut.-P.	Volu-ĕro.	-eris.	-erit.	-erimus.	-eritis.	-erint.

Subjunctive Mood.

Pres.	Vel-im.	-is.	-it.	-īmus.	-ītis.	-int.
Imp.	Vel-lem.	-les.	-let.	-lēmus.	-lētis.	-lent.
Perf.	Volu-ĕrim.	-eris.	-erit.	-erīmus.	-erītis.	-erint.
Plup.	Volu-issem.	-isses.	-isset.	-issēmus.	-issētis.	-issent.

(*No Imperative.*)

Infinitive Mood.

Pres. and *Imp.* Velle.   *Perf.* and *Plup.* Voluisse.

Participle, Pres. and *Imp.* Volens, *willing,* is commonly used as an Adjective. *The rest not used.*

Nolo, *I am unwilling.*

Nŏlo, nolui, nolle, *to be unwilling.* (*non* and *volo.*)

Indicative Mood.

Pres.	Nŏlo.	nonvis.	nonvult.	nolŭmus.	nonvultis.	nolunt.
Imp.	Nol-ēbam.	-ebas.	-ebat.	-ebāmus.	-ebātis.	-ebant.
Perf.	Nolu-i.	-isti.	-it.	-ĭmus.	-istis.	{ -ērunt, or -ēre.
Plup.	Nolu-ĕram.	-eras.	-erat.	-erāmus.	-erātis.	-erant.
Fut.	Nol-am.	-es.	-et.	-ēmus.	-ētis.	-ent.
Fut.-P.	Nolu-ĕro.	-eris	-erit.	-erimus.	-eritis.	-erint.

Subjunctive Mood.

Pres.	Nol-im.	-is.	-it.	-īmus.	-itis.	-int.
Imp.	Nol-lem.	-les.	-let.	-lēmus.	-lētis.	-lent.
Perf.	Nolu-ĕrim.	-eris.	-erit.	-erīmus.	-erītis.	-erint.
Plup.	Nolu-issem.	-isses.	-isset.	-issēmus.	-issētis.	-issent.

Imperative Mood.

Pres.   —   Nol-i, *or* -īto.   — -īte, *or* -itōte.   —

Infinitive Mood.

Pres. and **Imp.** Nolle.   **Perf.** and **Plup.** Noluisse.

Participle. **Pres.** and **Imp.** Nolens, **unwilling**, is commonly used as an Adjective. *The rest not used.*

MALO, I am more willing, I prefer.

Mǎlo,   malui,   **malle**, *to be more willing, to prefer.*
(*mage* and *volo.*)

Indicative Mood.

Pres.	Mǎlo.	mavis.	mǎvult.	malŭmus.	mavultis.	malunt.
Imp.	Mal-ĕbam.	-ebas.	-ebat.	-ebāmus.	-ebātis.	-ebant.
Perf.	Malu-i.	-isti.	-it.	-īmus.	-istis.	-ērunt, or -ēre.
Plup.	Malu-ĕram.	-eras.	-erat.	-erāmus.	-erātis.	-erant.
Fut.	Mal-am.	-es.	-et.	-ēmus.	-ētis.	-ent.
Fut.-P.	Malu-ĕro.	-eris.	-erit.	-erimus.	-eritis.	-erint.

Subjunctive Mood.

Pres.	Mal-im.	-is.	-it.	-īmus.	-ītis.	-int.
Imp.	Mal-lem.	-les.	-let.	-lēmus.	-lētis.	-lent.
Perf.	Malu-ĕrim.	-eris.	-erit.	-erīmus.	-erītis.	-erint.
Plup.	Malu-issem.	-isses.	-isset.	-issēmus.	-issētis.	-issent.

(*No Imperative.*)

Infinitive Mood.

Pres. and **Imp.** Malle.   **Perf.** and **Plup.** Maluisse.

The rest not used.

Volo, nolo, and *malo,* retain something of the **Third** Conjugation ; *ois, vult, vultis, &c.* being contracted for *volis, volit, volītis, &c.*

ACTIVE VOICE.

FERO, I carry, I bring, I suffer.

Fĕro,   tŭli,   lātum,   ferre, *to carry, to bring, to suffer.*

Indicative Mood.

Pres.	Fĕro.	fers.	fert.	ferĭmus.	fertis.	ferunt.
Imp.	Fer-ĕbam.	-ebas.	-ebat.	-ebāmus.	-ebātis.	-ebant.
Perf.	Tŭl-i.	-isti.	-it.	-ĭmus.	-istis.	{ -ērunt, *or* -ēre.
Plup.	Tul-ĕram.	-eras.	-erat.	-erāmus.	-erātis.	-erant.
Fut.	Fer-am.	-es.	-et.	-ēmus.	-ētis.	-ent.
Fut.-P.	Tul-ĕro.	-eris.	-erit.	-erimus.	-eritis.	-erint.

Subjunctive Mood.

Pres.	Fer-am.	-as.	-at.	-āmus.	-ātis.	-ant.
Imp.	Fer-rem.	-res.	-ret.	-rēmus.	-rētis.	-rent.
Perf.	Tul-ĕrim.	-eris.	-erit.	-erĭmus.	-erĭtis.	-erint.
Plup.	Tul-issem.	-isses.	-isset.	-issēmus.	-issētis.	-issent.
Fut.	Lat-ūrus sim.	sis.	sit.	-i simus.	sitis.	sint.

Imperative Mood.

Pres.—Fer,* *or* ferto.   ferto.   — ferte, *or* fertōte.   ferunto.

Infinitive Mood.	*Participles.*
Pres. and *Imp.* Ferre.	*Pres.* and *Imp.* Ferens.
Perf. and *Plup.* Tulisse.	*Fut.* Lat-ūrus, -a, -um.
Fut. Lat-ūrus, -a, -um esse ;	
and Lat-ūrus, -a, -um fuisse.	

Gerunds.	*Supines.*
Nom. Feren-dum. -di ; &c.	Lāt-um. Lāt-u.

PASSIVE VOICE.

Fĕror,   lātus,   ferri, *to be carried, &c.*

Indicative Mood.

Pres. Fĕror. ferris, *or* ferre. fertur. ferĭmur. ferimĭni. feruntur.

Imp. Fer-ĕbar. { -ebāris, *or* -ebāre. -ebātur. -ebāmur. -ebamĭni. -ebantur.

Perf. Lāt-us sum, *or* fui, &c.   -i sumus, *or* fuĭmus, &c.

Plup. Lāt-us eram, *or* fuĕram, &c. -i erāmus, *or* fuerāmus, &c.

Fut. Fer-ar. -ēris, *or* -ēre. -ētur. -ēmur. -emĭni. -entur.

Fut.-P. Lāt-us ero, *or* fuĕro, &c.   -i erimus, *or* fuerimus, &c.

---

* *Dico,* I say ; *duco,* I lead ; and *facio,* I make, have the Imperative formed in a similar manner ; *dic, duc, fac ;* and in the compounds
effer, educ, calĕfac ; except in those compounds of *facio,* which change
a into i : as, *confice, perfĭce.*

Subjunctive Mood.

Pres. Fer-ar. -āris, *or* -āre. -ātur. -āmur. -amīni. -antur.
Imp. Fer-rer. -rēris, *or* -rēre. -rētur. -rēmur. -remīni. -rentur.
Perf. Lāt-us sim, *or* fuĕrim, &c. -i simus, *or* fuerĭmus. &c.
Plup. Lāt-us essem, *or* fuissem, &c. -i essēmus, *or* fuissēmus, &c.

Imperative Mood.

Pres. — Ferre, *or* fertor. fertor. — ferimĭni. feruntor.

Infinitive Mood.	*Participles.*
Pres. and *Imp.* Ferri.	*Perf.* Lāt-us, -a, -um.
	Fut. Feren-dus, -da, -dum.

Perf. and *Plup.* Lāt-us, -a, -um esse, *or* fuisse.
Fut. Lāt-um iri.

Fero is a Verb of the Third Conjugation, *fers, fert, fertis, &c.* being contracted for *feris, ferit, ferĭtis, &c.*

The compounds of *fero* are conjugated in the same way; *affĕro* (*ad* and *fero*), *attŭli, allātum, afferre,* to bring to; *aufĕro* (*ab* and *fero*), *abstŭli, ablātum, auferre,* to take away; *confĕro, contŭli, collātum, conferre,* to bring together; *diffĕro* (*dis* and *fero*), *distŭli, dilātum, differre,* to disperse; *effĕro* (*ex* and *fero*), *extŭli, elātum, efferre,* to bring out; *infĕro, intŭli, illātum, inferre,* to bring into; *offĕro* (*ob* and *fero*), *obtŭli, oblātum, offerre,* to offer; and *suffĕro* (*sub* and *fero*), *sufferre,* to endure, which wants both Perfect and Supine.

Fɪo, *I am made,* or *I become.*

Fīo, factus, fiĕri, *to be made,* or *to become.*

Indicative Mood.

Pres. Fīo. fis. fit. fīmus. fītis. fiunt.
Imp. Fi-ēbam. -ebas. -ebat. -ebāmus. -ebātis. -ebant.
Perf. Fact-us sum, *or* fui, &c. -i sumus, *or* fuĭmus, &c.
Plup. Fact-us eram, *or* fuĕram, &c. -i erāmus, *or* fuerāmus, &c.
Fut. Fi-am. -es. -et. -ēmus. -ētis. -ent.
Fut.-P. Fact-us ero, *or* fuĕro, &c. -i erimus, *or* fuerimus, &c.

Subjunctive Mood.

Pres. Fi-am. -as. -at. -āmus. -ātis. -ant.
Imp. Fi-ĕrem. -eres. -eret. -erēmus. -erētis. -erent.
Perf. Fact-us sim, *or* fuĕrim, &c. -i simus, *or* fuerĭmus, &c.
Plup. Fact-us essem, *or* fuissem, &c. -i essēmus, *or* fuissēmus, &c.

Imperative Mood.

Pres. — Fi, *or* fīto. fīto. — fīte, *or* fitōte. fiunto.

Infinitive Mood.

Pres. and *Imp.* Fiĕri.
Perf. and *Plup.* Factus, -a, -um esse, *or* fuisse.
Fut. Fact-um iri.

Participles.

Perf. Fact-us, -a, -um.   *Fut.* Facien-dus, -da, -dum.
                    Supine. Fact-u.

The Third Person Singular is often used impersonally : as, *fit*, it happens ; *fiĕbat*, it happened ; &c.

Fio is used as the Passive of *facio*, from which it takes the Participles. The compounds of *facio*, which retain *a*, have *fio* in the Passive : as, *calefacio*, I warm ; *calefío* ; *&c.* But those compounds which change *facio* into *ficio* have the regular Passive in *ficior* : as, *conficio*, *conficior* ; *&c.*

To the Irregular Verbs may be added *edo*, **I eat**, which, in some of its tenses, agrees with *sum* : thus,

Edo,   ĕdi,   ēsum,   edĕre, *or* esse, *to eat.*

Indicative Mood.

Pres. Edo. { ĕdis, { edit, edĭmus. { edĭtis, edunt.
            { *or* es. { *or* est. { *or* estis.

Subjunctive Mood.

Imp. { Edĕrem, ederes, ederet, ederēmus, ederētis, ederent,
       { *or* essem. *or* esses. *or* esset. *or* essēmus. *or* essētis. *or* essent.

Imperative Mood.

Pres. ——— { Ede, *or* edĭto, edĭto, ——— edīte, *or* editōte, edunto.
              { *or* es, *or* esto. *or* esto. *or* este, *or* estōte.

                Infinitive. *Pres.* and *Imp.* Edĕre, *or* esse.

The compounds of *edo* are conjugated in the same manner, but, in the other Tenses, they are regular Verbs of the Third Conjugation.

DEFECTIVE VERBS.

Verbs are called *Defective* which are used only in a few Tenses and Persons.

I. The following most frequently occur : *Aio, inquam, forem, ausim, faxo,* **ave, salve,** *cedo,* and **quæso.**

Aio, *I say.*
Indicative Mood.

Pres. Aio. aïs. aït. ——— ——— aiunt.
Imp. Ai-ēbam. -ebas. -ebat. -ebāmus. -ebātis. -ebant.
Perf. ——— aisti. ——— ——— ——— ———

Subjunctive Mood.

Pres. ——— aias. aiat. ——— aiātis. aiant.
Imperative. **Pres.** Ai.   *Participle.* *Pres.* and *Imp.* Aiens.

Inquam, *I say.*

Indicative Mood.

Pres. In-quam. -quis. -quit. -quimus. -quitis. -quiunt.
Imp. —— —— inquiēbat. —— —— inquiēbant.
Perf. —— inquisti. —— —— —— ——
Fut. —— inquies. inquiet. —— —— ——

Imperative. Pres. Inque, *or* inquito.
Participle. Pres. and Imp. Inquiens.

Forem, *I might be, or I might have been.*

Subjunctive Mood.

Imp. and Plup. For-em. -es. -et. -ēmus. -ētis. -ent.
Infinitive. Pres. and Imp. Fore, *to be, or to be about to be.*

Forem, contracted for *fuĕrem,* seems to be the Imp. Sub. of the old Verb *fuo,* and is therefore used for *essem,* and sometimes for *fuissem.* *Fore* is properly the Pres. and Imp. Infinitive, but is commonly used as the Future for *futūrus esse.*

Ausim, *I may dare.*

Subjunctive Mood.

Pres. Aus-im. -is. -it. —— —— -int.

Ausim is contracted for *ausĕrim,* which was anciently used for *ausus sim.*

Faxo, *I shall see to it, or do it.*

Indicative Mood.

Fut.-P. Faxo. -is. -it. —— -itis. -int.

Subjunctive Mood.

Perf. Fax-im. -is. -it. —— —— -int.

Faxo and *faxim* are contracted for *fecĕro* and *fecĕrim,* and are used in the same sense.

Ave, and Salve, *God save you, hail, good morrow.*

Imperative Mood.

Pres. —— Av-e, *or* -ēto. —— —— av-ēte, *or* -etōte. ——
Infinitive. Pres. and Imp. Avēre.

Imperative Mood.

Pres. —— Salv-e, *or* -ēto. —— —— salv-ēte, *or* -etōte. ——
Infinitive. Pres. and Imp. Salvēre.

Salves the 2. Sing. Pres. Ind, and *salvēbis* the 2. Sing. Fut. Ind. are also found.

CEDO, *tell,* or *give.*

Imperative Mood.

Pres. —— Cedo. —— —— cedĭte. ——

Cedo is used both as Singular and Plural; *cedĭte,* as Plural only, and contracted *cette.*

QUÆSO, *I pray,* or *I beseech.*

Indicative Mood.

Pres. Quæso. —— —— quæsŭmus. —— ——

II. These three Verbs, *ōdi, memĭni, cœpi,* are called *Preteritive Verbs,* because they have only the Perfect and the Tenses formed from it.

The first two have, in the Perfect, the signification of the Present and Perfect; in the Pluperfect, that of the Imperfect and Pluperfect; and in the Future-Perfect, that of the Future and Future-Perfect.

ODI, *I hate,* or *I have hated.*

Indicative Mood.

Perf. Od-i.	-isti.	-it.	-ĭmus.	-istis.	{-ērunt, or -ēre.
Plup. Od-ĕram.	-eras.	-erat.	-erāmus.	-erātis.	-erant.
Fut.-P. Od-ĕro.	-eris.	-erit.	-erimus.	-eritis.	-erint.

Subjunctive Mood.

Perf. Od-ĕrim.	-eris.	-erit.	-erĭmus.	-erĭtis.	-erint.
Plup. Od-issem.	-isses.	-isset.	-issēmus.	-issētis.	-issent.

Infinitive. *Perf.* and *Plup.* Odisse.
Participles. *Perf.* Osus, *having hated.* *Fut.* Osūrus.

Odĕrit and *Odĕrint* sometimes supply the place of an Imperative.

In the same manner *Memĭni,* I remember, *or* I have remembered; and *Cœpi,* I have begun, are conjugated. *Memĭni* has *memento* and *mementōte,* the Second persons Singular and Plural of the Imperative; and to *Cœpi* are assigned the Perfect Participle *cœptus,* begun, *or* having begun, the Future Participle *cœptūrus,* and the Supine *cœptu.* *Cœpi* has also a Perfect Passive *cœptus sum,* of the same meaning as the Active, but used with Passive Infinitives.

To these some add *Novi,* because it frequently has the signification of the Present, *I know,* as well as *I have known,* though it comes from *nosco,* which is complete.

III. *Fari,* to speak, and *dari,* to be given, are not used in the First Person Sing. of the Pres. Indicative and Subjunctive. Of *fari,* only *fatur, fabor;* the Imperative, *fare;* the Participles, *fans, fatus, fandus;* the Gerunds, *fandi,* and *fando;* and the Supine, *fatu,* are commonly used.

Furĕre, to be mad, wants the First Per. Sing. and the Sec. Per.
Plur. of the Pres., and probably all the Future of the Indicative;
and the Imperative. It likewise wants the Perfect and Supine.

Of the following Verbs the 'subjoined persons only are found:
apăge, be gone; *infit,* he begins; *confit,* it is done; *confīet, con-*
fiĕret, confiĕri; defit, it is wanting, *def'īet, def'īat, defiĕri; ovas,* thou
rejoicest, *ovat, ovet, ovāret, ovans, ovātus, ovandi.*

IMPERSONAL VERBS.

Verbs are called *Impersonal,* which are used only in
the Third Person Singular, and which do not admit a
person as their Nominative.

They belong to all the Conjugations, and, when literally
translated, have the Pronoun *it* before them.

FIRST CONJUGATION.   SECOND CONJUGATION.

Delectat, *it delights.*   Decet, *it becomes.*
Delect-at, -āvit, -āre.   Dec-et, -uit, -ēre.

Indicative Mood.

Pres.   Delect-at, *it delights.*   Dec-et, *it becomes.*
Imp.   Delect-ābat, *it delighted.*   Dec-ēbat, *it became.*
Perf.   Delectāv-it, *it has delighted.*   Decu-it, *it has become.*
Plup.   Delectav-ērat, *it had delighted.*   Decu-ērat, *it had become.*
Fut.   Delect-ābit, *it will delight.*   Dec-ēbit, *it will become.*
Fut.-P. Delectav-ērit, *it shall have de-*   Decu-ērit, *it shall have become.*
[*lighted.*

Subjunctive Mood.

Pres. Delect-et, *it may delight.*   Dec-eat, *it may become.*
Imp. Delect-āret, *it might delight.*   Dec-ēret, *it might become.*
Perf. Delectav-ērit, *it may have delighted.* Decu-ērit, *it may have become.*
Plup. Delectav-isset, *it might have de-* Decu-isset, *it might have be-*
[*lighted.*   [*come.*

Infinitive Mood.

Pres. and *Imp.* Delect-āre, *to delight, &c.*   Dec-ēre, *to become, &c.*
Perf. and *Plup.* Delectav-isse, *to have delight-* Decu-isse, *to have be-*
[*ed, &c.*   *come, &c.*

THIRD CONJUGATION.   FOURTH CONJUGATION.

Accĭdit, *it happens.*   Evĕnit, *it happens.*
Accĭd-it, -it, -ĕre.   Evĕn-it, evĕn-it, -īre.

Indicative Mood.

Pres. Accĭd-it, *it happens.*   Evĕn-it, *it happens.*
Imp. Accid-ēbat, *it happened.*   Eveni-ēbat, *it happened.*
Perf. Accĭd-it, *it has happened; &c.*   Evĕn-it, *it has happened; &c.*

Most Verbs may be used impersonally in the Passive Voice, especially Neuter and Intransitive Verbs, which otherwise have no Passive: as, *pugnātur, favētur, currītur, venītur;* from *pugno,* I fight;
aveo, I favour; *curro,* I run; *venio,* I come.

FIRST CONJUGATION.	SECOND CONJUGATION.
Pugnätur, *it is fought*.	Favētur, *it is favoured*.
Pugn-ätur, -ätum est, -äri.	Fav-ētur, fautum est, favēri.

Indicative Mood.

Pres.	Pugnätur, *it is fought*.	Favētur, *it is favoured*.
Imp.	Pugnabätur, *it was fought*.	Favebätur, *it was favoured*.
Perf.	Pugnätum **est**, *it has been* [*fought*.	Fautum **est**, *it has been favoured*. [*voured*.
Plup.	**Pugnätum erat**, *it had been* [*fought*.	Fautum erat, *it had been favoured*. [*voured*.
Fut.	Pugnabïtur, *it will be fought*.	Favebïtur, *it will be favoured*.
Fut.-P.	**Pugnätum** fuĕrit, *it shall have* [*been fought*.	Fautum fuĕrit, *it shall have* [*been favoured*.

Subjunctive Mood.

Pres.	Pugnētur, *it may be fought*.	Faveätur, *it may be favoured*.
Imp.	Pugnarētur, *it might be fought*.	Faverētur, *it might be favoured*.
Perf.	Pugnätum **sit**, *it may have been* [*fought*.	Fautum **sit**, *it may have been* [*favoured*.
Plup.	Pugnätum **esset**, *it might have* [*been fought*.	Fautum **esset**, *it might have* [*been favoured*.

Infinitive Mood.

Pres. and *Imp.* Pugnäri, *to be fought, &c.*
Perf. and *Plup.* Pugnätum esse, *to have been fought, &c.*
Fut. Pugnätum iri, *to be about to be fought, &c.*
Pres. and *Imp.* Favēri, *to be favoured, &c.*
Perf. and *Plup.* Fautum **esse**, *to have been favoured, &c.*
Fut. Fautum iri, *to be about to be favoured, &c.*

THIRD CONJUGATION.	FOURTH CONJUGATION
Currïtur, *it is run*.	Venïtur, *it is come*.
Currïtur, cursum est, curri.	Venïtur, ventum est, venïri.

Indicative Mood.

Pres.	Currïtur, *it is run*.	Venïtur, *it is come*.
Imp.	Currebätur, *it was run*.	Veniebätur, *it was come*.
Perf.	**Cursum est**, *it has been run; &c.*	Ventum est, *it has been come; &c.*

Verbs, which, in the Active Voice, do not govern the Accusative, are used only impersonally in the Passive: as, *persuadētur mihi*, I am persuaded; not, *persuadeor.*

Impersonal Verbs want the Imperative, and generally the Participles, Gerunds, and Supines. The Imperative, when necessary, is supplied by the Present Subjunctive: as, *delectet*, let him delight.

Impersonal Verbs are applied to any person or number, by putting the words which form the Nominative to regular Verbs, after them, in the cases which they govern: as, *delectat me*, it delights me, *or* I delight; *delectat te*, thou delightest; *delectat hominem*, the man delights; *delectat nos, vos, homines*, we, ye, the men delight. *Placet*

mihi, tibi, homini, it pleases me, thee, the man ; *or*, I please, thou
pleasest, the man pleases, &c.   *Pugnatur a me, a te, ab homine*, I
fight, thou fightest, the man fights, &c.

ADVERB.

An Adverb is a word added to a Verb, Adjective, or
other Adverb, to express the Time, Place, or Manner in
which any thing is done.

I. The Adverbs of *Time* are, *nunc*, now ; *tunc*, then ; &c.

II. The Adverbs of *Place* are, *ubi*, where ? *hic*, here ; &c.

III. The Adverbs of *Manner, Quality*, &c. are, *profecto*, truly ;
satis, enough ; *itidem*, in like manner; &c.

The *Simple*, or *Primitive* Adverbs are few in number: as, *non*,
haud, not; *ibi*, there; *mox*, presently; *tunc*, then; &c.

The *Derivative* Adverbs are numerous, and are formed in the following manner :

1. Adverbs derived from Adjectives of the First and Second Declension generally end in *e* : as, *alte*, highly, from *altus*; *libère*,
freely, from *liber*.   They sometimes end in *o*, *um*, or *ter* : as, *tuto*,
safely, from *tutus* ; *tantum*, so much, from *tantus* ; *dure*, and *duriter*,
hardly, from *durus*.

2. Adverbs derived from Adjectives of the Third Declension generally end in *ter* : as, *feliciter*, happily, from *felix*.   They sometimes
end in *e* : as, *facile*, easily, from *facilis*.   One ends in *o* : *omnino*,
altogether, from *omnis*.

The Neuter Gender of Adjectives is often used adverbially : as,
recens, recently, for *recenter* ; *torva*, sternly, for *torve*.

3. Adverbs derived from Nouns generally end in *im*, or *itus* ; as,
viritim, man by man, from *vir* ; *funditus*, from the ground, from
fundus.   Many Adverbs in *im* are derived from Participles : as,
sensim, by degrees, from *sensus* (*sentio*, I perceive).   A few Adverbs
in *itus* are derived from Adjectives : as, *antiquitus*, anciently, from
antiquus.

4. Adverbs are formed by Composition in various ways : as, *hodie*,
to-day, from *hoc die* ; *scilicet*, truly, from *scire licet* ; *quomodo*, how,
from *quo modo* ; *quamobrem*, wherefore ? from *ob quam rem*.

Adverbs derived from Adjectives are compared, and are
subject to the same irregularities and defects as their Primitives.   The Positive generally ends in *e*, or *ter* ; the
Comparative in *ius* ; the Superlative in *ime* : as,

Pos.	*Comp.*	*Sup.*
Alte, *highly :*	Altius,	Altissime.
Fortiter, *bravely :*	Fortius,	Fortissime.
Libère, *freely ;*	Liberius,	Liberrime.
Tuto, *safely ;*	Tutius,	Tutissime.

The following Adverbs are compared *irregularly*, like the Adjectives from which they are derived :

Bene, *well ;*	Melius,	Optĭme.
Facĭle, *easily ;*	Facilius,	Facillĭme.
Male, *badly ;*	Pejus,	Pessĭme.
Multum, *much ;*	Plus,	Plurĭmum.
Parum, *little ;*	Minus,	{ Minĭme. Minĭmum.
Prope, *near ;*	Propius,	Proxĭme.

Positive wanting.

Magis, *more*, maxĭme; ocius, *more swiftly*, ocissĭme; prius, *sooner*, primo, *or* primum ; potius, *rather*, potissĭmum.

Comparative wanting.

Pene, *almost*, penissĭme ; nuper, *lately*, nuperrĭme ; nove, *or* novĭter, *newly*, novissĭme; merĭto, *deservedly*, meritissĭmo.

Superlative wanting.

Satis, *enough*, satius ; secus, *otherwise*, secius.

Two Adverbs not derived from Adjectives are also compared : *diu*, long, *diutius*, *diutissĭme ; sæpe*, often, *sæpius*, *sæpissĭme*.

PREPOSITION.

A Preposition is a word placed before Nouns and Pronouns, to show their relation to other words.

Prepositions are placed before, or govern the Accusative, or Ablative.

There are twenty-eight Prepositions which govern the Accusative :

Ad, *to, at.*
Apud, *at, near.*
Ante, *before.*
Adversus, }
Adversum, } *against, towards.*
Contra, *against, overagainst.*
Cis, }
Citra, } *on this side.*
Circa, }
Circum, } *about.*
Erga, *towards.*
Extra, *without, out of.*
Inter, *between, among.*
Intra, *within.*

Infra, *beneath.*
Juxta, *nigh to.*
Ob, *for, on account of.*
Propter, *for, because of.*
Per, *by, through.*
Præter, *beside, except.*
Penes, *in the power of.*
Post, *after, since.*
Pone, *behind.*
Secus, *by, along.*
Secundum, *according to.*
Supra, *above.*
Trans, *across, on the further side.*
Ultra, *beyond.*

D

There are fifteen Prepositions which govern the Ablative :

A,
Ab, } *from, by.*
Abs,

Absque, *without.*
Cum, *with, along with.*
Clam, *without the knowledge of.*
Coram, *before, in presence of.*
De, *of, concerning.*

E,
Ex, } *of, out of.*
Pro, *for.*

Præ, *before, in comparison of.*
Palam, *with the knowledge of.*
Sine, *without.*
Tenus, *up to, as far as.*

There are four Prepositions which govern sometimes the Accusative, and sometimes the Ablative.

In, *in, into.*   Sub, *under.*   Super, *above.*   Subter, *beneath.*

Tenus is placed after its case ; and also *cum*, when joined to *me, te, se, quo, quî*, and *quibus :* as, *mecum, &c.* *Clam* sometimes governs the Accusative : as, *Clam patre,* or *patrem.*

Circĭter, about ; *prope*, nigh ; *usque*, as far as ; *versus*, towards ; are Adverbs, and seem to govern the Accusative by means of *ad,* which is generally understood, but sometimes expressed. So likewise *procul,* far, which governs the Ablative by means of *a.*

Prepositions are often considered as Adverbs, when the word which they would govern is not expressed.

Prepositions in Composition.

Prepositions are often prefixed to other words, especially to Verbs, and modify the meaning of the Simple word, by their own.

Ad, *to :* as, *duco,* I lead ; *addūco,* I lead to ; *fero,* I bring ; *adfĕro.* I bring to.

Per, *through, entirely :* as *perdūco,* I lead through ; *perfĕro,* I carry through ; *facio,* I do ; *perficio,* I do entirely, I finish.

A, ab, abs, *from,* or *away :* as *abdūco,* I lead away ; *aufĕro,* I carry away.

In, *in, into, upon, against :* as *infĕro,* I bring in, *or* into ; *impono,* I place upon ; *ruo,* I rush ; *irruo,* I rush upon, *or* against. It sometimes *increases* the meaning : as, *duro,* I harden ; *indūro,* I harden much.

The following syllables *am, di,* or *dis. re, se, con,* are called *Inseparable Prepositions,* because they are never found except in compound words.

Am-, signifies *about, around :* as, *ambio,* I go about, I surround. The *m* is changed into *n,* before *c, q, f, h :* as, *anceps,* that may be taken two ways, doubtful ; and *b* is inserted before a vowel : as, *ambio.*

Di-, or dis-, *asunder, separately :* as, *didūco,* I lead asunder, I separate. It sometimes reverses the meaning : as, *facĭlis,* easy ; *difficĭlis,* difficult; *fido*, I trust; *diffido*, I distrust. It sometimes *increases* the meaning: as, *cupio*, I desire; *discupio*, I desire much. *Dis* is used before *c, f, j, p, q, s, t;* and *di* before the other consonants.

Re-, *back, again, against :* as, *redūco*, I lead back; *refēro*, I carry back; *relēgo*, I read again; *reclāmo*, I cry against. It sometimes *reverses* the meaning: as, *tendo*, I bend; *retendo*, I unbend. *D* is inserted before a vowel, and *h :* as, *redeo*, I return.

Se, *apart,* or *aside*: as, *sedūco*, I lead aside, *or* apart. With Adjectives, it denotes *privation :* as, *cura,* care; *secūrus,* free from care, careless.

Con-, (for cum,) *together, along with :* as, *condūco*, I lead together, I bring along with me; *confēro*, I carry together. It sometimes *increases* the meaning: as, *premo,* I press; *comprĭmo,* I press together, I press much. The *n* is dropt before a vowel, or *h ;* and is changed into *m*, before *b, p, m :* as, *cogo (conăgo,)* I drive together; *cohæres,* a coheir, an heir in participation.

Ne-, and *ve-,* are also prefixed to words, and have a *negative* signification : as, *fas,* justice; *nefas,* injustice, impiety; *scio,* I know; *nescio,* I know not, I am ignorant; *sanus,* healthy; *vesānus,* sickly.

INTERJECTION.

An Interjection is a word which expresses some passion or emotion of the mind : as, *oh, hei, heu,* ah, alas !

Nouns and Adjectives in the Neuter Gender are sometimes used as Interjections : as, *malum,* with a mischief ! *infandum,* O shame ! *misĕrum,* O wretched ! *nefas,* O the villany !

CONJUNCTION.

A Conjunction is a word which connects sentences, or words : as, *et, ac, atque, que,* and ; *etiam,* also ; &c.

Some words, as, *deinde,* thereafter ; *denĭque,* finally ; *cætĕrum,* moreover, but ; *videlĭcet,* to wit ; &c. may be considered either as Adverbs or Conjunctions.

Autem, enim, vero, quoque, quidem, are never put first in a clause or sentence. *Que, ve,* and *ne,* are always annexed to some other word.

SYNTAX.

Syntax is the correct arrangement of words in a sentence, and consists of *Concord* and *Government.*

Concord is when one word agrees with another in Gender, Number, Case, or Person.

Government is when one word requires another to be put in a certain Case or Mood.

General Principles.

1. In every sentence there must be a Verb and a **Nominative** expressed or understood.

2. Every Adjective must have a Substantive expressed or understood.

3. All the Cases of Nouns, except the Nominative and Vocative, must be governed by some other word.

4. The Genitive is governed by a Noun expressed or understood.

5. The Dative is governed by Adjectives and Verbs.

6. The Accusative is governed by an Active Verb, or by a Preposition, or is placed before the Infinitive.

7. The Vocative stands by itself, or has an Interjection joined with it.

8. The Ablative is governed by a Preposition expressed or understood.

9. The Infinitive is governed by a Verb or Adjective expressed or understood.

CONCORD.

RULE I.—An Adjective agrees with its Substantive in Gender, Number, and Case: as,

> *Vir bonus,* a good man.
> *Femĭna casta,* a chaste woman.
> *Dulce pomum,* a sweet apple.

Note 1.—The Substantive *negotium* is often understood to an Adjective in the Neuter Gender: as, *triste,* supply *negotium.*

Note 2.—The Infinitive sometimes supplies the place of a Substantive: as, *Scire tuum.* PERS.

RULE II.—A Verb agrees with its Nominative in Number and Person: as,

> *Ego lego,* I read.
> *Tu scribis,* you write.
> *Præceptor docet,* the master teaches.

Note 1.—The Nominative of the Pronouns is expressed only when some particular distinction of the Person is necessary.

Note 2.—An Infinitive, or part of a sentence, often supplies the place of a Nominative of the Third Person: as, *Mentiri est turpe; Vacare culpâ est magnum solatium.*

Note 3.—A Collective Noun, though **Singular**, may be joined with a Verb in the Plural: as, *Multitudo convenerant*.

RULE III.—Substantive Verbs, Passive Verbs of Naming, and Verbs of Gesture, have a Nominative both **before** and after them, belonging to the same thing: as,

> *Ego sum discipŭlus*, I am a scholar.
> *Tu vocāris Joannes*, you are named John.
> *Illa incēdit regīna*, she walks as a queen.

Or—Any Verb may have the same Case after it as before it, when both words refer to the same thing.

Note.—When a Verb comes between two Nominatives of different numbers, it generally agrees with the first: as, *Ossa fiunt lapis*. Ov.

RULE IV.—The Infinitive Mood has an Accusative before it: as,

> *Gaudeo te valēre*, I am glad that you are well.

Note.—The Accusative of the Pronouns is often understood; and *esse*, or *fuisse*, is frequently omitted after Participles.

RULE V.—*Esse* has the same Case after it that it has before it: as,

> *Petrus cupit esse vir doctus*, Peter desires to be a learned man.
> *Scio Petrum esse virum doctum*, I know that Peter is a learned man.

Or—The Infinitive of a Substantive Verb, of a Passive Verb of Naming, and of a Verb of Gesture, takes the same Case after it that it has before it.

Note.—When the Dative precedes the Infinitive, the Noun which follows is sometimes put in the Accusative: as, *Licet omnibus esse bonos*; sup. *eos*.

RULE VI.—The Relative *Qui, quæ, quod*, agrees with its Antecedent in Gender, Number, and Person: as,

> *Vir sapit qui pauca loquĭtur*, the man is wise who speaks little.
> *Ego qui scribo*, I who write.

Note 1.—The *Antecedent* is the Noun going before the Relative and to which it refers. The Relative is properly an Adjective, and agrees with the Antecedent, which is again understood to it: as, *Vir sapit qui (vir) pauca loquitur*, the man is wise which (man), &c.

Note 2.—Part of a sentence sometimes forms the Antecedent, in which case the Relative must be in the Neuter Gender: as, *In tempore veni quod rerum omnium est primum*. TER.

RULE VII.—If no Nominative come between the Relative and the Verb, the Relative shall be the Nominative to the Verb: as,

Præceptor qui docet, the master who teaches.

RULE VIII.—If a Nominative come between the Relative and the Verb, the Relative is governed by the Verb, Noun, or Adjective following, or by the Preposition which goes before it: as,

Deus quem colĭmus, God whom we worship.
Cujus munĕre vivĭmus, by whose gift we live.

Note.—Words of relative quantity and quality, as, *qualis, quantus, quotus,* are often construed as the Relative: thus, *Tanta multitudo quantam capit urbs nostra.* CIC.

RULE IX.—Two or more Substantives Singular, connected by the Conjunctions, *et, ac, atque, &c.* generally have a Verb, Adjective, or Relative Plural: as,

Petrus et Joannes qui sunt docti, Peter and John who are learned.

Note 1.—A Conjunction is not always necessary: as, *Dum ætas, metus, magister prohibebant.* TER.

Note 2.—If the Substantives be of different Genders, and signify Persons, the Adjective is Masculine, agreeing with *homines,* understood. But, if the Substantives signify things without life, the Adjective is Neuter, agreeing with *negotia,* understood.

Note 3.—When the Nominatives are of different Persons, the Verb agrees with the First rather than the Second, and with the Second rather than the Third: as, *Si tu et Tullia valetis, ego et Cicero valemus.* CIC.

RULE X.—Substantives signifying the same thing agree in Case: as,

Cicero orātor, Cicero the orator.
Urbs Edinburgum, the city Edinburgh.

Note.—A sentence, or clause, may supply the place of one of the Substantives: as, *Cogitet oratorem institui, rem arduam.* QUINT.

GOVERNMENT.

Government of Substantives.

RULE XI.—One Substantive governs another, signifying a different thing, in the Genitive: as,

Amor Dei, the love of God.
Lex natūræ. the law of nature.

Note 1.—The Genitive is sometimes changed into the Dative : as, *Urbi pater est, urbique maritus.* Luc.

Note 2.—The governing Substantive is sometimes understood : as, *Ubi ad Dianæ veneris.* Ter. Sup. *templum*, or *ædem.*

Rule XII.—If the latter of two Substantives have an Adjective signifying Praise, Dispraise, or any sort of Distinction, joined with it, it may be put in the Genitive or Ablative : as,

Vir summæ prudentiæ, or *summâ prudentiâ*, a man of great wisdom.
Puer probæ indŏlis, or *probâ indŏle*, a boy of a good disposition.

Note.—The latter Substantive must denote a part or property of the former, otherwise it does not belong to this Rule.

Rule XIII.—An Adjective in the Neuter Gender, without a Substantive, governs the Genitive : as,

Multum pecuniæ, much money.
Quid rei est ? what is the matter ?

Note 1.—The Adjectives which govern the Genitive like Substantives generally signify quantity : as, *multum, plus, tantum, &c.* To these add the Pronouns, *id, hoc, quid,* and its compounds. *Quid* and *plus* always govern the Genitive. *Quod* and its compounds agree in Case with their Substantives.

Note 2.—Plural Adjectives in the Neuter Gender also govern the Genitive : as, *Angusta viarum.* Virg.

* Rule XIII.—*Opus* and *Usus*, signifying *need*, govern the Ablative of the thing wanted : as,

Auctoritāte tuâ nobis opus est, we have need of your authority.
Nunc virĭbus usus (est vobis), now you have need of strength.

Note.—*Opus* and *usus* sometimes govern the Genitive : as, *Lectionis opus est.* Quint.

Government of Adjectives.

Rule XIV.—Verbal Adjectives, or such as signify an Affection of the Mind, govern the Genitive : as,

Avĭdus gloriæ, desirous of glory.
Ignārus fraudis, ignorant of fraud.
Memor beneficiōrum, mindful of favours.

To this Rule belong Verbal Adjectives in *ax, ns,* and *tus* ; Adjectives denoting Affection ; as, Desire and Disdain ; Knowledge and Ignorance ; Innocence and Guilt.

RULE XV.—Partitives, and words placed Partitively, Comparatives, Superlatives, Interrogatives, and some Numerals, govern the Genitive Plural: as,

Alīquis philosophŏrum, some one of the philosophers.
Senior fratrum, the elder of the brothers.
Quis nostrûm, which of us.

A *Partitive* is a word which signifies a part of any number of persons or things, in contradistinction to the whole.

Note 1.—Partitives, &c. agree in Gender with the Substantives which they govern: as, *Nulla sororum*. But if there be two Substantives of different Genders, the Partitives, &c. generally agree with the former: as, *Indus fluminum maximus*. CIC.

Note 2.—Partitives, &c. govern the Genitive Singular of Collective Nouns: as, *Præstantissimus nostræ civitatis*. CIC. Sup. *vir*.

RULE XVI.—Adjectives signifying Profit or Disprofit, Likeness or Unlikeness, govern the Dative: as,

Utĭlis bello, profitable for war.
Simĭlis patri, like his father.

Or—Any Adjective may govern the Dative in Latin, which has *to* or *for* after it in English.

To this Rule also belong Adjectives signifying Pleasure or Pain; Friendship or Hatred; Clearness or Obscurity; Nearness; Ease or Difficulty; Equality or Inequality; and several compounded with *con*: as, *cognātus, &c.*

Note 1.—Some of these Adjectives govern also the Genitive: as, *amĭcus, inimĭcus, socius, vicīnus, par, æquālis, simĭlis, commūnis, proprius, &c.*

Note 2.—Adjectives signifying *Motion* or *Tendency* to a thing, take after them the Accusative with *ad*, rather than the Dative: as, *proclīvus, pronus, propensus, velox, celer, tardus, piger, &c.*: as, *Piger ad pænas*. Ov.

Note 3.—Adjectives signifying *Usefulness, Fitness*, and the contrary, often take the Accusative with *ad*: as, *Utĭlis ad nullam rem*. CIC.

Note 4.—*Propior* and *proxĭmus* take after them the Dative, or the Accusative governed by *ad* understood: as, *Propius vero*. LIV. *Proximus Pompeium*. CIC. Sup. *ad*.

RULE XVII.—Verbal Adjectives in *bilis* and *dus* govern the Dative: as,

Amandus, or *amabĭlis omnĭbus*, to be beloved by all men.

RULE XVIII.—Nouns denoting Measure are put in the Accusative: as,

Columna sexaginta pedes alta, a pillar sixty feet high.

Note 1.—The names of *Measure* are *digitus, palmus, pes, cubitus, ulna, passus, stadium.*

Note 2.—The word denoting *Measure* is sometimes put in the Ablative: as, *Fossam sex cubitis altam.* L*iv.* The *difference* of Measure is always put in the Ablative: as, *Turris est sex pedibus altior quam murus.* To which may be referred, *tanto, quanto, hoc, eo, quo, multo, paulo, &c.*

RULE XIX.—The Comparative Degree governs the Ablative of the Object with which any thing is compared: as,

> *Dulcior melle*, sweeter than honey.
> *Præstantior auro*, better than gold.

Note.—When the Comparative is followed by *quam*, the objects compared are put in the same Case: as, *Dulcior quam mel*; *Præstantior quam aurum.* The Nominative and Accusative only can be repeated after *quam :* and if any other case precede the Comparative, the Verb *sum*, with the Nominative, are used: as, *Loquor de viro sapientiore quam tu es.*

RULE XX.—*Dignus, indignus, contentus, præditus, captus,* and *fretus;* also *natus, satus, ortus, editus,* and the like, govern the Ablative: as,

> *Dignus honōre*, worthy of honour.
> *Præditus virtūte*, endued with virtue.
> *Contentus parvo*, content with little.

Note.—*Dignus, indignus,* and *contentus,* are sometimes construed with the Genitive: as, *Indignus avorum.* V*irg.*

RULE XXI.—Adjectives of Plenty or Want govern the Genitive, or Ablative: as,

> *Plenus iræ,* or *irâ,* full of anger.
> *Inops ratiōnis,* or *ratiōne,* void of reason.

Note.—Some adjectives of *Plenty* or *Want* govern the Genitive only: as, *benignus, exsors, impos, impōtens, liberālis, &c.* Some the Ablative only: as, *beātus, distentus, tumĭdus, turgĭdus, &c.* Some the Genitive and Ablative: as, *compos, expers, gravis, dives, &c.*

Government of Verbs.

RULE XXII.—*Sum,* when it signifies Possession, Property, or Duty, governs the Genitive: as,

Est regis punīre rebelles, it belongs to the king to punish rebels. *Militum est suo duci parēre,* it is the duty of soldiers to obey their general.

Note.—The Genitive is not properly governed by *sum*, but by such words as *officium, munus, opus, negotium, res, proprium, &c.* understood.

RULE XXIII.—These Nominatives, *meum, tuum, suum, nostrum, vestrum,* are excepted : as,

Tuum est id procurāre, it is your duty to manage that.

Note.—That is, instead of the Genitives of the Substantive Pronouns, *ego, tu, sui,* the Nominative Neuter of the Possessives is used, agreeing with *officium, munus, &c.*

RULE XXIV.—*Misereor, miseresco,* and *satāgo,* govern the Genitive : as,

Miserēre civium tuōrum, take pity on your countrymen.
Satāgit rerum suārum, he is busy with his own affairs.

Note.—Many other Verbs, signifying some *affection* of the mind, likewise govern the Genitive : as, *ango, decipior, fallo, invideo, lætor, miror, studeo, pendeo, vereor, &c.*

RULE XXV.—*Est* taken for *habeo* (to have) governs the Dative of a Person : as,

> *Est mihi liber,* I have a book.
> *Sunt mihi libri,* I have books.

Note.—*Foret* and *suppĕtit* are construed in the same way : as, *Si mihi cauda foret.* MART. *Cui rerum suppetit usus.* HOR.

RULE XXVI.—*Sum* taken for *affĕro* (to bring) governs two Datives, the one of a Person, and the other of a Thing : as,

Est mihi voluptāti, it is (*or* it brings) a pleasure to me.

Note 1.—Some other Verbs, as, *forem, do, duco, verto, tribuo, habeo, relinquo, &c.* also govern two Datives.

Note 2.—To this Rule may be referred the form of naming, *Est mihi nomen Joanni ;* in which the Dative is more elegant than the Nominative or Genitive.

RULE XXVII.—Verbs signifying Advantage or Disadvantage govern the Dative : as,

Fortūna favet fortĭbus, fortune favours the brave.
Nemīni noceas, do hurt to no man.

Or—Any Verb may govern the Dative in Latin, which has *to* or *for* after it in English.

The Verbs which more particularly belong to this Rule, are,

Verbs signifying,

1. To Profit and Hurt : as, *commŏdo, placeo, noceo, &c.* But *lædo* and *offendo* govern the Accusative.

2. To Favour or Help, and the contrary : as, *faveo, auxilior, invideo, &c.* But *juvo* governs the **Accusative**.

3. To Command, Obey, Serve, and Resist: as, *impĕro, pareo, servio, resisto, &c.* But *jubeo* governs the **Accusative**.

4. To Threaten, **or to be Angry with**: as, *minor, indignor, irascor, &c.*

5. To Trust: as, *fido, confido, credo :* also, *diffido, despĕro.*

6. Verbs compounded with *satis, bene,* and *male :* as, *satisfacio, benefacio, maledico, &c.*

7. *Sum,* and its compounds, except *possum :* as, *adsum, &c.*

8. Many verbs compounded with these ten *Prepositions ; ad, ante, cum, in, inter, ob, post, præ, sub,* and *super :* as, *adsto, antecello, consto, &c.*

Rule XXVIII.—Verbs signifying Actively govern the Accusative : as,

Ama Deum, love God.
Reverĕre parentes, reverence your parents.

Note 1.—An Infinitive, or part of a Sentence, sometimes supplies the place of an Accusative : as, *Pœnitere tanti non emo.* Gell.

Note 2.—Neuter Verbs govern an Accusative of their own, or a similar signification : as, *Vivere vitam.* Plaut.

Rule XXIX.—*Recordor, memĭni, reminiscor,* and *obliviscor,* govern the Accusative, or Genitive : as,

Recordor lectiōnis, or *lectiōnem,* I remember my lesson.
Obliviscor injuriæ, or *injuriam,* I forget an injury.

Note.—*Memini,* when it signifies *to make mention,* is joined with the Genitive, or the Ablative with the Preposition *de :* as, *Memini alicujus,* or *de aliquo.*

Rule XXX.—Verbs of Accusing, Condemning, Acquitting, and Admonishing, govern the Accusative of a Person, with the Genitive of the Crime, or Thing: as,

Arguit me furti, he accuses me of theft.
Monet me officii, he puts me in mind of my duty.

Note 1.—The *Crime* is often put in the Ablative, with or without a Preposition : as, *Accusare de negligentia.* Cic. *Suspicione absolverent.* Liv.

Note 2.—Verbs of *Accusing* and *Admonishing* sometimes govern two Accusatives, the latter of which is generally a Pronoun, or a word referring to number or quantity : as, *hoc, id, unum, multa, &c.*

Rule XXXI.—Verbs of Comparing, Giving, Declaring, and Taking away, govern the Accusative and Dative : as,

Compăro Virgilium Homĕro, I compare Virgil to Homer.
Eripuit me morti, he rescued me from death.

Or—Any Active Verb may govern the Accusative and the Dative, when the Object of the action, and the Person or Thing upon which the action is exerted, are expressed.

Note.—Verbs of *Comparing* and *Taking away*, instead of the Dative, have often the Ablative after them, with a Preposition: as, *Composuit dicta cum factis.*

Rᴜʟᴇ XXXII.—Verbs of Asking and Teaching govern two Accusatives, the first of a Person, and the second of a Thing: as,

> *Posce Deum veniam,* beg pardon of God.
> *Docuit me grammatĭcam,* he taught me grammar.

Celo (I conceal) also governs two Accusatives: as, *Celo te hanc rem.* Tᴇʀ.

Note 1.—Verbs which, in the Passive Voice, take a Nominative both before and after them, govern, in the Active, two Accusatives referring to the same thing.

Note 2.—These Verbs are often construed with a Preposition.

Note 3.—*Doceo, edoceo, dedoceo,* and *erudio,* are the only Verbs of *Teaching* which govern two Accusatives. The others, as, *addoceo, instruo, &c.* take an Ablative, sometimes with *in.*

* Rᴜʟᴇ XXXII.—Verbs of Filling, Loading, Binding, Depriving, Clothing, and some others, govern the Accusative and Ablative: as,

> *Implet patĕram mero,* he fills the bowl with wine.
> *Onĕrat navem auro,* he loads the ship with gold.

Note 1.—*Compleo, impleo,* and *expleo,* sometimes govern the Genitive: as, *Animum explêsse juvabit ultricis flammæ.* Vɪʀɢ.

Note 2.—The Ablative is governed by Prepositions, which are sometimes expressed: as, *Solvere aliquem ex catenis.* Cɪᴄ.

Rᴜʟᴇ XXXIII.—The Passives of such Active Verbs as govern two Cases retain the latter case: as,

> *Accūsor furti,* I am accused of theft.
> *Doceor grammatĭcam,* I am taught grammar.
> *Patĕra implētur mero,* the bowl is filled with wine.

Note.—Passive Verbs of *Clothing,* such as, *Induor, amicior, cingor, accingor,* also *exuor, discingor,* and their Participles, are often, by the Poets, joined to the Accusative: as, *Protinus induitur faciem cultumque Dianæ.* Oᴠɪᴅ. With the Prose-writers, they govern the Ablative: as, *Hispano cingitur gladio.* Lɪᴠ.

Rᴜʟᴇ XXXIV.—Nouns denoting Price are put in the Ablative: as,

Emi librum duōbus assĭbus, I bought a book for two shillings.
Vendĭdit hic auro patriam, this man sold his country for gold.

Note.—The Ablative is often governed by the Preposition *pro :* as, *Dum pro argenteis decem aureus unus valeret.* Liv.

RULE XXXV.—These Genitives, *tanti, quanti, pluris, minōris,* are excepted : as,

> *Quanti constĭtit ?* how much cost it ?
> *Asse et pluris,* a shilling and more.

Note.—When the Substantive is expressed, these words are put in the Ablative : as, *Tanto pretio mercatus est.* Cic.

RULE XXXVI.—Verbs of Valuing govern the Accusative with such Genitives as these : *magni, parvi, nihili, &c. :* as,

> *Æstĭmo te magni,* I value you much.

Note 1.—*Æstĭmo* sometimes governs the Ablative : as, *Æstimo te magno.*

Note 2.—*Æqui* and *boni* are put in the Genitive after *facio* and *consŭlo :* as, *Hoc consulo boni, æqui bonique facio.*

RULE XXXVII.—Verbs of Plenty and Scarceness generally govern the Ablative : as,

> *Abundat divitiis,* he abounds in riches.
> *Caret omni culpâ,* he is free from every fault.

Note.—*Egeo* and *indigeo* frequently govern the Genitive : as, *Eget æris.* Hor.

RULE XXXVIII.—*Utor, abūtor, fruor, fungor, potior, vescor,* govern the Ablative : as,

> *Utĭtur fraude,* he uses deceit.
> *Abutĭtur libris,* he abuses books.

Note 1.—To these Verbs add, *nitor, gaudeo, muto, dono, munĕro, communico, victĭto, beo, fido, impertior, dignor, nascor, creor, afficio, consto, labōro* (I am ill,) *prosĕquor, &c. ;* but the Ablative, after most of these, may be referred to Rule LV.

Note 2.—*Potior, fungor, vescor, epŭlor,* and *pascor,* sometimes govern the Accusative : as, *Potiri summam imperii.* Nep. *Potior* sometimes governs the Genitive : as, *Potiri regni.* Cic.

Government of Impersonal Verbs.

RULE XXXIX.—Impersonal Verbs govern the Dative : as,

> *Expĕdit reipublicæ,* it is profitable for the state.
> *Licet nemĭni peccāre,* no man is allowed to sin.

Note 1.—Besides the Dative, Impersonal Verbs have commonly an Infinitive, or part of a sentence, joined to them, which is supposed to supply the place of a Nominative: as, *Cui peccare licet.* Ovid. These Nominatives, *hoc, illud, id, idem, quod, &c.* are sometimes joined to Impersonal Verbs: as, *Sin tibi id minus libebit.* Cic.

Note 2.—The Verbs, *potest, cœpit, incīpit, desĭnit, debet,* and *solet,* become Impersonal, when joined to Impersonal Verbs: as, *Non potest credi tibi.*

Rule XL.—*Refert* and *interest* govern the Genitive: as

> *Refert patris,* it concerns my father.
> *Intĕrest omnium,* it is the interest of all.

Note.—*Refert* and *interest* sometimes admit Nominatives: as, *Magni refert studium atque voluntas.*—Lucr.

Rule XLI.—*Mea, tua, sua, nostra, vestra,* are put in the Accusative Plural: as,

> *Non mea refert,* it does not concern me.

Note 1.—That is, *mea, tua, &c.* are put in the Acc. Plural, when joined to *refert* and *interest,* instead of the Genitives of the Substantive Pronouns.

Note 2.—*Cujā,* and *cujus interest,* are used indifferently.

Rule XLII.—*Misĕret, pœnĭtet, pudet, tædet,* and *piget,* govern the Accusative of a Person, with the Genitive: as,

> *Misĕret me tui,* I pity you.
> *Pœnitet me peccāti,* I repent of my sin.

Note 1.—The Infinitive, or part of a sentence, sometimes supplies the place of the Genitive: as, *Te id puduit facere.* Ter.

Rule XLIII.—*Decet, delectat, juvat,* and *oportet,* govern the Accusative of a Person, with the Infinitive: as,

> *Delectat me studēre,* it delights me to study.
> *Non decet te rixāri,* it does not become you to scold.

Note 1.—*Decet* sometimes governs the Dative: as, *Ita nobis decet.* Ter.

Note 2.—*Attĭnet, pertĭnet,* and *spectat,* when used *impersonally,* take the Accusative with *ad:* as, *Nihil ad me attinet.* Ter.

* Rule XLIII.—The principal Agent, after a Passive Verb, is put in the Ablative, with the Preposition *a* or *ab;* and sometimes in the Dative: as,

> *Mundus gubernātur a Deo,* the world is governed by God.
> *Neque cernĭtur ulli,* nor is he seen by any.

Note 1.—The Dative of the Agent is used chiefly by the Poets.

Note 2.—The secondary Agent is governed in the Accusative by the Preposition *per;* or is expressed in the Ablative without a Preposition: as, *Per me defensa est respublica.* Cic.

Government of the Infinitive, Participles, Gerunds, and Supines.

Rule XLIV.—One Verb governs another in the Infinitive: as,

Cupio discĕre, I desire to learn.

Note 1.—The Infinitive is sometimes governed by Adjectives: as, *Dignus amari.* Virg.—and sometimes also by Substantives: as, *Tempus equûm fumantia solvere colla.* Virg.

Note 2.—The Infinitive is used as a Neuter Noun, in all the Cases of the Singular Number. It is governed by Nouns, Adjectives, Verbs, and Prepositions; and Adjectives and Pronouns agree with it in Gender. It is sometimes also used as a participle: as, *Quin te conspicer fodere, aut arare, aut aliquid ferre denique.* Ter.

Note 3.—*Cœpit, cœpērunt,* or some other governing word, is frequently understood: as, *Omnes mihi invidere,* Ter. sup. *cœperunt.*

Rule XLV.—Participles, Gerunds, and Supines, govern the Case of their Verbs: as,

Amans virtūtem, loving virtue. By Rule XXVIII.
Carens fraude, wanting guile. By Rule XXXVII.

Note 1.—The latter Supine does not govern a Case.

Note 2.—*Verbal* Nouns and Adjectives sometimes govern the Case of the Verbs from which they are derived: as, *Justitia est obtemperatio legibus.* Cic. *Facta consultaque ejus æmulus erat.* Sall.

Note 3.—*Exōsus, perōsus,* and often, also, *pertæsus,* govern the Accusative: as, *Tædas exosa jugales.* Ovid.

Rule XLVI.—The Gerund in *dum* of the Nominative Case with the Verb *est* governs the Dative: as,

Vivendum est mihi recte, I must live well.
Moriendum est omnibus, all must die.

Note 1.—*Gerunds* are construed like Nouns of the same case.

Note 2.—This Gerund always denotes *Obligation,* or *Necessity,* and governs the Dative of the object with which the obligation, or necessity lies.

Note 3.—The Dative is frequently understood: as, *Eundum est* sup. *nobis.*

Rule XLVII.—The Gerund in *di* is governed by Substantives and Adjectives: as,

Tempus legendi, time of reading.
Cupidus discendi, desirous to learn.

See Rules XI. and XIV.

Note.—This Gerund is sometimes construed with the Genitive Plural: as, *Facultas agrorum condonandi,* for *agros.* Cic.

RULE XLVIII.—The **Gerund** in *do* of the Dative Case is governed by Adjectives signifying Usefulness or Fitness: as,

>*Charta utilis scribendo,* paper useful for writing.

See Rule XVI.

Note 1.—The Adjective is sometimes omitted : as, *Non est solvendo,* sup. *par,* or *habilis.*

Note 2.—This Gerund is sometimes governed by a Verb : as, *Epidicum quærendo operam dabo.* PLAUT. See Rule XXXI.

RULE XLIX.—The Gerund in *dum* of the Accusative Case is governed by the Preposition *ad,* or *inter :* as,

>*Promptus ad audiendum,* ready to hear.
>*Attentus inter docendum,* attentive in time of teaching.

See Rule LXVIII.

Note.—It is likewise sometimes governed by *ante, circa,* or *ob :* as, *Ante domandum.* VIRG.

RULE L.—The Gerund in *do* of the Ablative Case is governed by the Prepositions *a, ab, de, e, ex,* or *in :* as,

>*Pæna a peccando absterret,* punishment frightens from sinning.

See Rules LXIX. and LXXI.

RULE LI.—The Gerund in *do* of the Ablative Case is used without a Preposition, as the Ablative of Manner, or Cause : as,

>*Memoria excolendo augetur,* the memory is improved by exercising it.
>*Defessus sum ambulando,* I am wearied with walking.

See Rule LV.

RULE LII.—Gerunds governing the Accusative are varied by the Participles in *dus,* which agree with their Substantives in Gender, Number, and Case : as,

Gerunds.	Participles.
Petendum est pacem.	*Petenda est pax.*
Tempus petendi pacem.	*Tempus petendæ pacis.*
Ad petendum pacem.	*Ad petendam pacem.*
A petendo pacem.	*A petenda pace.*

Note.—The Gerunds of Verbs which do not govern the Accusative are never changed into the Participles, except those of *utor, abutor, fruor, fungor,* and *potior :* as, *Ad hæc utenda idonea est.* TER.

RULE LIII.—The Supine in *um* is put after a Verb of Motion : as,

>*Abiit deambulatum,* he has gone to walk.

Note.—It is also put after Verbs which **do** not strictly denote motion: as, *Do filiam nuptum.* TER.

RULE LIV.—**The Supine in** *u* **is** put after **an Adjective**: as,

> *Facĭle dictu,* easy to tell, *or* to be told.

I. THE CAUSE, MANNER, AND INSTRUMENT.

RULE LV.—**The Cause, Manner,** and Instrument, are put in the Ablative: **as,**

> *Palleo metu,* I am pale for fear.
> *Fecit suo more,* he did it after his **own way.**
> *Scribo calămo,* I write with a pen.

Note.—To this Rule are referred the Ablatives **of** the *Matter* **of** which any thing is made ; and of the **Adjunct** or **Noun** expressive of some circumstance, joined **to a** Verb or Adjective: as, *Ære cavo clypeus.* VIRG. *Floruit acumine ingenii.* CIC.

II. PLACE.

RULE LVI.—*In* or *At* a place is put in the Genitive, if the Noun be of the **First or Second** Declension, and Singular Number: as,

> *Vixit Romæ,* he lived at Rome.
> *Mortuus est Londĭni,* he died at London.

Note.—*Humi, militĭæ,* and *belli,* **are also construed** in the Genitive: as, *Humi nascentia fraga.* VIRG.

RULE LVII.—*In* or *At* a place is put in the Ablative, if the Noun be of the Third Declension, or of the Plural **Number**: as,

> *Habĭtat Carthagĭne,* he dwells at Carthage.
> *Studuit Parisiis,* he studied at Paris.

RULE LVIII.—*To* a place is put in the Accusative: as,

> *Venit Romam,* he came **to** Rome.
> *Profectus est Athēnas,* he went to Athens.

RULE LIX.—*From* or *By* a place is put in the Ablative: as,

> *Discessit Corintho,* he departed from Corinth.
> *Laodicēâ iter faciēbat,* he went by Laodicea.

Note.—Motion *by* or *through* a Town is generally expressed by the Preposition *per :* as, *Quum iter per Thebas faceret.* NEP.

RULE LX.—*Domus* and *Rus* are construed the same way as Names of Towns: as,

Manet domi, he stays at home.
Domum revertĭtur, he returns home.
Vivit rure, or *ruri,* he lives in the country.
Rediit rure, he has returned from the country.

Note.—*Domi* is used only when joined with the Adjectives, *meæ,* *tuæ, suæ, nostræ, vestræ, alienæ.* With other adjectives, *domo* is used for *domi ;* as, *In domo paternâ.*

RULE LXI.—To names of Countries, Provinces, and all other places, except Towns, the Preposition is generally added : as,

Natus in Italiâ, in Latio, in urbe, &c. born in Italy, in Latium, in a city, &c.

Abiit in Italiam, in Latium, in urbem, &c. he has gone to Italy, to Latium, to a city, &c.

See Rules LXVIII, LXIX, LXX, and LXXI.

Note 1.—The Preposition is often expressed before names of Towns, especially when Apellatives or Adjectives are added to them : as, *in Epheso,* for *Ephesi ;* *ad Capuam,* for *Capuam ;* *ex Epheso,* for *Epheso ; in Hispali oppido.* The Preposition is sometimes omitted after names of Countries, Provinces, &c.: as, *Inde Sardiniam cum classe venit.* CIC.

Note 2.—*Peto,* signifying *I make for, I go to,* always governs the Accusative, without a Preposition: as, *Ægyptum petere decrevit.* CURT.

RULE LXII.—Nouns denoting *Space,* or *Distance,* are put in the Accusative, and sometimes in the Ablative : as,

Urbs distat triginta millia, or *millibus passuum,* the city is thirty miles distant.

Note 1.—One of the Substantives expressing *Distance,* is sometimes omitted : as, *Castra aberant bidui,* CIC. sup. *spatium.*

Note 2.—The *difference* of Measure or Distance is put in the Ablative : as, *Superat capite et cervicibus altis.* VIRG. See Rule XVIII.

III. TIME.

RULE LXIII.—Nouns denoting a *Point* of Time are put in the Ablative : as,

Venit horâ tertiâ, he came at the third hour.

RULE LXIV.—Nouns denoting *Continuance* of Time are put in the Accusative, or Ablative, but oftener in the Accusative : as,

Mansit paucos dies, he staid a few days.
Sex mensĭbus abfuit, he was absent six months.

RULE LXV.—A Substantive and a Participle, whose

Case depends upon no other word, are put in the Ablative Absolute : as,

Sole oriente, fugiunt tenebræ, the sun rising, *or,* when the sun rises, darkness flies away.
Opere peracto, ludēmus, our work being finished, *or,* when our work is finished, we will play.

Note 1.—The Perfect Participles of *Deponent* Verbs are not used in the Ablative Absolute, but agree in Case with the Nominative to the Verb : as, *Cicero locutus hæc concedit,* and not *his locutis.* The Perfect Participles of *Common* Verbs are seldom used in a Passive sense, and therefore rarely occur in the Ablative Absolute.

Note 2.—Part of a sentence sometimes supplies the place of a Noun : as, *Exposito quid iniquitas loci posset.* CÆS.

Construction of Indeclinable Words.

I. ADVERBS.

RULE LXVI.—Adverbs are joined to Verbs, Adjectives, and other Adverbs : as,

Bene scribit, he writes well.
Fortiter pugnans, fighting bravely.
Satis bene, well enough.

Note.—Adverbs are sometimes, though seldom, joined to Nouns : as, *Homerus plane orator.* CIC.

RULE LXVI.*—Some Adverbs of Time, Place, and Quantity, govern the Genitive : as,

Pridie illius diēi, the day before that day.
Ubique gentium, every where.
Satis est verbōrum, there is enough of words.

Note 1.—*Ergó* (for the sake of,) *instar,* and *partim,* also govern the Genitive : as, *Donari virtutis ergó.* CIC.

Note 2.—*Pridie* and *Postridie* govern the Genitive or Accusative : as, *Pridie Kalendas,* sup. *ante ; Postridie Kalendas,* sup. *post.*

Note 3.—*En* and *Ecce* govern the Nominative or Accusative : as, *En causa.* CIC. *Ecce hominem.* CIC.

RULE LXVII.—Some Derivative Adverbs govern the Case of their Primitives : as,

Omnium elegantissīme loquĭtur, he speaks the most elegantly of all. By Rule XV.
Vivĕre convenienter natūræ, to live agreeably to nature.
By Rule XVI.

II. PREPOSITIONS.

Rule LXVIII.—The Prepositions *ad, apud ante*, &c. govern the Accusative : as,

Ad patrem, to the father.

Rule LXIX.—The Prepositions *a, ab, abs*, &c. govern the Ablative : as,

A patre, from the father.

Note.—*Tenus*, when subjoined to a Noun in the Plural Number, generally governs the Genitive : as, *Crurum tenus.* Virg.

Rule LXX.—The Prepositions *in, sub, super*, and *subter*, govern the Accusative when *Motion* to a place is signified : as,

Eo in scholam, I go into the school.
Sub mœnia tendit, he goes under the walls.
Incīdit super agmīna, it fell upon the troops.

Rule LXXI.—When *Motion* or *Rest* in a place is signified, *in* and *sub* govern the Ablative, *super* and *subter* either the Accusative or Ablative : as,

Sedeo, or *discurro in scholâ*, I sit, *or* run up and down, in the school.
Sedens super arma, sitting above the arms.
Subter littŏre, beneath the shore.

Note 1.—*In*, when used for *erga, contra, per, ad, usque ad, apud, super*, governs the Accusative : as, *Amor in patriam.* Cic. When used for *inter*, it generally governs the Ablative : as, *In bonis.* Cic.

Note 2.—*Sub*, when it refers to *time*, governs the Accusative : as, *Sub noctem.* Cæs.

Note 3.—*Super*, when used for *ultra, præter*, and *inter*, governs the Accusative ; when used for *de, pro*, or *ab*, it governs the Ablative : as, *Super Garamantas.* Virg. *Hac super re scribam.* Cic.

Note 4.—*Subter* rarely governs the Ablative, and only among the poets.

Note 5.—Prepositions are frequently omitted : as, *Devenēre locos.* Virg. sup. *ad.*

Rule LXXII.—A Preposition often governs the same Case in Composition that it does out of it : as,

Adeāmus scholam, let us go to the school.
Exeāmus scholâ, let us go out of the school.

Note.—This Rule takes place only when the Preposition may, without injuring the sense, be separated from the Verb, and placed before the Case by itself : as, *Alloquor patrem*, i. e. *loquor ad patrem*. And even then, the Preposition is frequently repeated : as, *Exire e finibus suis.* Cæs.

III. INTERJECTIONS.

RULE LXXIII.—The Interjections *O, heu,* and *proh,* govern the Vocative and sometimes the Accusative : as,

> *O formōse puer !* O fair boy !
> *Heu me misĕrum !* ah, wretch that I am !

Note 1.—These Interjections are sometimes joined to the Nominative: as, *O vir fortis.* TER.

Note 2.—O is often understood : as, *Tityre, coge pecus.* VIRG.

RULE LXXIV.—*Hei* and *væ* govern the Dative : as,

> *Hei mihi !* ah me !
> *Væ vobis !* wo to you !

IV. CONJUNCTIONS.

RULE LXXV.—The Conjunctions *et, ac, atque, nec neque, aut, vel,* and some others, connect like Cases and Moods : as,

> *Honōra patrem et matrem,* honour your father and mother
> *Nec scribit nec legit,* he neither writes nor reads.

Note.—To these add *quam, nisi, præterquam, an,* &c. and Adverbs of Likeness : as, *ut, ceu, tanquam, quasi,* &c.

RULE LXXVI.—*Ut, quo, licet, ne, utinam,* and *dummŏdo,* are generally joined to the Subjunctive Mood : as,

> *Accĭdit ut terga vertĕrent,* it happened that they turned their backs.
> *Utinam sapĕres,* I wish you were wise.

Note 1.—All *Indefinite* words require the Subjunctive : as, *Quι est ? Nescio quis sit. Nescit vitāne fruatur, An sit apud manes.* OVID. *Nescio ubi sit.*

Note 2.—*Ut* is omitted after *volo, nolo, malo, rogo, precor,* &c. and after the Imperatives *sine, cave,* and *fac :* as, *Ducas volo.* TER. *Fac cogites.*

---

* *Additional Rules for the Construction of* Qui *and* Quum.

In the application of the following Rules, it is necessary to distinguish between the Subjunctive and Potential Mood. When the meaning is contingent, the Potential Mood must be employed ; and, in all such examples, it deserves particular attention, that the form of

---

* For these Rules and Observations the Editor is indebted to Dr CROMBIE's *Gymnasium,* 4th Edit.

the Verb is not affected by the relative, or any antecedent particle
but is strictly potential, the sense itself requiring that form. Thus
if we say, " I read, that I may learn," *Lego ut discam*—" He sent
men, who might tell the king," *Misit homines, qui regi nunciarent*—
the two Verbs, *Discam* and *Nunciarent*, are not each *subjoined* to any
preceding word, as its regimen ; but are to be considered as in the
Potential Mood, the sentiment to be expressed clearly demanding that
form of the Verb. But, when this form is used, not because the sentiment requires it, as being contingent or conditional, but because the
Verb is *subjoined* to some Adverb, Conjunction, or indefinite term,
which requires that form, it is then properly the Subjunctive Mood.
If I say, " He was so cruel a tyrant, that all men feared him," *Ty-
rannus tam crudelis erat, ut omnes eum metuerent*—" You err, who
think," *Erras, qui censeas*—the Verbs *Metuerent* and *Censeas* must
be considered as Subjunctive : for, were they not subjoined to *Ut* and
Qui, they would be put in the Indicative form, the sense being as-
sertive and unconditional.

RULE 1.—*Qui* is uniformly joined to the Subjunctive Mood when
. the relative clause does not express any sentiment of the author's, but
refers it to the person or persons of whom he is speaking : as,

Socrates dicere solebat, omnes in eo, *quod scirent*, satis esse elo-
quentes. CIC.

Obs. 1.—Or, *Qui* is joined to the Subjunctive Mood when the discourse is *oblique* or *indirect*. In oblique narration, the only Moods
admissible are, the *Infinitive* and *Subjunctive :* and, as the relative is
never employed except in the secondary and subordinate members of
a sentence, it must always, in oblique statements, be followed by the
Subjunctive.

Obs. 2.—In the same manner *Ubi* for *in quo loco*, *Quo* for *ad quem
locum*, and *Unde* for *e quo loco*, taken relatively, and not expressing
an observation of the author's, or an object of his knowledge, govern
the Subjunctive Mood : as, Cognovit, non longe ex eo loco oppidum
Cassivellauni abesse, *quo* satis magnus hominum pecorisque numerus
convenerit. CÆS.

Obs. 3.—The same principle extends also to the Conjunctions *quia,
quam, quum, quod, quando, atque*, and other such relative words : as,
Eos inter se, *quia* nemo unus satis dignus regno *visus sit*, partes regni
rapuisse. LIV.

RULE II.—*Qui* is joined to the Subjunctive Mood, when the relative clause expresses the motive, reason, or cause of the action or
event : as,

Male fecit Hannibal, *qui* Capuæ *hiemârit*, Hannibal did wrong in
wintering, *or* because he wintered, at Capua.

RULE III.—*Qui* is joined to the Subjunctive Mood, when it is
equivalent to *quanquam*, or *etsi is, si, modo*, or *dummodo is :* as,

Scilicet etiam illum, *qui* libertatem publicam *nollet,* tam projectæ servientium patentiæ tædebat. **T**AC.

RULE IV.—*Qui* is joined to the Subjunctive Mood when it follows an Interrogative, Negative, or Indefinite word : as,

Quis est enim, *cui* non perspicua *sint* illa ? **C**IC.

Obs. 1.—This rule takes effect only when the antecedent and relative clauses refer to the same subject, and logically express but one subject and one attribute.

Obs. 2.—The following are the most common forms of expression referred to in this Rule: *Quis est ? Quantus est ? Ecquis est ? An quisquam est ? Quotusquisque est ?* &c. *Nemo est, Nullus est, Nihil est, Non quisquam est, Nego esse quenquam, Vix ullus est,* &c.

Obs. 3.—This rule is applicable to those cases only in which the interrogation is equivalent to an affirmation or negation. When the sentence implies a question, put for the sake of information, the relative takes the Indicative Mood : as, **Quis hic est,** *qui* operto capite Æsculapium *salutat ?* **P**LAUT. **Quis est,** *qui salutet ?* would signify, " Who is there that salutes ?" implying " Nobody salutes."

RULE V.—*Qui* is very generally joined to the Subjunctive Mood, when a periphrasis with the Verb *Sum* is employed, instead of simply the Nominative with the principal Verb : as,

Sunt, *qui dicant,* " There are persons, who say," instead of *Nonnulli dicunt,* " Some say."

Obs. 1.—This Rule, like the preceding, takes effect only when the relative clause forms the predicate of the sentence.

Obs. 2.—The periphrastic form of expression is employed with other Verbs besides *Sum* : as, *Reperio, invenio, existo, exorior :* also, *tempus fuit, tempus veniet,* &c. *adest, præsto sunt,* &c.

RULE VI.—*Qui* is joined to the Subjunctive Mood, when it is used for *ut ego, ut tu, ut ille, ut nos, ut vos, ut illi,* through all their cases : as,

At ea fuit legatio Octavii, in *quâ* periculi suspicio non *subesset.* **C**IC.

RULE VII.—*Qui* is joined to the Subjunctive Mood after *Solus* and *Unus,* when they are employed to restrict to a single person the qualities implied in the relative clause : as,

Solus hic homo est, *qui sciat* divinitus. **P**LAUT.

Quum—a Conjunction.

RULE I.—*Quum* taken for *quoniam,* or *quandoquidem,* " since," is very generally joined to the Subjunctive Mood : as, " *Quum* Athenas *sis* profectus." **C**IC.

RULE II.—*Quum* taken for *quod,* " because," is generally joined to the Indicative Mood : as, Ego redigam vos in gratiam hoc fretus, *quum* e medio *excessit.* **T**ER.

RULE III.—*Quum* taken for *etsi*, "although," is uniformly juined to the Subjunctive Mood: as, Cui *quum* Cato et Caninius *intercessissent*, tamen est perscripta. CIC.

Quum—an Adverb.

RULE I.—*Quum* taken for *quoties*, or *quandocunque*, "as often as," or "whenever," is joined to the Indicative Mood: as, *Quum* prospero ejus flatu *utimur*, ad exitus pervehimur optatos, et *quum* reflavit, *affligimur*. CIC.

RULE II.—*Quum* taken for *quando*, "at the time when," *or* "at which time," is joined to the Indicative Mood: as, Ne stridorem quidem serræ tunc audiunt, *quum acuitur;* aut grunnitum *quum jugulatur* sus. CIC.

RULE III.—*Quum* is joined to the Indicative Mood, when it is used to express the point of time at which an action or state commenced, conceived to be continued to the present period: as, Jam anni prope quadraginta sunt, *quum* hoc *probatur.* CIC.

RULE IV.—*Quum* is joined to the Indicative Mood when it signifies "as soon as," and is emphatically used with *primum*, denoting an action or event in close succession to another: as, *Quum* ad nos *allatum est* de temeritate eorum, graviter commotus sum. CIC. *Quum primum* Romam *veni.* CIC.

RULE V.—*Quum* is joined to the Subjunctive Mood, when it is taken for *postquam*, "after," denoting simply the posteriority of one event to another, but not implying close succession: as, Hæc *quum animadvertisset*, vehementer eos incusavit. CÆS.

RULE VI.—*Quum*, when joined to a secondary clause, expressing a past action or event as in progression, to which another action or event, in the primary clause, is expressed as contemporary, is joined to the Subjunctive Mood: as, *Quum* civitas armis jus suum exsequi *conaretur*, Orgetorix mortuus est. CÆS.

Obs.—It is necessary to observe, that the preceding rules for joining *Quum* with the Indicative Mood, do not take place in the two following cases: 1*st*, If the clause be oblique—we say, for example, "Tempus fuit, *quum* homines *vagabantur*," CIC. but, "Scio tempus fuisse, *quum* homines *vagarentur*." 2*dly*, When any thing doubtful, contingent, or fortuitous, is implied, the sense requires the Potential Mood: as, "Sed tu omnia consilia differebas in id tempus, *quum sciremus*." CIC. "When we should know." It must be observed also, that though usage be very generally conformable to these rules, it is not universally so. Cicero says, "Tempus fuit, *quum* homines *vagabantur*." Varro, in a sentiment precisely similar, says, "Tempus fuit, *quum* homines rura *colerent*."

APPENDIX.

FIRST DECLENSION.

1. In the declension of the word *familia*, when compounded with *pater, mater, filius,* and *filia*, an old form of the Genitive Singular in *as* has been retained : as, *pater-familias, patres-familias.* The regular forms *familiæ* and *familiarum* are, however, not uncommon.

There is also a poetical form of the Genitive Singular in *äi*, for *æ:* as, *auläi, auräi.*

2. Patronymics in *es* and *a*, compound words ending in *cŏla* and *gĕna,* and a few national names, sometimes form the Genitive Plural, in the poets, in *ûm* instead of *arum :* as, *Æneadûm, Cœlicolûm, Lapithûm.* This contraction is very unusual in prose.

SECOND DECLENSION.

3. The Genitive Singular of Nouns in *ius* and *ium*, in the purest age of the Latin language, was formed in *i*, and not in *ii*, both in prose and verse: as, *fili, Tulli, ingeni.*

4. Proper names in *ius* which continue Adjectives, and *Pius* when used as a surname, form the Vocative Singular in *e :* as, *Delie, Pie.*

5. Some Nouns, especially those which denote value, measure, and weight, commonly form the Genitive Plural in *ûm,* instead of *orum :* as, *nummûm, sestertiûm.* Neuter Nouns have sometimes *ôn* instead of *orum.*

THIRD DECLENSION.

Genitive Singular.

6. Cicero and other writers of the best age sometimes form, from Greek proper names in *es*, especially from those in *cles* a Genitive in *i* instead of *is :* as, *Achilli, Agathocli.* In Nouns in *is, ĭdis,* the poets often use the Greek termination *os* for *is :* as, *Daphnis, Daphnĭdos.* The Greek form is not common in prose. Feminines in *o* have commonly *us :* as, *Dido, Didus.*

E

Accusative Singular.

7. The following Nouns in *is* have *im* in the Accusative:

Amussis, f. *a mason's rule.*	Ravis, f. *hoarseness.*
Buris, f. *the beam of a plough.*	Sinăpis, f. *mustard.*
Cannăbis, f. *hemp.*	Sitis, f. *thirst.*
Cucŭmis, m. *a cucumber.*	Tussis, f. *a cough.*
Gummis, f. *gum.*	Vis, f. *strength.*
Mephītis, f. *a strong smell.*	

8. Proper Names in *is* have *im* in the Accusative:

Names of Cities and other places: as, *Bilbĭlis*, f. a city in Spain; *Syrtis*, f. a quicksand on the coast of Africa.

Names of Rivers: as, *Tibĕris*, m. the Tiber; *Bætis*, m. the Guadalquivir.

Names of Gods: as, *Anūbis*, m. *Osīris*, m. Egyptian deities.

Note.—These Nouns have sometimes *in* in the Accusative: as, *Bilbĭlin, Bætin, Serāpin.*

9. The following Nouns in *is* have *em* or *im* in the Accusative:

Aquālis, m. *a water-pot.*	Puppis, f. *the stern of a ship.*
Clavis, f. *a key.*	Restis, f. *a rope.*
Cutis, f. *the skin.*	Secūris, f. *an axe.*
Febris, f. *a fever.*	Sementis, f. *a sowing.*
Lens, f. *lentiles.*	Strigĭlis, f. *a curry-comb.*
Navis, f. *a ship.*	Turris, f. *a tower.*
Pelvis, f. *a bason.*	

Puppis, restis, secūris, and *turris,* have much more frequently *im;* the others have commonly *em.* The oldest Latin writers form the Accusative of some other Nouns in *im:* as, *avis, auris,* &c.

10. Nouns which have been adopted from the Greek, sometimes retain *a* in the Accusative: as, *heros,* m. a hero, *herōa; Tros,* m. a Trojan, *Troa.* See page 8.

This form is seldom employed by the best prose writers, and is chiefly confined to Proper Names, except in *aër,* m. the air; *æther,* m. the sky; *delphin,* m. a dolphin; and *Pan,* m. the God of the shepherds, which commonly have *aëra, æthĕra, delphīna,* and *Pana.*

Many Greek Nouns in *es* have *en* as well as *em* in the Accusative: as, *Euphrāten, Oresten, Pylāden.*

Ablative Singular.

11. Nouns in *is* which have *im* in the Accusative, have *i* in the Ablative: as, *sitis, sitim, siti.*

But *cannăbis, Bætis, sināpis,* and *Tigris,* have *e* or *i.*

12. Nouns in *is* which have *em* or *im* in the Accusative, have *e* or *i* in the Ablative: as, *clavis, clave,* or *clavi.*

But *cutis* and *restis* have *e* only: *secūris, sementis,* and *strigĭlis* have seldom *e.*

13. The following Nouns which have *em* in the Accusative, have *e* or *i* in the Ablative:

Amnis, m. *a river.*	Occĭput, n. *the hind-head.*
Anguis, m. *and* f. *a snake.*	Orbis, m. *a circle*
Avis, f. *a bird.*	Pars, f. *a part.*
Civis, c. *a citizen.*	Postis, m. *a door-post.*
Classis, f. *a fleet.*	Pugil, c. *a pugilist.*
Finis, m. *and* f. *an end.*	Rus, n. *the country.*
Fustis, m. *a staff.*	Sors, f. *a lot.*
Ignis, m. *fire.*	Supellex, f. *furniture.*
Imber, m. *a shower.*	Unguis, m. *a nail.*
Mugil, m. *a mullet.*	Vectis, m. *a lever.*

Finis, mugil, occĭput, pugil, rus, supellex, and *vectis,* have *e* or *i* indifferently; the others have much more frequently *e.*

Names of Towns, when they denote the place *in* or *at* which any thing is done, take *e* or *i:* as, *Carthagĭne,* or *Carthagĭni.*

Canālis, m. *or* f. a water-pipe, has *canāli* only. Likewise names of months in *is* or *er:* as, *Aprīlis, September, Aprīli, Septembri;* and those Nouns in *is* which were originally Adjectives: as, *ædīlis, affīnis, bipennis, familiāris, natālis, rivālis, sodālis, volucris,* &c. though the last class also admit of *e.* *Rudis,* f. a rod; and *juvenis,* c. a youth, have *e* only.

14. The following **Neuter Nouns** in *al* and *ar* have *e* in the Ablative:

Baccar, *lady's glove.*	Jubar, *a sunbeam.*	Sal, *salt.*
Far, *corn.*	Nectar, *nectar.*	

Par, when used as a Substantive, forms the Ablative Singular, and Genitive Plural, in the same way as the Adjective. *See Adjectives.*

Genitive Plural. See page 6.

15. The following Nouns have *ium* in the Genitive Plural:

Caro, f. *flesh.*	Fauce, f. *the jaws.*	Nox, f. *night.*
Cohors, f. *a cohort.*	Lar, m. *a household god.*	Os, n. *a bone.*
Cor, n. *the heart.*	Linter, m. *or* f. *a boat.*	Quiris, m. *a Roman.*
Cos, f. *a whetstone.*	Mus, m. *a mouse.*	Samnis, m. *a Samnite.*
Dos, f. *a dowry.*	Nix. f. *snow.*	Uter, m. *a bottle.*

The Compounds of *uncia* and *as* have likewise *ium:* as, *septunx,* m. seven ounces, *septuncium; sextans,* m. two ounces, *sextantium.*

Apis, f. a bee, has *apum* and *apium;* and *opis,* f. power, has *opum* only. *Gryps,* m. a griffon: *lynx,* m. *or* f. a lynx; and *Sphinx,* f. the Sphinx, have *um.*

16. *Bos,* c. an ox, has *boum* in the Genitive, and *bobus,* or *bubus,* in the Dative; and *sus,* c. a sow, has *suĭbus,* or *subus.* Nouns in *ma* have *tis* as well as *tibus:* as, *poēma,* n. a poem, *poematĭbus,* or

poemătis. The Greek termination *si* or *sin* is very uncommon in prose, and is admissible only in words which are purely Greek. See page 8. -

17. The form of the Accusative Plural in *as* is admissible in all words which have that termination in Greek, but is rarely used in prose. Livy, however, frequently uses *Macedŏnas ;* and *Allobrŏgas* is found in Cæsar.

IRREGULAR NOUNS.

Irregular Nouns are divided into *Variable, Defective,* and *Redundant.*

I. VARIABLE NOUNS.

Nouns are variable either in Gender, or Declension, or in both.

18. Masculine in the Singular, Neuter in the Plural.

Avernus, *a hill in Campania.*	Pangæus, *a promontory in Thrace.*
Dindўmus, *a hill in Phrygia.*	Tænărus, *a promontory in Laconia.*
Ismărus, *a hill in Thrace.*	Tartărus, *hell.*
Mænălus, *a hill in Arcadia.*	Taygĕtus, *a hill in Laconia.*
Massĭcus, *a hill in Campania, famous for its wines.*	

19. Masc. in the Singular, Masc. and Neut. in the Plural.

Jocus, *a jest.* Pl. -i, and -a.   Locus, *a place.* Pl. -i, and -a.

20. Feminine in the Singular, Neuter in the Plural.

Carbăsus, *a sail.* Pl. -a.   Pergămus, *the citadel of Troy.* Pl. -a.

21. Neuter in the Singular, Masculine in the Plural.

Argos, *a city in Greece.* Pl. -i.   Elysium, *the Elysian fields.* Pl. -i.
Cœlum, *heaven.* Pl. -i.

Note.—Argos, in the Singular, is used only in the Nominative and Accusative.

22. Neut. in the Singular, Masc. and Neut. in the Plural.

Frenum, *a bridle.* Pl. -i, and -a.   Rastrum, *a rake.* Pl. -i, and -a.

23. Neuter in the Singular, Feminine in the Plural.

Balneum, *a bath.* Pl. -æ, and -a.   Epŭlum, *a banquet.* Pl. -æ.
Delicium, *a delight.* Pl. -æ.

24. *Vas, vasis,* n. a vessel, of the Third Declension : Plural, *vasa, vasōrum,* of the Second. *Jugĕrum, jugĕri,* n. an acre, of the Second Declension ; Plur. *jugĕra, -um,* of the Third. *Jugĕris,* and *jugĕre* from *jugus,* are also found in the Singular. *See Num.* 27.

II. DEFECTIVE NOUNS.

Nouns are defective in Cases or Number.

25. Some Nouns are altogether indeclinable : as, *pondo,* n. a pound,

or pounds; *semis*, n. the half; *mille*, n. a thousand; *cœpe*, n. an onion; and *opus*, n. need, needful, which is used both as a Substantive, and an Adjective. To these may be added, any word used for a Noun: as, *velle suum*, for *sua voluntas*, his own inclination; and Proper Names adopted from a foreign language: as, *Elisäbet, Jerusalem*.

I. Some Nouns are defective only in Particular Cases.

26. The following Nouns are used only in one Case:*

Nom.
Inquies, f. *want of rest.*

Abl.
Admonitu, m. *an admonition.*
Ambāge, f. *a winding.*
Casse, m. *a net.*
Diu, *by day.*
Ergô, *on account of.*

Fauce, f. *the jaws.*
Ingratiis, f. *in spite of.*
Injussu, m. *without order.*
Interdiu, *by day.*
Natu, m. *by birth.*
Noctu, f. *by night.*
Promptu, m. *in readiness.*

Note.—A great many Verbal Nouns of the Fourth Declension are used only in the Abl. Singular: as, *accitu, promptu*, &c. *Dicis*, f. and *nauci*, n. are used only in the Gen. Sing.: as, *dicis gratiâ*, for form's sake; *res nauci*, a thing of no value. *Inficias*, f. and *incita*, f. or *incitas*, have only the Acc. Plural: as, *inficias ire*, to deny; *ad incitas redactus*, reduced to extremities. *Ambāges, casses*, and *fauces* are regularly declined in the Plural.

27. The following Nouns are used only in two Cases:

Nom. and *Acc.*
Astu, n. *the city Athens.*
Inferiæ, -as, f. *sacrifices to the dead.*
Instar, n. *likeness, bigness.*
Suppetiæ, -as, f. *help.*

Nom. and *Abl.*
Astus, -u, m. *cunning.*
Vesper, -e, *or* -i, m. *the evening.*

Gen. and *Abl.*
Compēdis, -e, f. *a fetter.*
Impētis, -e, m. *force.*
Jugēris, -e, n. *an acre.*
Spontis, -e, f. *of one's own accord.*
Verbēris, -e, n. *a stripe.*
Repetundārum, -is, f. *extortion.*

Note.—*Compēdes, jugēra*, and *verbēra* are regularly declined in the Plural. *Astus* is found in the Nom. and Acc. Plural.

28. The following Nouns are used only in three Cases:

Nom. Acc. and *Voc.*
Cacoëthes,† n. *a bad custom.*
Cete, n. *whales.*
Dica, -am, f. *a process*; Pl. -*as.*

Epos, n. *an heroic poem.*
Fas, n. *divine law.*
Grates, f. *thanks.*
Melos, n. *a song*; Pl. -*e.*

---

* Nouns which are used only in one case are called *Monoptotes*; in two cases, *Diptotes*; in three cases, *Triptotes*; in four cases, *Tetraptotes*; in five cases, *Pentaptotes*.

† Also other Greek Neuter Nouns in *es*. See *Rules for the Gender of Nouns*, 29.

Nefas, n. *impiety.*   Mane, -e, -e, n. *the morning.*
Nihil, *and* Nil, n. *nothing.*   Tabes, f. *consumption.*
Tempe, n. *the vale of Tempe.*   Vepres, *or* -is, m. *a brier.*
    Nom. Acc. and *Abl.*
Lues, f. *a plague.*

       Nom. Gen. and *Abl.* Tabum, n. *putrid gore.*
       Nom. Gen. and *Acc.* Munia, -ōrum, n. *offices.*

Opis, f. Gen. help (from *ops*), has *opem* and *ope* in the Acc. and
Ablative, with the Plural complete, *opes, opum,* &c. wealth; and
preci, f. Dat. a prayer (from *prex*), has *precem*, and *prece*, with the
Plural entire, *preces, precum,* &c. *Feminis*, n. Gen. the thigh (from
femen), has *femĭni*, and -*e*, in the Dat. and Abl. Singular; and *femĭna*
in the Nom. Acc. and Voc. Plural.

Note.—Vepres has the Plural entire ; and *tabes*, and *gratĭbus*, the
Nominative and Ablative Plural of *tabes*, and *grates* are also found

The following Nouns want the Genitive, Dative, and Ablative Plural :

Far, n. *corn.*   Mel, n. *honey.*   Rus, n. *the country.*
Hiems, f. *winter.*   Metus, m. *fear.*   Thus, n. *frankincense.*

For Nouns of the Fifth Declension, See page 10.

29. The following Nouns want the Nominative and Vocative,
and are therefore used only in four Cases :

      Ditiŏnis, f. *power.*   Sordis, f. *filth.*
      Pecŭdis, f. *a beast.*   Vicis, f. *a change.*

To these may be added *daps*, f. a dish ; *frux*, f. corn ; and *nex*, f.
slaughter, which are seldom used in the Nominative. The Plural of
frux is entire; *daps* wants the Genitive ; and *nex* seems to have the
Nom. Acc. and Voc. only.

Chaos, n. a confused mass, wants the Gen. and Dat. Singular, and
is not used in the Plural.

Note.—Pecŭdis and *sordis* have the Plural entire : *vicis* is defective in the Genitive ; *ditiŏnis* has no Plural.

30. Some Nouns are defective in one Case.

The following want the Genitive Plural :

      Fæx, f. *dregs.*   Proles, f. *offspring.*
      Fax, f. *a torch.*   Ros, m. *dew.*
      Labes, f. *a stain.*   Sobŏles, f. *offspring.*
      Lux, f. *light.*   Sol, m. *the sun.*
      Os, n. *the mouth.*

Satias, f. a glut of any thing, and *salum*, n. the sea, want the Gen.
Sing. and the Plural entirely. *Situs*, m. a situation, nastiness, wants
the Gen. and perhaps the Dat. Sing. and probably the Gen. Dat and

Abl. Plural. *Nemo,* c. nobody, wants the Voc. Sing. and has no Plural.

II. Many Nouns are defective in Number.

31. Some Nouns, from the nature of the things which they express, cannot be used in the Plural. Such are the names of virtues and vices, of arts, herbs, metals, liquors, different kinds of corn, abstract nouns, &c. : as, *justitia,* justice ; *luxus,* luxury ; *musĭca,* music ; *apium,* parsley ; *aurum,* gold ; *lac,* milk ; *tr%itĭcum,* wheat ; *magnĭtŭdo,* greatness ; *senectus,* old age ; *macies,* leanness, &c. But some of the Nouns included in these classes are occasionally found in the Plural.

32. **The** following Masculine Nouns are scarcely used in the Plural :

Aër, aĕris, *the air.*
Æther, -ĕris, *the sky.*
Fimus, -i, *dung.*
Hespĕrus, -i, *the evening star.*
Limus, -i, *mud.*
Meridies, -iĕi, *mid-day.*
Mundus, -i, *a woman's ornaments.*
Muscus, -i, *moss.*

Penus, -i, *or* -ûs, *all manner of provisions.*
Pontus, -i, *the sea.*
Pulvis, -ĕris, *dust.*
Sanguis, -ĭnis, *blood.*
Sopor, -ōris, *sleep.*
Veternus, -i, *a lethargy.*

Note.—Aër, pulvis, and *sopor,* are found in the Plural.

33. **The** following Feminine Nouns are scarcely used in the Plural :

Argilla, -æ, *potter's earth.*
Fames, -is, *hunger.*
Humus, -i, *the ground.*
Indŏles, -is, *a disposition.*
Plebs, -is, *the common people.*
Pubes, -is, *the youth.*

Salus, -ûtis, *safety.*
Sitis, -is, *thirst.*
Supellex, -ctĭlis, *household furniture.*
Venia, -æ, *pardon.*
Vespĕra, -æ, *the evening.*

The following are sometimes found in the Plural :

Bilis, -is, *bile.*
Cholĕra, -æ, *choler.*
Cutis, -is, *the skin.*
Fama, -æ, *fame.*
Gloria, -æ, *glory.*
Labes, -is, *a stain.*
Pax, -cis, *peace.*

Pituïta, -æ, *phlegm.*
Pix, -cis, *pitch.*
Proles, -is, *offspring.*
Quies, -ētis, *rest.*
Sobŏles, -is, *offspring.*
Tellus, -ûris, *the earth.*

34. The following Neuter Nouns are scarcely used in the Plural :

Album, -i, *a list of names.*
Barăthrum, -i, *any deep place.*
Dilucŭlum, -i, *the dawn of day.*
Ebur, -ōris, *ivory.*

Fœnum, -i, *hay.*
Gelu, *frost,* ind.
Hilum, -i, *the black speck of a bean, a trifle.*

Jubar, -ăris, *the sunbeam.*

Justitium, -i, *a vacation, the time when courts do not sit.*

Lardum, -i, *bacon.*

Lethum, -i, *death.*

Lutum, -i, *clay.*

Nectar, -ăris, *nectar.*

Pelăgus, -i, *the sea.*

Penum, -i, *and* penus, -ŏris. *all kinds of provisions.*

Pus, puris, *matter.*

Sal, salis, *salt.*

Ver, veris, *the spring.*

Virus, -i, *poison.*

Viscum, -i, *the mistletoe.*

Vitrum, -i, *glass.*

Vulgus, -i, *the rabble.*

Note.—*Ebur, lardum, lutum,* and *pus* are found in the Plural ; and *pelăge* is found, in some cases, as the Plural of *pelăgus* ; *sal,* as a Neuter Noun, is not used in the Plural.

35. Many Nouns want the Singular ; as the Names of feasts, books, games, and of many cities and places : as,

Apollinăres, -ium, *games in honour of Apollo.*

Bacchanălia, -um, *and* -ōrum, *the feasts of Bacchus.*

Bucolĭca, -ōrum, *a book of pastorals.*

Hierosolўma, -ōrum, *Jerusalem.*

Olympia, -ōrum, *the Olympic games.*

Syracūsæ, -ārum, *Syracuse.*

Thermopўlæ, -ārum, *the straits of Thermopylæ.*

36. The following Masculine Nouns are scarcely used in the Singular :

Antes, *the front rows of vines.*

Cancelli, *lattices,* or *windows made with cross-bars.*

Cani, *gray hairs.*

Celĕres, -um, *the light-horse.*

Codicilli, *writings.*

Fasti, -ōrum, *or* fastus, -uum, *calendars, in which were marked festival days, &c.*

Fori, *the gangways of a ship,* or *seats in the Circus.*

Infĕri, *the gods below.*

Lemŭres, -um, *ghosts, hobgoblins.*

Libĕri, *children.*

Majōres, -um, *ancestors.*

Manes, -ium, *ghosts.*

Minōres, -um, *successors.*

Penātes, -um, *or* -ium, *household gods.*

Postĕri, *posterity.*

Procĕres, -um, *the nobles.*

Pugillāres, -ium, *writing tables.*

Supĕri, *the gods above.*

Note.—*Libĕri* and *procĕres* (*procĕrum*) are also found in the Singular. Some of the others, as, *infĕri, majōres,* &c. are properly Adjectives, and agree with the Substantives which are implied in their signification.

37. The following Feminine Nouns want the Singular :

Clitellæ, *a pannier.*

Cunæ, *a cradle.*

Diræ, *imprecations.*

Divitiæ, *riches.*

Excubiæ, *watches.*

Exsequiæ, *funerals.*

Exuviæ, *spoils.*

Feriæ, *holidays.*

Gerræ, *trifles.*

Induciæ, *a truce.*

Induviæ, *clothes to put on.*

Insidiæ, *snares.*

Kalendæ, Nonæ, Idus, -uum, *names which the Romans gave to certain days in each month.*

Lactes, *the small guts.* Nuptiæ, *a marriage.* Scopæ, *a besom.*
Lapicidīnæ, *stone quar-* Parietīnæ, *ruinous* Tenebræ, *darkness.*
   ries.   *walls.* Thermæ, *hot baths.*
Manubiæ, *spoils taken* Phalēræ, *trappings.* Tricæ, *toys.*
   in war. Primitiæ, *first fruits.* Valvæ, *folding doors.*
Minæ, *threats.* Reliquiæ, *a remainder.* Vindiciæ, *a claim of*
Nugæ, *trifles.* Salīnæ, *salt-pits.*   *liberty, a defence.*
Nundīnæ, *a market.* Scalæ, *a ladder.*

The following are sometimes found in the Singular :

Argutiæ, *quirks, witticisms.*   Charĭtes, -um, *the Graces.*
Bigæ, *a chariot drawn by two* Facetiæ, *pleasant sayings.*
  horses.   Ineptiæ, *silly stories.*
Trigæ, — *by three.*   Præstigiæ, *enchantments.*
Quadrīgæ, — *by four.*   Salebræ, *rugged places.*
Braccæ, *breeches.*

38. The following Neuter Nouns want the Singular :

Acta, *public acts,* or *records.*   Lautia, *provisions for the entertain-*
Æstīva, *summer quarters.*   *ment of foreign ambassadors.*
Arma, *arms.*   Magalia, -um, *cottages.*
Bellaria, *dainties.*   Mœnia, -um, *the walls of a city.*
Brevia, -um, *shallows.*   Orgia, *the sacred rites of Bacchus.*
Cibaria, *victuals.*   Parentālia, -um, *solemnities at the*
Crepundia, *children's toys.*   *funeral of parents.*
Cunabŭla, *a cradle, an origin.*   Præcordia, *the midriff, the bowels.*
Exta, *the entrails.*   Sponsālia, -um, *espousals.*
Februa, *purifying sacrifices.*   Statīva, *a standing camp.*
Flabra, *blasts of wind.*   Talaria, -um, *winged shoes.*
Fraga, *strawberries.*   Tesqua, *rough places.*
Hyberna, *winter quarters.*   Transtra, *the seats where the rowers*
Ilia, -um, *the entrails.*   *sit in ships.*
Justa, *funeral rites.*   Utensĭlia, -um, *utensils.*
Lamenta, *lamentations.*

Note.—*Acta* and *transtra* are also found in the Singular. Some
of the others, as, *æstīva, brevia, hyberna, statīva,* &c. are properly
Adjectives ; and agree with the Substantives which are necessary to
complete their meaning.

III. REDUNDANT NOUNS.

39. Nouns are redundant in Termination, Gender, or form
of Declension : as, *arbor,* or *arbos,* a tree ; *vulgus,* the rabble,
Masc. *or* Neut. *menda, -æ,* or *mendum, -i,* a fault.

The most numerous class of Redundant Nouns is composed
of those which express the same meaning by different terminations : as,

Æther, -ĕris, & æthra, -æ, *the air.* Amarăcus, & -um, *sweet marje-*
Alvear, & -e, & -ium, *a bee-hive.*   *ram.*

Ancīle & -ium, *an oval shield.*

Angiportus, -ûs. & -i, & -um, *a narrow lane.*

Aphractus, & -um, *an open ship.*

Aplustre, & -um, *the flag, colours.*

Arbor, & -os, *a tree.*

Bacŭlus, & -um, *a staff.*

Balteus, & -um, *a belt.*

Batillus, & -um, *a fireshovel.*

Capus, & -o, *a capon.*

Cassis, -ĭdis, & -ĭda, -ĭdæ, *a helmet.*

Cepa, -æ, & -e, indec. *an onion.*

Clypeus, & -um, *a shield.*

Colluvies, & -io, *filth, dirt.*

Compāges, & -go, *a joining.*

Conger, & -grus, *a large eel.*

Crocus, & -um, *saffron.*

Cubĭtus, & -um, *a cubit.*

Diluvium, & -es, *a deluge.*

Elĕgi, -ōrum, & -ĭa, *an elegy.*

Elephantus, & Elephas, -antis, *an elephant.*

Essēda, & -um, *a chariot.*

Eventus, & -a, -ōrum, *an event.*

Gausăpa, & -e, -es ; & -e, -is ; & -um, *a rough cloth.*

Gelu, & -um, *frost.*

Gibbus, & -a ; & -er, -ĕris, *or* -ĕri, *a bunch, a swelling.*

Glutĭnum, & -en, *glue.*

Grus, -uis, & -uis, -uis, *a crane.*

Laurus, -i, & -ûs, *a laurel tree.*

Macēria, & -ies, -iēi, *a wall.*

Materia, -æ, & -ies, -iēi, *matter.*

Menda, -æ, & -um, -i, *a fault.*

Milliāre, & -ium, *a mile.*

Monĭtum, & -us, -ûs, *an admonition.*

Muria, & -ies, -iēi, *brine, or pickle.*

Nasus & -um, *the nose.*

Obsidio, & -um, *a siege.*

Ostrea, -æ, & -ea, -ōrum, *an oyster.*

Penus, -ûs, & -i ; & -um ; & -us, -ŏris, *provisions.*

Peplus, & -um, *a veil, a robe.*

Pistrīna, & -um, *a grinding-house.*

Plebs, & -es, *the common people.*

Prætextus, -ûs, & -um, *a pretext.*

Rapum, & -a, *a turnip.*

Ruma, & -men, *the cud.*

Ruscum, & -us, *butcher's broom.*

Segmen, & -mentum, *a paring.*

Sepes & Seps, *a heage.*

Sibĭlus, & -a, -ōrum, *a hissing.*

Sinus, & -um, *a milk-pail.*

Stramen, & -tum, *straw.*

Suffimen, & -tum, *a perfume.*

Tignus, & -um, *a plank.*

Toral, & -āle, *a bed-covering.*

Tonitrus, -us, & -u, & -uum, *thunder.*

Torcŭlar, & -āre, *a wine-press.*

Veternus, & -um, *a lethargy.*

Viscum, & -us, *the mistletoe.*

Note.—Some of the above nouns may be used in either, or any of the terminations, and in the Singular or Plural, indifferently; some, as *auxilium, laurus, -ús,* are used only in one or two cases ; or in one number, as *elĕgi ;* while others, as *prætextus* (a pretext) and *prætextum* (a border), though sometimes synonymous, are commonly employed in a different meaning.

40. The following Nouns have a double meaning in the Plural—one in addition to that which generally belongs to them in the Singular :

Singular.	*Plural.*
Aedes, *a temple.*	Aedes, *a house.*
Auxilium, *assistance.*	Auxilia, *auxiliary troops.*
Bonum, *any thing good.*	Bona, *goods, property.*
Carcer, *a prison.*	Carcĕres, *the barriers of a race-course.*

Singular.	Plural.
Castrum, *a fort.*	Castra, *a camp.*
Comitium, *a place in the Roman forum where the comitia were held.*	Comitia, *an assembly of the people for the purpose of voting.*
Copia, *plenty.*	Copiæ, *troops.*
Cupedia, *daintiness.*	Cupediæ, *or -a, dainties.*
Facultas, *power, ability.*	Facultātes, *wealth, property.*
Fascis, *a bundle of twigs, a fagot.*	Fasces, *a bundle of rods carried before the chief magistrates of Rome.*
Finis, *the end of any thing.*	Fines, *the boundaries of a country.*
Fortūna, *fortune.*	Fortūnæ, *an estate, possessions.*
Gratia, *grace, favour.*	Gratiæ, *thanks.*
Hortus, *a garden.*	Horti, *pleasure-grounds.*
Litĕra, *a letter of the alphabet.*	Litĕræ, *a letter, an epistle.*
Lustrum, *a period of five years.*	Lustra, *dens of wild beasts.*
Natālis, *a birth-day.*	Natāles, *birth, descent.*
Opĕra, *labour.*	Opĕræ, *workmen.*
Opis (Gen.), *help.*	Opes, *wealth, power.*
Pars, *a part, a portion.*	Partes, *a party, a faction.*
Plăga, *a space, a tract of country.*	Plăgæ, *nets used by hunters.*
Principium, *a beginning, a first principle,* or element.	Principia, *a place in the camp where the general's tent stood.*
Rostrum, *the beak of a bird, the sharp part of the prow of a ship.*	Rostra, *a pulpit in the Roman forum, from which orators used to address the people.*
Sal, *salt.*	Sales, *witticisms.*

Note.—All the Nouns in the preceding list, except *castrum* and *comitium,* are sometimes found in the Singular, in the sense in which they more commonly occur in the Plural.

IRREGULAR ADJECTIVES.

THIRD DECLENSION.

41. The following Adjectives have *e* only in the Ablative Singular, and *um* in the Genitive Plural:

Cœlebs, *unmarried.*	Pubis, *marriageable.*
Compos, *master of.*	Senex, *old.*
*Concŏlor, *of the same colour.*	Sospes, *safe.*
Hospes, *strange.*	Superstes, *surviving.*
Impos, *unable.*	*Tricorpor, *three-bodied.*
Impūbis, *beardless.*	*Tricuspis, *three-pointed.*
Juvĕnis, *young.*	*Tripes, *three-footed.*
Pauper, *poor.*	Vetus, *old.*

* The other compounds of *color, corpor, cuspis,* and *pes,* have likewise *e* and *um.*

Note.—Cælebs, compos, impos, and *superstes,* have sometimes, though rarely, *i* in the Ablative. Vetus has commonly *i,* but always *vetĕra* and *vetĕrum.*

42. The following Adjectives have *um* in the Genitive Plural:

Ales, *winged.*
Anceps, *double.*
Artĭfex, *artificial.*
Celer, *swift.*
*Compar, *equal.*
Consors, *sharing.*
Degĕner, *degenerate.*
Dives, *rich.*

Inops, *poor.*
Memor, *mindful.*
Partĭceps, *sharing.*
Præceps, *headlong.*
Supplex, *suppliant.*
Uber, *fertile.*
Vigil, *watchful.*
Volucris, *swift.*

* *Dispar,* different, *impar,* unequal, and *separ,* separate, have also *um.* *Par* has *i* only in the Ablative, and *ium* in the Genitive Plural, but its compounds have, in the poets, *e* or *i* indifferently.

Note.—Celer, memor, and *volucris,* have *i* only in the Ablative; and the last, with *vigil,* has sometimes *um* in the Genitive Plural.
Locuples, rich, has *locuplētum,* or *locupletium.*

Adjectives ending in *ns,* Comparatives, and Participles, particularly when used in an *Absolute sense,* have much more frequently *e* than *i* in the Ablative Singular.

DEFECTIVE ADJECTIVES.

43. *Quot,* how many? *tot,* so many; *alĭquot,* some; *quotquot,* and *quotcunque,* how many soever; *totĭdem,* just so many, are indeclinable, and used only in the Plural Number. *Nequam,* worthless, is also indeclinable, but used in both Numbers.

44. *Exspes,* hopeless; and *potis, pote,* able, are used only in the Nominative. They are of all Genders, and the latter is also found joined with Plural Nouns.

Tantundem, as much, has *tantĭdem,* in the Genitive, and *tantundem,* m. and n. in the Nominative and Accusative Singular.

Necesse, or *-um,* necessary; and *volŭpe,* pleasant, are used only in the Nominative and Accusative Singular.

45. *Mactus, -e,* and Pl. *-i,* a common word of encouragement, brave! gallant! is used only in the Nominative, and Vocative Singular, and Nominative Plural.

Plus, more, is Neuter only in the Singular; wants the Dative, and probably the Vocative; has *e* only in the Ablative, and *a,* seldom *ia,* in the Nominative, Accusative, and Vocative Plural Neuter.

Primōris, Gen. first, wants the Nominative and Voc. Singular, and the Nom. Acc. and Voc. Plural Neuter; likewise *seminĕcis,* half-dead, which is not used in the Neuter and has *seminĕcum,* in the Genitive Plural.

Pauci, few, and *plerīque*, the most part, are seldom used in the Singular.

46. The following classes of words want the Vocative: Partitives; as, *quidam, alius:* Relatives; as, *qualis, quantus:* Negatives; as, *nullus, neuter:* Interrogatives; as, *quotus? uter?*

Except *alīquis, quicunque, quilĭbet,* and *quisque.* See pages 20, and 21.

47. The following Adjectives of one termination in *er, es, or, os,* and *fex,* with the others contained in the subjoined list, are scarcely used in the Nominative, Accusative, and Vocative Plural Neuter.

Adjectives in ER: as, *pauper, puber, celer, degĕner, uber.*

Adjectives in FEX: as, *artĭfex, carnĭfex.*

Adjectives in OR: as, *memor, concŏlor, bicorpor.*

Adjectives in ES: as, *ales, dives, locuples, sospes, superstes, deses, reses, hebes, teres, præpes.*

Adjectives in OS: as, *compos, impos, exos.*

Also *pubis, impŭbis, supplex, comis, inops, vigil, sons, insons, intercus, redux,* and, perhaps, some others.

Cæter, or *cætĕrus,* the rest, is scarcely used in the Nom. Sing. Masculine.

Victrix, victorious, and *ultrix,* revengeful, are Feminine only in the Sing. but Fem. and Neut. in the Plural: as, *victrīces, victricia.*

REDUNDANT ADJECTIVES.

48. Some Adjectives compounded of *clīvus, frēnum, bacillum, arma, ĭugum, līmus, somnus,* and *anĭmus,* have two forms of Declension; one in *us,* of the First and Second Declension; and another in *is,* of the Third: as, *acclīvus, -a, -um,* and *acclīvis, -e,* steep; *imbecillus,* and *imbecillis,* weak; *semisomnus,* and *semisomnis,* half-sleeping; *exanĭmus* and *exanĭmis,* dead. Also *hilăris* and *hilărus,* merry.

Note.—Some of these Compounds do not admit of this variation: as, *magnanĭmus, flexanĭmus, effrēnus, levisomnus,* not *magnanĭmis, &c.* On the contrary, *pusillanĭmis, injŭgis, illīmis, insomnis, exsomnis,* are used, and not *pusillanĭmus, &c. Semianĭmis, inermis, sublīmis, acclīvis, declīvis, proclīvis,* are more common than *semianĭmus, &c. Inanĭmis* and *bijŭgis* are scarcely used.

IRREGULAR AND DEFECTIVE COMPARISON.

See page 17.

49. The following Adjectives form the Superlative in *limus:*

Facĭlis, *easy,*	facilior,	facillĭmus.
Gracĭlis, *lean.*	gracilior,	gracillĭmus.

Humĭlis, *low*,	humilior,	humillĭmus.
Imbecillis, *weak*,	imbecillior,	imbecillĭmus.
Simĭlis, *like*.	similior,	simillĭmus.

50. The following Adjectives have the Comparative regular but the Superlative irregular:

Citer, *near*,	citerior,	citĭmus.
Dexter, *right*,	dexterior,	dextĭmus.
Exter, *outward*,	exterior,	extrĕmus, *or* extĭmus.
Infĕrus, *low*,	inferior,	infĭmus, *or* imus.
Intĕrus, *inward*,	interior,	intĭmus.
Matūrus, *ripe*,	maturior,	maturrĭmus, *or* maturissĭmus.
Postĕrus, *behind*,	posterior,	postrĕmus, *or* postŭmus.
Sinister, *left*,	sinisterior,	sinistĭmus.
Supĕrus, *high*,	superior,	suprĕmus, *or* summus.
Vetus, *old*,	veterior,	veterrĭmus.

Note.—Dives, rich, has commonly *ditior* and *ditissĭmus*, for its Comparative and Superlative; contracted for *divitior* and *divitissĭmus*.

51. Compounds in *dĭcus, fĭcus, lŏquus*, and *vŏlus*, form the Comparative in *entior* and the Superlative in *entissĭmus*.

Maledĭcus, *railing*,	maledicentior,	maledicentissĭmus.
Benefĭcus, *beneficent*,	beneficentior,	beneficentissĭmus.
Mirifĭcus, *wonderful*,	mirificentior,	mirificentissĭmus.
Magnilŏquus, *boasting*,	magniloquentior,	
Benevŏlus, *benevolent*,	benevolentior,	benevolentissĭmus.

Note.—Mirifĭcus has also *mirifĭcissĭmus* in the Superlative. The Compounds of *loquus* are not found in the Superlative.

52. The following Adjectives want the Positive:

Deterior, *worse*, deterrĭmus. Propior, *nearer*, proxĭmus.
Ocior, *swifter*, ocissĭmus. Ulterior, *farther*, ultĭmus.
Prior, *former*, primus.

53. The following Adjectives want the Comparative:

Inclўtus, *renowned*, inclytissĭmus. Par, *equal*, parissĭmus.
Invictus, *invincible*, invictissĭmus. Persuāsus, *persuaded*, persuasissĭ-
Merĭtus, *deserving*, meritissĭmus. mus.
Novus, *new*, novissĭmus. Pius, *holy*, piissĭmus.
Nupĕrus, *late*, nuperrĭmus. Sacer, *sacred*, sacerrĭmus.

54 The following Adjectives want the Superlative:

Adolescens, *young*, adolescentior. Pronus, *inclined downwards*, pro-
Diuturnus, *lasting*, diuturnior. nior.
Ingens, *huge*, ingentior. Satur, *full*, saturior.
Juvĕnis, *young*, junior. Senex, *old*, senior.
Opĭmus, *rich*, opimior.

Note.—The Superlative of *juvĕnis*, and *adolescens*, is supplied by *minĭmus natu*, the youngest ; *senex* takes *maxĭmus natu*, the oldest.

55. Almost all Adjectives in *ĭlis* (penult long), *ālis* and *bĭlis*, want the Superlative : as, *civīlis, civilior*, civil ; *regālis, regalior*, regal ; *flebĭlis, -ior*, lamentable.

Note.—Some **Adjectives of these** terminations are also compared, as, *æquālis, frugālis, hospitālis, liberālis, vocālis—affabĭlis, amabĭlis, habĭlis, ignobĭlis, mirabĭlis, mobĭlis, mutabĭlis, nobĭlis, stabĭlis.*

Some Adjectives of other terminations also want the Superlative : as, *arcānus, -ior*, secret ; *declīvis, -ior*, bending downwards ; *longinquus, -ior*, far off ; *propinquus, -ior*, near ; *salutāris*, healthful, *salutarior.*

Anterior, former, and *sequior*, worse, are only found in the comparative.

Nequam, worthless (indeclinable), has *nequior, nequissĭmus.*

56. Many Adjectives, which are capable of having their signification increased, do not admit of comparison : as, *albus*, white ; *almus*, gracious : *egēnus*, needy ; *lacer*, torn ; *memor*, mindful ; *mirus*, wonderful ; *precox*, early ripe ; *sospes*, safe, &c.

Participles in *rus* and *dus*, and Adjectives in *īvus, īnus, ōrus*, and *īmus : as, fugitīvus*, fugitive ; *matutīnus*, early ; *canōrus*, shrill ; *legitīmus*, lawful.

Adjectives compounded with Nouns and Verbs : as, *versicŏlor*, of various colours ; *degĕner*, degenerating ; *pestĭfer*, poisonous, &c.

Diminutives, which, in themselves, involve a sort of comparison : as, *tenellus*, somewhat tender ; *majuscŭlus*, somewhat big.

Adjectives, in which a vowel precedes *us*, except those in *quus*, form the Comparative by putting *magis* before the Positive ; and the **Superlative** by putting *valde*, or *maxime* before it : as, *arduus*, high ; *magis* arduus ; *valde*, or *maxime* arduus.

VERBS.

General Rules for Compound Verbs.

1. Compound Verbs form the Perfect and Supine in the same manner as Simple **Verbs** : as, *amo, amāvi, amātum ; red-amo, red-amāvi, red-amātum.*

2. When the Simple Verbs double the first syllable in the Perfect, the Compounds drop the former Syllable : as, *pello, pepŭli ; re-pello, re-pŭli.* Except the Compounds of *do, sto, disco, posco*, and some of the Compounds of *curro.* See p. 122.

3. Compound Verbs which change *a* of the Present into *i*, have *e* in the Supine : as, *facio : per-ficio, per-fēci, per-fectum.* Except Verbs ending in *do, go*, with *displiceo*, and the Compounds of *habeo, salio*, and *statuo.*

4. Verbs which are defective in the Perfect likewise want the Supine. *Cico,—cĭtum, ciēre*, to stir up, is probably the only exception.

FIRST CONJUGATION.

RULE.—Verbs of the First Conjugation have *āvi* in the Perfect, and *ātum* in the Supine : as,

Amo,	amāvi,	amātum,	*to love.*
Muto,	mutāvi,	mutātum,	*to change.*

EXCEPTIONS.

The Tenses of some Verbs included in the lists of Exceptions are also found, especially in the earliest authors, conjugated according to the General Rules. The form here given is that which is in common use.

Do,[1]	dĕdi,	dătum,	*to give.*
Sto,[2]	stĕti,	stātum,	*to stand.*
Lăvo,	lāvi,	{ lavātum, lautum, lōtum, }	*to wash.*
Pŏto,[3]	potāvi,	{ potātum, *or* pōtum, }	*to drink.*
Jŭvo,[4]	jūvi,	jŭtum,	*to assist.*

Do dedit atque *dătum* format, compostaque primæ
Quæ *venum*, *circum*, *pessum*que, *satis*que creârunt.
Sto stetit et *statum* poscit : STITIT at sibi proles
Exigit atque STITUM, multò sed crebriùs ATUM.

[1] *Circumdo*, to surround ; *pessundo*, to ruin ; *satisdo*, to give surety ; and *venundo*, to sell, are conjugated like *do*. The other Compounds belong to the third Conjugation, and have *dĭdi* in the Perfect, and *dĭtum* in the Supine : as, *abdo, abdĭdi, abdĭtum, abdĕre*, to hide ; *reddo, reddĭdi, reddĭtum*, to give back. *See* p. 107, *Rule* 2.

[2] The Compounds of *sto* have *stĭti* in the Perfect, and *stātum* in the Supine : as, *consto, constĭti, constātum*, to stand together. Some of the Compounds are said to have also *stĭtum* in the Supine : as, *præsto, præstĭti, præstĭtum, or præstātum*, to stand before, to excel ; but the Future Participle is always formed from *stātum*. *Adsto*, to stand by, *prosto*, to stand, to be sold, and *resto*, to remain over and above, have no Supine. *Antesto*, to stand before ; *circumsto*, to stand round ; *intersto*, to stand between ; and *supersto*, to stand over, have *stĕti*, in the Perfect, and want the Supine. *Disto*, to be distant, and *substo*, to stand under, have neither Perfect nor Supine. *See* p. 107, *Rule* 2.

A *lavo* fit *lavi, lautum, lotum*, atque *lavatum*.
Poto *potatum* vel *potum* flecte : *juvoque*
Dat *juvi* ; at soboles *jutum* propè sola reservat.

[3] The Perfect Participle *pōtus*, is used both in a Passive sense, *that has been drunk*, and in an active sense, *having drunk*. The compounds *epōtus* and *perpōtus* are used only in the Passive sense.

[4] *Jutus*, the Perfect Participle from *jutum*, is found ; but the

Cŭbo,[5]	cubui,	cabĭtum,	to lie.
Dŏmo,	domui,	domĭtum,	to subdue.
Sŏno,[6]	sonui,	sonĭtum,[*]	to sound.
Tŏno,[7]	tonui,	tonĭtum,	to thunder.
Vĕto,[8]	vetui,	vetĭtum,	to forbid.
Crĕpo,[9]	crepui,	crepĭtum,	to make a noise.
Mĭco,[10]	micui,	—————	to glitter.
Frĭco,[11]	fricui,	frictum,	to rub.
Sĕco,	secui,	sectum,	to cut.
Nĕco,[12]	{ necāvi, or necui,	necātum,	to kill.

Future Participle is *juvatūrus*. *Adjŭvo*, to help, has *adjutūrus*, the other form being scarcely in use.

> Hæc per UI per ITUMque, *cubo, domo* cum *sono* flectes,
> Et *tono*, junge *veto*, simul et *crepo*: *discrepo* normam
> Sed potiùs sequitur: *mico* vult *micui*que, supini
> Impatiens: AVI tamen ATUM *dimico* præfert;
> Quam tenuit legem *replico* cum *supplico*, et omne
> Quod *plico* componit verbum cum nomine junctum.
> Cætera sed soboles ritu variantur utroque.
> At *frico* vult *fricui, frictum; secui, seco, sectum;*
> Interdumque *neco, necui;* quod sæpiùs AVI
> Atque ATUM poscit. *Labo, nexo,* cum *plico* nil dant.

[5] In the same manner those Compounds are conjugated which do not assume an *m*: as, *accŭbo*, to lie next to; *excŭbo*, to watch; *incŭbo*, to lie anywhere; *occŭbo*, to lie in a place; *procŭbo*, to lie before; *recŭbo*, to lie down; *secŭbo*, to lie alone. The Compounds which assume an *m* belong to the Third Conjugation, and have *ui* and *ĭtum* in the Perfect and Supine: as, *incumbo, incubui, incubĭtum*, to lie upon.

[6] The Future Participle is *sonatūrus*.

[7] *Intŏno* has *intonātus* in the Perfect Participle.

[8] *Vĕto* has sometimes *vetāvi* in the Perfect.

[9] *Discrĕpo*, to differ, and *incrĕpo*, to chide, have sometimes *āvi* and *ātum*, as well as *ui* and *ĭtum. Increpo* has seldom the latter form.

[10] *Emĭco*, to shine forth, has *emicui, emicātum;* and *dimĭco*, to fight, has *dimicāvi*, rarely *dimicui, dimicātum.*

[11] Some of the Compounds of *frĭco* have the Participles formed from the regular Supine in *ātum:* as, *confricātus, infricātus.*

[12] *Enĕco*, to kill, and *internĕco*, to destroy, have more frequently *ui* and *ectum:* the Participle of *enĕco* is usually *enectus.*

---

[*] The Supine *sonĭtum* has been retained in deference to general usage; but there does not appear to be any authority for it except the verbal substantive *sonĭtus;* while *sonatūrus*, which is used by Horace Sat. I. 4. 44. and the adjective *sonabilis*, which is found in Ovid, Art. Am. I. 106., seem to prove that the Supine ought to be *sonātum.*

Lăbo,	—— ——	—— ——	*to fall*, or *faint.*
Nexo,	——— ——	=== ——	*to bind.*
Plĭco,[13]	——— ——	—— ——	*to fold.*

SECOND CONJUGATION.

RULE.—Verbs of the Second Conjugation have *ui* in the Perfect, and *ĭtum* in the Supine: as,

| Mŏneo, | monui, | monĭtum, | *to advise.* |
| Hăbeo,[1] | habui, | habĭtum, | *to have.* |

EXCEPTIONS.

Neuter Verbs which have *ui* in the Perfect, want the Supine: as, *splendeo, splendui,* to shine; *mădeo, madui,* to be wet.

The following Neuter Verbs have *ui* and *ĭtum,* according to the general rule:

Căleo, *to be hot.*	Lĭceo, *to be valued.*
Căreo, *to want.*	Mĕreo, *to deserve.*
Coăleo, *to grow together.*	Nŏceo, *to hurt.*
Dŏleo, *to grieve.*	Păreo, *to appear.*
Jăceo, *to lie.*	Plăceo, *to please.*[8]
Lăteo,[2] *to lie hid.*	Văleo, *to be in health.*

> Quod dat UI neutrum, *timeo, sileo*que supina
> Nulla dabunt. *Valeo, placeo, caret,* et *licet* aufer,
> *Paret,* item *jaceo, caleo, noceo, doleo*que;
> Queis *coalet, latet,* atque *meret* sociabis, *olet*que.

| Dŏceo, | docui, | doctum, | *to teach.* |

---

[13] *Duplĭco,* to double, *multiplĭco,* to multiply; *replĭco,* to unfold; and *supplĭco,* to entreat humbly, have *āvi* and *ātum.* The other Compounds of *plĭco* have either *ui* and *ĭtum,* or *āvi* and *ātum:* as, *applĭco,* to apply, *applicui, applicĭtum,* or *applicāvi, applicātum.* *Explĭco,* in the sense of *explain,* has *āvi* and *ātum;* in the sense of *unfold,* it has *ui* and *ĭtum.*

[1] The Compounds of *hăbeo* change *a* into *i:* as, *adhĭbeo, adhibui, adhibĭtum,* to admit; *prohĭbeo, prohibui, prohibĭtum,* to forbid. *See* p. 107, *Rule* 3.

[2] The Compounds of *lăteo* want the Supine: as, *delĭteo, delitui,* to lurk; *perlăteo, perlatui,* to lie hid.

[8] *Plăceo,* when compounded with *per,* retains *a;* when compounded with *dis,* it changes *a* into *i:* as, *displĭceo, displicui, displicĭtum,* to displease. *Complăceo,* to please, has *complacui,* and *complacĭtus sum* in the Perfect. *See* p. 107, *Rule* 3.

> Dat *doceo doctum;* a *teneo* deducito *tentum:*
> *Mistum* vel *mixtum* dat *misceo: censeo, censum;*
> *Torreo*que et *tostum* capient; et *sorbeo, sorptum.*

Tĕneo,[4]	tenui,	tentum,	*to hold.*
Misceo,	miscui,	{ mistum, *or* mixtum,	*to mix.*
Censeo,[5]	censui,	censum,	*to think, to judge*
Torreo,	torrui,	tostum,	*to roast.*
Sorbeo,[6]	sorbui,	sorptum,	*to sup.*
Tĭmeo,	timui,	————	*to fear.*
Sĭleo,	silui,	————	*to be silent.*
Arceo,[7]	arcui,	————	*to drive away.*
Tăceo,[8]	tacui,	tacĭtum,	*to be silent.*
Prandeo,[9]	prandi,	pransum,	*to dine.*
Vĭdeo,	vīdi,	vīsum,	*to see.*
Sĕdeo,[10]	sēdi,	sessum,	*to sit.*
Strĭdeo,	strīdi,	————	*to make a noise.*
Frendeo,	frendi,	fressum,	*to gnash the teeth.*
Mordeo,[11]	momordi,	morsum,	*to bite.*
Pendeo,	pependi,	pensum,	*to hang.*
Spondeo,	spopondi,	sponsum,	*to promise.*

[4] The Compounds of *tĕneo* change *e* into *i:* as, *contĭneo, continui, contentum,* to hold together. *Attĭneo,* to hold; *pertĭneo,* to belong to, and *abstĭneo,* to abstain from, have no Supine.

[5] *Censeo* has also *census sum* in the Perfect, and *crnsĭtum* in the Supine. *Accenseo,* to reckon with, and *percenseo,* to recount, want the Supine; and *recenseo,* to review, has *recensum,* and *recensĭtum.*

[6] *Absorbeo,* to sup up, and *exsorbeo,* to sup out, have sometimes *absorpsi,* and *exsorpsi* in the Perfect. The latter, with *resorbeo,* to draw back, has no Supine.

> *Arceo* quod simplex nescit, dant nata supinum :
> Quod retinent *taceo, lateo,* sobolique recusant.

[7] The Compounds of *arceo* have *ĭtum* in the Supine: as, *exerceo, exercui, exercĭtum,* to exercise.

[8] The Compounds of *tăceo* want the Supine: as, *contĭceo, conticui,* to keep silence; *retĭceo, reticui,* to remain silent, to conceal.

> Dant DI SUM *prandet, videt* et *sedet ;* at geminabit
> S *sessum : stridet stridi* facit absque supino.

[9] The Participle *pransus* is used in the Active sense of *having dined.*

[10] *Dĕsĭdeo,* to sit idle, *dissĭdeo,* to disagree, *persĭdeo,* to continue, *præsĭdeo,* to sit before, *resĭdeo,* to sit down, to rest, and *subsĭdeo,* to subside, want the Supine.

> DI SUM præterito geminato *mordeo* donat :
> *Spondeo* lege pari, *pendet, tondet*que jugantur.

[11] The Compounds of *mordeo, pendeo, spondeo,* and *tondeo,* do not double the first syllable of the Perfect. *See* p. 107, *Rule* 2. *Impendeo,* to overhang, has no Perfect or Supine.

Tondeo,	totondi,	tonsum,	*to clip.*
Mŏveo,[12]	mŏvi,	mōtum,	*to move.*
Fŏveo,	fōvi,	fōtum,	*to cherish.*
Vŏveo,	vōvi,	vōtum,	*to vow.*
Făveo,	făvi,	fautum,	*to favour.*
Căveo,	căvi,	cautum,	*to beware of.*
Păveo,	păvi,	———	*to be afraid.*
Ferveo,[13]	ferbui,	———	*to boil.*
Connīveo,	connīvi, *or* -ixi,	———	*to wink.*
Dĕleo,	delēvi,	delētum,	*to destroy.*
Compleo,[14]	complēvi,	complētum,	*to fill.*
Fleo,	flēvi,	flētum,	*to weep.*
Neo,	nēvi,	nētum,	*to spin.*
Vieo,	viēvi,	viētum,	*to hoop a vessel.*
Cieo,[15]	(cīvi),	cītum,	*to stir up.*
Oleo,[16]	olui,	(olītum),	*to smell.*
Suādeo,	suāsi,	suāsum,	*to advise.*
Rīdeo,	rīsi,	rīsum,	*to laugh.*

Ex VEO fit VI, TUM : *faveo* sed dicito *fautum,*
Et *caveo, cautum.* Mutilantur neutra supinis :
Ferbuit at *fervet ;* VI, XI. *conniveo* donat.

[12] Verbs in *veo* undergo a contraction in the Supine. Neuter Verbs in *veo* want the Supine : as, *păveo, păvi,* to be afraid.

[13] *Fervo, fervi,* another form of this Verb belonging to the Third Conjugation, is used in a few persons, and in the Present Infinitive.

Deleo, nata *pleo, flet, net, viet,* EVIT et ETUM
Accipiunt, *cieoque citum : civi* dato quartæ.
Nunc *oleo* per UI dat ITUM : sic pignora patris
Quæ retinent sensum : EVI, ETUM vult cætera proles.
Fert *abolevit* ITUM : sed dic *adolevit adultum.*

[14] The other Compounds of the obsolete Verb *pleo* are conjugated in the same way : as, *expleo, impleo, repleo, supp!eo.*

[15] *Cīvi* is the Perfect of *cio* of the Fourth Conjugation, having *cītum* in the Supine. The Compounds, in the sense of *calling,* are generally conjugated according to this form : as, *excio, excītum.* See p. 107, *Rule* 4. *See also* p. 149, *Note.*

[16] The Compounds of *ŏleo* which retain the sense of the Simple Verb have *ui* and *ītum :* as, *obŏleo, obolui, obolītum,* to smell strongly. The Compounds which adopt a different signification have *ēvi* and *ētum :* as, *exŏleo, exolēvi, exolētum,* to fade ; *obsŏleo, obsolēvi, obsolētum,* to grow out of use ; *inŏleo, inolēvi, inolētum,* or *inolītum,* to come into use. *Abŏleo,* to abolish, has *abolēvi, abolītum ;* and *adŏleo,* to grow up, to burn, has *adolēvi, adultum.*

Dant Si SUM *suadet, ridet, manet, hæret* et *ardet,*
Et *terget, mulcet, mulget :* sed et Ş geminato
Vult *jubeo, jussi, jussum*que. *Indulgeo* SI TUM,
Torqueo dat *torsi tortum.* Viduata supinis
SI capiunt *urget,* cum *fulget, turget* et *alget.*

Măneo,	mansi,	mansum,	*to stay.*
Hæreo,	hæsi,	hæsum,	*to stick.*
Ardeo,	arsi,	arsum,	*to burn.*
Tergeo,	tersi,	tersum,	*to wipe.*
Mulceo,	mulsi,	mulsum,	*to stroke.*
Mulgeo,	mulsi,	{ mulsum, *or* mulctum,	*to milk.*
Jŭbeo,	jussi,	jussum,	*to order.*
Indulgeo,	indulsi,	indultum,	*to indulge.*
Torqueo,	torsi,	tortum,	*to twist.*
Augeo,	auxi,	auctum,	*to increase.*
Urgeo,	ursi,	——	*to press.*
Fulgeo,	fulsi,	——	*to shine.*
Turgeo,	tursi,	——	*to swell.*
Algeo,	alsi,	——	*to be cold.*
Lûgeo,	luxi,	——	*to mourn.*
Lûceo,	luxi,	——	*to shine.*
Frĭgeo,	frixi,	——	*to be cold.*

Lugeo XI solum, cum *luceo, frigeo,* poscit :
Augeo sic *auxi,* comitabitur inde sed *auctum.*

The following Verbs want both Perfect and Supine :

Aveo, *to desire.*
Denseo, *to grow thick.*
Flăveo, *to be yellow.*
Glabreo, *to be smooth.*
Hĕbeo, *to be blunt.*
Lacteo, *to grow milky.*

Līveo, *to be black and blue.*
Mœreo, *to be sorrowful.*
Renĭdeo, *to shine.*
Polleo, *to be powerful.*
Scăteo, *to flow out.*

Nil formant *lactet, livet, scateoque renidet,*
Mœret, avet, pollet, flavet, cum *denseo glabret.*

THIRD CONJUGATION.

Verbs of the Third Conjugation form the Perfect and Supine variously.

IO.

Făcio,[1]	fĕci,	factum,	*to do, to make.*

Dat *facio, feci, factum : jacio* quoque *jeci*
Accipit, et *jactum : specio lacioque* creata
Dant XI CTUM : verùm *elicui* dic *elicitum*que.

[1] *Făcio,* when compounded with a Preposition, changes *a* into *i ;* as, *afficio, affeci, affectum,* to affect. In the other Compounds the *a* is retained. A few Compounds end in *fico,* and *ficor,* and belong to the First Conjugation : as, *amplifico,* to enlarge ; *sacrifico,* to sacrifice : *gratificor,* to gratify ; and *ludificor,* to mock. *See* page 63.

Jăcio,[2]	jēci,	jactum,	*to throw.*
Aspĭcio,[3]	aspexi,	aspectum,	*to behold.*
Allĭcio,	allexi,	allectum,	*to allure.*
Fŏdio,	fōdi,	fossum,	*to dig.*
Fŭgio,	fūgi,	fugĭtum,	*to fly.*
Căpio,[4]	cēpi,	captum,	*to take.*
Răpio,	rapui,	raptum,	*to seize.*
Săpio,	sapui,	——	*to taste, to be wise.*
Cŭpio,	cupīvi,	cupĭtum,	*to desire.*
Părio,[5]	pĕpĕri,	{ partum, *or* { parĭtum,	*to bring forth.*
Quătio,[6]	(quassi),	quassum,	*to shake.*

UO.

Acuo,	acui,	acūtum,	*to sharpen.*
Arguo,	argui,	argūtum,	*to show, to prove.*
Batuo,	batui,	batūtum,	*to beat.*
Exuo,	exui,	exūtum,	*to put off clothes.*
Imbuo,	imbui,	imbūtum,	*to moisten, to wet.*
Induo,	indui,	indūtum,	*to put on clothes.*

[2] The Compounds of *jăcio* change *a* into *i:* as, *abjĭcio, abjēci, abjectum,* to throw away. *See* p. 107, *Rule* 3.

[3] The Compounds of the obsolete Verbs *spĕcio,* and *lăcio,* have *exi,* and *ectum;* except *elĭcio,* to draw out, which has *elicui,* and *elicĭtum.*

> Dic *fodio, fodi, fossum : fugio* dato *fugi,*
> Et *fugĭtum : capio, cepi, captum*que requirit :
> At *rapio, rapui, raptum :* viduumque supino
> Dat *sapio, sapui : cupio* volet *ivit* et *itum.*

[4] The Compounds of *căpio, răpio,* and *săpio,* change *a* into *i:* as, *accĭpio, accēpi, acceptum,* to receive; *abrĭpio, abripui, abreptum,* to carry off; *consĭpio, consipui,* to be in one's senses. *See* p. 107, *Rule* 3.

> Dat *pario peperi, partum,* vel ITUM : *quatio*que
> *Quassum,* vix *quassi ; cussi* at *cussum* bene proles.

[5] The Compounds of *părio* have *perui* and *pertum,* and belong to the Fourth Conjugation : as, *apĕrio, aperui, apertum, aperīre,* to open. So *opĕrio,* to shut, to cover. But *compĕrio* (which also has a Deponent form in the Present Indicative and Infinitive, *comperior, comperīri,*) to know a thing for certain, has *compĕri, compertum ;* and *reperio,* to find, has *repĕri, repertum.*

[6] The Compounds of *quatio* take the form *cătio,* and have *cussi* and *cussum :* as, *concŭtio,* to shake violently, *concussi, concussum.*

> Queis UO dat finem, per UI labuntur, et UTUM.
> At *fluo* vult *fluxi, fluxum : struxi, struo, structum.*
> Vultque *ruo, ruitum :* dat UTUM proles tibi solum
> Nulla supina dabunt *metuo, pluo, congruo,* sicut
> *Annuo,* cum sociis ; quibus *ingruo, respuo* junges.

Mĭnuo,	minui,	minūtum,	*to lessen.*
Spuo,[7]	spui,	spūtum,	*to spit.*
Stătuo,[8]	statui,	statūtum,	*to set, to place.*
Sternuo,	sternui,	sternūtum,	*to sneeze.*
Suo,	sui,	sūtum,	*to sew, to stitch.*
Trĭbuo,	tribui,	tribūtum,	*to give, to divide.*
Fluo,	fluxi,	fluxum,	*to flow.*
Struo,	struxi,	structum,	*to build.*
Luo,[9]	lui,	luĭtum,	*to pay, to wash.*
Ruo,[10]	rui,	ruĭtum,	*to rush, to fall.*
Mĕtuo,	metui,	————	*to fear.*
Pluo,	plui,	————	*to rain.*
Congruo,	congrui,	————	*to agree.*
Ingruo,	ingrui,	————	*to assail.*
Annuo,[11]	annui,	————	*to assent.*

BO.

Bĭbo,	bĭbi,	bibĭtum,	*to drink.*
Scăbo,	scăbi,	————	*to scratch.*
Lambo,	lambi,	————	*to lick.*
Scrībo,	scripsi,	scriptum,	· *to write.* [*ried.*
Nūbo,[12]	nupsi,	nuptum,	*to veil, to be mar-*
Glūbo,	————	————	*to strip, to flay.*

CO.

Dīco,	dixi,	dictum,	*to say.*
Dūco,	duxi,	ductum,	*to lead,*
Vinco,	vīci,	victum,	*to overcome.*

[7] *Respuo*, to spit out, to reject, has no Supine.

[8] The compounds of *statuo* change *a* into *i* : as, *constituo, constitui, constitūtum*, to place. *See* p. 107, *Rule* 3.

[9] The Compounds of *luo* have *ūtum* in the Supine : as, *abluo, ablui, ablūtum*, to wash away, to purify.

[10] The Compounds of *ruo* have *ŭtum* in the Supine : as, *diruo, dirui, dirŭtum*, to overthrow. *Corruo*, to fall together, and *irruo*, to rush in furiously, have no Supine.

[11] The other Compounds of the obsolete *nuo*, as *abnuo*, to refuse ; *innuo*, to nod with the head : and *renuo*, to deny, likewise want the Supine. *Abnuitūrus*, the Fut. Participle from *abnuo*, is found.

BI BO BITUMque facit. *Scabo, lambo* carento supinis :
Orta *cubo*, ternum quibus M dedit indita flexum,
Dant *cubui, cubitum*. Vult *scribo, nuboque* PSI, PTUM.

[12] *Nupta sum*, another form of the Perfect, is sometimes used instead of *nupsi*.

Dant XI, CTUM *dico, duco* simul : Nque remotâ
Vult *vinco, vici, victum ;* geminato *peperci*
A *parco, parsum* adjiciens ; quod SI dat ITUMque
Rariùs. *Ico* sibi formavit et *icit* et *ictum*.

Parco,[13]	{ peperci, *or* { parsi,	{ parsum, *or* { parcĭtum,	to *spare*.
Ico,	ĭci,	ictum,	to *strike*.

SCO.

Cresco,	crēvi,	crētum,	to *grow*.
Nosco,[14]	nōvi,	nōtum,	to *know*.
Quiesco,	quiēvi,	quiētum,	to *rest*.
Scisco,	scīvi,	scītum,	to *ordain*.
Suesco,	suēvi,	suētum,	to *be accustomed*.
Pasco[15]	pāvi,	pastum,	to *feed*.
Disco,[16]	didĭci,	——	to *learn*.
Posco,[16]	poposci,	——	to *demand*.
Glisco,[17]	——	——	to *glitter, to grow*.

DO.

Accendo,	accendi,	accensum,	to *kindle*.
Cūdo,	cūdi,	cūsum,	to *forge*.
Defendo,'	defendi,	defensum,	to *defend*.
Edo,[18]	ēdi,	ēsum,	to *eat*.

[13] The form *parsi* and *parcĭtum* is seldom used.

Vertitur in VI, TUM, SCO. *Pasco* dat tibi *pastum*:
Agnosco sed ITUM capiet *cognoscoque*. *Disco*
Vult *didĭci* primam geminans: sic *posco, poposci*;
Dispescit, compescit UI dant: cuncta supinis
Orba. Nihil *glisco*, nihil Inceptiva creârunt.

[14] The Fut. Part. is *noscitūrus* from *noscĭtum*, the old form of the Supine. *Agnosco*, to own, has *agnŏvi, agnĭtum*; and *cognosco*, to know, has *cognōvi, cognĭtum*.

[15] *Compesco*, to feed together, to restrain; and *dispesco*, to separate, have *compescui*, and *dispescui*, without the Supine.

[16] *See* p. 107, *Rule* 2.

[17] *Fatisco*, to be weary, likewise wants both Perfect and Supine; and also all Inceptive Verbs, unless when they adopt the Tenses of their Primitives: as, *ardesco*, to grow hot, *arsi, arsum*. See page 51.

DO finita petunt DI, SUM. Sed *divido, rado*,
Dant SI, SUM, *claudo, plaudo*, cum *ludere, trudo*,
Et *lædo, rodo*, compostaque *vado* (quod ipsum
Præteritum vix dat), geminans ac S quòque *cedo*.
At *pando, pandi, passum pansum*que: *comedi*
Estum sæpe capit; N perdens *fundo*que *fudi*,
Et *fusum*: sic *scindo, scidi*, sic *findo fidi*que;
At *scissum, fissum*, duplicans S, redde supinis.

[18] All the Compounds of *ĕdo* are conjugated in the same manner, except *comĕdo*, to eat up, which has *comēsum*, or *comestum*, in the Supine. *See* page 63.

Mando,	mandi,	mansum,	*to chew.*
Prehendo,	prehendi,	prehensum,	*to take hold of.*
Scando,	scandi,	scansum,	*to climb.*
Divǐdo,	divīsi,	divīsum,	*to divide.*
Rādo,	rāsi,	rāsum,	*to shave.*
Claudo,[19]	clausi,	clausum,	*to close.*
Plaudo,[20]	plausi,	plausum,	*to applaud.*
Lūdo,	lūsi,	lūsum,,	*to play.*
Trūdo,	trūsi,	trūsum,	*to thrust.*
Lædo,[21]	læsi,	læsum,	*to hurt.*
Rōdo,	rōsi,	rōsum,	*to gnaw.*
Vādo,[22]	——	——	*to go.*
Cĕdo,	cessi,	cessum,	*to yield.*
Pando,	pandi,	{ passum, *or* pansum,	*to open.*
Fundo,	fūdi,	fūsum,	*to pour forth.*
Scindo,	scǐdi,	scissum,	*to cut.*
Findo,	fǐdi,	fissum,	*to cleave.*
Tundo,[23]	tutŭdi,	{ tunsum, *or* tūsum,	*to beat.*
Cădo,[24]	cecǐdi,	cāsum,	*to fall.*

[19] The Compounds of *claudo* change *au* into *u:* as, *conclŭdo, conclūsi, conclūsum*, to conclude. *Circumclaudo* is found in Cæsar.

[20] The Compounds of *plaudo*, except *ap-* and *circum-plaudo*, change *au* into *o:* as, *explōdo, explōsi, explōsum*, to reject.

[21] The Compounds of *lædo* change *æ* into *i:* as, *allīdo, allīsi, allīsum*, to dash against.

[22] The Compounds of *vādo* have the Perfect and Supine: as, *evādo, evāsi, evāsum*, to escape.

> *Tundo* facit *tutudi tunsum*, compostaque *tusum*.
> Et *cado* vult *cecidi casum:* sed nata supinum
> (*Incido* si demas, *recido,* simul *occido*) spernunt.
> *Cædo cecidit* habet *cæsum:* sic *tendo, tetendi,*
> *Tensum* vel *tentum;* mage *tentum* sed dato proli:
> Vultque *pepedit,* ITUM, *pedo: pensum*que *pependi,*
> *Pendo* capit: DIDIT atque DITUM cum *vendere, credo,*
> Et prope cuncta sibi quæ DO cum præposituris
> Gignit: at *abscondo* potius DIT quàm DIDIT effert.
> Præterito DI *strido, rudo* dant, absque supinis,
> *Sidoque,* sed soboli *sedeo* dat mutuò *sedi.*

[23] The Compounds of *tundo* have *tŭdi,* and *tūsum:* as, *contundo,* to bruise, *contŭdi, contūsum. See Rule 2, page* 107. Some of the Compounds have also a Perfect Participle formed from *tunsum:* as, *obtunsus,* and *retunsus,* from *obtundo,* and *retundo.*

[24] The Compounds of *cădo* want the Supine: as, *accǐdo, accǐdi,* to happen; except *incǐdo, incǐdi, incāsum,* to fall in; *occǐdo, occǐdi, occāsum,* to fall down; and *recǐdo, recǐdi, recāsum,* to fall back.

Cædo,[25]	cecīdi,	cæsum,	to cut, to kill.
Tendo,[26]	tetendi,	tensum, or tentum,	to stretch.
Pendo,	pependi,	pensum,	to hang.
Crēdo,[27]	credīdi,	credītum,	to believe.
Vendo,	vendīdi,	vendītum,	to sell.
Abscondo,	abscondi,	absconditum,	to hide.
Strīdo,	strīdi,	——	to creak.
Rudo,	rūdi,	——	to bray as an ass.
Sīdo,[28]	sīdi,	——	to sink down.

GO.

Cingo,	cinxi,	cinctum,	to surround.
Flīgo,[29]	flixi,	flictum,	to dash.
Jungo,	junxi,	junctum,	to join.
Lingo,	linxi,	linctum,	to lick.
Mungo,	munxi,	munctum,	to wipe the nose.
Plango,	planxi,	planctum,	to beat.
Rĕgo,[30]	rexi,	réctum,	to rule.

[25] The Compounds of *cædo* change *æ* into *i* : as, *accīdo, accīdi, accīsum*, to cut about ; *decīdo, decīdi, decīsum*, to cut off. *Percīdo*, to cut in pieces, has *percīdi*, and *percecīdi*, in the Perfect.

[26] The Compounds of *tendo* have generally *tentum* in the Supine, except *extendo*, to stretch out, and *ostendo*, to show, which have also *tensum* ; the latter, almost always.

[27] The other Compounds of *do* which belong to the Third Conjugation have also *dīdi* and *dītum* : as, *condo, condīdi, condītum*, to build. *Abscondo* has sometimes *abscondīdi. See page* 108, *note* 1.

[28] The Compounds of *sīdo* adopt the Perfect and Supine of *sedeo* ; as, *consīdo, consēdi, consessum*, to sit down.

> GO vel GUO, XI, CTUMque facit. Cum *surgere, pergo*
> Accipit at REXI, RECTUM.   Sed et ista supinis
> N tria deperdunt, *fingo*, cum *pingere, stringo*.
> Dat *frango, fregi, fractum* ; sicut *egit* et *actum*
> Vult *ago* ; sed soboles, *satago*, cum *prodigo, dego*,
> Nulla supina dabunt ; caret *ambigo* præteritoque.
> *Tango* facit *tetigi, tactum* : *legi, lego, lectum* :
> *Negligo* sed poscunt, *intelligo, diligo*, XI, CTUM.
> *Pungo* capit *pupugi, punctum*, sed pignora *punxi* :
> Præteritum sed utrumque petit sibi ritè *repungo*.
> Vult *pango, panxi, pactum* ; *pepigi*que vetustum
> Dat *pago*, quod *pegi* genitis de *pango* reservat.

[29] The Compounds of *fligo* are conjugated in the same way, except *profligo*, to dash down, which is a regular Verb of the First Conjugation.

[30] The Compounds of *rego* change *e* into *i* : as, *dirigo, direxi, directum*, to direct ; *corrigo, correxi, correctum*, to correct.

Stinguo,[31]	stinxi,	stinctum,	*to dash out.*
Sûgo,	suxi,	suctum,	*to suck.*
Tĕgo,	texi,	tectum,	*to cover.*
Tinguo,	tinxi,	tinctum,	*to dip.*
Unguo,	unxi,	unctum,	*to anoint.*
Surgo,	surrexi,	surrectum,	*to rise.*
Pergo,	perrexi,	perrectum,	*to go forward.*
Stringo,	strinxi,	strictum,	*to bind.*
Fingo,	finxi,	fictum,	*to feign.*
Pingo,	pinxi,	pictum,	*to paint.*
Frango,[32]	frēgi,	fractum,	*to break.*
Ago,[33]	ēgi,	actum,	*to do, to drive.*
Tango,	tetĭgi,	tactum,	*to touch.*
Lĕgo,[34]	lēgi,	lectum,	*to gather, to read.*
Pungo,[35]	pupŭgi,	punctum,	*to prick.*
Pango,[36]	panxi,	pactum,	*to drive in.*
Spargo,[37]	sparsi,	sparsum,	*to spread.*
Mergo,	mersi,	mersum,	*to dip, to plunge.*
Tergo,	tersi,	tersum,	*to wipe.*
Fīgo,	fixi,	fixum,	*to fix.*

[31] *Stinguo, tinguo,* and *unguo,* are also written *stingo, tingo, ungo.*

[32] The Compounds of *frango* and *tango* change *a* into *i* : as, *confringo, confrēgi, confractum,* to break to pieces ; *attingo, attĭgi, attactum,* to touch gently.

[33] *Circumăgo,* to drive round ; *perăgo,* to finish ; and *coăgo* (contracted *cōgo*), to collect, retain the *a* : the other Compounds change *a* into *i* : as, *abĭgo, abēgi, ăbactum,* to drive away. *Dēgo* (for *deăgo*), to live, to dwell : *prodĭgo,* to lavish or squander ; and *satăgo,* to be busy, want the Supine. *Ambĭgo,* to doubt, has neither Perfect nor Supine.

[34] *Lĕgo,* when compounded with *ad, per, prœ, re,* and *sub,* retains the *e* : as, *allĕgo,* to choose. The other Compounds change *e* into *i* : as, *collĭgo,* to collect. *Dilĭgo,* to love ; *intellĭgo,* to understand, and *neglĭgo,* to neglect, have *exi,* and *ectum. Neglĭgo* has sometimes *neglēgi* in the Perfect.

[35] The Compounds of *pungo* have *punxi* in the Perfect : as, *compungo,* to sting, *compunxi, compunctum.*

[36] *Pango,* in the sense of *to bargain,* has *pepĭgi ;* the Present is rarely used in this meaning ; but instead of it *paciscor* is commonly employed. The Compounds which change *a* into *i* have *pēgi,* and *pactum :* as, *compingo,* to fasten together, *compēgi, compactum. Oppango,* to fasten to, has also *pēgi* and *pactum.* Of the other Compounds which retain *a,* the Perfect and Supine are not found.

Dant SI, SUM *spargo, mergo, tergo*que. Requirit
At XI, XUM *figo* cum *frigere :* nec male *frictum*
Invenies quandoque datum. Nil *vergo* capessit.
XI *clango, ningo* dat et *ango,* supinaque nulla.

[37] The Compounds of *spargo* change *a* into *e* : as, *aspergo, aspersi, aspersum,* to besprinkle.

Frĭgo,	frixi,	frixum, *or* frictum,	*to fry.*
Vergo,	——	——	*to lie toward.*
Clango,	clanxi,	——	*to sound a trum-*
Ningo,	ninxi,	——	*to snow.* [*pet.*
Ango,	anxi,	——	*to vex.*

HO.

Trăho,	traxi,	tractum,	*to draw.*
Věho,	vexi,	vectum,	*to carry.*
Mejo,[38]	minxi,	mictum,	*to make water.*

LO.

Cŏlo,[39]	colui,	cultum,	*to till, to inhabit.*
Consŭlo.	consului,	consultum,	*to consult.*
Alo,	alui,	alĭtum, *or* altum,	*to nourish.*
Mŏlo,	molui,	molĭtum,	*to grind.*
Antecello,[40]	antecellui,	——	*to excel.*
Pello,	pepŭli,	pulsum,	*to drive away.*
Fallo,[41]	fefelli,	falsum,	*to deceive.*
Vello,[42]	velli, *or* vulsi,	vulsum,	*to pull.*
Sallo,	salli,	salsum,	*to salt.* [*strument.*
Psallo,	psalli,	——	*to play on an in-*

Postulat HO, XI, CTUM. *Minxi, mictum* cape *mejo.*

[38] *Mingo* is also used as the Present of *minxi.*

LO, LUIT efformat: *colo, consulit, occulit,* ULTUM.
Ast *alo* dic *altum,* vel ITUM: *molitum molo* donat.
Nulla supina manent genitis de *cello:* sed unum
Excipe *percello,* quod *perculit* optat et ULSUM.
Pello facit *pepuli, pulsum; falloque fefelli,*
Et *falsum. Velli* vel *vulsi, vello* reposcit,
Inde petens *vulsum: sallo, salli,* quòque *salsum.*
At *psallo, psalli,* tantùm: pariterque supinis
Deficiunt *malo, volo, nolo,* junge *refello.*
More sed insolito dat *tollo sustulit,* atque
Sublatum; attollo proles sed nil sibi quærit.

[39] *Cŏlo,* when compounded with *ob,* changes *o* into *u:* as, *occŭlo,* to hide. *Accŏlo,* to dwell near, and *circumcŏlo,* to dwell round, have no Supine.

[40] The other Compounds of the obsolete *cello* likewise want the Supine; except *percello, percŭli, perculsum,* to strike, to astonish. *Recello* likewise wants the Perfect.

[41] *Refello, refelli,* to confute, wants the Supine.

[42] *Vello,* when compounded with *de, di,* or *per,* has usually *velli* in the Perfect. The other Compounds take either form indifferently.

| Tollo,[43] | sustŭli, | sublātum, | *to lift up.* |

MO.

Frĕmo,	fremui,	fremĭtum,	*to rage, to roar.*
Gĕmo,	gemui,	gemĭtum,	*to groan.*
Vŏmo,	vomui,	vomĭtum,	*to vomit.*
Trĕmo.	tremui,	——	*to tremble.*
Dēmo,[44]	dempsi,	demptum,	*to take away.*
Prŏmo,	prompsi,	promptum,	*to bring out.*
Sūmo,	sumpsi,	sumptum,	*to take.*
Cŏmo,	compsi,	comptum,	*to deck, to dress.*
Emo,[44]	ēmi,	emptum,	*to buy.*
Prĕmo,[45]	pressi,	pressum,	*to press.*

NO.

Pŏno,	pŏsui,	posĭtum,	*to place.*
Gigno,	genui,	genĭtum,	*to beget.*
Căno,[46]	cecĭni,	cantum,	*to sing.*
Temno,[47]	——	——	*to despise.*
Sperno.	sprēvi,	sprētum,	*to disdain.*
Sterno,[48]	strāvi,	strātum,	*to lay flat.*
Sĭno,	sīvi, *or* sii,	sĭtum,	*to permit.*

[43] *Attollo* and *extollo*, to raise up, have no Perfect or Supine of their own; but those of *affĕro* and *effĕro*, which agree with them in meaning, are sometimes assigned to them.

MO per UI dat ITUM. *Tremo* flectitur absque supino.
Dant PSI, PTUM, *demo, promo,* cum *sumere, como;*
Emi, emptum sed *emo* capiet, *pressi, premo, pressum.*

[44] *Dēmo, prŏmo,* and *sūmo,* are Compounds of *emo.* The other Compounds change *e* into *i,* and are conjugated like the Simple Verb: as, *adĭmo, adēmi, ademptum,* to take away.

[45] The Compounds of *prĕmo* change *e* into *i;* as, *comprĭmo, compressi, compressum,* to press together.

Pono facit *posui, positum : genui, genitum*que
Gigno creat : *cecini, cantum, cano* poscit ; habeto
Sed CINUI, CENTUM proles. Prope nil sibi servans,
Temno dedit nato PSI, PTUM. Vult *spernoque sprevi,*
Et *spretum ;* sterno, stravi, stratum : *sino, sivi,*
Atque *situm ; livi, levive, litum, lino ; cerno*
Dat *crevi, cretum*que, magis quæ nata frequentant.

[46] The Compounds of *căno* have *cinui,* and *centum :* as, *concino, concinui, concentum,* to sing in concert. Of *accĭno,* to sing to, and *intercĭno,* to sing between, or during, no Perfect or Supine is found.

[47] *Contemno,* to despise, has *contempsi, contemptum.*

[48] *Consterno* and *externo,* when they signify *to alarm,* are regular Verbs of the First Conjugation. The other Compounds are conjugated like *sterno :* as, *insterno, instrāvi, instrātum,* to spread upon.

Lĭno,	lĭvi, *or* lēvi,	lĭtum,	*to anoint.*
Cerno,⁴⁹	crēvi,	crētum,	*to see, to decree.*

PO, QUO.

Carpo,⁵⁰	carpsi,	carptum,	*to pluck.*
Clĕpo,	clepsi,	cleptum,	*to steal.*
Rēpo,	repsi,	reptum,	*to creep.*
Scalpo,	scalpsi,	scalptum,	*to engrave.*
Sculpo,	sculpsi,	sculptum,	*to carve.*
Serpo,	serpsi,	serptum,	*to creep.*
Strĕpo,	strepui,	strepĭtum,	*to make a noise.*
Rumpo,	rūpi,	ruptum,	*to break.*
Coquo,	coxi,	coctum,	*to boil.*
Linquo,⁵¹	lĭqui,	———	*to leave.*

RO.

Quæro,⁵²	quæsīvi,	quæsītum,	*to seek.*
Tĕro,	trĭvi,	trĭtum,	*to wear.*
Verro,	verri,	versum,	*to sweep.*
Uro,	ussi,	ustum,	*to burn.*
Curro,⁵³	cucurri,	cursum,	*to run.*
Gĕro,	gessi,	gestum,	*to carry.*
Fŭro,⁵⁴	———	———	*to be mad.*

---

⁴⁹ The Perfect *crēvi* is used in the sense of *to declare one's self heir,* or *enter on an inheritance.* In the sense of *seeing,* cerno has properly neither Perfect nor Supine.

    PO, PSI, PTUMque facit. *Strepo* vult *strepui, strepitum*que : At *rumpo, rupi, ruptum.* *Coquo* flectito XI, CTUM. *Linquo* tenet *liqui* tantum, compostaque *lictum.*

⁵⁰ The Compounds of *carpo* change *a* into *e:* as, *discerpo, discerpsi, discerptum,* to tear in pieces.
  ⁵¹ The Compounds of *linquo* have *lictum* in the Supine: as, *relinquo, reliqui, relictum,* to forsake; so *delinquo,* to fail.

>   *Quæro, quæsivi, quæsitum* dat: *tero, trivi,*
>   Et *tritum: verro, verri, versum*que requirit :
>   *Uro, ussi* ac *ustum: cursum* vult *curro, cucurri :*
>   Flecte *gero, gessi, gestum: latum*que *tulique*
>   Dat *fero:* præteritum nullum *furo, suffero* nòrunt :
>   A *sero* fit *sevique satum:* sic EVIT, ITUMque
>   Dant composta quibus plantandi significatus
>   Inditur; at SERUI, SERTUM vult cætera proles.

⁵² The Compounds of *quæro* change *æ* into *i:* as, *acquīro, acquisīvi, acquisītum,* to acquire.
  ⁵³ *Curro,* when compounded with *circum, re, sub,* and *trans,* seldom takes the reduplication. The other Compounds sometimes take the reduplication, and sometimes not. *See* p. 107, *Rule* 2.
  ⁵⁴ See page 66.

Sĕro,[55]	sĕvi,	sătum,	*to sow.*

SO.

Arcesso,	arcessīvi,	arcessītum,	*to call*, or *send for.*
Capesso,	capessīvi,	capessītum,	*to take.*
Facesso,	facessīvi,	facessītum,	*to do, to go away.*
Lacesso,	lacessīvi,	lacessītum,	*to provoke.*
Vīso,	vīsi,	————	*to go to visit.*
Incesso,	incessi,	————	*to attack.*
Depso,	depsui,	depstum,	*to knead.*
Pinso,	pinsui, or pinsi,	pinsum, pistum, *or* pinsĭtum,	*to bake.*

TO.

Flecto,	flexi,	flexum,	*to bend.*
Plecto,	plexi & plexui,	plexum,	*to plait.*
Necto,	nexi & nexui,	nexum,	*to tie*, or *knit.*
Pecto,	pexi & pexui,	pexum,	*to dress*, or *comb.*
Mĕto,	messui,	messum,	*to reap.*
Pĕto,	petīvi,	petītum,	*to seek.*
Mitto,	mīsi,	missum,	*to send.*
Verto,[56]	verti,	versum,	*to turn.*
Sterto,	stertui,	————	*to snore.*
Sisto,[57]	stĭti,	stătum,	*to stop.*

[55] The Compounds of *sĕro* which retain the sense of *planting* and *sowing*, have *sĕvi* and *sĭtum:* as, *consĕro, consĕvi, consĭtum*, to plant together. Those which adopt a different signification have *serui* and *sertum:* as, *assĕro, asserui, assertum*, to claim. The latter class of Compounds properly belongs to the old verb *sĕro*, to knit, to plait.

> SO, SIVI, SITUMque capit : sed trunca supinis
> SI *viso, incesso* retinent : at *depso* reposcit
> *Depsuit* et *depstum. Pinso* dat *pinsuit* atque
> *Pinsit*, et hinc *pinsum, pistum* formabit ITUMque.

> *Flecto* XI, XUM vult : sic *plecto, nectoque, pecto:*
> Quæ XUIT et pariter formant. *Meto* sed geminans S
> *Messuit* et *messum:* peto suscipit IVIT, et ITUM :
> At *mitto, misi, missum* dat : vertoque *verti,*
> Et *versum:* sterto vult *stertuit*, absque supino.
> *Sisto, stitique, statum* dat agens : neutrale sequetur
> *Sto* verbum, unde STITI, atque STITUM composta tulerunt.

[56] The Compounds of *verto* are conjugated in the same manner except *revertor*, to return, which is often used as a Deponent Verb and *divertor*, to turn aside, and *prævertor*, to outrun, which are likewise Deponent, but want the Perfect Participle.

[57] *Sisto*, to stand still (a neuter verb), has neither Perfect nor Supine. The Compounds have *stĭti*, and *stĭtum:* as, *assisto, astĭti, astĭtum*, to stand by. But these are seldom found in the Supine.

VO, XO.

Vīvo,	vixi,	victum,	*to live.*
Solvo,	solvi,	solūtum,	*to loose.*
Volvo	volvi,	volūtum,	*to roll.*
Texo,	texui,	textum,	*to weave.*

Dat *vivo* XI, CTUM : *solvo* VI format et UTUM,
Ut *volvo.* *Texo* vult *texuit,* indeque *textum.*

FOURTH CONJUGATION.

RULE.—Verbs of the Fourth Conjugation have ĭvĭ in the Perfect,
and ĭtum in the Supine: as,

Audio,	audīvi,	audītum,	*to hear.*
Mūnio,	munīvi,	munītum,	*to fortify.*

EXCEPTIONS.

Singultio,	singultīvi,	singultum,	*to sob.*
Sepĕlio,	sepelīvi,	sepultum,	*to bury.*
Vĕnio,	vĕni,	ventum,	*to come.*
Vĕneo,[1]	venii,	——	*to be sold.*
Sălio,[2]	salui, *or* salii,	saltum,	*to leap.*
Amĭcio,	{ amicui, *or* amixi,	amictum,	*to clothe.*
Vincio,	vinxi,	vinctum,	*to tie.*
Sancio,	{ sanxi, *or* sancīvi,	{ sanctum, *or* sancītum,	*to ratify.*
Cambio,	campsi,	campsum,	*to change money.*

Singultit vult singultum, sepelitque sepultum :
Dat venio, veni, ventum : sed veneo solum
Veniit efficiet : salio, salui, saliique,
Extulit, et saltum : capiunt at pignora sultum.

[1] For the Conjugation of *veneo,* see page 59.
[2] The Compounds of *sălio* have generally *silui,* sometimes *silii,* or
silīvi, in the Perfect, and *sultum* in the Supine: as, *transilio, transi-
lui, transilii,* or *transilīvi, transultum,* to leap over. *Absultum, cir-
cumsultum,* and *prosultum,* are scarcely used. *See* p. 107, *Rule* 3.

Vult *amicit* vel UI, vel XI, CTUM : *vincio* XI, CTUM.
Sancio jungatur, quod et IVI format, et ITUM.

Cambio vult PSI, PSUM : sed sepsi, sepio, septum :
Haurio SI, STUM dat ; SUM rariùs effer. Habebit
Sentio sed sensi, sensum : sic raucio, rausi,
Et rausum : sarcit, farcit, cum fulcio, SI, TUM.
At PERUI, PERTUMque sibi composta jugârunt
Ex pario ternæ : RI comperit et reperit vult.

Sĕpio,	sepsi,	septum,	*to enclose.*
Haurio,	hausi,	{ haustum, *or* haustum,	*to draw out.*
Sentio,	sensi,	sensum,	*to feel.*
Raucio,	rausi,	rausum,	*to be hoarse.*
Sarcio,	sarsi,	sartum,	*to mend,* or *repair.*
Farcio,[a]	farsi,	fartum,	*to cram.*
Fulcio,	fulsi,	fultum,	*to prop.*
Fĕrio,	———	———	*to strike.*

The following Verbs have the Perfect formed regularly, but want the Supine :

Cæcūtio, *to be dim-sighted.*
Dementio, *to be mad.*
Ferōcio, *to be fierce.*

Gestio, *to show one's joy by the gestures of the body.*
Glōcio, *to cluck as a hen.*
Ineptio, *to play the fool.*

Cæcutit, gestit, glocit, et *dementit, ineptit,*
Nulla supina dabunt; cum *prosilit* atque *ferocit.*

For Desiderative Verbs which belong to this Conjugation, *See* page 51.
For the Compounds of *pario,* which belong to this Conjugation, *See* page 114, *Note* 5.

DEPONENT AND COMMON VERBS.

RULE.—Deponent and Common Verbs form the Perfect Participle in the same manner as if the Active Voice existed. *See* pages 51 and 52.

Note.—All Deponent Verbs seem to have been originally Passives. Hence there are many Verbs which, though found in the Active Voice, are used deponently in the Passive; others, under the name of Common Verbs, have become obsolete in the Active, and, in the Passive, are employed either as Deponents or Passives; and many which have laid aside their Passive signification in the other Tenses, still retain it in the Perfect Participle.

Exceptions in the Second Conjugation.

Reor,	rătus,	rēri,	*to think.*
Misereor,[1]	misertus,	miserēri,	*to pity.*
Făteor,[2]	fassus,	fatēri,	*to confess.*
Medeor,	———	medēri,	*to heal.*

---

[a] The Compounds of *farcio* change *a* into *e :* as, *refercio, refersi, refertum,* to fill up.

Nam *ratus* a *reor* est ; *misereri* vultque *misertus ;*
Et *fateor, fassus :* FESSUS sed reddito proli.

[1] *Misereor* has also *miserītus* in the Perfect Participle.
[2] The Compounds of *fāteor* change *a* into *i,* and have *fessus ;* as,

Exceptions in the Third Conjugation.

Lābor,	lapsus,	labi,	*to slide.*
Ulciscor,	ultus,	ulcisci,	*to revenge.*
Utor,	ūsus,	ūti,	*to use.*
Lŏquor,[3]	loquūtus,	loqui,	*to speak.*
Sĕquor,	sequūtus,	sequi,	*to follow.*
Quĕror,	questus,	queri,	*to complain.*
Nītor,[4]	nīsus, *or* nixus,	niti,	*to strive.*
Paciscor,	pactus,	pacisci,	*to bargain.*
Grădior,	gressus,	gradi,	*to go.*
Proficiscor,	profectus,	proficisci,	*to go a journey.*
Nanciscor,	nactus,	nancisci,	*to obtain.*
Pătior,	passus,	pati,	*to suffer.*
Apiscor,[5]	aptus,	apisci,	*to get.*
Comminiscor,	commentus,	comminisci,	*to devise.*
Fruor,	fruĭtus, *or* fructus,	frui,	*to enjoy.*
Obliviscor,	oblītus,	oblivisci,	*to forget.*
Expergiscor,	experrectus,	expergisci,	*to awake.*
Mŏrior,[6]	mortuus,	mori,	*to die.*
Nascor,[7]	nātus,	nasci,	*to be born.*
Orior,[8]	ortus,	orīri,	*to rise.*

---

confĭteor, confessus, to confess. *Diffĭteor,* to deny, wants the Perf. Participle.

Insuper a *labor lapsus* sibi tertia format :
Ultus ab *ulciscor* manat : venit *usus* ab *utor ;*
Vult UTUS *loquor* atque *sequor : queror* accipe *questus,*
Nisus vel *nixus nitor, pactus*que *paciscor ;*
Dat *gradior gressus ; proficiscor* funde *profectus ;*
*Nanciscor nactus, patior passus*que requirit ;
Aptus apiscor habet ; *commentus comqueminiscor*
Accipit : at *fructus* pariter *fruĭtus*que jugari
Vult *fruor : oblitus* sed et *obliviscor* adoptat ;
Ast *expergiscor* cupit *experrectus* habere.
Mortuus aque *mori* est, *natus nasci, ortus oriri :*
Queis tribus extremis per ITURUS flecte Futurum.

[3] *Lŏquor* and *sĕquor* have likewise *locūtus* and *secūtus* in the Perfect Participle.

[4] *Nītor,* when compounded with *con, in, ob, re, sub,* has *nixus* oftener than *nīsus. Adnītor,* to lean to, has either indifferently. *Enītor,* in the sense of *to bring forth,* generally takes *enixa* in the Participle.

[5] *Adipiscor* and *indipiscor,* to obtain, have *adeptus* and *indeptus.*

[6] *Morior* seems to have originally belonged to the Fourth Conjugation. The Infinitive *morīri* occurs in Plautus and Ovid; and *morīmur,* with the penult long, is also found. The Imperative is *morĕre.* This verb, with *nascor* and *orior,* has *itūrus* in the Fut. Part. : as, *moritūrus, nascitūrus, oritūrus.*

[7] *Nascor* is Passive in signification, but has no Active Voice.

[8] *Orior* has *orīre,* and always *orirētur* in the Imperfect Subjunc-

The following Verbs want the Perfect Participle :

Defetiscor, -i, *to be weary.*
Irascor, -i, *to be angry.*
Liquor, -i, *to melt.*

Reminiscor, -i, *to remember.*
Ringor, -i, *to grin like a dog.*
Vescor, -i, *to feed.*

Nil formant *vescor, liquor, medeor, reminiscor,*
Irascor, ringor, prævertor, diffiteorque :
Queis demum adjungas *divertor,* deque*fetiscor.*

Exceptions in the Fourth Conjugation.

Metior,	mensus,	metiri,	*to measure.*
Ordior,	orsus,	ordiri,	*to begin.*
Experior,	expertus,	experiri,	*to try.*
Opperior,	oppertus,	opperiri,	*to wait for.*

Metior in quartâ *mensus* dabit, *ordior orsus ;*
Experior PERTUS, simul *opperior*que tenebunt.

IMPERSONAL VERBS.—*See* page 66.

1. There are only ten **real** Impersonal Verbs, and these are all of the Second Conjugation. Six of them have a double Perfect, one Active, and the other Passive : as,

Libet, *it pleases,*	libuit, *or* libitum est.
Licet, *it is lawful,*	licuit, *or* licitum est.
Miseret, *it pities,*	miseruit, *or* misertum est.
Piget, *it irks,*	piguit, *or* pigitum est.
Pudet, *it shames,*	puduit, *or* puditum est.
Tædet, *it wearies,*	tæduit, *or* pertæsum est.

The others form the Perfect regularly : as, *decet,* it becomes ; *oportet,* it behoves ; *pœnitet,* it repents ; and *liquet,* it appears, which is scarcely used in the Perfect.

2. There are besides a great many Verbs of all the Conjugations, both Active and Passive, which are used Impersonally in the Third Pers. Sing., sometimes with a slight change of signification : as,

First Conj. *Spectat, vacat, stat, constat ; datur, pugnatur, statur.*
Second Conj. *Apparet, pertinet, debet, dolet, nocet ; placet, displicet, favetur, nocetur.*
Third Conj. *Contingit, incipit, conducit, desinit, curritur.*
Fourth Conj. *Convenit, evenit, expedit, venitur, itur.*
Also Irregular Verbs : *as, est, obest, fit, præterit, nequit.*

3. Those Verbs which denote the operations and appearances of nature are also Impersonals : as, *fulgurat, fulminat, tonat, pluit.*

---

tive, according to the Fourth Conjugation. Likewise in the Compounds *adoriretur, exoriretur ;* and not *adoreretur, exoreretur.* The Present follows the Third, though *oriris* and *oritur,* with the penult long, are also found.

REDUNDANT VERBS.

Redundant Verbs are those which have different forms to express the same sense: as, *assentio* and *assentior*, to agree; *fabrīco* and *fabrīcor*, to frame; *mereo* and *mereor*, to deserve. The Passive form of these Verbs is also used in a Passive sense.

1. Some Verbs are usually of the First Conjugation and rarely of the Third: as,

  Lavo, lavas, lavāre, *and* lavo, lavis, lavĕre, *to wash*.
  Sono, sonas, sonāre, *and* sono, sonis, sonĕre, *to sound*.

2. Some are usually of the Second and rarely of the Third: as,

  Ferveo, ferves, fervēre, *and* fervo, fervis, fervĕre, *to boil*.
  Fulgeo, fulges, fulgēre, *and* fulgo, fulgis, fulgĕre, *to shine*.
  Strideo, strides, stridēre, *and* strido, stridis, stridĕre, *to creak*.
  Tergeo, terges, tergēre, *and* tergo, tergis, tergĕre, *to wipe*.
  Tueor, tuĕris, tuĕri, *and* tuor, tuĕris, tui, *to defend*.

3. Some are usually of the Third and rarely of the Fourth: as,

  Arcesso, arcessis, arcessĕre, *and* arcessio, arcessīre, *to send for*.
  Fodio, fodis, fodĕre, *and* fodio, fodis, fodīre, *to dig*.
  Sallo, sallis, sallĕre, *and* sallio, sallis, sallīre, *to salt*.
  Morior, morĕris, mori, *and* morior, morīris, morīri, *to die*.
  Orior, orĕris, *and* orior, orīris, orīri, *to rise*.
  Potior, potĕris, *and* potior, potīris, potīri, *to obtain*.

Note.—Orior and *potior* are always of the Fourth Conjugation in the Infinitive.

There is also one Verb which is usually of the Second and more rarely of the Fourth: *cieo, cies, ciēre,* and *cio, cis, cīre,* to stir up.—*See* page 112, *Note* 15.

FIGURES OF SPEECH.

The Figures of Speech are included in the following lines:

  PROSTHESIS *apponit capiti, sed* APHÆRESIS *aufert.*
  SYNCOPA *de medio tollit, sed* EPENTHESIS *addit.*
  Abstrahit APOCOPE *fini, sed dat* PARAGOGE.
  Constringit CRASIS, *distracta* DIÆRESIS *effert.*
  Litera si legitur transposta, METATHESIS *exit.*
  ANTITHESIN *dices, tibi litera si varietur.*

FIGURATIVE SYNTAX.

Figurative Syntax comprehends those forms of expression which cannot be reduced to any of the general rules.

I. ELLIPSIS.

Ellipsis is the omission of one or more words necessary to com-

plete the regular Syntax : as, *Aberant bidui*, sup. *iter ; Expleri men-
tem nequit*, sup. *secundum*, or *quod ad ; Et genus, et virtus, nisi cum
re vilior algâ est*, sup. *vilius ; Caper tibi salvus, et hædi*, sup. *salvi.*

II. PLEONASM.

Pleonasm is the redundance of one or more words not necessary to
complete the sense : as, *Oculis vidi ; Sic ore locutus est ; Pateris li-
bamus et auro*, for *aureis pateris ; Urbs Troja*, for *Troja.*

III. ENALLAGE.

Enallăge is the change or substitution of one number, case, tense,
&c. for another : as, *Vestra indicatio est*, for *vestrum indicare ; Po-
pulum late regem*, for *regnantem ; Scelus*, for *scelestus ; Romanus*, for
Romani ; Expediti militum, for *milites ; Dare classibus austros*, for
classes austris.

IV. HYPERBATON.

Hyperbăton is the violation of the common arrangement of words
in a sentence : as, *Italiam contra*, for *contra Italiam ; Valet atque
vivit*, for *vivit atque valet ; Saxa vocant Itali mediis quæ in fluctibus
Aras*, for *quæ saxa in mediis fluctibus Itali vocant Aras ; Adeo super
unus eram*, for *supereram.*

RULES FROM RUDDIMAN'S GRAMMAR.

I. RULES FOR THE GENDER OF NOUNS.

I. GENERAL RULES.

1. **Quæ maribus solùm tribuuntur, mascula sunto.**

Names of Males, and Nouns referring to the Male Sex, are Masculine: as, *Homērus*, Homer; *pater*, a father; *Tros*, a Trojan; *fur*, a thief; *Mars*, the god of war; *equus*, a horse.

2. **Esto femineum, quod femina sola reposcit.**

Names of Females, and Nouns referring to the Female Sex, are Feminine: as, *Helĕna*, Helen; *mater*, a mother; *Troas*, a Trojan woman; *Venus*, the goddess of love; *equa*, a mare.

3. **Sit commune duûm, sexum quod signat utrumque.**

Nouns denoting either the Male or Female Sex are of the Common Gender: as, *parens*, a parent; *canis*, a dog, or bitch.

The following lines comprehend nearly all the Nouns of the Common Gender:

Conjux *atque* parens, infans, patruelis *et* hæres,
Affinis, vindex, judex, dux, miles *et* hostis,
Augur *et* antistes, juvenis, conviva, sacerdos,
Muni*que*ceps, vates, adolescens, civis *et* auctor.
Custos, nemo, comes, testis, sus, bos*que*, canis*que*,
Interpres*que*, cliens, princeps, præs, martyr *et* obses,
Atque index, hospes, *queis adde* satelles *et* exsul.

Conjux, a husband, *or* wife; *parens*, a parent; *infans*, an infant; *patruēlis*, a cousin by the father's side: *hæres*, an heir, *or* heiress; *affīnis*, a relation by marriage; *vindex*, an avenger; *judex*, a judge; *dux*, a leader; *miles*, a soldier; *hostis*, an enemy; *augur*, a soothsayer; *antistes*, a high-priest; *juvĕnis*, a young man, *or* woman; *convīva*, a guest; *sacerdos*, a priest, *or* priestess; *munĭceps*, a burgess; *vates*, a prophet; *adolescens*, a young man, *or* woman; *civis*, a citizen; *auctor*, an author; *custos*, a keeper; *nemo*, nobody; *comes*, a companion; *testis*, a witness; *sus*, a swine; *bos*, an ox, *or* cow; *canis*, a dog, *or* bitch; *interpres*, an interpreter; *cliens*, a client; *princeps*, a prince, *or* princess; *præs*, a surety; *martyr*, a martyr; *obses*, a hostage; *index*, an informer; *hospes* a stranger; *satelles*, a life-guardsman; *exsul*, an exile.

4. Multa, quibus sexus promiscuus, uuaque vox est,
Nomina sunt, quorum genus est a fine petendum.

> Some Nouns, referring to both Sexes, have their Gender regulated by their terminations: as, *passer*, a sparrow, Masc. because Nouns in *er* are Masculine; *aquĭla*, an eagle, Fem. because Nouns in *a* of the First Declension are Feminine. This class of Nouns includes many names of wild beasts, and the names of most birds, fishes, and insects. Difference of sex is indicated by the words *mas* and *femina*: as, *mas passer; femina passer.*
> Such Nouns are said to be of the *Epicœne* Gender.

5. Menses cum Ventis generi conjunge virili.

> Names of Months and Winds are Masculine: as, *Aprīlis*, April; *Aquĭlo*, the north-wind; *Eurus*, the east-wind.

6. Masculeum Fluvii nomen Montisque repone:
Sæpe tamen norma est finalis syllaba utrique.

> Names of Rivers and Mountains are Masculine: as, *Tibĕris*, the Tiber; *Othrys*, a hill in Thessaly. Many of these, however, particularly those ending in *a*, *e*, and *um*, adopt the Gender of their terminations: as, *Matrŏna*, f. the Marne in France; *Ætna*, f. a mountain in Sicily; *Soracte*, n. a hill in Italy; because Nouns in *e* of the Third Declension are Neuter.—*See Rules* 16 and 18.

7. *As* partesque dabis maribus: sit at *uncia* dempta.

> *As*, a pound, or any thing that may be divided into twelve parts,[*] is Masculine. The various component parts of *as* are also Masculine, except *uncia*, an ounce, which is Feminine.

8. Jungito femineis nomen Regionis et Urbis;
Præcipuè quod in *n* ternæ fit, *us os*ve secundæ.
Est *Tuder* atque *Argos* neutrum, quibus adjice *Gadir*.
Rariùs HIC *Marathon* capit, et *Pharsalus, Abydos.*
Mascula in *us* ternæ, *Pontus, Sasonque, Canopus,*
Atque *Tunes, Tecmon.* HIC, at HOC vult sæpius
Anxur.
Cætera turba suos fines plerumque sequuntur.

> Names of Countries and Cities are Feminine, especially those in *n* of the Third Declension, and in *us* or *os* of the Second: as, *Britannia*, Britain; *Persis*, Persia; *Roma*, Rome; *Carthăgo*, Carthage. This, as a general rule, refers chiefly to those Nouns which have a Masculine termination: as, *Ægyptus*,

---

[*] The Component parts of *as* are, *uncia*, an ounce, Fem.; *sextans*, 2 ounces; *quadrans*, 3; *triens*, 4; *quincunx*, 5; *semis*, 6; *septuns* 7; *bes*, 8; *dodrans*, 9; *dextans*, or *decunx*. 10; *deunx*, 11 ounces.

Egypt; *Samos*, the island of Samos; *Corinthus*, Corinth; *Lacedæmon*, Lacedemon.

The following names of cities and towns do not follow the general rule. *Tuder*, *Argos*, and *Gadir*, are Neut. *Marăthon*, *Pharsălus* and *Abȳdos*, are generally Fem. but sometimes Masc. Those in *us* of the Third Declension are Masc. : as, *Pessĭnus;* and also *Pontus*, when used as the name of a country; *Sason*, a small island; *Canōpus*, *Tunes*, *Tecmon*, names of towns. *Anxur* is sometimes Masc. but more frequently Neuter.

But many names of Countries and Cities adopt the Gender ot their terminations : as, *Sulmo*, m. *Ilium*, n. *Prœneste*, n. names of cities. Some of the exceptions are also found Feminine in reference to the general word *urbs :* as, *gelida Prœneste*. Juv.

9. Arbor femineis dabitur : sed mas *oleaster,*
   Et *rhamnus :* petit HIC potiùs *cytisus*que *rubus*que :
   HIC quandoque *larix, lotus* volet, atque *cupressus :*
   Hoc quod in *um, suber*que, *siler*, dant *robur acer*que.

Names of trees are Feminine : as, *abies*, the silver-fir ; *pomus*, an apple-tree ; *pirus*, a pear-tree ; *quercus*, an oak.

Oleaster, the wild olive-tree ; and *rhamnus*, the white bramble, are Masc. *Cytĭsus*, the shrub trefoil ; and *rubus*, the bramble-bush, are generally Masculine. *Larix*, the larch-tree ; *lotus*, the lote-tree ; *cupressus*, the cypress, are sometimes Masculine. Those in *um* are Neut ; as, *buxum*, the box-tree ; also *suber*, the cork-tree ; *siler*, the osier ; *robur*, oak of the hardest kind ; and *acer*, the maple-tree.

Note.—Sentis, a brier, is also Masculine.

10. Femineum Naves genus atque Poëmata quærunt.

Names of Ships and Poems are Feminine : as, *Argo*, the ship Argo ; *Ænēis*, the Æneid ; *Ilias*, the Iliad.

Proper Names, when applied to Ships or Poems, retain their Gender : as, *Python*, m. *Triton*, m.; and names of Poems which want the Singular take the Gender of their termination : as, *Adelphi*, m. *Georgĭca*, n.

11. Adjicito neutris quodcunque inflexile nomen.

Indeclinable Nouns are Neuter : as, *gummi*, gum ; *fas*, right.

12. Literæ amant neutrum : sic pars pro nomine sumpta ;
    Et verbum quodvis pro nudâ voce repóstum.

Names of letters are generally Neuter : as, *a parvum ; i longum :* also Verbs and other parts of speech used as Nouns : as, *Scire tuum ; Cras istud :* likewise any word used objectively without reference to its meaning : as, *lux est monosyllabum*.

13. Sæpe genus vocum trahit ad se vox generalis :
    Sic volucrem sequitur *bubo*, sic flumen *Iader*.

The general word frequently regulates the gender of the various words included under it: thus *Bubo*, an owl, is sometimes Fem. taking the gender of *avis*, or *volucris;* and *Iäder* is Neut. because *flumen*, the general word to which it refers, is Neuter.

14 Adjectiva trium generum sunt cuncta : sed unum
Quædam, multa duos, capiunt tres plurima fines.

Adjectives have three Genders; some under one, some under two, and some under three terminations.

15. Pro fixo positum, genus optat mobile fixi.

An Adjective, when used for a Substantive, takes the Gender of the Substantive which it represents.

II. SPECIAL RULES.
A.

16. Hæc dat A quod primæ est: sed neutrum *Pascha* requirit.
Hadria mas æquor, pariterque *cometa, planeta :*
Mascula et interdum *talpam damam*que videbis.

Nouns in A of the First Declension are Feminine : as, *mensa*, a table ; *ripa*, a bank ; *unda*, a wave.
Pascha, the passover, is Neut. *Hadria*, the Hadriatic Sea ; *cŏmēta*, a comet ; and *planēta*, a planet, are Masculine ; likewise all Nouns applied to males : as, *poëta*, a poet ; *nauta*, a sailor. *Talpa*, a mole ; and *dama*, a doe, are sometimes Masculine.
Note.—Hadria, the town Hadria, is Feminine.

17. Sit neutri generis per A quicquid tertia flectit.

Nouns in A of the Third Declension are Neuter : as, *poēma*, a poem ; *diadēma*, a crown.

E.

18. Hæc petit E primæ; neutrum deposcit E ternæ.

Nouns in E of the First Declension are Feminine : as, *epitŏme*, an abridgment ; *grammatĭce*, grammar. Nouns in E of the Third are Neuter : as, *mare*, the sea ; *rete*, a net.

I. U. Y.

19. Dant quibus I fines, Y, vel U, sunt omnia neutra.

Nouns in I, Y, and U, are Neuter: as, *sinăpi*, mustard ; *misy*, vitriol ; *cornu*, a horn ; *genu*, the knee.

O.

20. Hic dat O : femineis *halo* cum *caro* dantur et *echo ;*
Quæque in IO, seu sint verbo, seu nomine nata,

Rem (numeris demptis) aliquam sine corpore sig-
nant.

Nouns in O are Masculine: as, *sermo*, speech; *carbo*, a coal.

Halo, a circle round the sun or moon; *caro*, flesh; and *echo*, an
echo, are Fem.; also Nouns in IO denoting any thing incor-
poreal, whether derived from verbs or nouns: as, *legio*, a le-
gion; *oratio*, a speech; *rebellio*, rebellion.

Nouns in IO denoting any bodily substance, with Names of
Number, are Masc. according to the general rule: as, *scipio*,
a staff; *ternio*, the number three.

21. Adjice femineis, DO, GO : sed mascula *cudo*,
    Harpago, sic *ordo*, simul *udo, tendo, ligo*que.
    Rariùs HÆC *margo* vati est, HIC sæpe *cupido*.
    Arrhabo cum *cardo* muliebria vix imitanda.

Nouns in DO, and GO, are Feminine: as, *arundo*, a reed;
formīdo, fear; *imāgo*, an image; *orīgo*, an origin.

Cudo, a leather cap; *harpăgo*, a drag; *ordo*, order; *udo*, a kind
of shoe; *tendo*, a tendon; and *ligo*, a spade, are Masc. *Margo*, the brink of a river, is generally Masculine. *Cupīdo*, desire, is often Masc. with the poets, but always Fem. in prose
writers. *Arrhăbo*, an earnest; and *cardo*, a hinge, are seldom
Feminine.

C. L. M. T.

22. Quod fit in L, vel T, C, vel M, neutralibus adde :
    Mascula *sol, mugil*, ceu *sal*, quod rariùs HOC vult.

Nouns in L, T, C, and M, are Neuter: as, *anĭmal*, an animal;
toral, a bed-cover; *caput*, the head; *lac*, milk; *regnum*, a
kingdom; *donum*, a gift.

Sol, the sun, and *mugil*, a mullet-fish, are Masc. *Sal*, salt, is
Masc. sometimes Neuter; *Sales*, Plural, is always Masculine.

N.

23. Masculeum capit N.   Finita in MEN dato neutris,
    Quæque secunda creat, cum *gluten* et *inguen* et *un-
    guen :*
    Addideris *pollen.   Sindon* petit HÆC, et *aëdon ;*
    Alcyonem junges, data postea queis comes *icon.*

Nouns in N are Masculine: as, *pecten*, a comb; *canon*, a rule.

Nouns in MEN are Neuter: as, *carmen*, a song; *lumen*, light;
also Greek Nouns in ON of the Second Declension: as, *sym-
bŏlon*, a symbol; likewise *gluten*, glue; *inguen*, the groin;
unguen, ointment; *po'len*, fine flour. *Sindon*, fine linen;
aëdon, a nightingale; *Alcyon*, the kingsfisher, and *icon*, an
image, are Feminine.

AR.

24. Postulat AR neutrum : sed masculeum *salar* optat.

Nouns in A R are Neuter : as, *calcar*, a spur ; *jubar*, the sun-beam. *Salar*, a trout, is Masculine.

ER.

25. ER capit HIC. Neutrum plantæ fructusve requir-unt ;

At *tuber* HIC fructus ; *tuber* quemcunque tumorem
Significans neutrale petit ; cumque *ubere spinther,*
Verque, *cadaver, iter.* Dabit HIC aut HÆC tibi *linter.*

Nouns in ER are Masculine : as, *liber*, a book ; *aër*, the air.
Names of Plants and Fruits are Neuter : as, *papaver*, a poppy ;
piper, pepper. *Tuber*, when it signifies the fruit of the tuber-tree, is Masc. : but *tuber*, denoting any kind of swelling, is
Neuter ; also *uber*, a pap ; *spinther*, a clasp ; *ver*, the spring ;
cadaver, a carcass ; and *iter*, a journey. *Linter*, a boat, is
Masc. or Feminine.

OR.

26. HIC dat OR. HÆC *arbor : cor, ador*que, HOC *mar-mor,* et *æquor.*

Nouns in OR are Masculine : as, *color*, a colour ; *honor*, honour.
Arbor, a tree, is Feminine. *Cor*, the heart ; *ador*, wheat ; *mar-mor*, marble ; and *æquor*, the sea, are Neuter.

27. Hoc dat UR. HIC *furfur* capiet, cum *vulture turtur.*

Nouns in UR are Neuter : as, *murmur*, a noise ; *guttur*, the
throat ; *fulgur*, lightning.
Furfur, bran ; *vultur*, a vulture ; and *turtur*, a turtle-dove, are
Masculine.

AS.

28. AS petit HÆC. Neutrum est *vas vasis,* queisque
Pelasgi
Dant *ătis* in patrio : quibus *antis*, mascula sunto ;
Adjicito quotquot format tibi flexio prima.

Nouns in AS are Feminine : as, *ætas*, an age ; *piĕtas*, piety.
Vas, vasis, a vessel, and Greek nouns having *ătis* in the Geni-tive, are Neuter: as, *artocreas, artocreătis*, a pie. Greek
Nouns having *antis* in the Gen. are Masc. : as, *adămas, -an-tis*, an adamant ; *gigas, -antis*, a giant ; also Nouns in *as* of
the First Declension : as, *tiăras*, a turban.

ES.

29. HÆC dabit ES. Capient *ales* HIC HÆCve, *palumbes,*
Atque *dies :* sed mas proles : mas *poples* et *ames,*

Fomes, pes, paries, palmes cum *limite stipes,*
Queis addes *trames, termes,* cum *gurgite cespes ;*
Et quæ fonte fluunt Graio : sed neutra capessunt
Hippomanes, panaces, nepenthes, sic *cacoëthes.*

Nouns in ES are Feminine : as, *rupes,* a rock ; *res,* a thing.

Ales, a bird ; *palumbes,* a ring-dove ; and *dies,* a day, are Masc.
or Feminine. The following Nouns are Masculine : *meridies,*
the mid-day ; *poples,* the ham of the leg ; *ames,* a fowler's
staff ; *fomes,* fuel ; *pes,* the foot ; *paries,* a wall ; *palmes,* a
vine-branch ; *limes,* a limit ; *stipes,* the stock of a tree ;
trames, a path ; *termes,* an olive-bough ; *gurges,* a whirl-
pool ; *cespes,* a turf ; also all Greek Nouns, either of the
First or Third Declension : as, *comētes,* a comet ; *acinăces,* a
Persian sword. The following Greek Nouns are Neuter,
hippomănes, a kind of poison ; *panăces,* all-heal ; *nepenthes,*
kill-grief ; *cacoëthes,* a bad custom.

Note.—Dies is always Masculine in the Plural.

IS.

30. IS dabo femineis. Sunt mascula *piscis* et *axis,*
*Glis, callis, vermis, vectis, mensis, cucumis*que,
Mugilis et *postis,* cum *sanguine, fascis,* et *orbis,*
Fustis item, *collis, caulis*que, et *follis,* et *ensis,*
Serpentemque notans *cenchris,* cum **vomere torris**
In NIS finitum Latium, *lapis, unguis, aqualis.*

Nouns in IS are Feminine : as, *classis,* a fleet ; *turris,* a tower.

The following are Masculine : *piscis,* a fish ; *axis,* an axle-tree ;
glis, a rat ; *callis,* a beaten path ; *vermis,* a worm ; *vectis,* a
lever ; *mensis,* a month ; *cucămis,* a cucumber ; *mugĭlis,* a
mullet-fish ; *postis,* a post ; *sangnis,* blood ; *fascis,* a bundle ;
orbis, a circle, the world ; *fustis,* a staff ; *collis,* a hill ; *caulis,*
the stalk of an herb ; *follis,* a pair of bellows ; *ensis,* a sword ;
cenchris, Gen. *cenchris,* a serpent ; *vomis,* a ploughshare ;
torris, a firebrand ; *lapis,* a stone ; *unguis,* a nail ; *aquălis,* a
water-pot ; also Nouns of Latin origin in NIS : as, *panis,*
bread. But Greek Nouns in NIS are Feminine, according to
the general rule : as, *tyrannis,* tyranny.

Note.—Cenchris, -ĭdis, a kind of hawk, is Feminine.

31. HIC aut HÆC *finis, clunis,* cum *torque canalis,*
Dant, *scrobis,* ac *anguis : corbis* muliebre præoptat :
Masculeo potiùs gaudent *pulvis, cinis, amnis.*

Finis, the end ; *clunis,* a buttock ; *torquis,* a chain ; *canālis,*
a water-pipe ; *scrobis,* a ditch ; *anguis,* a serpent, are Masc.
or Fem., but more frequently Masculine. *Corbis,* a twig-
basket, is usually Feminine. *Pulvis,* dust ; *cinis,* ashes ;

amnis, a river, are more commonly Masc. sometimes also Feminine.

Note.—Fines, when it signifies the borders or territories of a country, is always Masculine.

OS.

32. OS maribus detur. Sunt neutra *chaos, melos, os, os :*
Postulat HÆC *arbos, cos, dos,* et origine Græcâ
Orta *eos, arctos, perimetros* cum *diametro.*

Nouns in OS are Masculine: as, *flos,* a flower ; *ros,* dew.
Chaos, a confused mass; *melos,* a song ; *os, oris,* the mouth ; *os, ossis,* a bone, are Neuter. *Arbos,* a tree ; *cos,* a whetstone ; *dos,* a dowry, are Feminine ; also the following Nouns of Greek origin ; *eos,* the morning ; *arctos,* the constellation of the Bear ; *perimetros,* the circumference ; and *diametros,* the diameter of a circle.

US *of the Second and* **Fourth Declension.**

33. Nomen in US mas est, seu quartæ sive secundæ.

Nouns in US of the Second and Fourth Declensions are Masculine : as, *annus,* a year ; *vultus,* the countenance.

34. HÆC *domus* et *vannus,* pro fructu *ficus,* et *alvus,*
Sic *humus* atque *manus,* poscunt: *acus* addito quartæ,
Porticus atque *tribus.* Capit HOC *virus, pelagus* que.

The following Nouns of the Second Declension are Feminine : *vannus,* a sieve ; *alvus,* the belly ; *humus,* the ground : also *manus,* the hand ; *acus,* a needle ; *porticus,* a gallery ; *tribus,* a tribe, which are of the Fourth. Likewise *domus,* a house, which is partly of the Second, and partly of the Fourth ; and *ficus,* a fig, which is declined according to both. *Virus,* poison ; and *pelagus,* the sea, of the Second, are Neuter.

35. Nomen in OS Græcum, quod in US mutare Latini
Sæpe solent, normam sequitur plerumque virilem :
Femineum sed **multa** petunt : ut, *abyssus, eremus,*
Antidotus que, *pharus, dialectus, carbasus :* adde
Ex *odos* et *phthongos* genitum, quæque a generali
Voce genus plantæ et gemmæ capiunt muliebre.

Greek Nouns in OS which the Latins change into US, are generally Masculine : as, *cyäthus,* a cup ; *gyrus,* a circle. Many, however, are Feminine: as, *abyssus,* a bottomless pit ; *erēmus,* a desert ; *antidŏtus,* an antidote ; *pharus,* a watchtower ; *dialectus,* a dialect ; *carbăsus,* a sail ; the Compounds of *odos* and *phthongos :* as, *periŏdus,* a period ; *diphthongus,* a diphthong ; also some names of plants and gems following the Gender of the general words *planta* and *gemma :* as, *papŷrus,* an Egyptian plant ; *amethystus,* the amethyst.

36. Postulat US neutrum, quoties id tertia flectit.

> Nouns in US of the Third Declension are Neuter: as, *pectus*,
> the breast; *littus*, a shore; *nemus*, a grove.

37. Femineum voluere *palus, subscus*que, *salus*que,
Quæque *senex, juvenis*, cum *servio*, nomina formant,
Et *virtus, incus*.   At mascula sunt *lepus* et *mus*,
Et *pus* compositum: petit at muliebre *lagopus.*

> The following Nouns are Feminine: *palus*, a fen; *subscus*, a
> dovetail; *salus*, health, safety; *senectus*, old age; *juventus*,
> youth; and *servĭtus*, slavery (from *senex, juvĕnis* and *servio*);
> *virtus*, virtue; *incus*, an anvil. *Lepus*, a hare; *mus*, a
> mouse; and the Compounds of *pus*; as, *tripus*, a tripod, are
> Masculine. *Lagōpus*, hare's foot, is Feminine.

38. Hic aut HÆC donant *balanus, specus*, atque *phaselus*,
Barbitus, atque *penus, grossus*: sed *grus, atomus*que
Femineum potiùs cupiunt; *colus* adde, virile
Quod rarò invenies: muliebre at contrà *camelus*
Est ubi nonnunquam videas. Vult HIC dare *vulgus*,
Sed magis HOC. Ternæ *specus* et *penus* addito neu-
tris.

> The following Nouns in US are sometimes Masculine, and some-
> times Feminine; *balănus*, the fruit of the palm-tree; *specus*,
> *-ŭs*, a den: *phasēlus*, a yacht; *barbĭtus*, a harp; *penus, -i*,
> or *-ŭs*, all kinds of provisions; *grossus*, a green fig. *Grus*, a
> crane; and *atŏmus*, an atom; are generally Feminine, seldom
> Masculine. *Colus*, a distaff, is seldom Masculine. *Camēlus*,
> a camel, is sometimes Feminine; but more commonly Mas-
> culine. *Vulgus*, the rabble, is sometimes Masculine, but
> more often Neuter. *Specus* and *penus*, of the Third Declen-
> sion, are Neuter.

YS.

39. Nomen in YS Græcum est, genus et sibi femineum
vult.

> Greek Nouns in YS are Feminine: as, *chelys*, a harp; *chlamys*,
> a soldier's cloak.

40. *Æs* neutrale petit: *laus, fraus*, muliebria sunto.

> *Æs*, brass, or money, is Neuter: *laus*, praise; and *fraus*, fraud,
> are Feminine.

S preceded by a consonant.

41. S dato femineis, si consona ponitur ante.
  Mascula sed *pons, fons, mons, seps,* dum denotat an-
    guem ;
  Et queis P præit S polysyllaba, *forcipe* dempto,
  Densque, chalybs, cum *gryphe, rudens,* quod rariùs
    HÆC vult.
  Hic aut HÆC *serpens* dat, *scrobs, stirps* truncus,
    adepsque.
  Dans *animans* genus omne, tamen muliebre præoptat.

  Nouns in S preceded by a consonant are Feminine : as, *mors,*
    death ; *pars,* a part ; *trabs,* a beam.
  The following are Masculine : *pons,* a bridge ; *fons,* a fountain ;
    mons, a mountain ; *seps,* a kind of serpent; nouns of more
    than one syllable in PS : as, *hydrops,* a dropsy ; (except *for-
    ceps,* a pair of tongs, f.) ; *dens,* a tooth ; *chalybs,* steel ; **gryps,**
    a griffon ; and *rudens,* a cable, which last is sometimes Femi-
    nine. *Serpens,* a serpent ; *scrobs,* a ditch ; *stirps,* the trunk
    of a tree ; and *adeps,* fatness, are Masculine or Feminine.
    Animans, an animal, is of all Genders, but most commonly or
    the Feminine.
  Note.—*Seps,* a hedge, and *stirps,* offspring, kindred, are Femi-
    nine only.

X.

42. HÆC petit X. *Ax, ex* maribus polysyllaba junge :
  Dic tamen HÆC *fornax, smilax, carex,* velut *halex,*
  Et cum prole *panax,* et *forfex* atque *supellex.*

  Nouns in X are Feminine : as, *pax,* peace ; *vox,* a voice.
  Polysyllables in AX and EX are Masculine : as, *thorax,* the
    breast ; *frutex,* a shrub. Of these, however, the following
    are Feminine : *fornax,* a furnace ; *smilax,* bindweed ; *carex,*
    a sedge ; *halex,* a herring ; *panax,* all-heal ; *opopanax,* the
    juice of the herb all-heal ; *forfex,* a pair of scissors ; *supel-
    lex,* furniture.

43. Mascula sunto *calix, phœnix,* pro vermeque *bombyx,*
  Et *coccyx, fornix,* et *onyx* vas, aut lapis unde
  Vas fit ; *oryx, tradux,* **grex** his adjunge *calyx*que.
  Femineo interdum data *tradux* cum *grege* cernes.

  The following Nouns in X are Masculine : *calix,* a cup ; *phœ-
    nix,* a bird called a phenix ; *bombyx,* a silk-worm ; *coccyx,* a
    cuckoo ; *fornix,* a vault ; *onyx,* alabaster, *or* an alabaster
    box ; *oryx,* **a wild goat ;** *tradux,* a graft of a vine, *grex,* a
    flock ; *calyx,* the bud of a flower. *Tradux* and *grex* are
    sometimes Feminine.
  Note.—*Bombyx,* when it signifies a silk garment ; **and** *onyx,* a
    gem, are Feminine.

44. Hæc modò femineis, maribus modò juncta videbis ;
    Calx pro parte pedis metâve laboris, et *hystrix,*
    Imbrex; sardonychem jungas, *rumicem, silicem*que :
    Hic mage **vult** *cortex,* et *obex,* cum *pumice varix ;*
    Hæc potiùs *lymax, lynx,* et cum *sandice perdix :*
    Atriplici neutrum meliùs dabo quàm muliebre.

> The following Nouns are sometimes Masculine and sometimes
> Feminine : *calx,* the heel, or the end of any thing, the goal ;
> *hystrix,* a porcupine ; *imbrex,* a gutter-tile ; *sardŏnyx,* a pre-
> cious stone ; *rumex,* the herb sorrel ; *silex,* a flint ; and also
> *cortex,* the bark of a tree ; *obex,* a bar ; *pumex,* a pumice-
> stone ; *varix,* a swollen vein, which are seldom Feminine.
> *Limax,* a snail ; *lynx,* an ounce ; *sandix,* a sort of purple ;
> *perdix,* a partridge ; are more commonly Feminine. *Atri-*
> *plex,* the herb orach, is generally Neuter.
>
> *Note.*—*Calx,* when it signifies limestone, is always Feminine.

I, Æ, A, and E *Plural.*

45. I maribus plurale dabis : muliebre sed Æ vult :
    Ast A, et E Græcum, cupiunt neutralibus addi.

> Plural Nouns in I are Masculine : as, *lĭbĕri,* children ; those in
> Æ are Feminine : as, *cunæ,* a cradle ; those in A are Neuter :
> as, *arma,* arms.
>
> Plural Nouns in E from the Greek are also Neuter : as, *mele,*
> songs ; *cete,* whales. *See page 97.*

Defective Nouns.

46. In reliquis primo numero primive carentûm
    Recto, animo, qualem vocum natura reposcat,
    Concipito talem : sic a *prece prex* tibi forma.
    Hic dat *casse* tamen, dat et *impete ; verbere* vult
    hoc ;
    Hic *veprem, pecudis* capit hæc ; hæ postulat *Idus.*

> In Nouns of other Terminations which are defective in the No-
> minative, or in the whole of the Singular, the Gender is regu-
> lated by the termination of the Nominative from which they
> are supposed to have come : Thus *preci* (Dat.), a prayer, is
> Feminine, because it comes from the old Nominative *prex,*
> which is Feminine, by *Rule* 42. *Femĭnis,* (Gen.) the thigh,
> is Neuter, because the supposed Nominative *femen* is Neuter,
> by *Rule* 23.
>
> The following are Exceptions : *casse,* a net ; *impĕtis,* force, and
> *vepres,* a brier, Masculine : *verbĕris,* a scourge, Neuter : *pe-*
> *cŭdis,* a beast, and *Idus,* the Ides of a month, Feminine. *See*
> *Defective Nouns,* pages 97 and 98.

8 88 88 88 8 8 88 88 8 8 88 8888888888888888888888888 888888888888888888888888888888888888888888888888888888888888888888888888888888

EXERCISES ON THE RULES FOR THE GENDER OF NOUNS.

RULE 1. Jupiter, Mars, Homerus, Virgilius, Tros, pater, consul, flamen, ædilis, optio, fur, equus. 2. Juno, Diana, Troas, Helena, Venus, Siren, mater, uxor, anus, nurus, socrus, equa. 3. Conjux, parens, &c. 4. Passer, aquila, liberi, homo, elephantus, hirundo, vulpes, salmo, balæna.

5. Januarius, Aprilis, September—Aquilo, Eurus, Notus, Iapyx. 6. Tiberis, Rhodanus, Tagus, Eurotas, Euphrates, Ganges, Tigris—Othrys, Olympus—*Allia, Matrona, Lethe, Ætna, Styx, Soracte, Alpes.* 8. Italia, Britannia, Ægyptus, Samos, Roma, Carthago, Lacedæmon, Persis, Pylos,—*Tuder, Argos, Gadir—Marathon, Pharsalus, Abydos—Pessinus, Hydrus, Opus, Pontus, Sason, Canopus, Tunes, Tecmon,—Anxur —Sulmo, Acragas, Londinum, Zeugma, Reate, Præneste, Care, Albion, Ilion, Tibur, Veii, Athenæ, Gades, Susa, Hierosolyma.*

7. As, sextans, semis, quincunx, bes—*uncia.* 9. Quercus, abies, pinus, taxus, pirus, fraxinus—*oleaster, rhamnus—cytisus, rubus—larix, lotus, cupressus*—buxum, ligustrum, *suber, siler, robur, acer—sentis.* 10. Argo, Centaurus, Chimæra, Tigris, Spes, Victoria, Æneis, Ilias. 11. Gummi, fas, nefas, pondo, mille, cæpe.

16. Ala, litera, turba, mensa, hedera, invidia, rana—*Hadria, cometa, planeta—talpa, dama—Pascha.* 17. Dogma, poema, diadema, epigramma, stemma. 18. Epitome, rhetorice, grammatice—ancile, cubile, mare, ovile, præsepe. 19. Sinapi, gummi —cornu, genu, tonitru—moly, misy.

20. Sermo, bufo, carbo, pulmo, mucro—*halo, caro, echo*— oratio, opinio, rebellio, communio, legio, seditio—scipio, scorpio, papilio, pugio, unio, ternio, quaternio, senio. 21. Arundo, imago, grando, caligo, testudo, origo—*cudo, harpago, ordo, udo, tendo, ligo—margo—cupido—cardo, arrhabo.*

22. Animal, puteal, vectigal—lac, halec—caput, sinciput, occiput—bellum, regnum, donum, prælium, armentum—*sol, mugil—sal.* 23. Canon, delphin, ren, pæan, pecten—flumen, agmen, carmen, cognomen, cacumen—symbolon, symposion, barbiton— *gluten, inguen, unguen, pollen—sindon, aëdon, alcyon, icon.*

24. Calcar, nectar, jubar, far, lacunar—*salar.* 25. Liber, imber, aër, ager, carcer, anser, agger, culter—papaver, cicer, piper—*tuber* (a swelling), uber, spinther, ver, cadaver, iter— linter. 26. Dolor, color, honor, timor, sopor—*arbor—cor, ador, marmor, æquor.* 27. Guttur, murmur, robur, sulphur—*furfur, vultur, turtur.*

28. Ætas, pietas, voluptas, lampas, anas—*vas* (a vessel)— artocreas, erysipelas—adamas, elephas—tiäras, paréas. 29. Ædes, fames, sedes, res, facies, soboles, proles, spes, vulpes, merces. quies, seges—*ales, palumbes, dies—meridies—poples,*

ames, fomes, pes, paries, palmes, limes, stipes, trames, termes, gurges, **cespes**—cometes, achates, lebes, **magnes**, acinaces—*hippomanes, panaces, nepenthes, cacoethes.*

30. Avis, vallis, ovis, classis, naris, **lis**, pestis, apis, pellis, cenchris (a kind of hawk)—*piscis, axis, glis, callis, vermis, vectis, mensis, cucumis, mugilis, postis, sanguis, fascis, orbis, fustis, collis,* **caulis,** *follis, ensis, cenchris* (a kind of serpent), *vomis, torris, lapis, unguis, aqualis—panis, crinis, ignis, funis,*—tyrannis, coronis. 31. *Finis, clunis, torquis, canalis, scrobis, anguis—corbis—pulvis, cinis, amnis.*

32. Flos, ros, honos, mos—*chaos, melos, os* (a bone), *os* (the mouth)—*arbos, cos, dos, eos, arctos, perimetros, diametros.* 33. Annus, oculus, ventus, terminus, vultus, gradus, currus, impetus. 34. *Domus, vannus, ficus, alvus, humus, manus, acus* (a needle), *porticus, tribus—virus, pelagus.* 35. Cyathus, gyrus, dialogus, bolus—*abyssus, eremus, antidotus, pharus, dialectus,* **carbasus**—periodus, methodus, synodus, diphthongus, —amethystus, chrysolithus, crystallus, sapphirus, &c.—papyrus, nardus, byssus, hyssopus, costus, crocus, &c.

36. Corpus, onus, littus, nemus, pignus, thus. 37. *Palus, suoscus, salus, senectus, juventus, servitus, virtus, incus—* **lepus,** *mus—tripus—lagopus.* 38. *Balanus, specus* (4th decl.), **phaselus,** *barbitus,* **penus** (2d and 4th) *grossus—grus, atomus —colus—camelus—vulgus.* 39. Chlamys, chelys. 40. Æslaus, fraus.

41. Mors, **pars,** gens, juglans, hyems, **mens, trabs,** stirps (an offspring), **seps** (a hedge)—*pons, fons,* **mons, seps** (a kind of serpent), *dens, chalybs, gryps—rudens*—hydrops, merops, epops —*forceps—serpens, scrobs,* **stirps** (the stock of a **tree**), *adeps—animans.*

42. Pax, lex, vox, calx (limestone), **falx,** arx, onyx (a gem), cervix, cornix, radix, bombyx (a silk garment)—thorax, corax, murex, vertex, vortex, frutex—*fornax, smilax,* **carex,** *halex,* **panax, opopanax,** *forfex, supellex.* 43. *Calix, phœnix, bombyx* (a silkworm), *coccyx, fornix, onyx* (alabaster, or an alabaster-box), *oryx, tradux, grex, calyx—tradux, grex.* 44. *Calx* (the heel, a goal), *hystrix, imbrex, sardonyx, rumex, silex, —cortex,* **obex, pumex,** *varix—limax, lynx, sandyx, perdix—atriplex.*

45. Liberi, fasti, posteri—divitiæ, **cunæ,** induciæ, nuptiæ, tenebræ—arma, castra, **comitia,** mœnia, rostra—mele, cete, **Tempe.** 46. Spontis, preci, **grates,** ditionis, vicis, necis—*casse,* **impete,** *veprem—verbere—pecudis,* **Idus.**

II. RULES FOR THE QUANTITY OF SYLLABLES.

That part of **Grammar** which treats of the quantity of Syllables, and the Construction of **Verse**, is called *Prosody*.

By the Quantity of a Syllable is meant, the time occupied in pronouncing it.

Syllables are either long or short. A long syllable occupies, in pronouncing, double the time which is assigned to a short syllable. Long syllables are marked thus, ¯: as, *Dīdō :* short syllables are marked thus, ˘: as, *pătĕr*.

I. GENERAL RULES.

1. Vocalem breviant aliâ subeunte Latini.

> A vowel before another vowel or a diphthong, in words of Latin origin, is short : as, *dĕus, pŭer, dĕæ ;* or before *h* and a vowel : as, *trăho, mĭhi, nĭhil;* because *h*, in verse, is considered merely as a breathing.

2. Ni capit *r, fīo* produc: et nomina quintæ
   E servant longum, si præsit *i*, ceu *speciēi*.
   Anceps *ius* erit patrio: sed protrahe *alīus*,
   Alterīus brevia tantùm : commune sit *ohe*.
   Pompēi Cāi produc, conformia jungens.
   Dianam varia: longa *āĕr, dīus* et *ēheu*,
   Et patrius primæ cum sese solvit in *āi*.

> *Exc.* The i is long in *fīo* when not followed by *r :* as, *fīebam :* in the other Tenses it is short: as, *fĭerem*. The *e* in the penult of the Gen. and Dat. of Nouns of the Fifth Declension, when preceded by *i*, is long: as, *speciēi*.[*] Genitives in *ius* have the i long in prose, but common† in verse: as, *unius :* but *alīus* is always long, and *altĕrius* is always short. Proper names in *eïus*, and *aïus :* as, *Pompēius, Cāius*, with Vocatives of the same kind, are long; also the old form of the Genitive of the First Declension : as, *terrāi ;* likewise *āĕr, dīus*, and *ēheu*.

> *Ohe, Diana* and *Io* (a Proper Name) have the first syllable common ; but *io* (the interjection) follows the general rule.

3. Hic Græci variant, nec certâ lege tenentur.

> The Quantity of a Vowel before another vowel or a diphthong,

---

[*] All Nouns of the Fifth Declension have the *e* long in the penult of the Genitive Singular, except *fides* and *res*, in which it is common, and *spes*, in which it is always short.

† The quantity of a syllable is said to be *common*, or *doubtful*, when it is found sometimes long, and sometimes short.

in words derived from the Greek, cannot be reduced to any precise Rule. It is short in some words: as, *Danăe, idĕa*; and long in others: as, *Lycāou, Cytherēa.*

4. Si postponatur vocali consona bina,
Aut duplex, longa est positu: sin utraque vocem
Incipiat, rarò præeunti est ultima longa.

A Vowel before two Consonants, either in the same, or in consecutive words, or before a double Consonant, is long: as, *bĕllum, dīscors, āxis:* and in this case the vowel is said to be long by *Position.* The Double Consonants are *X, Z,* and *J,* except in Compound words: as, *bĭjugus, quadrĭjŭgus.*

The Latin poets after the time of Lucretius, seldom, if ever, allowed a vowel in the end of a word to remain short, when followed by a word beginning with *sc, sp, sq, st,* though from the few examples which occur, they appear to have carefully avoided such a collocation. The quantity of a vowel in the end of a word is not affected by any other combination of consonants, or by a double consonant in the beginning of the following word.

5. Si mutæ liquida est subjuncta in syllabâ eâdem,
Quae brevis antevenit vocalis, redditur anceps.
Hanc tamen in prosâ semper breviare memento.
Sunt *l, r,* liquidæ, queis rarò jungimus *m, n.*

A Vowel naturally short, when followed by a Mute[*] and either of the Liquids, *l, r,* in the same syllable, is common in verse, but always short in prose: as, *agris, pharetra, volucris.* In a few words taken immediately from the Greek, a vowel is allowed to remain short before a Mute, and either of the two other Liquids, *m, n:* as, *cȳcnus, Prŏcne.*

If the Liquid stand before the Mute, or belong to a different syllable, the preceding vowel is necessarily long: as, *ārte, āb-luo, ōb-ruo, quamōb-rem.*

A Vowel naturally long is never made short before a Mute and a Liquid: as, *mātris, salūbris,* from *māter, salūber.*

6. Vocalem efficiet semper Contractio longam.

Contracted Syllables are long: as, *cogo,* for *coăgo; alĭus,* for *aliius; sīs,* for *si vis; tibīcen,* for *tibiicen,* or *tibiacen.*

7. Diphthongum produc in Græcis atque Latinis:
In Græcis semper: at PRÆ composta sequente
Vocali brevia: veluti *praĕit* atque *praĕustus.*

---

[*] There are ten Mutes: b, c, d, f, j, k, p, q, t, v; and four Liquids: l, r, m, n, of which the first two only come within the limits of this rule, except in Greek words.

Diphthongs are long in Latin and Greek words : as, *Cæsar, aurum, fænus ; Eubæa, Æneas, Harpyia.*

Exc. The Preposition *præ,* when prefixed to a word beginning with a Vowel, is short : as, *praëeo, praëustüs.*

II. SPECIAL RULES.

First and Middle Syllables.

8. Derivata tenent mensuram primigenorum :
   Orta tamen brevibus, *suspĭcio, rēgula, sēdes,*
   Sēcius, hūmanus, pēnuria, mōbilis, hūmor,
   Jūmentum, fōmes, primam producere gaudent.
   Corripiunt sed *ărista, vădum, sŏpor* atque *lŭcerna,*
   Duxque dŭcis, stabilisque, fĭdes, dĭtioque, quăsillus,
   Nata licet longis ; quæ pluraque suggeret usus.

   Derivative words usually retain the quantity of the words from which they are formed : as, *ămicus, păvidus,* from *ămo, păveo ; mäternus, nātivus,* from *mäter, nālus ; lĕgam, lĕgeram,* from *lĕgo, lēgi ; virgĭneus, sanguĭneus,* from *virgĭnis* and *sanguĭnis.*

   Exc. 1. The following Derivatives are long, although the corresponding syllables in their Primitives are short : *suspĭcio* from *suspĭcor, rēgula* from *rĕgo, sēdes* from *sĕdeo, sēcius* from *sĕcus, hūmanus* from *hŏmo, pēnuria* from *pĕnus, mōbilis* from *mŏveo, hūmor* from *hŭmus, jūmentum* from *jŭvo, fōmes* from *fŏveo.*

   Exc. 2. The following are short, from Primitives which have the corresponding syllables long : *ărista* from *āreo, vădum* from *vādo, sŏpor* from *sōpio, lŭcerna* from *lūceo, dŭcis* from *dūco, stăbilis* from *stātum, fĭdes* from *fīdo, dĭtio* from *dītis, quăsillus* from *quālus.*

Note 1.—*Mōbilis, jūmentum,* and *fōmes* are necessarily long, being derived from the Supines, *mōtum, jūtum,* and *fōtum ;* these Supines being probably lengthened by contraction.

Note 2. The following Derivative words, which are of frequent occurrence, also differ in quantity from their Primitives : *jūgerum* from *jŭgum, lāterna* from *lăteo, mācero* from *măcer, mōlestus* from *mŏles, nŏta* and *nŏto* from *nōtus, perfĭdus* from *fīdus, tēgula* from *tĕgo, vŏco* from *vox, vōcis.*

9. Simplicium servant legem composta suorum,
   Quamvis diphthongus vel vocalis varietur.
   At breviant *nihĭlum,* cum *pejĕro, dejĕro,* nec non
   Veridĭcus, sociis junctis, et *semisŏpitus.*
   Cognĭtus his addes, relut *agnĭtus, innŭbus,* atque
   Pronŭbus : at longis *ambĭtus* mobile junges,
   Imbēcillus item : sed *connubium* variabis.

Compounds usually retain the quantity of the Simple words of which they are composed: as, *perlĕgo, invĭdeo*, from *lĕgo, vĭdeo; perlēgi, invīdi*, from *lēgi, vīdi; imprŏbus, perjŭrus*, from *prŏbus, jūris.*

The quantity of the simple word is not altered by the change of a vowel or diphthong in the Compound: as, *concīdo, irrītus*, from *eŭdo, rătus; concīdo, inīquus*, from *cædo, æquus.*

Exc. The following Compounds differ in quantity from the Simple words: *nihĭlum* from *ne* and *hĭlum, pejĕro* and *dejĕro* from *jūro, vĕridĭcus* and other Adjectives in *dĭcus* from *dīco, semisŏpitus* from *sōpitus, cognĭtus* and *agnĭtus* from *nōtus, innŭbus* and *pronŭbus* from *nūbo, imbēcillus* from *băculus, ambĭtus* from *ĭtum. Connŭbium* from *nūbo* has the second syllable common.

10. Quam disjuncta dabat mensuram præpositura,
　　Juncta tenet: subiens illam nisi litera mutet.

Prepositions, when compounded with other words, retain their original quantity: as, *āmitto, dēduco; ăboleo, pĕrimo*, because *ā* and *dē* are long, and *ăb* and *pĕr* short. *Trans* frequently drops the last two letters in composition, but retains its proper quantity: as, *trāduco*, for *transduco.*

Prepositions ending in a Vowel become short, when prefixed to words which begin with a vowel: as, *dĕosculor, prŏhibeo. Ob* sometimes drops the *b* before a Consonant, in which case the *o* remains short: as, *ŏmitto*, for *obmitto.* The Prepositions which end in a Consonant become long by *Position*, when placed before another Consonant: as, *ădmitto.*

11. Est PRO breve in Græcis, PRO longum rite Latinis.
　　At rape quæ *fundus, fugio, neptis*que, *nepos*que,
　　Et *festum, fari, fateor, fanum*que creârunt.
　　Hisce *prŏfecto* addes, pariterque *prŏcella, prŏtervus*,
　　Atque *prŏpago* genus; *prōpago* protrahe vitis.
　　Propino varia, verbum *propago, profundo*:
　　Cum *pello, curo* genitis, *Proserpina* junge.

The Preposition *pro* is short in Greek words: as, *Prŏmetheus, prŏlogus, prŏpheta:** it is generally long in Latin words: as, *prōdo, prōmitto, prōveho.*

Exc. 1. In the following Latin words *pro* is short; *prŏfundus, prŏfugio, prŏfugus, prŏneptis, prŏnepos, prŏfestus, prŏfari, prŏfiteor, prŏfanus, prŏfano, prŏfecto, prŏficiscor, prŏfectus, prŏcella, prŏtervus*, and *prŏpago* when it signifies *a race* or *lineage*; but when it signifies *a vine-stock*, the first syllable is long.

---

* *Pro*, in words transferred from the Greek, represents the Greek Preposition προ, in which the vowel is short.

Exc. 2. In the following words *pro* is common: *propino, pro-pago* (a Verb), *profundo, propello, propulso, procuro,* and *Pro-serpina,* though **not a** Compound.

Note.—The rule here given **for the quantity** of *pro* in *profundo, propello,* and *procuro,* is not supported by sufficient authority: in the first, *pro* is always found short in the best writers; and in the other two, it is always long. The first syllable of *propago* is common both in the noun and verb. The distinction mentioned above is not observed by the best writers.

12. SE produc et DI, præter *dĭrimo,* atque *dĭsertus.*
   Est RE breve: at viduum personis protrahe *rēfert.*

   The Inseparable Prepositions *se* and *di* are long in Compound words: as, *sēparo, dīvello:* except in *dĭrimo* and *dĭsertus.*

   Re is short: as, *rĕmitto;* also in verbs beginning with a vowel, where *d* is inserted for the sake of euphony: as, *rĕdamo.* *Re* in the Impersonal Verb *rēfert,* **is long; but is here to be con-** sidered not as the inseparable **Preposition, but as the dative** or ablative of *res.*

   Re, though naturally short, is made long **in the following** Compound **words:** *rēcĭdo, rēduco, rēligio, rēligiosus, rēliquiæ, rēlatum, rēmotum;* it is always long **in the three** Preterites, *rēperit, rēpulit,* and *rētulit.*

   The prefix *ve,* signifying *small,* **is** long in composition, and *ne* (negative) and *si,* which are long as monosyllables, are short: as, *vēsanus, nĕfas, sĭquidem.*

13. Pars si componens fini prior *i* vel *o* donat,
   Sit breve: *vatĭcinor* monstraverit *Arctŏphylax*que.

   I and *o* in the end of the first component part of a word **are** generally short: as, *omnĭpotens, hŏdie.* The exceptions are contained in the following rule:

14. *I* quibus est flexu mutabile, jungito longis,
   Quæque queunt sensu salvo divellier, addens
   De quibus aut Crasis aliquid vel Syncopa tollit.
   Idem masculeum produc, et *ubĭque,* et *ibĭdem;*
   Huic dein agglomerans turbæ composta *diei.*
   His *intro, retro, contro*que, et *quando* creata
   (*Quandōquidem* excepto,) bene junxeris, atque *aliŏquin.*
   Quæque per *o* magnum scribuntur **nomina Graiis.**

   The following words have **i and** *o* long **in the end** of the first component part:

   1. **Those in** which i is the Termination of a case: as, *quĭdam, tantīdem, reĭpublicæ, qualīcunque.*
   2. Those in which the component parts may be separated **with-** out injuring the sense: as, *ludīmagister, lucrīfacio, sīquis;* which are also written, *ludi magister, lucri facio, si quis.*

3. Those in which a syllable has been dropped by Crasis or Syncope : as, *tibīcen* for *tibiacen*, *bīgæ* for *bijugæ*, *scīlicet* for *scirelicet*.

4. *Idem* has i long in the Nom. and Voc. Singular Masc., but short in the Neuter. *I* is long in *ubīque* and *ibīdem*, but short in *ubīvis*, and doubtful in *ubicunque*.

5. The compounds of *dies :* as, *bīduum*, *merīdies*. But *quotidie* and *quotidianus* have the second syllable sometimes short.

6. Latin words compounded with *intro, retro, contro* and *quando :* as, *intrŏduco, retrŏduco, contrŏversia, quandŏque :*; likewise *aliŏquin, cæterŏquin, utrŏbique.*

7. Words transplanted from the Greek in which o represents ω : as, *geŏmetra, Minŏtaurus, lagŏpus.*

Note.—The two preceding rules would have been more simple had the principle stated in *Rule* 9 been kept in view, that words when joined in composition retain their natural quantity, unless they are modified by contraction or otherwise. Thus the i in *quīdam, tantīdem, ludīmagister, sīquis, &c.* is long, because it is long in *qui, tanti, ludi, si, &c.* In *bīduum, īdem, scīlicet,* the first syllable is long by contraction. The same principle applies to some words which have o long in the end of the first component part : as, *aliŏquin, cæterŏquin, utrŏbique,* because it is long in *aliŏ, cæterŏ* and *utrŏ.* So likewise in *quāre, quāpropter, &c.,* the a is long because it is long in *quā.* In *omnīpotens, semīvir, &c.,* the s of *omnis* and *semis* is dropped before the consonants, and the i consequently remains short.

The following facts concerning the Compounds of *facio* are taken from Professor Ramsay's excellent work on Latin Prosody : In *calĕfacio, calĕfacto, labĕfacio, labĕfacto, madĕfacio, pavĕfacio, rubĕfacio, stupĕfacio, tremĕfacio, tumĕfacio,* the e is uniformly short. *Patefacio* has the second syllable generally short ; it is lengthened by Lucretius in two passages, of which the one is a disputed reading. *Tepefacio,* with one exception, has the e always short ; in *liquefacio* it is generally short. *Putrefacio,* which is an unusual word, appears to have the e common. *Expergĕfacta* and *confervĕfacit,* are found with the e long, but not in poets of the Augustan age.

Perfects and Supines of Verbs.

15. Præterita assumunt primam dissyllaba longam.
Tolle *bibit, scidit,* et *fidit,* ac *tulit,* ortaque *do, sto.*

> Preterites of two syllables and the Tenses formed from them, have the first syllable long : as, *vēni, vīdi, vīci, īvi ; vēneram, &c.*

> *Exc.* *Bĭbi, scĭdi* from *scindo, fĭdi* from *findo, tŭli, dĕdi,* and *stĕti,* or *stĭti,* have the first syllable short.

16. Præteritum geminans primam, breviabit utramque,
Ut *pario pĕpĕri ;* vetet id nisi consona bina.
At quod *cædo* creat tardat, ceu *pedo* secundam.

Preterites which double the first syllable have the first two syllables short: as, *pĕpĕri, tĕtĭgi, cĕcĭdi;* except *cecīdi* from
cædo, pepēdi, and those in which the middle syllable is made
long by Position: as, *fefelli.*

17. Cuncta Supina tenent primam dissyllaba longam :
Præter nata *sero, cieo, lino,* cum *sino, sisto,*
Quæ breviant; *eo, do*que, *ruo, queo* junge, *reor*que.

Supines of two syllables, and the parts of the Verb formed from
them, have the first syllable long: as, *vīsum, cāsum, mōtum ;
vīsus, &c.*

Exc. Sătum from *sero, cĭtum** from *cieo (See* page 112, *Note* 15),
lĭtum from *lino,* **sĭtum** from *sino, stătum* from *sisto, ĭtum* from
eo, dătum from *do, rŭtum* in the compounds of *ruo, quĭtum*
from *queo, rătum* from *reor,* have the first syllable short.

18. Cætera præsentis mensuram verba reservant.
Excipe sed *pŏsui, pŏsitum, gĕnui, gĕnitum*que,
Et *pŏtui;* quæ dant quoque *solvo* et *volvo* supina.

All Preterites and Supines, except those included in the preceding Rules, retain, in the first syllable, the quantity of the first
syllable of the Present: as, *vŏco, vŏcavi, vŏcatum ; clāmo,
clāmavi, clāmatum ; mŏneo, mŏnui, mŏnitum.*

Exc. Pŏsui, pŏsitum, from *pōno ; gĕnui, gĕnitum,* from *gīgno :
sŏlutum,* and *vŏlutum,* from *sōlvo,* and *vōlvo,* have the first
syllable short, though the corresponding syllable in the Present is long.

19. Præ *tum* vocalem polysyllaba cuncta supina
Producunt, *ātum,* quibus *ētum* finis, et *ūtum :*
Ivi præterito veniens sociabis et *ĭtum.*
Cætera corripies in *ĭtum* quæcunque residunt.

Supines of more than two syllables in *ātum, ētum,* and *ūtum,*
have the penult long: as, *amātum, delētum, minūtum.* So
also Supines in *ĭtum* from Preterites in *īvi ;* as *cupīvi, cupī-
tum,* (except *eo* and its compounds, *See* page 59); but all
other Supines in *ĭtum* have the penult short: as, *monui,
monĭtum ; abolēvi, abolĭtum. Recenseo,* has *recensĭtum.*

20. In *rus* Participî semper penultima longa est.

Participles in *rus* have the penult always long : as, *amatūrus.*

---

* The Compounds which are found in the Perfect Participle with
the penult short are *concĭtus, excĭtus, incĭtus,* and *percĭtus ; concĭtus*
is also supported by authority, and *excĭtus* and *excĭtus* are used indifferently. These appear to be the only Compounds which are found in
the poets.

INCREASE OR CREMENT OF NOUNS.

Nouns are said to *increase* when they have more syllables in the oblique cases than in the Nominative: as,
sermo, sermōnis; cardo, cardĭnis.

21. Vocalis numero coëat nisi bina priòre,
    Casibus obliquis non crescunt nomina primæ,
    Nec quæ quarta dedit, dedit aut inflexio quinta.

22. Quæ sequitur primam tantùm producit *Ibēri.*

23. Semper A curtat *ătis* ternæ : sit *dogmătis* index.

24. O breviabit *ĭnis :* sed porrigit *ēnis* et *ōnis.*
    Mensuram variant at in his gentilia quædam.

25. I breve mittit *ĭtis.* Sed ab EC producitur *ēcis.*

26. In D crementum breve nomina pauca tulerunt.

27. AL mas curtat *ălis :* sed neutrum protrahit *ālis.*
    Elis cum *Sōlis* produc ; reliquis breviatis.

28. ON nimis incertum est : EN *ĭnis* rape : cætera produc.

29. *Aris* ab AR neutro produc : sed demito *bacchar,*
    Par cum compositis, *jubar* his cum *nectăre* jungens.
    Protrahe *Nar Năris, fŭris, vēris, Recimēris,*
    Byzer, Ser, et *Iber,* in *ter* Græcum, *æthĕre* dempto.
    Oris ab OR longum est : cum neutris corripe Græca.
    Arbŏris et *memŏris* brevies, indictaque cuncta.

30. *Atis* ab AS tardant, *anătis* nisi, quæque Latina.
    Cætera, sed *văsis* dempto, correpta dabuntur.

31. ES patrium breviat : demas *locuplesque, quiesque,*
    Et *mansues, hæres, merces,* et Græca per *ētis.*

32. Corripit IS crescens patrium : sed porrige *glīris,*
    Et quod Romuleum Genitivum format in *ītis,*
    Et *Psophis, Crenis, Nesis,* Græcumque quod *in* dat.

33. OS patrii cremata dedit producta : sed aufer
    Quæ tria correptis gaudent, *bos, compos,* et *impos.*

34. US cremata rapit : sed in *ūris,* et *ūtis,* et *ūdis,*
    Quod præit *u* longum est : *Ligus* hinc at tolle, *pecusque,*
    Intercusque. Gradus medius producit US *ōris.*

35. YS celerabit *ўdos :* sed tardè proferet *ўnis.*

36. Consona cum præit S, patrii penultima curta est.
    Hinc *Cyclops, seps, gryps, Cercops, plebs,* aufer et *hydrops.*

37. T breve crementum patrii per *ĭtis* sibi poscit.

38. Præ *gis* vocalem rapit X. Producito *lex, rex,*
    EX ĭcis abbreviat, *vibex* nisi. Cætera produc.
    Præter *abax, smilax, atrax,* cum *dropăce,* et *anthrax,*

Fax, et *Atax*, *climax*que, *panax*que, *styrax*que, *colarque* ;
Quæque *phylax*que, *corax*que creant, et cum *nece*, rectis
Orba suis, *vicis* atque *preci* ; cum *appendice*, *fornix*,
Coxendix, *chœnix*que, *Cilix*, *natrix*que, *calix*que,
Pix, et *onyx*, *illix*, *histrix*, cum *mastiche*, *varix*,
Queis *Ercÿcis*, *filicis*, *salicis*, *laricis*que, *nivis*que,
Cappadŏcis, *calÿcis*, cum *Narÿce*, *præcŏce* nectes :
Adde *dŭcis*, pariterque *crŭcis*, *nŭce* cum *trŭce* junctis.
At patrio variato *Syphax*, cum *Bebryce*, *sandix*.

39. Pluralis casus, si crescit, protrahit A, E,
Et simul O. *Bŭbus* dempto, sed corripit I, U.

INCREASE OR CREMENT OF VERBS.

A Verb is said to *increase* when any part of it exceeds
the Second Person Singular of the Present of the Indicative Active, by one or more syllables : as, *rogas, rogāmus
rogabātis, rogabāmĭni.*

40. A verbum crescens auctu producit in omni.
Excipe crementum *dăre* primum quod breve poscit.

41. E quoque producunt verba increscentia : verùm
Prima E corripiunt ante *r* duo tempora ternæ.
Rēre sit et *rēris* longum, *bĕris* at *bĕre* curtum.
Semper E corripitur præ *ram, rim, r*oque locatum.
Curtat et interdum *stetĕrunt, dedĕrunt*que poeta.

Note.—Besides *stetĕrunt* and *dedĕrunt*, various other verbs are
shortened by the poets in the penult of the Third Person Plural of the
Perfect Indicative. Virgil uses *tulĕrunt* : Horace, *annuĕrunt, vertĕ-
runt :* Ovid, *contigĕrunt, defuĕrunt, fuĕrunt, horruĕrunt, præbuĕ-
runt, &c.*

42. Corripit I crescens verbum : sed deme *velīmus,
Nolīmus, sīmus,* quæque his sata cætera ; jungens
Ivi præteritum, prima incrementaque quartæ.
Præterito curtabis *īmus* tamen undique : vates
Exacto variant *rimus, ritis*que futuro.

43. O produc verbis crescentibus ; U breve profer.

FINAL SYLLABLES.
A.

44. Casibus A flexum brevia. Sed protrahe sextum,
Et quintum, Græco quando hic de nomine in AS fit.
Casibus haud flexum produc. *Ităa*, cum *quiă*, et *ejă,*
Et *pută* non verbum subduxeris, *hallequelujă.*

> A in the end of words declined by cases, i. e. in Nouns, and
> Adjectives, is short : as, *musă, lampadă, Tydcă, bonă, eă.*

> *Exc.* The Ablative of Nouns and Adjectives of the First De-
> clension, and the Vocative of Greek Nouns in *as* of the First
> and Third Declensions are long : as, *Musā, Æneā, Atlā.*

Note.—Vocatives in *a* of Greek Nouns in *tes* are short : as, *Æetă,
Orestă.* Those from Nominatives in *es* are sometimes, though rarely,
found long : as, *Anchisā, Æacidā.* But these more commonly follow
the general Rule.

> A in the end of words not declined by cases, i. e. in Verbs,
> and indeclinable words, is long : as, *amā, frustrā, prætereā,
> ergā, intrā, ā.*

> *Exc. Ită, quiă, ejă, pută* put adverbially, and *hallelujă,* are
> short.

Note.—*Alphă, Betă,* the names of letters, have the *a* short.

E.

45. **E brevia.** Primæ produc, et nomina quintæ
    Cum natis. Addes pluralia cuncta : secundæ
    Induperativum socians. Monosyllaba, demptis
    Encliticis ac syllabicis, quoque longa repones.
    Adde a mobilibus flexûs quæcunque secundi
    Manârunt, summique gradûs adverbia quævis.
    Sed *benĕ* cum *malĕ* corripies, *infernĕ, supernĕ.*
    Productis *fermē* atque *ferē* jungantur, et *ohē.*

> E in the end of a word is short : as, *natĕ, cubilĕ, patrĕ, currĕ.*

> *Exc.* 1. The following words have *e* long. Nouns of the First
> and Fifth Declension : as, *Calliopē,* * *Anchisē ; rē* and *diē,*
> with their Compounds, *quarē, hodiē, &c. ;* Plural Greek
> Nouns : as, *cetē, Tempē ;* and the Second Per. Sing. of the
> Imperative of the Second Conjugation : as, *docē, manē.*

Note.—The Doric Vocatives of Greek Nouns are long : as,
Ulyssē, Achillē ; contracted cases : as, *Diomedē* for *Diomedea ;* the
contracted Genitive and Dative of the Fifth Declension : as, *diē, fidē ;*
likewise *famē,* which originally belonged to the Fifth. The Imperative *cave* has the last syllable common. This license is usually extended to *vale, vide,* and *responde,* but not on good authority ; in the
best writers, where the reading is undisputed, they are always long.

> *Exc.* 2. Monosyllables are long : as, *ē, mē, tē ;* except the en-
> clitic particles, *quĕ, vĕ, nĕ* (interrogative), and the syllabic
> adjections *ptĕ, cĕ, tĕ :* as, *suaptĕ, hujuscĕ, tutĕ.*

> *Exc.* 3. Adverbs derived from Adjectives of the Second Declen-

---

* Final *e* is always long when it represents the Greek *η.*

sion are long: as, *placidē, pulchrē, doctissimē ;* except *benĕ, malĕ, infernĕ,* and *supernĕ,* which are short. *Fermē, ferē,* and *ohē* are also long.

I.

46 I longum pono. Vocitantem corripe Græcis.
His tamen at ternus dabitur crescentibus anceps.
Sic variato *mihi, tibi,* cum *sibĭ ;* sed mage curtis.
Vult *ibĭ,* vultque *cui, nisĭ,* mox *ubĭ,* cum *quasi,* jungi.
Sicutĭ sed breviant, cum *necubĭ, sicubĭ* vates.

I in the end of a word is long : as, *dominī, patrī, amavī, ī.*

> *Exc.* 1. The Vocatives of Greek Nouns have the i short : as, *Alexī, Amaryllī.*

Note.—The Vocatives of Greek Nouns having *entes* in the Genitive are long : as, *Simois, -entos, Simoī.*

> *Exc.* 2. Of the Datives of Greek Nouns which increase in the Genitive, some are short: as, *Palladĭ, Minoidĭ ;* and others are long: as, *Thctidī, Paridī, Tyndaridī.* The Datives and Ablatives Plural in *si :* as, *heroisī,* are short. *Mihi, tibi, sibi, ibi, ubi,* and *cui* (a dissyllable), are common ; *nisĭ* and *quasĭ* are always short.

Note.—The Compounds of *ibi, ubi,* and *uti* are peculiar. *Ibĭ* and *ubi* have the i common ; but in *alibī* it is always long, and in *necubi* and *sicubi,* it is always short. The i is always long in *utī* and *velutī,* but is always found short in *sicutĭ.*

O.

47. O commune loces. Dabis at monosyllaba longis,
Græcaque ceu *Didō,* ternum sextumque secundæ,
Et patrium Græcum, atque adverbia nomine nata,
Quō jungens et *eō.* Variant at *denuo, sero,*
Mutuo, postremo, vero : modŏ sed breve pones.
Sæpiùs *ambo, duo, scio* corripe, et *illico* et *imo,*
Et *cedo da* signans, *ego,* queis *homo,* cum *cito,* junge.
Sunt aliis variata Gerundia, longa Maroni.
Ergō pro *causâ* produc ; secus editur anceps.

O in the end of a word is common : as, *leo, virgo, amo.*

Note.—The poets of the Augustan age very rarely shortened final *o* in Verbs, or in Nouns of the Third Declension. *Sciŏ* and *nesciŏ* are often found short, and *credŏ, putŏ, rogŏ, volŏ,* when used parenthetically or in colloquial discourse. Instances of *o* being shortened in other verbs are very rare. *Homŏ* is found short in Catullus, *ncmŏ* and *leŏ* in Ovid, and *mentiŏ* in the Satires of Horace. The later poets appear to have considered *o* common, and accordingly in their works it is very often found short.

Exc. 1.—Monosyllables are long: as, *ō, dō, stō ;* Greek Nouns!
as, *Didō,* Sapphō, Athō* (Gen.) ; the Datives and Ablatives
of the Second Declension : as, *dominō, bonō ;* Adverbs derived from Adjectives : as, *certō, crebrō, falsō,* and *ergō,* on
account of ; likewise *quō* and *eō,* with the Compounds, *quō-
vis, quōcunque.*

Exc. 2.—*Denuo, sero, mutuo, postremo, vero,* are generally long,
but sometimes short. *Ambo, duo, scio, illico, imo, cedo* (Defective Verb), *ego, homo,* and *cito,* are commonly short. *Modŏ,*
and its Compounds, *quomodŏ, dummodŏ, &c.* are short.

Note.—There appears to be a want of precision in the latter part
of the preceding rule. The result of Professor Ramsay's minute examination is as follows : Final *o* in *ambō, ergō, ideō, imō, porrō,
postremō, quandō, serō, verō,* is perhaps never found short except in
writers posterior to the Augustan age. It is always short in the following words, in good writers : *citŏ, duŏ, egŏ, octŏ, modŏ* the Adverb,
and its Compounds, *dummodŏ, postmodŏ, quomodŏ, tantummodŏ.* There
does not appear to be any good authority for the distinction which is
made in the rule between *ergo,* signifying *on account of,* and *ergo,* signifying *therefore.*

Exc. 3. The Gerund in *dō* is always long in Virgil, but is sometimes found short in the later poets.

U and Y.

48. U semper longis, sed Y raptis jungere oportet.

U in the end of a word is long : as, *vultū, cornū, dictū.*
Y in the end of a word is short : as, *molў, Tiphў.*

B.

49. Corripe B Latium : peregrinum at tendere malim.

B in the end of a word is short : as, *ăb, ŏb, săb.* Words adopted
from a foreign language are long : as, *Jōb, Jacōb.*

C.

50. C produc, præter *nĕc, donĕc :* sed variabis
Hic bene pronomen : *fac* verbum jungimus isti.

C in the end of a word is long : as, *āc, sīc, illūc, dūc.*

Exc. Nĕc and *donĕc* are short. The Pronoun *hic,* and the Verb
fac, are common.

Note.—*Hic,* the Adverb is always long ; *hic,* the Pronoun is twice
found short in Virgil, but is generally long ; *hoc,* which is also said
to be common, is always found long, except in the comic writers. *Fac*
appears to be always short.

---

* Final *o* is always long when it represents the Greek *ω.*

D.

51. D breve ponatur. Variare at Barbara possis.

D in the end of a word is short: as, *ăd, apŭd, quĭd.* Foreign words are common: as, *David, Bogud.*

L.

52. L breve sit. Cum *sōl, sāl, nīl,* tolluntur Hebræa.

L in the end of a word is short: as, *animăl, vigĭl, consŭl.*

Exc. Sōl, sāl, nīl, with words adopted from the Hebrew, are long: as, *Daniēl, Nabūl.*

Note.—Nil is long, because it is a contraction for *nihil.*

M.

53. M nunc vocalis perimit: rapuére vetusti.

M in the end of a word is cut off before a vowel; the earlier writers often preserved it, and made the syllable short.

N.

54. N produc. Demas EN *ĭnis* dans, quæque priore
Græca per ON casus numero tenuére secundæ;
Et quartum casum, si sit brevis ultima recti.
Sĭn quoque pluralis ternæ conjunge Pelasgum:
Forsităn, ĭn, forsăn, tamĕn, ăn, vidĕn' insuper addens.

N in the end of a word is long: as, *ēn, splēn, quīn, Titān.*

Exc. 1. Nouns in *en,* having *ĭnis* in the Genitive, are short: as, *carmĕn, pectĕn ;* the Singular Cases of Greek Nouns in *on :* as, *Ilĭon ;* the Acc. Sing. of Greek Nouns which have the last syllable of the Nom. short: as, *Maiăn, Orpheŏn ;* and *sin,* the Greek termination of the Dat. Plural: as, *Arcasĭn, Troasĭn.*

Exc. 2. The following words are also short: *forsităn, ĭn, forsăn, tamĕn, ăn, vidĕn', satĭn'.*

R.

55. R brevies. Produc cujus dat patrius *ēris :*
Addito *Ibēr, aēr, œthēr.* Sit *Celtiber* anceps.
At *pār, fār, lār, Nār,* quoque *cūr, fūr,* adjice longis.

R in the end of a word is short: as, *imbĕr, patĕr, Hectŏr, supĕr.*

Exc. Nouns in *er* having *ēris* in the Genitive are long: as, *cratēr, vēr ;* also, *Ibēr, aēr, œthēr, pār,* with its compounds, *compār, &c., fār, lār, Nār, cūr, fūr. Celtiber* has the last syllable common.

---

* Nouns in *on* which, in Greek, are written with *o,* are short those having *ω* are long.

AS.

56. AS produc. Patrio sed *ădis* quod flectit, *ănas*que
Sit breve : plurales ternæ quibus addito quartos.

AS in the end of a word is long : as, *pietās, mensās, amās.*

> *Exc.* Greek Nouns having *ădis* or *ădos,* in the Genitive are
> short : as, *Arcăs, lampăs ;* also *anăs ;* and the Acc. Plural
> of Greek Nouns of the Third Declension : as, *craterăs,
> Troăs.*

Note.—Latin Nouns in *as,* formed after the manner of Greek patronymics, are short : as, *Appiăs, Adriăs.* Greek Nouns in *as,* which
have *antis* in the Genitive, are long : as, *Pallas, -antis.*

ES.

57. Ponitur ES longum. Pluralia corripe Græca
Quæ crescunt ; velut *ĕs* de *sum : penĕs* additur illi ;
Cum neutris ; et queis patrii penultima curta est
Ternæ. Tolle *Cerēs, pariēs, ariēs, abiēs, pēs.*

ES in the end of a word is long : as, *quiēs, amēs, rēs, Circēs.*

> *Exc.* 1. Greek Neuter Nouns, and those which increase in the
> Genitive, are short : as, *hippomanĕs, Arcadĕs, delphinĕs :* also
> *ĕs* from *sum,* with its Compounds *abĕs, adĕs ;* and the Pre-
> position *penĕs.*

Note.—Latin Nouns in *es,* in which *es* represents the Greek *ns,* are
long : as, *Alcidēs, Palamedēs ;* and the Nominative and Vocative
Plural in *es* of Greek Nouns, which form the Genitive Singular in
eos : as, *hæresēs, crisēs ;* because in such words the *e* represents the
Greek diphthong. E is always short in those words which, in Greek,
are written with *ι :* as, in the Vocatives, *Demosthenĕs, Socratĕs.*

> *Exc.* 2. Nouns of the Third Declension which have the penult
> of the Genitive short : as, *alĕs, alĭtis, divĕs, divitis ;* except
> *Cerēs, pariēs, ariēs, abiēs, pēs,* with its Compounds *bipēs,
> tripēs, &c.,* which follow the general rule.

IS.

58. IS brevio. Verùm plurales protraho casus ;
ISque quod in patrio mutatur in *ĭtis,* et *inis,*
Aut *entis ; gratis*que *foris, glis, vis* quoque, nomen
Seu verbum fuerit : sic et persona secunda
Protrahit IS, quoties *ĭtis* plurale reponit.
In subjunctivi *ris* est commune futuro.

IS in the end of a word is short : as, *turrĭs, magĭs, bĭs, ĭs, Jovĭs.*

> *Exc.* 1. Plural Cases are long : as, *pennīs, nobīs, omnīs* for *om-
> neis ;* also Nouns in *is* which have *ītis, īnis,* or *entis,* in the
> Genitive : as, *līs, Samnīs, Salamīs, Simoīs ;* likewise *gratīs,
> forīs, glīs,* and *vīs,* whether it be a Noun or a Verb.

Exc. 2. *Is* in the Second Per. Sing. is long, when the Second
  Per. Plur. is in *itis :* as, *audīs, possīs. Ris* in the Second
  Per. Sing. of the Future Perfect Indicative, and Perfect Sub-
  junctive, is common.

OS.

59. OS produc.   Patrius brevis est, et *compŏs,* et *impŏs,*
  Osque *ossis* præbens.   Rectos breviato secundæ
  (*O* nisi det patrius): neutra his dein addito Graiûm.

  OS in the end of a word is long: as, *flŏs, bonŏs, vŏs, Minōs.*

  Exc. 1. Greek Genitives are short: as, *Arcadŏs, Tethyŏs ;* also
  compŏs, impŏs, and *ŏs* (a bone), with its Compound *exŏs.*

  Exc. 2. Greek Neuter Nouns are short: as, *chaŏs, melŏs ;* also
  Greek Nouns of the Second Declension: as, *Clarŏs,* * *Tenedos ;* except those which have *o* in the Genitive: as, *Andro-
  geōs, Athōs.*

US.

60. US correpta datur.   Monosyllaba cum genitivis
  Ternæ vel quartæ produc: numerique secundi
  In quartâ primum, quartum, quintumque ; et in *ūris,*
  Dumve *ūtis* patrius, vel in *ūdis,* et *untis, ŏdis* ve est ;
  Aut quintus fit in *u ;* longus tum rectus habetur.
  Ergo produces venerabile nomen *Jesus.*

  US in the end of a word is short: as, *annŭs, tempŭs, amamŭs.*

  Exc. 1. Monosyllables and Genitives of the Third Declension
  are long: as, *grūs, sūs, Clitūs,*† *Sapphūs ;* also the Gen.
  Singular, and the Nom. Acc. and Voc. Plural of the Fourth
  Declension: as, *frūctus ;* and Nouns of the Third, which
  have *ūris, ūtis, ūdis* (the penult long), *untis,* or *ŏdis,* in the
  Genitive: as, *tellūs, virtūs, incūs, Amathūs, tripūs.*

  Exc. 2. Nouns in *us,* which have *u* in the Vocative, are long :
  as, *Panthūs* (Voc. *Panthu*) ; also *Jesūs.*

YS.

61. YS junges brevibus.   *Tethys* reperitur at anceps.
  Longaque sunt, rectis aliter quæ casibus YN dant.

  YS in the end of a word is short : as, *Capỹs, chelỹs, chlamỹs.*

  Exc. Nouns in *ys,* which have likewise *yn* in the Nom. are
  long : as, *Gortỹs. Tethys* is sometimes found long.

T.

62. T breve semper erit: nisi quondam Syncopa tardet.

---

* *OS* is always short in those words which, in Greek, are written
with *s,* and long in those in which *os* represents the Greek *ος.*

† *U* in these and similar words represents the Greek diphthong.

T in the end of a word is short : as, *capŭt*, *amăt* ; unless when
the preceding Vowel is lengthened by a Syncope : as, *abĭt* for
abiit, *amarát* for *amaverat*.

63. Ultima cujusque est communis Syllaba versûs.

The last syllable of every line may be made long or short, according to the pleasure of the poet.

EXERCISES ON THE RULES FOR THE QUANTITY
OF SYLLABLES.

1. Deus, puer, moneo, faciam, eo, ea, meus, tineæ, traho, mihi,
ı hil, reprehendo, ahenus, cohæreo, dehisco, audiit.

2. Fio, fiunt, ficbam—fieri, fierem—diei, speciei, aciei—rei,
fidei, spei—unius, illius, totius—*alius—alterius—ohe*, Diana,
Io—aër, dius, eheu—aulaï, terraï—Pompeius, Caius, Veius.

3. Greek—Simois, Deucalion, Danaë, Hyades—Arion, Ixion,
Briseis, Menelaus, Æneas, Peneus, Darius, Medea, Iphigenia,
Troes, heroes—Chorea, platea, Malea, Nereides.

4. Bellum, mortem, amant, est, arcessere—pax, exul, thorax
—Amazon, gaza, horizon—major, pejor, hujus, cujus, rejicio
—*bijugus*, *quadrijugus*—āriete, ābiete, ābiegnæ, pārietibus,
tēnuis, gēnua, princĭpium, consĭlium, flūviorum.

5. Agri, peragro, patres, patrius, bœrathrum, pharetra, illece-
bra, cathedra, integrum, funebris, muliebris, libri, migro, demi-
gro, nigrum, impigra, ludibrium, reciprocus, mediocris, coch-
lear, Patroclus, volucris—matres, fratres, acris, atrum, aratrum,
theatrum, simulacrum, spectatrix, crebra, tetra, delubrum,
salubres, adjutrix—gubernaclum, spectaclum—abluo, ablatus,
obruo, oblitus, subrideo, quamobrem. Greek—cycnus, Atlas,
daphne, Tecmessa.

6. Nil, mi, it, petît, Juli, cogo, cogito, debeo, nolo, malo,
alius, tibicen, sodes, bigæ, scilicet, junior, jucundus, jumentum,
motum, fotum, momentum, fomentum, fomes, ala, mala, palus,
velum, seni, deni—Phaethon, deero, cui, iidem, deinde.

7. Aurum, musæ, mœnia, Cæsar, Graia, plebeiæ—præit,
præustus, præaltus.

8. Amicitia, natura, virgineus, augurium, custodio, oratio,
audacia, felicitas, utilitas, largitio, relatio, ratio, irritus, proditio,
superstitio, competitor, onerare, præcipitare, saluber, probabilis,
monimentum, munimentum, initium, involucrum, volumen,
moveam, moverem, moveram, movissem, legam, legerim, legens,
niveus, ferrugineus, regius, ambiguus, plurimus, divinitùs, con-
vivium.   For the exceptions, see the Rule.

9. Perlego, perlegi, invidet, invidit, perjurus, excĭdo, excĭdo,
appăro, appăreo, consolor, depeculor, despero, enodo, erudio,
investigo, eradico, indĭco, indico, desolo, enato, consideo, con-
sĭdo, permăneo, permāno, suffŏco, suffŏco, irrĭto.   See Rule.

11. Prometheus, prologus, propheta, Propontis—prodo, promitto, proveho, promulgo, provincia. See Rule.

12. Separo, semoveo, securus, secretus—diligo, dimitto, dimico—*dirimo, disertus ;* remitto, reclamo, refert ; vesanus.

13. Laniger, thurifer, opifer, semiviri, omnipotens, armipotens, tubicen, cornicen, sacrifico, significo, causidicus, magnificus, multiplex, biceps, bidens, bipatens, triceps, triplex, Trivia, siquidem, Agricola—duodecim, duodeni, sacrosanctus, Argonauta, Philomela, philosophus, metropolis, bibliotheca, Cleopatra, hodie.

14. Lucrifacio, agricultura, ludimagister—tibicen, bigæ—biduum, triduum, meridies, pridie, postridie, quotidie—geometra, minotaurus, lagopus. See Rule and *Note.*

15. Veni, vidi, vici, feci, crevi, ivi, movi. fodi—*bibi, scidi, fidi* (findo), *tuli, dedi, steti.* 16. Peperi, cecini, tetigi, pepuli, memini, pupugi—*cecidi, pepedi*—cucurri, tetendi, momordi, spopondi, pependi, poposci. 17. Visum, motum, potum, fletum, stratum, cretum, cusum—*satum, citum, litum, situm, statum* (sisto), *itum, datum, rutum* (from ruo: as, *dirutum, obrutum, &c.*), *quitum, ratus*—*insitus, illitus, circumdatus, concitus, excitus, incitus, percitus.* 18. Voco, vocavi, vocatum ; clamo, clamavi, clamatum ; moneo, monui, monitum—*pono, posui, positum ; gigno, genui, genitum ; solvo, solutum ; volvo, volutum.* 19. Mutatum, aratum, deletum, oletum, minutum, exutum, auditum, cupitum, recensitum, monitum, territum, placitum. 20. Amaturus, docturus, lecturus, politurus.

44. Penna, galea, regna, bella, sedilia, cornua, bona, meliora, tria, ea, siqua, aliqua—musâ, pennâ, galeâ, eâ, siquâ, aliquâ—*s,* da, ama, voca, frustra, præterea, interea, erga, extr.i, intra—*ita, quia, eja, puta, halleluja*—triginta, sexaginta, contra, ultra. Greck—Aenea, Palla, Atla—Anchisa, Æacida—Oresta, Polydecta, Thyesta.

45. Domine, nate, cubile, sedile, sermone, rupe, ille, iste, curre, lege, legere, regere, canere, audire, esse, unde, sæpe, dulcè, facilè, sublimè, suavè, impunè, ante, sine, atque—re, die, rabie, quare, hodie, pridie, quotidie, (die, fide *Gen.*), fame—doce, mone, habe, gaude—*cave*—me, te, se, e, de, ne—pennaque, aliusve, tantane, suapte, hujusce, tute—placide, pulchre, valde, minime, maxime—*bene, male, inferne, superne—ferme, fere, ohe.* Greek—Penelope, Anchise, Tydide—cete, mele, pelage, Tempe—Ulysse, Achille, Diomede (for Diomedea).

46. Domini, classi, audiri, fieri, amavi, fregi, i, viginti, fili, geni, Juli, Ovidi, Virgili—*mihi, tibi, sibi, ibi, ubi, cui*—*nisi, quasi—sicuti, necubi, sicubi—alibi, veluti.* Greek—Alexi, Amarylli, Pari, Daphni, Theti—Simoi—Palladi, Minoidi, Tethyi.

47. Leo, sermo, virgo, amo, peto, esto, ero, volo, octo—*scio, nescio, credo, puto, rogo, volo, homo, nemo, leo, mentio*—o, do,

sto, pro, proh—domino, genero, vento, bono, pulchro—crebro, falso, certo, raro, merito—*quo, eo,* quocunque, quovis, eodem— *denuo, sero, mutuo, postremo, vero, adeo, idco—modo, ambo,* *duo, scio, nescio, illico, imo, cedo* (give thou), *ego, homo, cito—* quomodo, dummodo, postmodo—vigilando, cunctando—*ergo.* Greek—Dido, Atho, Clio, Alecto, Sappho.

48. Cornu, fructu, manu, dictu, lectu, tu, Panthu—moly, chely, Tiphy. 49. Ab, ob, sub—Job, Jacob. 50. Ac, sic, illuc, hic (here), lac, huc, duc—*nec, donec, fac*—hic (this), hoc. 51. Ad, apud, illud, quid, id, David. 52. Animal, vigil, consul, Hannibal, mel, fel, nihil, procul—*sol, sul, nil*—Daniel, Israel, Nabul.

54. Non, en, Siren, Hymen, Pan, Titan, quin, Orion, Ænean —carmen, pecten, nomen, agmen, tibicen.—*forsitan, forsan, in, an, tamen, viden', satin'.* Greek—Rhodon, Cerberon, Pelion, Ilion—Maian, Parin, Thetin, Ityn—Athōn, Androgeōn, Demo- leōn—Arcasin, Troasin, heroisin.

55. Calcar, imber, vir, cor, honor, vultur, amor, sequor, ter, per, præter—crater, ver, stater, Ser—*aër, æther, Iber—Celtiber* —*par, far, lar, Nar, cur, fur.*

56. Mensas, Æneas, pietas, amas, nefas, Arpinas, Antias, Pallas (a man's name)—Pallas (a goddess), lampas, Arcas, Ap- pias, Adrias, anas—heroas, delphinas, lampadas.

57. Rupes, patres, quies, res, dies, ames, doces, esses, toties, quoties—*es,* ades, potes—*penes*—miles, limes, eques, dives— *Ceres, paries, aries, abies, pes,* sonipes, quadrupes. Greek— Anchises, Atrides, Penelopes, Circes—Tritones, Troes, Amaz- ones, dæmones, Socrates (Voc.)—cacoëthes, hippomanes—here- ses, phrases.

58. Classis, patris, is, quis, amabis, legis, legitis, ais, bis, magis, fortassis—pennis, viris, regnis, nobis, vobis, illis, quis for quibus, omnis for omnes, humilis for humiles—Quiris, Samnis, lis, Salamis, Simois—*gratis, ingratis, foris, glis, vis, vis,* quam- vis—audis, venis, fis, sis, adsis, possis, velis, nolis, malis—dede- ris, fueris, dixeris, placâris.

59. Flos, dominos, custos, bonos, vos, heros—*compos, impos, os* (a bone), *exos.* Greek—Minos, Androgeos, Athos—Claros, Tenedos, Ilios—chaos, melos, Argos—Arcados, Pallados, Or- pheos, Prometheos.

60. Annus, tempus, montibus, rebus, fructus (Nom. & Voc. Sing.), legimus, sumus, penitus, tenus—jus, rus, grus, plus, sus —fructus, luctus, portus, lacus—tellus, salus, servitus, palus, Amathus, tripus, Œdipus. Greek—Cliùs, Mantùs, Eratùs, Sapphûs—Panthus, Jesus.

61. Capys, chelys, Erinnys—Phorcys, Trachys—Tethys.
62. Et, at, ut, tot, quot, amat, docet, legat, audivit, abit.

SCANNING.

Scanning is the division of a verse into the several *Feet* of which it is composed.

A verse is a certain number of syllables disposed so as to form a line of poetry.

A Verse, when it contains the exact number of syllables, is called *Acatalectic ;* when it wants one syllable at the end to complete the measure, it is called *Catalectic ;* when it wants two syllables, it is called *Brachycatalectic ;* when it has a redundant syllable or foot, it is called *Hypercatalectic*, or *Hypermeter.*

A Foot is a portion of a Verse consisting of two or more syllables.

The feet most commonly employed in Latin verse are the following :—

1. *A Spondee*, which consists of two long syllables : as, *rūpēs.*
2. *An Iambus*—a short and a long syllable : as, *dŏcēs.*
3. *A Trochee*—a long and short syllable : as, *nātŭs.*
4. *A Pyrrhic*—two short syllables : as, *dĕŭs.*
5. *A Dactyl*—a long and two short syllables : as, *pōnĕrĕ.*
6. *An Anapæst*—two short and a long syllable : as, *bŏnĭtās.*
7. *A Tribrach*—three short syllables : as, *lĕgĕrĕ.*
8. *A Choriambus*—a long, two short, and a long syllable : as, *cōmmĕmŏrās.*

CÆSURA.

Cæsura is the syllable which remains in the end of a word after the completion of a foot.

The Cæsura has received various names from the different positions which it occupies in the verse. When it comes after the first foot, or falls on the third half-foot, it is called *Triemimĕris*, or the *Triemimeral Cæsura ;* when it falls on the fifth half-foot, it is called *Penthemimĕris ;* when it falls on the seventh half-foot, it is called *Hephthemimĕris ;* when it falls on the ninth half-foot, it is called *Enneemimĕris :* as,

Ille la-*tus* nive-*um* mol-*li* ful-*tus* hya-cintho.—*Virg.*

where *tus, um, li, tus*, are examples of the *Triemimeris*, the *Penthemimeris*, the *Hephthemimeris*, and the *Enneemimeris.*

The Cæsura is commonly a long syllable ; but, when it falls on a syllable naturally short, it sometimes renders it long : as,

Omnia vincit am-*ōr*, et nos cedamus amori.—*Ovid.*

The lengthening of a short syllable in the *cæsura* may probably be accounted for by the circumstance that the ancients in reciting their verses were in the habit of resting the voice emphatically on the cæsural syllables, and longer time being thus assigned to them in pronunciation, they would be artificially lengthened, though naturally short.

FIGURES IN SCANNING.

Figures in Scanning comprehend the various changes which are made upon words to adapt them to the Verse.

SYNALŒPHA.

Synalœpha is the elision of the final Vowel or Diphthong, when the following word begins with a vowel : as,

Conticuere omnes intentique ora tenebant.—*Virg.*

The Interjections *o, heu,* and *ah,* are not elided : as,

O et de Latiâ, o et de gente Sabinâ.—*Ovid.*

Other long Vowels and Diphthongs sometimes remain un-elided, and are then generally made short : as,

Glaucō, et Panopeă̆ et Inoo Melicertæ.—*Virg.*

ECTHLIPSIS.

Ecthlipsis is the elision of *M* with the preceding Vowel, when the following word begins with a vowel : as,

O curas hominum ! o quantum est in rebus inane !—*Pers.*

Sometimes, however, the syllable is not elided : as,

Et tantum venerata virum, hunc sedula curet.—*Tib.*

SYNÆRESIS.

Synærĕsis is the contraction of two Vowels, which naturally make separate syllables, into one : as, *Phæthon,* for *Pha-ethon ; aurcâ,* for *aure-â.*

Inarime Jovis imperiis impôsta Typhöeo.—*Virg.*

Synæresis is frequently employed in the following words : `

Antehac, anteit, alveo, eadem, eodem, cui, huic, deest, deerat, deerit, dehinc, dein, deinceps, deinde, dii, diis, ii, iidem, iisdem, &c.

I and *u* are frequently changed into *j* and *v,* and joined, in pronunciation, with the following vowel : as, *abjete,* for *abiete ; genu* for *genua.*

Ædificant, sectâque intexunt ăbjŏte costas.—*Virg.*
Genva labant, gelido concrevit frigore sanguis.—*Virg.*

DIÆRESIS.

Diærĕsis is the division of a Diphthong into two syllables : as, *au-lāi* for *aulæ ; să̆adent* for *suadent.*

Aulāi in medio libabant pocula Bacchi.—*Virg.*

J and *v* are sometimes changed into *i* and *u,* and form separate syllables : as, *subĭecta,* for *subjecta ; silüæ,* for *silvæ.*

Si qua ferventi subĭecta Cancro est.—*Senec.*
Aurarum et silüæ metu.—*Hor.*

DIFFERENT KINDS OF VERSE.

I. HEXAMETER.

Hexameter or Heroic verse consists of **six feet**, of which the fifth is a Dactyl, and the sixth a Spondee; the other four may be either Dactyls or Spondees indiscriminately: as,

> Tītўrĕ- tū pătŭ- læ rĕcŭ- bāns sŭb- tĕgmĭnĕ- fāgi.—*Virg.*
> Intŏn- sī crī- nēs lōng- gā cĕr- vīcĕ flŭ- ēbāt.—*Tib.*

Sometimes a Spondee occurs in the fifth place; whence verses so constructed are called *Spondaic :* as,

> Cārā dĕ- ūm sŭbŏ- lēs māg- nūm Jŏvīs- īncrĕ- mēntūm.—*Virg.*

Spondaic verses are sometimes employed in solemn and mournful descriptions, to express dignity, gravity, &c., and generally end in a word of four syllables, with a Dactyl in the fourth foot.

II. PENTAMETER.

Pentameter verse consists of **five feet**. It is commonly divided into two parts; the former consisting of **two feet,** either Dactyls, or Spondees, and a Cæsura; the latter always containing two Dactyls and a Cæsura: as,

> Cārmĭnĭ- būs vīv- ēs- tēmpūs īn- ōmnĕ mĕ- īs.—*Ovid.*

This verse is generally combined with Hexameter in alternate lines, and from this union is constituted, what is termed *Elegiac verse.*

III. ASCLEPIADEAN.

Asclepiadēan verse consists of a Spondee, a Dactyl, a Cæsura, and two Dactyls: as,

> Maēcē- nās ătă- vīs- ēdītĕ- rēgĭbŭs.—*Hor.*

This species of verse, which is otherwise called *Choriambic Trimeter Acatalectic,* may also be scanned by a Spondee, two Choriambi, and an Iambus.

IV. GLYCONIAN.

Glyconian **Verse consists of three feet;** a Spondee, and two Dactyls: as,

> Rĕddās- īncŏlŭ- mēm prĕcŏr.—*Hor.*

This species of verse, is otherwise called *Choriambic Dimeter Acatalectic,* and may be scanned by a Spondee, a Choriambus, and an Iambus. Glyconian verse is usually combined with Asclepiadean.

V. SAPPHIC and ADONIAN.

Sapphic verse consists of five feet; a Trochee, a Spondee, a Dactyl, and two Trochees: as,

> Jām ză- tĭs tĕr- rĭs nĭvīs- ātquĕ- dīræ.—*Hor.*

Adonian verse, otherwise called *Dactylic Dimeter Aca-talectic,* consists of a Dactyl and a Spondee : as,

Tĕrrŭĭt- ûrbĕm.—Hor.

Sapphic and Adonian verses are always combined by the lyric poets, in stanzas, consisting of three lines of the former, followed by one of the latter.

VI. PHERECRATIAN.

Pherecratian verse consists of three feet ; a Spondee, a Dactyl, and a Spondee : as,

Quāmvīs- Pŏntĭcă- pīnūs.—Hor.

Pherecratian verse is otherwise called *Choriambic Dimeter Catalectic,* and may also be scanned by a Spondee, a Choriambus, and a Catalectic syllable. This verse is combined by Horace with Asclepiadean and Glyconian.

VII. PHALEUCIAN.

Phaleucian verse consists of five feet ; a Spondee, a Dactyl, and three Trochees : as,

Sūmmām- nĕc mĕtŭ- ās dĭ- ĕm nĕc- ŏptĕs.—Mart.

VIII. ALCAIC or HORATIAN.

The Alcaic or Horatian stanza consists of four lines, of which the first two are *Greater Dactylic Alcaic ;* the third, *Archilochian Iambic ;* and the fourth, *Lesser Dactylic Alcaic.*

Greater Dactylic Alcaic consists of a Spondee (varied sometimes by an Iambus), an Iambus, a Cæsura, and two Dactyls : as,

Cēdēs- cŏĕm- tīs- sāltĭbŭs- ĕt dŏmŏ.—Hor.
Vīdēs- ŭt āl- tā- stĕt nīvĕ- cāndĭdŭm.—Id.

Archilochian Iambic has a Spondee in the first and third places, an Iambus in the second and fourth, with a Cæsura in the end of the line. The first foot is sometimes an Iambus : as,

Nĕc sū- mīt aūt- pōnīt- sĕcū- res.—Hor.
Stĕtĕ- rĕ cāu- saĕ cūr- pĕrī- rĕnt.—Id.

Lesser Dactylic Alcaic consists of two Dactyls followed by two Trochees : as,

Arbĭtrĭ- ŏ pŏpŭ- lārīs- aūræ.—Hor.

Alcaic verse is called *Horatian* from its being used by Horace more frequently than any other description of lyric metre.

IX. IAMBIC.

There are two kinds of Iambic verse, the one consisting of four feet, the other of six. The former is called *Iambic*

Dimeter Catalectic; the latter, *Iambic Trimeter Acatalectic.*

Iambic Verse originally admitted of no other foot but the Iambus : as,

> Ĭnār- sĭt aē- stŭŏ- sĭūs.—*Hor.*
> Sŭīs- ĕt ĭp- să Rō- mă vī- rĭbūs- rŭīt.—*Id.*

Afterwards, other feet, as the Spondee, the Dactyl, the Anapæst, and the Tribrach were admitted into the first, third, and fifth places, and sometimes, but very rarely, into the second and fourth. The last continued invariably an Iambus : as,

> Cānĭdĭ- ă rō- dĕns pōl- lĭcĕm.—*Hor.*
> Vĭdē- rĕ prŏpĕ- rantĕs- dŏmūm.—*Id.*
> Quōquō- scĕlēs- tī rŭī- tīs aūt- cūr dēx- tĕrīs.—*Id.*
> Păvĭdūm- quĕ lĕpŏ- rum aūt- ăd- vĕnām- lăquĕŏ- grŭĕm.—*Id.*
> Alĭtĭ- bŭs āt- quĕ cănĭ- bŭs hōmĭ- cīdam Hēc- tŏrĕm.—*Id.*

Comic writers sometimes use an Iambic verse consisting of eight feet, and therefore called *Tetrameter,* or *Octonarius.*

Besides these, the following kinds of verse are employed in the lyric writings of Horace :

1. *Dactylic Trochaic Archilochian,* consisting of seven feet, of which the first four are either Dactyls or Spondees, the remaining three are Trochees : as,

> Sōlvĭtŭr- ācrĭs hĭ- ēms grā- tă vĭcĕ- vērĭs- ĕt Fă- vōnĭ.—*Hor.*

This verse is used in alternate lines with the following, B. I. Od. IV.

2. *Iambic Trimeter Catalectic,* consisting of five feet and a Cæsura, and admitting of the same varieties as Iambic Trimeter. It must, however, have an Iambus in the fifth place, on account of the deficiency of a syllable in the sixth : as,

> Trāhūnt- quĕ sīc- cās mā- chĭnaē- cărī- nās.—*Hor.*

This verse is used B. I. Od. IV. and is combined with the following in alternate lines, B. II. Od. XVIII.

3. *Trochaic Dimeter Catalectic,* consisting of three Trochees, with a Cæsura : as,

> Nōn ĕ- būr nĕ- que aūrĕ- ūm.

4. The eighth Ode of the First Book contains two kinds of verse ; *Choriambic Dimeter,* consisting of a Dactyl and two Trochees ; and *Greater Sapphic,* consisting of a Trochee, a Spondee, a Dactyl, a Cæsura, another Dactyl, and two Trochees : as,

> Lўdĭā- dīc pĕr- ōmnĕs
> Tē dĕ- ōs ō- rō Sўbă- rīm- cūr prŏpĕ- rēs ă- māndo.

5. *Greater Asclepiadean* or *Choriambic Pentameter,* consisting of

a Spondee, a Dactyl, a Cæsura, another Dactyl and Cæsura, and two Dactyls : as,

Tū nĕ- quæsĭĕ- rĭs- scīrĕ nĕ- fās- quēm mĭhĭ- quēm tĭbĭ.

This verse is used, B. I. Odes XI. and XVIII.; and B. IV. Od. X. It may also be measured by a Spondee, three Choriambi, and an Iambus.

6. *Dactylic Tetrameter Acatalectic,* consisting of the last four feet of Hexameter : as,

Aūt Ephĕ- sūm bĭma- rĭsvĕ Cŏ- rīnthī.
O fōr- tēs pē- jŏrăquē- pāssī.

This verse is combined in alternate lines with Hexameter, in the 7th and 28th Odes of the First Book, and in the 12th Epode.

7. *Ionic a minore,* employed B. III. Od. XII. may be divided into eight feet, consisting of a Pyrrhic and a Spondee alternately : as,

Mĭsĕ- rārum ĕst- nĕque ă- mōrĭ- dărĕ- lūdūm- nĕquĕ- dūlcī.

8. *Dactylic Trimeter Catalectic,* otherwise called the *Lesser Archilochian,* consisting of two Dactyls and a Cæsura : as,

Arbŏrĭ- būsquĕ cŏ- mæ.

This verse is combined with Hexameter in alternate lines, B. IV. Od. VII.

9. The 11th Epode consists of *Iambic Trimeter* in the first verse, and, in the second, of the latter part of *Pentameter,* followed by *Iambic Dimeter,* which is called *Archilochian Elegiambic :* as,

Scrībĕrĕ- vērsĭcŭ- lōs- ămō- rĕ pĕr- cūssūm- grăvĭ.

10. The 13th Epode, in the second verse, consists of *Iambic Dimeter,* followed by the latter half of *Pentameter,* and is called *Iambelegiac :* as,

Nĭvēs- quĕ dĕ- dūcūnt- Jŏvēm- nūnc mărĕ- nūnc sĭlŭ- æ.

METRICAL TABLE

OF THE

ODES OF HORACE.

B Ode.	M.	B. Ode.	M.	B. Ode.	M.
I. 1.	III.	II. 1.	VIII.	III. 19.	IV, III.
2.	V.	2.	V.	20.	V.
3.	IV, III.	3.	VIII.	21.	VIII.
4.	1, 2.	4.	V.	22.	V.
5.	III, VI, IV.	5.	VIII.	23.	VIII.
6.	III, IV.	6.	V.	24.	IV, III.
7.	I, 6.	7.	VIII.	25.	IV, III.
8.	4.	8.	V.	26.	VIII.
9.	VIII.	9.	VIII.	27.	V.
10.	V.	10.	V.	28.	IV, III.
11.	5.	11.	VIII.	29.	VIII.
12.	V.	12.	III, IV.	30.	III.
13.	IV, III.	13.	VIII.	IV. 1.	IV, III.
14.	III, VI, IV.	14.	VIII.	2.	V.
15.	III, IV.	15.	VIII.	3.	IV, III.
16.	VIII.	16.	V.	4.	VIII.
17.	VIII.	17.	VIII.	5.	III, IV.
18.	5.	18.	3, 2.	6.	V.
19.	IV, III.	19.	VIII.	7.	I, 8.
20.	V.	20.	VIII.	8.	III.
21.	III, VI, IV.	III. 1.	VIII.	9.	VIII.
22.	V.	2.	VIII.	10.	5.
23.	III, VI, IV.	3.	VIII.	11.	V.
24.	III, IV.	4.	VIII.	12.	III, IV.
25.	V.	5.	VIII.	13.	III, VI, IV.
26.	VIII.	6.	VIII.	14.	VIII.
27.	VIII.	7.	III, VI, IV.	15.	VIII.
28.	I, 6.	8.	V.	Ep. 1—10.	IX.
29.	VIII.	9.	IV, III.	11.	IX, 9.
30.	V.	10.	III, IV.	12.	I, 6.
31.	VIII.	11.	V.	13.	I, 10.
32.	V.	12.	7.	14.	I, IX.
33.	III, IV.	13.	III, VI, IV.	15.	I, IX.
34.	VIII.	14.	V.	16.	I, IX.
35.	VIII.	15.	IV, III.	17.	IX.
36.	IV, III.	16.	III, IV.	Secular	
37.	VIII.	17.	VIII.	Hymn.	V.
38.	V.	18.	V.		

INDEX

TO THE IRREGULAR AND DEFECTIVE NOUNS AND ADJECTIVES
CONTAINED IN THE APPENDIX.

The Numbers refer to the Sections of the Appendix, from page 93 to 107.

A

Accitu	26
Acclivus	48
Achilli	6
Acta	38
Admonitu	26
Adolescens	54
Ædes	40
Ædilis	13
Æneadûm	2
Æqualis	55
Aer	10, 32
Æstiva	38
Æther	10, 32, 39
Affabilis	55
Affinis	13
Agathocli	6
Album	34
Albus	56
Ales	42, 47
Aliquis	46
Aliquot	43
Alius	46
Allobrogas	17
Almus	56
Alvear	39
Amabilis	55
Amaracus	39
Ambage	26
Amnis	13
Amussis	7
Anceps	42
Ancile	39
Angiportus	39
Anguis	13
Anterior	55
Antes	36
Anûbis	8
Aphractus	39

Apis	15
Apium	31
Aplustre	39
Apollinares	35
Aprilis	13
Aqualis	9
Arbor	39
Arcănus	55
Arduus	56
Argilla	33
Argos	21
Argutiæ	37
Arma	38
Artifex	42, 47
Astu	27
Astus	27
Aulai	1
Aurai	1
Auris	9
Aurum	31
Auxilium	39, 40
Avernus	18
Avis	9, 13

B

Baccar	14
Bacchanalia	35
Baculus	39
Bætis	8, 11
Balneum	23
Balteus	39
Barathrum	34
Batillus	39
Bellaria	38
Beneficus	51
Benevolus	51
Bicorpor	47
Bigæ	37
Bijŭgis	48

Bilbilis	8
Bilis	33
Bipennis	13
Bonum	40
Bos	16
Braccæ	37
Brevia	38
Bucolica	35
Buris	7

C

Cacoëthes	28
Cæpe	25
Cæter	47
Canalis	13
Cancelli	36
Cani	36
Cannăbis	7, 11
Canorus	56
Capus	39
Carbăsus	20
Carcer	40
Carnifex	47
Caro	15
Carthagine	13
Casse	26
Cassis	39
Castrum	40
Celer	42, 47
Celĕres,	36
Cepa	39
Cete	28
Chaos	29
Charites	37
Cholĕra	33
Cibaria	28
Citer	50
Civilis	55
Civis	13

Classis	13	Dispar	42	Feriæ	37
Clavis,	9, 12	Ditiōnis	29	Fili	3
Clitellæ	37	Diu	26	Fimus	32
Clypeus	39	Diuturnus	54	Finis	13, 40
Codicilli	36	Dives	42, 47, 50	Flabra	38
Cœlebs	41	Divitiæ	37	Flebĭlis	55
Cœlicŏlûm	2	Dos	15	Flexanĭmus	48
Cœlum	21			Fœnum	34
Cohors	15	**E**		Fori	36
Colluvies	39	Ebur	34	Fortūna	40
Comis	47	Effrēnus	48	Fraga	38
Comitium	40	Egēnus	56	Frenum	22
Compāges	39	Elĕgi	39	Frugālis	55
Compar	42	Elephantus	39	Frux	29
Compĕdis	27	Elisăbet	25	Fugitīvus	56
Compos	41, 47	Elysium	21	Fustis	13
Concŏlor	41, 47	Epos	28		
Conger	39	Epŭlum	23	**G**	
Consors	42	Ergô	26	Gausăpa	39
Copia	40	Essĕda	39	Gelu	34, 39
Cor	15	Euphrātes	10	Gerræ	37
Cos	15	Eventus	39	Gibbus	39
Crepundia	38	Exanĭmus	48	Gloria	33
Crocus	39	Excubiæ	37	Glutĭnum	39
Cubĭtus	39	Exos	47	Gracĭlis	49
Cucŭmis	7	Exsequiæ	37	Grates	28
Cunabŭla	38	Exsomnis	48	Gratia	40
Cunæ	37	Exspes	44	Grus	39
Cupedia	40	Exta	38	Gryps	15
Cutis	9, 12, 33	Exter	50	Gummis	7
		Exuviæ	37		
D				**H**	
Daphnis	6	**F**		Habĭlis	55
Daps	29	Facetiæ	37	Hebes	47
Declīvis	48, 55	Facĭlis	49	Heros	10
Degĕner	42, 47, 56	Facultas	40	Hespĕrus	32
Delicium	23	Fæx	30	Hiems	28
Delie	4	Fama	33	Hierosolȳma	35
Delphin	10	Fames	33	Hilăris	48
Deses	47	Familiăris	13	Hilum	34
Deterior	52	Far	14, 28	Hortus	40
Dexter	50	Fas	28	Hospes	41
Dica	28	Fascis	40	Hospitālis	55
Dicis	26	Fasti	36	Humĭlis	49
Dido	6	Fauce	15, 26	Humus	33
Dilucŭlum	34	Fax	30	Hyberna	38
Diluvium	39	Febris	9		
Dindȳmus	18	Februa	38	**I**	
Diræ	37	Femĭnis	28	Idus	37

Ignis	13	**K**		Manes	36
Ignobĭlis	55	Kalendæ	37	Manubiæ	37
Ilia	38			Massĭcus	18
Illīmis	48	**L**		Materia	39
Imbecillis	48, 49	Labes	30, 33	Matūrus	50
Imber	13	Lac	31	Matutīnus	56
Impar	42	Lacer	56	Mel	28
Impĕtis	27	Lactes	37	Melos	28
Impos	41, 47	Lamenta	38	Memor	42, 47, 56
Impūbis	41, 47	Lapicidīnæ	37	Menda	39
Inanĭmis	48	Lapithûm	2	Mephītis	7
Incĭta	26	Lar	15	Meridies	32
Inclÿtus	53	Lardum	34	Merĭtus	53
Indŏles	33	Laurus	39	Metus	28
Induciæ	37	Lautia	38	Mille	25
Induviæ	37	Legitīmus	56	Milliāre	39
Ineptiæ	37	Lemŭres	36	Minæ	37
Inermis	48	Lens	9	Minōres	36
Infĕri	36	Lethum	34	Mirabĭlis	55
Inferiæ	27	Lævisomnus	48	Mirifĭcus	51
Infĕrus	50	Liberālis	55	Mirus	56
Inficias	26	Libĕri	36	Mobĭlis	55
Ingĕni	3	Limus	32	Mœnia	38
Ingens	54	Linter	15	Monĭtum	39
Ingratiis	26	Litĕra	40	Mugil	13
Injŭgis	48	Locuples	42, 47	Mundus	32
Injussu	26	Locus	19	Munia	28
Inops	42, 47	Longinquus	55	Muria	39
Inquies	26	Lues	28	Mus	15
Insidiæ	37	Lustrum	40	Muscus	32
Insomnis	48	Lutum	34	Musĭca	31
Insons	47	Lux	30	Mutabĭlis	55
Instar	27	Luxus	31		
Intercus	47	Lynx	15	**N**	
Interdiu	26			Nasus	39
Intĕrus	50	**M**		Natālis	13, 40
Invictus	53	Macedŏnas	17	Natu	26
Ismārus	18	Maceria	39	Nauci	26
		Macies	31	Navis	9
J		Mactus	45	Necesse	44
Jerusălem	25	Mænălus	18	Nectar	14, 34
Jocus	19	Magalia	38	Nefas	28
Jubar	14, 34	Magnanĭmus	48	Nemo	30
Jugĕris	24, 27	Magnilŏquus	51	Nequam	43, 55
Jugĕrum	24	Magnitŭdo	31	Neuter	46
Justa	38	Majōres	36	Nex	29
Justitia	31	Majuscŭlus	56	Nihil	28
Justitium		...ĭcus	51	Nii	28
Juvĕnis	28	Nix	15		

Nobĭlis 55
Noctu 26
Nonæ 37
Novus 53
Nox 15
Nugæ 37
Nullus 46
Nummûin 5
Nundĭnæ 37
Nupĕrus 53
Nuptiæ 37

O

Obsidio 39
Occĭput 13
Ocior 52
Olympia 35
Opĕra 40
Opīmus 54
Opis 15, 28, 40
Opus 25
Orbis 13
Orestes 10
Orgia 38
Os 15, 30
Osīris 8
Ostrea 39

P

Pan 10
Pangæus 18
Par 14, 42, 53
Parentalia 38
Parietĭnæ 37
Pars 13, 40
Partĭceps 42
Pater-familias 1
Pauci 45
Pauper 41, 47
Pax 33
Pecŭdis 29
Pelăgus 34
Pelvis 9
Penātes 36
Penum 34
Penus 32, 39
Peplus 39
Pergămus 20
Persuāsus 53

Pestĭfer 56
Phalĕræ 37
Pistrīna 39
Pituïta 33
Pius 4, 53
Pix 33
Plăga 40
Plebs 33, 39
Plerīque 45
Plus 45
Poëma 16
Pondo 25
Pontus 32
Postĕri 36
Postĕrus 50
Postis 13
Potis 44
Præceps 42
Præcordia 38
Præpes 47
Præstigiæ 37
Prætextus 39
Preci 28
Precox 56
Primitiæ 37
Primōris 45
Principium 40
Prior 52
Procĕres 36
Proclīvis 48
Proles 30, 33
Promptu 26
Pronus 54
Propinquus 55
Propior 52
Puber 47
Pubes 33
Pubis 41, 47
Pugil 13
Pugillāres 36
Pulvis 32
Puppis 9
Pus 34
Pusillanĭmis 48
Pylădes 10

Q

Quadrīgæ 37
Qualis 46

Quantus 46
Quicunque 46
Quidam 46
Quies 33
Quilībet 46
Quiris 15
Quisque 46
Quot 43
Quotcunque 43
Quotquot 43
Quotus 46

R

Rapum 39
Rastrum 22
Ravis 7
Redux 47
Regālis 55
Reliquiæ 37
Repetundārum 27
Reses 47
Restis 9, 12
Rivālis 13
Ros 30
Rostrum 40
Rudis 13
Ruma 39
Rus 13, 28
Ruscum 39

S

Sacer 53
Sal 14, 34, 40
Salebræ 37
Salīnæ 37
Salum 30
Salus 33
Salutāris 55
Samnis 15
Sanguis 32
Satias 30
Satur 54
Scalæ 37
Scopæ 37
Secūris 9, 12
Segmen 39
Sementis 9, 12
Semianĭmis 48
Seminĕcis 45

Semis	25	Supĕrus	50	Tros		10
Semisomnus	48	Suppetiæ	27	Tulli		3
Senectus	31	Supplex	42, 47	Turris		9
Senex	41, 54	Sus	16	Tussis		7
Separ	42	Syracûsæ	35			
Sepes	39	Syrtis	8		U	
September	13			Uber		42, 47
Septunx	15		T	Ulterior		52
Sequior	55	Tabes	28	Ultrix		47
Serapis	8	Tabum	28	Unguis		13
Sestertiûm	5	Tænărus	18	Utensilia		38
Sextans	15	Talaria	38	Uter		15
Sibĭlus	39	Tantundem	44	Uter		46
Simĭlis	49	Tartărus	18			
Sinăpis	7, 11	Taygĕtus	18		V	
Sinister	50	Tellus	33	Valvæ		37
Sinus	39	Tempe	28	Vas		24
Sitis	7, 11, 33	Tenebræ	37	Vectis		13
Situs	30	Tenellus	56	Venia		33
Sobŏles	30, 33	Teres	47	Vepres		28
Sodălis	13	Tesqua	38	Ver		34
Sol	30	Thermæ	37	Verbĕris		27
Sons	47	Thermopÿlæ	35	Versicŏlor		56
Sopor	32	Thus	28	Vesper		27
Sordis	29	Tibĕris	8	Vespĕra		33
Sors	13	Tignus	39	Veternus		32, 39
Sospes	41, 47, 56	Tigris	11	Vetus		41, 50
Sphinx	15	Tonitrus	39	Vicis		29
Sponsalia	38	Toral	39	Victrix		47
Spontis	27	Torcûlar	39	Vigĭl		42, 47
Stabĭlis	55	Tot	43	Vindiciæ		37
Statīva	38	Totĭdem	43	Virus		34
Stramen	39	Transtra	38	Vis		7
Strigĭlis	9, 12	Tricæ	37	Viscum		31, 39
Sublīmis	48	Tricorpor	41	Vitrum		34
Suffīmen	39	Tricuspis	41	Vocālis		55
Supellex	13, 33	Trigæ	37	Volucris		13, 42
Supĕri	36	Tripes	41	Volŭpe		44
Superstes	41, 47	Tritĭcum	31	Vulgus		34, 39

THE END.

PRINTED BY OLIVER AND BOYD,

EDUCATIONAL WORKS published by OLIVER and BOYD, Edinburgh; Simpkin, Marshall, and Co., London.

A Medal was awarded by Her Majesty's Commissioners of the International Exhibition to Messrs Oliver and Boyd for their Educational Works, in which are now included the greater part of the Educational Publications of Mr James Gordon, to whom a Medal was also awarded.

ENGLISH READING, GRAMMAR, Etc.

	s.	d.
ARMSTRONG's English Composition, Part I. 1s. 6d.—Part II.	2	0
Both Parts in one, 3s.—Key to ditto	2	0
.... English Etymology	2	0
.... English Etymology for Junior Classes	0	4
CONNON's System of English Grammar	2	6
.... First Spelling Book	0	6
COWPER's Poems, with Life by M'Diarmid	2	0
DALGLEISH's Outlines of English Grammar and Analysis, with Exercises. *Just published.* [*Key*, nearly ready].	0	8
.... Progressive English Grammar [*Key*, 2s. 6d.]	2	0
.... Grammatical Analysis, with Exercises [*Key*, 2s.]	0	9
.... English Composition in Prose & Verse [*Key*, 2s. 6d.]	2	6
DEMAUS' Selections from Paradise Lost, with Notes	1	6
.... Analysis of Sentences	0	3
EWING's Principles of Elocution, *improved by Calvert*	3	6
FISHER's Assembly's Shorter Catechism Explained	2	0
FULTON's Edition of Johnson's Dictionary	1	6
LENNIE's Child's A, B, C, Part I. 1½d.—Part II. 3d.—Ladder	0	10
.... Principles of English Grammar [The *Key*, 3s. 6d.]	1	6
LESSONS from Dr M'Culloch's First Reading-Book, large type, for hanging on the wall, 10 sheets, 1s.; or mounted on Roller	1	8
M'CULLOCH's First Reading-Book, 1½d.—Second Reading-Book	0	3
.... Third Reading-Book	0	10
.... Fourth Reading-Book and Synopsis of Spelling	1	6
.... Series of Lessons in Prose and Verse	2	0
.... Course of Reading in Science and Literature	3	0
.... Manual of English Grammar	1	6
.... Prefixes and Affixes of the English Language	0	2
M'DOWALL's Rhetorical Readings for Schools	2	6
MILLEN's Initiatory English Grammar	1	0
MILTON's Poems, with Life and Notes. Oliver and Boyd's Edition	2	0
MORELL's Poetical Reading-Book	2	6
RAE's First Lessons in English Grammar	0	6
REID's Rudiments of English Grammar	0	6
.... Rudiments of English Composition [The *Key*, 2s. 6d.]	2	0
.... Pronouncing English Dictionary,.........Reduced to	5	0

English Reading, etc., continued.

	s.	d.
ROBINSON'S (Canon) Shakspeare's King Richard II.; with Historical and Critical Introductions; Grammatical, Philological, and Miscellaneous Notes. *Just published*	2	0
ROBINSON'S (Canon) Wordsworth's Excursion. The Wanderer. With Notes to aid in Analysis and Paraphrasing	0	8
SESSIONAL SCHOOL Etymological Guide	2	6
.... Old Testament Biography	0	6
.... New Testament Biography	0	6
SPALDING'S (Professor) History of English Literature	3	6
WHITE'S System of English Grammar	1	6

OBJECT LESSONS.

	s.	d.
OBJECT LESSON CARDS on the Vegetable Kingdom. Set of 20 in a Box	21	0
ROSS'S How to Train Young Eyes and Ears, a Manual of Object Lessons for Parents and Teachers	1	6

WRITING, ARITHMETIC, AND BOOK-KEEPING.

	s.	d.
GRAY'S Introduction to Arithmetic [The *Key*, 2s.]	0	10
HUTTON'S Arithmetic & Book-keeping, by S. & D. Entry, by Trotter	2	6
.... Book-keeping, by S. & D. Entry, by Trotter, separately	2	0
Two Ruled Writing Books for Ditto: Single Entry	1	6
.....................................Double Entry	1	6
INGRAM'S Principles of Arithmetic, *Improved Edition* [*Key*, 2s.]	1	0
MACLAREN'S Arithmetic for Junior Classes, with Answers annexed	0	6
.... System of Practical Book-keeping	1	6
A Set of Ruled Writing Books adapted for the Work	1	6
MELROSE'S Arithmetic, by Trotter, *Improved Edition* [*Key*, 2s. 6d.]	1	6
SCOTT'S First Lessons in Arithmetic [*Answers*, 6d.]	0	6
.... Mental Calculation Text-Book, Pupil's Copy	0	6
.....................................Teacher's Copy	0	6
.... Writing Copy-Books, with Engraved Headings, in a progressive Series of 20 Numbers: Post Paper, 4d.; Medium Paper, each	0	3
.... Copy Lines, 30 Sorts.....each	0	4
SMITH'S Practical Arithmetic for Junior Classes [*Answers*, 6d.]	0	6
.... Practical Arithmetic for Senior Classes [*Answers*, 6d.]	2	0
.... Key to Ditto	2	6
STEWART'S First Lessons in Arithmetic [*Answers*, 6d.]	0	6
.... Practical Arithmetic, *Improved Edition* [The *Key*, 2s.]	1	6
TROTTER'S Arithmetic for Junior Classes [*Answers*, 6d.]	0	6
.... Arithmetic for Advanced Classes [*Answers*, 6d.]	0	6
The above two Books bound together in leather	1	3
.... Complete System of Arithmetic [The *Key*, 4s. 6d.]	3	0

GEOGRAPHY AND ASTRONOMY.

	s.	d.
CLYDE's (Dr) Elementary Geography.....................................	1	6
.... School Geography..............................	4	0
EDINBURGH ACADEMY Modern Geography..............................	2	6
.... Ancient Geography.................................	3	0
EWING's Geography, with Astronomy and Physical Geography...	4	6
....with 14 Maps	6	0
.... General Atlas of Modern Geography, 29 Maps.............	7	6
LAWSON's Geography of the British Empire..............................	3	0
.... Mathematical and Physical Geography......................	1	3
MURPHY's Bible Atlas, 24 Maps, coloured, & Historical Descriptions	1	6
REID's Rudiments of Modern Geography (Map), 1s. ; with 5 Maps	1	3
First Book of Geography (Reid's Rudiments abridged).............	0	6
.... Outlines of Sacred Geography, with Map of Palestine......	0	6
.... Introductory Atlas of Modern Geography, 10 Maps.........	2	6
.... School Atlas of Modern Geography, 16 Maps..................	5	0
REID's (Hugo) Elements of Astronomy......................................	3	0
.... Physical Geography, with Astronomy (Phys. Chart).	1	0
STEWART's Modern Geography, with Physical Geography and Astronomy, Maps, and Physical Chart................................	3	6
WHITE's Abstract of General Geography (with 4 Maps, 1s. 3d.)...	1	0
.... System of Modern Geography (with 4 Maps, 2s. 9d.).....	2	6
.... School Atlas of Modern Geography, 24 Maps..............	6	0
.... Elementary Atlas of Modern Geography, 10 Maps........	2	6

SCHOOL SONGS.

HUNTER's School Songs for Junior Classes : 60 Songs, mostly for two voices, 4d.—Second Series, 63 Songs.......................	0	4
.... School Songs for Advanced Classes: 44 Songs, mostly for three voices, 6d.—Second Series, 46 Songs.....................	0	6
SCHOOL Psalmody. 58 pieces arranged for three voices.............	0	4

HOUSEHOLD ECONOMY.

GORDON's Household Economy, a Manual for Female Training Colleges and the Senior Classes of Girls' Schools...................	2	0

MATHEMATICS, NATURAL PHILOSOPHY, Etc.

INGRAM's Mathematics, by Trotter ['The Key, 3s. 6d.], reduced to...	4	6
.... Mensuration, by Trotter	2	0
INGRAM & TROTTER's Euclid's Plane Geometry and Trigonometry	1	6
.... Elements of Algebra...............................	3	0
LEE's Catechism of Natural Philosophy, Parts I. & II., each......	0	9
NICOL's (Professor) Introductory Book of the Sciences	1	6
TROTTER's Logarithms and Practical Mathematics	3	0

HISTORY.

	s.	d.
CORKRAN's History of England in Epochs, with Maps and Genealogical and Chronological Tables	2	6
GRAHAM's (Dr) Genealogical and Historical Diagrams	4	6
SIMPSON's History of Scotland, with Map	3	6
.... Goldsmith's History of England, with Map	3	6
.... Goldsmith's History of Rome, with Map	3	6
.... Goldsmith's History of Greece, with Map	3	6
TYTLER's Elements of General History, with 2 Maps, etc	3	6
WATTS' Scripture History, with Notice by Dr Tweedie	2	0
WHITE's History of England for Junior Classes	1	6
.... History of Scotland for Junior Classes	1	6
.... History of Scotland for Senior Classes	3	6
.... History of Great Britain and Ireland, with an Account of the Present State and Resources of the United Kingdom and its Colonies. With Map, *reduced to*	3	0
.... History of France, with Map	3	6
.... Sacred History	1	6
.... Outlines of the History of Rome	1	6
.... Outlines of Universal History	2	0
.... Elements of Universal History, 7s.; *or in separate Parts,* Ancient History—Middle Ages—Modern History ....each	2	6

MYTHOLOGY.

OLYMPUS AND ITS INHABITANTS: a Narrative Sketch of the Classical Mythology, by Agnes Smith. Edited by John Carmichael, M.A. 3 6

ITALIAN.

LEMMI's Theoretical and Practical Italian Grammar [KEY, 5s.]... 5 0
RAMPINI's Italian Grammar [KEY, 2s.] 2 6

GAELIC.

FORBES' Principles of Gaelic Grammar 3 0

LOGIC.

BAYNES' (Professor) Port Royal Logic 4 0

SCHOOL REGISTERS.

MYRON's School Register of Attendance, Absence, and Fees, arranged on a New and Improved Plan, and adapted to the Revised Code. Each folio serves 50 pupils for a Quarter 1 0
PUPIL's Daily Register of Marks. Spaces for 48 Weeks; with Spaces for a Summary and Order of Merit for each month, for each quarter, and for the year 0 2

LATIN AND GREEK.

	s.	d.
AINSWORTH's Latin Dictionary, by Duncan	9	0
CICERO's Orationes Selectae, by Professor Ferguson	1	6
.... Cato Major, Laelius, etc., by Professor Ferguson	1	6
.... De Officiis, by Professor Ferguson	1	6
CLYDE's (Dr) Greek Syntax, with Notice by Professor Blackie	4	0
DYMOCK's Cæsar, with Notes, Index, and Map of Gaul	4	0
.... Sallust, with Notes and Index	2	0
EDINBURGH ACADEMY CLASS-BOOKS :—		
Rudiments of the Latin Language	2	0
Latin Delectus, with Vocabulary	3	0
Rudiments of the Greek Language	3	6
Greek Extracts, with Vocabulary and Index	3	6
Ciceronis Opera Selecta, published at 4s. 6d.	3	0
Selecta e Poetis Latinis	3	0
FERGUSON's (Professor) Grammatical Exercises, with Notes and Vocabulary [Key, 2s.]	2	0
.... Introductory Latin Delectus, with Vocabulary	2	0
.... Ovid's Metamorphoses, with Notes and Index	2	6
FERGUSSON's (Dr J.) Greek Exercises, Vocab [The Key, 3s. 6d.]	3	6
.... Xenophon's Anabasis, Books I. and II., with Vocab.	2	6
GEDDES' (Professor) Greek Grammar, for Colleges and Schools	4	0
GREEK TESTAMENT, Griesbach's Readings, by Duncan, reduced to	3	6
HAMILTON's Functions of Si and Qui	6	0
.... True Theory of the Subjunctive	5	0
.... True Theory of the Greek Negative Mή	3	6
HOMER'S ILIAD, by Veitch, from Bekker's Text, and Index, reduced to	3	6
.... Books I., VI., XX., and XXIV., with a copious Vocabulary, by J. Fergusson, M.D.	3	6
HUNTER's Ruddiman's Latin Rudiments	1	6
.... Sallust, with Notes	1	6
.... Virgil, with Critical Notes	2	6
.... Horace, with various Readings	2	0
.... Livy's History, Books XXI. to XXV., with Notes	4	0
LATIN Testament by Beza, revised by Dickinson	3	6
M'DOWALL's Cæsar, with Vocabulary, Notes, Map, and Memoir	3	0
.... Virgil, with Vocabulary, Notes, and Memoir	3	0
MACGOWAN's First Latin Lessons, by Dr Halle, with Vocabulary	2	0
.... Second Latin Lessons, with Vocabulary	2	6
MAIR's Introduction to Latin Syntax, by Stewart, with Vocabulary	3	0
MASSIE's Latin Prose Composition, with Vocab. & Index Verborum	3	6
MELVILLE's Lectiones Selectæ, for Beginners, with Vocabulary	1	6
NEILSON's Eutropius and Aurelius Victor, New Edition, Improved by M'Dowall, with Vocabulary, etc.	2	0
STEWART's Cornelius Nepos, with Notes, Index, and Vocabulary	3	0

FRENCH.   *s.*

BELJAME's Grammar of the French Language, 2s.; or with Exercises, 3s. 6d. Exercises separately.. 2

CARON's First French Class-Book [The *Key*, 1s.]...................... 1

.... First French Reading-Book, with Vocabulary............. 1

.... French Grammar, with Exercises [The *Key* 2s.]........... 2

CHAMBAUD's Fables Choisies, by Scot & Wells, with Vocabulary 2

CHRISTISON's Easy Grammar of the French Language [*Key*, 8d.]... 1

.... Recueil de Fables et Contes Choisis, with Vocabulary 1

.... Fleury's Histoire de France, *with Translations of the more difficult and idiomatic passages*..................... 2

FRENCH TESTAMENT, Ostervald's Protestant Version, neat, gt. edges 1

GIBSON's Le Petit Fablier, with copious Vocabulary................. 1

HALLARD's French Grammar, with Exercises, *reduced to*............ 3

⸳ The KEY... 3

LONGMOOR's Catechism of French Grammar............................. 0

SCHNEIDER's Edinburgh High School French Conversation-Grammar [The *Key*, 2s. 6d.]............................. 3

.... Edinburgh High School New Practical French Reader, *with Questions in French on the subjects read* 3

.... Edinburgh High School French Manual of Conversation and Commercial Correspondence.......... 2

SURENNE's New French Dialogues.. 2

.... French Manual and Traveller's Companion.............. 3

.... French Reading Instructor, *reduced to*...................... 2

.... French and English Dictionary, without Pronunciation, 3

.... Pronouncing French and English Dictionary.   22d Thousand. [*Pronunciation shown by a re-spelling of the words.*].. 7

.... Pronouncing French Primer............................... 1

.... Fénélon's Télémaque, 2 vols, each 1s.; or bound together 2

.... Molière's L'Avare, stiff wrapper (bound, 1s. 6d)........ 1⸳

.... Molière's Le Bourgeois Gentilhomme (bound, 1s. 6d.) 1

.... Molière's Le Misanthrope and Le Mariage Forcé, 1 vol. stiff wrapper (bound, 1s. 6d.)......................... 1

.... Voltaire's Histoire de Charles XII, stiff wrapper (bd. 1/6) 1

.... Voltaire's Russie sous Pierre le Grand, 2 vols, each... 1

.... Voltaire's La Henriade, stiff wrapper (bound, 1s. 6d)... 1

SYNOPTICAL TABLES of the French Language........................... 1

WOLSKI's French Extracts for Beginners............................. 2

.... New French Grammar, with Copious Exercises.......... 3

⁎⁎ *A detailed Catalogue will be forwarded* POST FREE, *on applicat to Oliver and Boyd ; and a specimen copy of any Book will likewise be ↧* POST FREE *on receipt of the retail price in postage stamps.*

HISTORY AND GEOGRAPHY.

NEW AND REVISED EDITIONS.

OUTLINES OF UNIVERSAL HISTORY, in Three Parts.
Part I. Ancient History. Part II. Middle Ages. Part III. Modern History.
Edited by H. WHITE, B.A., Trinity College, Cambridge; M.A. and Ph. Dr.,
Heidelberg. 8th Edition, *continued to the Autumn of* 1866. Price 2s.

DR WHITE'S ELEMENTS OF UNIVERSAL HISTORY, on
a New and Systematic Plan. In Three Parts. Part I. Ancient History.
Part II. History of the Middle Ages. Part III. Modern History. With a
Map. 10th Edition, *continued to the Autumn of* 1866. 7s.; or in Parts, 2s. 6d. each.

This work contains numerous synoptical and other tables, to guide the re-
searches of the student, with sketches of literature, antiquities, and manners
during each of the great chronological epochs.

TYTLER'S ELEMENTS OF GENERAL HISTORY, Ancient
and Modern. To which are added, a Comparative View of Ancient and
Modern Geography, and a Table of Chronology. With two large Maps, etc.
New Edition, continued to the middle of 1866. 3s. 6d.

EDINBURGH ACADEMY MODERN GEOGRAPHY. *Eleventh
Edition* (Sept. 1866), *Revised and Enlarged.* A handsome Class-book printed
with large type. 2s. 6d.

SCHOOL GEOGRAPHY. By JAMES CLYDE, LL.D., one of the
Classical Masters of the Edinburgh Academy. With special Chapters on
Mathematical and Physical Geography, and Technological Appendix. 10*th
Edition* (Oct. 1866), *Corrected throughout.* 4s.

In composing the present work, the author's object has been, not to dissect
the several countries of the world, and then label their dead limbs, but to depict
each country, as made by God and modified by man, so that the relations
between the country and its inhabitants—in other words, the present geographical life of the country—may appear.

Athenæum.—" We have been struck with the ability and value of this work,
which is a great advance upon previous Geographic Manuals. . . . Almost
for the first time, we have here met with a School Geography that is quite
a readable book,—one that, being intended for advanced pupils, is well adapted
to make them study the subject with a degree of interest they have never yet
felt in it.

DR CLYDE'S ELEMENTARY GEOGRAPHY. 10*th Edition*
(Oct. 1866), *Corrected throughout.* 1s. 6d.

In the *Elementary Geography* (intended for less advanced pupils), it has been
endeavoured to reproduce that life-like grouping of facts—geographical portraiture as it may be called—which has been remarked with approbation in
the *School Geography.*

Edinburgh: OLIVER AND BOYD.   London: SIMPKIN, MARSHALL, AND CO.

School Geography. By JAMES CLYDE, LL.D., one of the

Classical Masters of the Edinburgh Academy. With special Chapters
on Mathematical and Physical Geography, and Technological Appendix. *10th Edition* (October 1866), *Corrected throughout.* 4s.

In composing the present work, the author's object has been, not
to dissect the several countries of the world, and then label their dead
limbs, but to depict each country, as made by God and modified by man,
so that the relations between the country and its inhabitants—in other
words, the present geographical life of the country—may appear.

Athenæum.—" We have been struck with the ability and value of this
work, which is a great advance upon previous Geographic Manuals. . . .
Almost for the first time, we have here met with a School Geography that
is quite a readable book,—one that, being intended for advanced pupils, is
well adapted to make them study the subject with a degree of interest they
have never yet felt in it. . . Students preparing for the recently-instituted
University and Civil Service examinations will find this their best guide."

Dr Clyde's Elementary Geography. *10th Edition*

(October 1866), *Corrected throughout.* 1s. 6d.

In the *Elementary Geography* (intended for less advanced pupils), it has
been endeavoured to reproduce that life-like grouping of facts—geographical
portraiture, as it may be called—which has been remarked with approbation
in the *School Geography.*

Greek Syntax, with a Rationale of the Constructions, by

JAMES CLYDE, LL.D., one of the Classical Masters of the Edinburgh
Academy. With Prefatory Notice by JOHN S. BLACKIE, Professor
of Greek in the University of Edinburgh. Third Edition. 4s.

Greek Grammar for the Use of Colleges and Schools.

By Professor GEDDES, University of Aberdeen. 7th Edition. 4s.

The author has endeavoured to construct such a book as might combine
the clearness and conciseness of the older Greek Grammars with the accu-
racy and fulness of more recent ones.

Geography of the British Empire. By WILLIAM LAWSON,

St Mark's College, Chelsea. 3d Edition, *with Corrections.* 3s.

PART I. Outlines of Mathematical and Physical Geography.

II. Physical, Political, and Commercial Geography of the British Islands.

III. Physical, Political, and Commercial Geography of the British Colonies.

The Museum.—" It is out of sight the best book on the subject that we
possess. It is as far as possible removed from being a dry book. . . .
The volume contains a vast amount of interesting and accurate information,
well arranged and happily illustrated."

Lawson's Outlines of Mathematical and Physical

GEOGRAPHY. 1s. 3d. Contains the First Part of the Author's
Geography of the British Empire.

Edinburgh Academy Modern Geography. *Eleventh*
Edition (Sept. 1866), *Revised and Enlarged.* 2s. 6d.

** *This is a handsome class-book, printed on fine* **paper with**
a large type, and is especially adapted for schools where a manual in
a small type and condensed form is considered objectionable.

A Compendium of Modern Geography, POLITICAL,
PHYSICAL and MATHEMATICAL: With a Chapter on the Ancient
Geography of Palestine, Outlines of Astronomy and of Geology,
a Glossary of Geographical Names, Descriptive and Pronouncing
Tables, Questions for Examination, etc. By the **Rev. ALEX.**
STEWART, LL.D. *20th Edition, Revised;* with 11 Maps, of which
5 are by W. & A. K. Johnston. 3s. 6d.

The work includes an Alphabetical table of the Chief Roots of Geographical Names. Such an analytical glossary, it is believed, will be of use in
exciting the interest of the scholar; while it both increases his knowledge,
and, by exercising his reflective faculties, makes him **more fully** master of
what he learns.

A Concise History of England in Epochs. By J. F.
CORKRAN. With **Maps and** Genealogical and Chronological **Tables,**
and comprehensive Questions to each **Chapter.** 5th Edition. 2s. 6d.

** *Intended chiefly for the Senior Classes of Schools, and for the*
Junior Students of Training Colleges.

The writer has endeavoured to convey a broad and full impression of the
great Epochs, and to develop with care, but in subordination to the rest of
the narrative, the growth of Law and of the Constitution.

History of English Literature; with an OUTLINE of the
Origin and Growth of the ENGLISH LANGUAGE. Illustrated by
EXTRACTS. For the Use of Schools and of Private Students.
By WM. SPALDING, A.M., late Professor of Logic, Rhetoric, and
Metaphysics, in the University of St Andrews. 3s. 6d. 9th Edition.

School Songs. By T. M. HUNTER. With Preface by
J. CURRIE, M.A., Principal of the Church of Scotland Training
College, Edinburgh.

For JUNIOR CLASSES: 60 Songs, principally **for two voices.** 4d.
 Do.   do.   *Second Series:* 63 Songs. **4d.** *Just Published.*
For ADVANCED CLASSES, 44 Songs, principally for three voices. 6d.
 Do.   do.   *Second Series:* 46 **Songs.** 6d. *Just Published.*

** *Notice.—The* SECOND SERIES *has been published to meet the desire of*
Teachers who wished a greater variety of Songs than were contained in the
FIRST SERIES.

School Psalmody. Containing 58 pieces for three voices. 4d.

www.ingramcontent.com/pod-product-compliance
Lightning Source LLC
Chambersburg PA
CBHW030556040726
47497CB00008B/2753